A kiss can never be undone...

Natalie studied the boldly handsome face, the dark, deep-set eyes, and the mouth she sensed could be harshly unyielding or tenderly sensuous according to his mood...she yearned for the first time to touch and kiss a man.

As if he had read her mind, Andrei leaned closer to her and said in a low, gentle voice, "If you felt that you desired something passionately, more passionately than anything else in the world, would you dare to risk defying society's petty rules?"

The attraction between them reached a fever pitch. They drew unconsciously together, both longing to savor their first kiss...

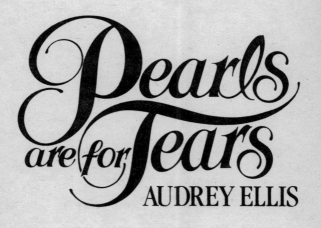

Pearls are for Tears

AUDREY ELLIS

A JOVE BOOK

PEARLS ARE FOR TEARS

A Jove Book/published by arrangement with
the author

PRINTING HISTORY
Jove edition/January 1987

ISBN: 0-515-08833-1

Jove Books are published by The Berkley Publishing Group,
200 Madison Avenue, New York, N.Y. 10016.
The words "A JOVE BOOK" and the "J" with sunburst
are trademarks belonging to Jove Publications, Inc.

PRINTED IN THE UNITED STATES OF AMERICA

Prologue
1886

"A visitor for you, ma'am," announced little Miss Knollys, Princess Alexandra's devoted secretary. She stood aside while a slender lady, wrapped in exquisite sable furs, entered the pretty mauve-and-white sitting room.

It was a favored retreat at Marlborough House, where the Princess of Wales, England's future Queen, received her dearest friends in a relaxed and intimate atmosphere. The beautiful Marchioness of Grandison was high on this exclusive list. As she cast aside her furs, revealing an elegant hourglass figure clad in gray moiré silk, Miss Knollys retreated, murmuring that there was a mountain of correspondence to attend to.

Sketching a brief curtsy, Alexandra's guest sank down gracefully on a brocaded sofa. Her mass of silver gilt hair was drawn back into glossy plaited braids, with a profusion of curls peeping out under a gray velvet bonnet onto her smooth white forehead.

"It is so kind of you to take tea with me, Louise," Alexandra began with her usual ingenuous charm. "I realize that you are still in half-mourning for your aunt Leonora. Otherwise I suppose you would have been with Lord Grandison at the same house party as

H.R.H. Duck shooting, isn't it, in Norfolk? But you are not too saddened by the old lady's death, I hope. After all, eighty-three is a great age!"

"No, ma'am, there was little sympathy between us. She became my guardian, somewhat reluctantly, when both my parents were killed in the Indian Mutiny. I was only an infant, and she was already a middle-aged spinster, whose only interest was hunting and horses in general. I suppose I was an unwelcome encumbrance."

Lady Grandison looked down at the gray silk roses embroidered on the backs of her delicate kid gloves. Her loveless childhood, spent on a lonely estate in Yorkshire, had made it hard for her to experience or express the ardent affections that came to Alexandra so easily. "I was glad to have an excuse to cry off going to the house party," she went on frankly. "I very much enjoy a ball in town, even dancing until the early hours, if my partners are agreeable. But a day out with the guns, followed by an interminable dinner, then gambling until dawn—or leaving the gentlemen to their cards while we ladies yawn over our coffee until we can decently trail off to bed—does not amuse me."

No sooner had she mentioned card-playing than Lady Grandison wished she had kept silent on this touchy subject. Alexandra's opinion of her royal husband's gambling cronies was known to be a bone of contention between them. So she continued smoothly, "Nothing pleases me more than the opportunity to play with my little girl before her bedtime. I shall be delighted to take tea with you, ma'am. Then I shall have a full hour with her in the nursery before dressing for dinner."

"Why, she must be running about and talking, the dear wee soul. I thought you might have left Cordelia at Grayle Abbey. I had no idea you had brought her up to town. Let me see, she must be two years old at least."

"Lord Grandison would not leave her behind at Grayle for the world," his wife said, smiling. "He adores his little girl, and unlike many other gentlemen who never enter the nursery, he is *au fait* with the arrival of each new tooth, and each new word she can pronounce. Delia is quite a self-possessed young miss and can already recite some nursery rhymes."

Alexandra, who doted on her own children, and had brought them up with far more familiarity than other royal princesses of her generation, glowed with approval. The danger point had been safely negotiated, the Prince's addiction to baccarat and endless cigars in dubious company, forgotten.

A footman brought in the silver tea tray and set it before his mistress, then respectfully withdrew. Lady Grandison, always finely tuned to the mood of her companion of the moment, sensed that the invitation to tea had been deliberately planned as an excuse for some confidence. Yet Alexandra seemed to be choosing her next words carefully.

"I heard from the Grand Duchess Voroshnikoff that she and the Grand Duke had invited you to visit them this summer in St. Petersburg. Dear Natalya is utterly charming, and Constantine has such polished manners. Extremely civilized, compared with others of the Russian nobility, whose conduct is often most bizarre. I like them both extremely. I was astonished that you refused the invitation."

At the very mention of Constantine's name Louise felt a sharp pang of yearning. Yet she could not understand why the refusal, so reluctantly given for a reason known only to herself, should affect the Princess of Wales.

"It would have meant being parted from our little girl for several months, and the journey is long and tedious..." she began, almost at random.

"But a stay in St. Petersburg at The Hermitage!" Alexandra urged. "There is to be a naval review that your husband, as a former officer in our own navy, would doubtless enjoy. The Voroshnikoffs are in attendance on the Russian imperial family, so you too would be staying at the palace. Then a few weeks on their estate in the Crimea when the weather is at its best. Quite delightful. But I should hope you would spend some time in St. Petersburg first."

The Princess picked up a rosewood fan with an embroidered panel to shield her face from the heat of the fire. Her fair skin, which reddened so easily, was becoming flushed.

Louise remained silent, certain that the real reason for this royal enthusiasm would now be disclosed.

"The fact is, I am desperately worried about the health of my sister, Dagmar," Alexandra continued in a low voice. "Russia is so far away, and since she became Empress she lives in constant fear, believing that the Nihilists have sworn to destroy the whole Romanoff family. Dagmar probably exaggerates the danger, yet there was that fearful train explosion when all of them, including the children's servants, were only saved because of my brother-in-law's fantastic strength. He held up the buckled wreckage of their railway compartment on his shoulders while they crawled to safety. It was explained away as an accident, but who can say for sure?"

"I understand your anxiety, ma'am," said Louise at once. "But suppose your sister is not mistaken, not falling prey to delusions?" She paused. "May I ask why you are urging us to visit St. Petersburg at the risk of some plot that might threaten our own lives?"

"Because I am almost certain that Dagmar is wrong, and I cannot go myself." Alexandra became quite agitated, her eyes brimming with tears. "Affairs of state, Bertie tells me, make it impossible to arrange a private meeting of the kind we used to have every year at home with Papa in Denmark. I can only judge Dagmar's state of mind by her letters. She writes more and more strangely, as though she considers herself doomed." She rose and began to pace the room. "It is so unfair. She and Alexander have the greatest concern for the sufferings of the Russian people, and they long to institute all sorts of reforms, although they are accused of being reactionary. But the customs of Romanoff rule forbid any changes to be made. My poor sister has come to imagine that they are hated, vilified, may even be murdered, not for anything infamous they have done, but for what they *are* . . . Romanoffs."

Alexandra sank down beside Louise and clasped her hand. "That's why I sincerely beg you to reconsider," she went on. "There would be no danger in any case for yourselves as English visitors, or I would not ask it. Go to St. Petersburg, talk to Dagmar, and when you return, tell me honestly how you find her."

Louise looked away, concealing the alarm she felt must be evident in her lovely blue eyes.

The Princess was unaware of the temptation she was placing in her friend's path. Until recently, Louise had thought herself above the sins of the flesh. Of course, she submitted to her husband's embraces, although there was little pleasure for her in his arms, because she must bear him children. But she had been overwhelmed by desire from the first moment of meeting the Grand Duke Constantine. He had seemed to draw her to him with every glance from those dark magnetic eyes. They had danced together at the Queen's birthday ball. She had allowed him to murmur outrageous words of love in her ear, caress her flaxen ringlets, his touch burning her bare shoulder as they swayed together to the strains of a waltz. She had made no demur when he steered her, still moving in the rhythm of the dance, from the brightly lit ballroom onto the shadowy, deserted terrace beyond.

"*Moya dushka*, my lovely snow bird, I adore your slim white neck, your glorious white breasts. Give yourself to me," he had whispered, gathering her close, pressing her soft bosom to his hard, muscular chest. "Don't draw away from me. I know there is fire beneath the ice of your cool beauty, Louise. I could draw wild music from your body with my fingers, as our peasants do when they play the balalaika. . . ."

She had melted, aware as never before of a warm, moist explosion within her, spreading, spreading, even as she turned her head away from his ardent entreaties, the voluptuous quest of his insistent mouth on hers. Where had she found the strength to refuse him? she had often asked herself afterward. But she had taken care never to be left alone with the Grand Duke Constantine again. Only in her imagination, night after night, shamed by her own lust, did she offer herself to him. . . .

When an invitation to visit the Voroshnikoffs had arrived, she knew it had not really come from Natalya. Pretty, languid Natalya, absorbed in trivialities; the new fashions from Worth, the latest jeweled trinkets from Fabergé, even the rose-scented pastilles she scooped endlessly from their heart-shaped satin box. It had been Constantine's invitation, his summons to her.

Louise wrenched her mind back to the present. She knew she must accede to Alexandra's request. Perhaps, she thought confusedly, she was fated to visit Russia and allow Constantine to become her lover. For she had no doubt this was what he intended and would certainly contrive, in spite of her scruples.

"I will persuade my husband that we should accept, after all," she found herself saying. "The imperial court, the naval review, and summer on the Voroshnikoff estates! As you say, it will be an unforgettable experience."

While Louise was unpinning the headdress of egret's feathers, secured with a crescent of diamonds, from her hair that night, her husband, Arthur, was undressing in the comfortable bedroom allotted to him at the Lodge, Mr. Nicholls's palatial country house in Norfolk. The Marquis of Grandison's appearance commanded respect. He was a man of impressive figure, in the prime of life, with chestnut hair and fine blue eyes. He called to his valet, who had just removed his tailcoat and was hanging it reverently on a polished mahogany shoulder stand.

"Give me my smoking jacket, Gaston. I'm going downstairs again for a nightcap with Mr. Nicholls."

The valet sensed that his master was disturbed by some event that had taken place that evening and was not really anxious to seek out his host at such a late hour. Indeed, Mr. and Mrs. Nicholls were among those *nouveaux riches* couples on whom the Prince of Wales bestowed the honor of a visit because the shooting was good at their place, the chef superb, and the entertainment smoothly geared to suit his particular tastes.

There was no lady present that weekend for whom the Prince had a penchant at the moment. So the object of the house party was not only to slaughter as many wild ducks as possible, but to send the ladies to bed early, while the gentlemen sat long over their port. After this, they would adjourn to the card room to play baccarat for exorbitant stakes. "Baccy," as the Prince called it, was his ruling passion, along with sensuous women, rich food, and rare wines. Usually, the other players would tactfully contrive that H.R.H. should win more than a little, or certainly not lose much. But tonight he had lost heavily, as had Lord Grandison himself.

Nicholls was a fool, Arthur concluded. Among the guests were two young army officers, close friends and gambling companions, who had been invited because they were both fine shots and knew how to amuse the Prince with bawdy jokes when ladies were not present. Arthur, having far more worldly knowledge than Mr. Nicholls, happened to know that this pair of young rips were up to their necks in debt. He had a shrewd suspicion that they were also in the hands of moneylenders and desperate to raise funds.

His sharp eye had, during the course of the evening, discerned that they were in collusion to cheat at cards. The result was that the three older men had risen from the table ruefully conscious of having "lost a packet", while the youngsters could hardly conceal their jubilation.

Lord Grandison judged it his duty to have a private chat with his host and point out that the offenders must be got rid of forthwith, in such a way that the Prince himself would not guess that he had literally been robbed by a pair of card sharps. Nor must he be allowed to notice for himself that two of the other guests were cheating. Rage often robbed him of discretion, and the vengeance he would seek might cause a resounding scandal. H.R.H. was an irritable fellow. Only the previous month a footman had spilled a drop of soup on his sleeve while serving the royal guest. Noticing that his immaculate broadcloth was sullied, the Prince had seized the ladle, poured a brimming dollop of soup onto his own lap, and roared at the top of his voice, "Why not make a good job of it?" before stalking out of the room.

Clad in a wine velvet smoking jacket with quilted satin revers to match, Lord Grandison descended the stairs swiftly but silently. He wanted no servant to hurry forward and inquire his pleasure.

It was probable he could corner Mr. Nicholls in the library, enjoying one more glass of port. He was not mistaken. The gentleman was busy pouring himself a generous measure from a cut-glass decanter and contentedly puffing a large cigar. Privately he was congratulating himself that the shooting party was going so well. However, he soon had good reason to look concerned, and his cigar was hurriedly stubbed out.

"Good gad, my dear Arthur," he stammered. "Are you certain? Marked cards, you say. I'd never have believed it of either of them."

"Perfectly certain, or I should not have mentioned it. I examined one of the cards myself. Very cleverly done, but quite obvious when you know what you're looking for. Dammit, man, we can't risk another evening's baccy with that pair at the table. Tell them early tomorrow you've rumbled it. Get them both to sign an undertaking never to play cards again for money, at least not in a gentleman's house. Threaten to inform the Prince unless they do, and let them think up some plausible excuse to cut their visit short. Certainly they ought to be on a train back to London before dinner."

Nervously, Mr. Nicholls agreed. But he was of the vacillating disposition that never knows when to let well alone. After all, the crime had taken place under his own roof. Somehow he felt compelled to tell H.R.H. what Lord Grandison had disclosed and, in the most sycophantic terms, begged the Prince to punish the perpetrators in any way he saw fit. The culprits were summoned to the library and accused. One of the young men caved in at once, admitted everything, actually wept a few contrite tears, and rushed away to pack his bags. The other was made of more impudent stuff. Lieutenant Francis Berryman, son of the distinguished banker Sir James Berryman, refused to sign any such undertaking, to admit his guilt, or to leave before the following day, when the house party was due to end. He was quite confident that his father's wealth and reputation in the world of high finance would deter any attempt to blacken his name. Indeed, as he pointed out, it would merely be Lord Grandison's word against his.

The Prince's face was literally purple with rage. Certainly the word of a peer of the realm with an unblemished reputation would be accepted against that of a jackanapes who was merely the son of a jumped-up bank clerk! Unexpectedly summoned to what he had supposed would be a discreet interview, at which the truth was no more than hinted, Lord Grandison found himself ordered by the enraged heir to the throne to inform the young man's father of the scandalous incident in the card room and to insist that H.R.H.'s wishes be carried out. The cheat must be severely punished, and it was his father's duty to see to it.

Furious at being placed in this invidious position when the matter could have been dealt with effectively, but without an ugly scene, Arthur had no choice but to bow and agree. Young Francis believed that when it came to the point, the threat would never be carried out. He was wrong.

His father was visited by a reluctant Lord Grandison in his aerie in Threadneedle Street, from which he controlled the destinies of many a vast industrial enterprise. A private investigator was summoned to ferret out the extent of Lieutenant Berryman's debts, which had only the previous year been settled by his father on the young man's promise not to gamble again. The truth proved to be far worse than his father had dreamed possible. Money was owed to bookmakers, tailors, landlords, jewelers, livery stables—even his mess bills had not been paid. This time, Sir James decided his son needed a really sharp lesson. He would pay none of them, even if it meant that young Francis would be cashiered by his regiment. He had not reckoned with the strain of weakness underlying the aggressive front that the boy maintained. Fearful of exposure and social disgrace, Francis took one last desperate flutter at the tables in Monte Carlo and lost heavily. He tottered unsteadily onto the Casino's palm-fronded terrace and blew out his brains.

When he heard this news, amid the excitement of packing and preparing for their trip to St. Petersburg, Lord Grandison told his wife, "I shall never forgive myself. I shouldn't have let that idiot Nicholls involve those wretched fools in a confrontation with the Prince. It was bound to lead to some sort of tragedy."

"You really need not blame yourself, Arthur," his wife replied gently. "They were taking a frightful chance of being found out. And it was your advice to Mr. Nicholls, from what you tell me, to deal with the matter himself. If anyone is to blame, it is he. He should never have mentioned it to H.R.H. If only Bertie had an equable character, like our darling Alix!"

But there was one person at least who did not agree with her. Sir James Berryman, brooding in his office over the loss of his only son, blamed Lord Grandison unreservedly. Magically all his boy's faults were forgotten. He had been mercilessly hounded to his death by the archfiend Grandison.

"Off to Russia, is he?" the banker muttered to himself. "No matter, I can wait until he gets back. I can wait for years if need be. But sooner or later, I'll punish him. Scandal, eh? I'll see him yet go down under such a scandal that he'll wish he'd never been born."

So the threads of destiny were woven.

The summer Lord and Lady Grandison spent with the Voroshnikoffs was indeed memorable. Louise was never to forget the ecstasy of her surrender to Constantine. Later, she was able to assure the anxious Princess of Wales that her sister, now Empress Marie Theodorovna, was not deranged. Rather, she acknowledged with courage the grim and inevitable fate that awaited the entire Romanoff dynasty, hoping that it might pass her own immediate family by.

The following spring four-year-old Delia bent over a crib draped and canopied in Chantilly lace, her fair ringlets touching the cheek of the baby girl who lay sleeping there.

"My little sister!" she whispered lovingly, quite awed by the sight of the tiny mortal whose silky wisps of raven-black hair crept out from under the embroidered bonnet. The baby awoke and stared back solemnly at Delia, with great dark eyes the color of drowned violets.

BOOK ONE

1904

The Lion, the Bear,
and the Shamrock

Chapter 1

It was a warm, almost breathless afternoon in Hyde Park, at the height of London's social season. The Ladies Cordelia and Natalie Grandison were strolling, unescorted, across a wide expanse of grass behind Speaker's Corner, where any individual, no matter how eccentric, might spout forth his views.

Their maid, Linnet, was comfortably seated on a park bench in the sun, with Marcus, Mama's overfed and indolent lapdog, curled up beside her. Linnet did not feel quite easy about letting her young ladies, both so charming in flounced écru lace, walk off alone together. She had strict instructions to accompany them everywhere. But they had absolutely insisted. Well, she supposed no harm could come of it. She dived into her pocket for a cheap paper novelette and was soon absorbed in a lurid tale of romance.

On entering the park at Brook Gate, Natalie had paused to speak to the old balloon woman. An urchin, kicking a pebble along the gutter, paused to look longingly at a huge red balloon in the center of the bunch.

To his surprise one of the visions in lace, the taller girl with the guinea-gold hair, opened her embroidered mesh purse and handed the balloon woman a coin. Then she turned a ravishing azure-blue gaze upon the dirty ragamuffin and said invitingly, "Choose one!"

He gaped. "Can I 'ave the red 'un, miss?" he inquired, not quite believing his luck. She nodded, and the other young lady, who was slighter in figure and not quite so tall, laughed. He stole a glance at her face, creamy complexioned, framed in ebony braids of hair under the straw hat piled with silk ribbons and flowers. Cor, he'd never seen such eyes, he thought. Exactly the color of the violets his auntie Pen sold off a tray in Piccadilly. Her skin was like the white camellia buttonholes the real toffs bought for a tanner, a whole sixpence, before a night out at the theater or music hall.

He snatched the long string and strutted off into Hyde Park, flapping his broken boots and holding his red balloon aloft with pride. He felt like one of the toffs himself, with his balloon bouncing high above his head.

"Let's make a tour of Kensington Gardens, as we used to do with the boys," Delia suggested. "I'm glad we left Marcus with Linnet. Ill-tempered little beast that he is, we don't want him to snap at the haunches of some great hound and be instantly swallowed up. It would be entirely his own fault, but Mama would never forgive us."

"What an awful thought," Natalie remonstrated lightly. "Poor Marcus! Anyway, we'd have to carry him, for he'd never keep up with us if we go all the way down to the Hermit's Well. I know we were supposed to rest this afternoon, before Lady Jessop's ball," she went on, "but it would be hateful, lying down with the blinds drawn on such a lovely day. And we don't often escape like this, do we?" Her face glowed with pleasure under the shady hat brim. "Oh, isn't it a pity that the boys are both away at school?" The glow faded a little. "We shan't see either of them until the summer holidays, and that's still ages away."

Julian, who bore the courtesy title of Viscount Grayle, was now fifteen and had been a pupil at Harrow for the last two years. His brother, Lord Justin, had joined him there the previous January. Natalie found the old school room in Grandison House oddly empty this summer without the boys' cheerful clutter of cricket bats, leg pads, stumps, and torn copies of the *Boy's Own Annual*.

Expertly looping up their trailing skirts, the sisters continued their walk, by mutual consent avoiding Speaker's Corner itself, which was not a pleasant place. On this hot day, however, only one preacher was ranting, before a sparse audience, on the evils of demon drink.

He surveyed the progress of the two girls stealthily until they were out of sight. Temptation was always at hand, he reminded himself, but these girls were exceptionally tempting. Tender young breasts thrusting up under their thin lace bodices. Tiny waists, needing no tight-laced corsets to pull them in. Such a seductive sway of rounded hips as they moved . . . Wistfully he noticed that two hopeful swains, dressed to kill in striped flannel blazers and straw boaters, were already pursuing them.

The cool green shelter of the trees ahead beckoned the girls on. Soon they reached the Flower Walk, which ran parallel to Bayswater Road. Delia bent to unlatch a small iron gate marking the border between Hyde Park and the tranquil peace of Kensington Gardens.

At this point, the two mashers gave up the chase, disappointed. It was obvious that the gorgeous creatures ahead were not in search of a flirtatious encounter. Leaning on the stone balustrade overlooking the Serpentine lake, they watched slanting rays of sunlight dance on an endless stream of water pouring from the mouths of two carved stone lions. The sky above was cerulean blue on this glorious afternoon.

Natalie sighed wistfully. "That poor boy was in seventh heaven with his balloon," she said. "I wish everyone could buy perfect happiness with a penny and keep it safe on the end of a string."

Delia looked at her affectionately. "It doesn't last, you know. By tomorrow the balloon will have burst, that boy will be hungry, and his father will have given him a black eye for missing school."

"But perhaps his father won't find out," Natalie answered reasonably. "I suppose we girls ought to be deliriously happy with all the advantages we have, as Mama so often reminds us."

"Most of which are burdens, but Mama never mentions that," Delia replied with a hint of sarcasm. "We have to set an example, obey stupid rules, pretend to enjoy dull company, and do a thousand other horrid things that are expected of us just because we're Lord Grandison's daughters."

Delia had seen a little more of life than her sheltered younger sister. Unknown to Mama, she often went riding by herself on an omnibus; she had observed the mean streets of Paddington and Notting Hill, and their miserable inhabitants, if only in safety from the top deck. She would not willingly embrace abject pov-

erty, but she was prepared to live frugally if the prize was freedom; and now it was within her grasp.

As the girls strolled on together Delia was about to share this
momentous news when Natalie laughed gaily, pointing ahead.

"Do you remember Julian walking backward into the Round
Pond that day when he was flying his kite for the first time?" she
asked. "It seems only a little while ago, but it must have been
years. The boys wouldn't deign to walk in the park with us now.
They'd think it terribly infra dig to be seen out with their sisters.
It's just as well we'll be at Grayle for the long summer holidays.
They can rampage there to their hearts' content. Besides, it's
always fun when we drive into Oxford with them in the wagonette."

Delia knew how much her sister loved the family's country
home, Grayle Abbey, and its proximity to the ancient university
nearby. "Speaking of Oxford, my dear Imp, I've a secret I've
been dying to share with you." Imp was a nickname reserved for
their special confidences, which Delia never dared use in her
parents' hearing. Now she caught Natalie's hand and, leading the
way down a verdant slope to the Hermit's Well, where genera-
tions of children had quenched their thirst, seated herself on the
crumbling rim.

"I haven't been sure until now that I really ought to tell you,
but I can't keep it to myself any longer. Natalie, I've been accepted as a student by Miss Rathbone, the principal of Somerville
College, and I'm going up to Oxford in October. I'll be reading
for a classics degree."

The healthy flush of exercise faded from Natalie's cheeks. She
was momentarily stunned by this bombshell. From the spectators
seated around the bandstand nearby came the sound of perfunc-
tory applause for the selection from Gilbert and Sullivan's *Mi-
kado* that had just ended.

"But do you really want so much to go, Delia?" Natalie finally
asked in a small, woebegone voice. "It's no more than a few
months since Justin went off to boarding school. I'll be the only
one left at home. I know you're extremely clever for a girl, and
it's wonderful to think of your being given a place at the college.
But the classics—Latin and Greek! I thought only absolute man-
haters were interested in such dry-as-dust subjects."

"Don't look so forlorn, dear," Delia broke in swiftly. "You
won't miss me as much as you think. There's your singing, and

you'll still be the leading light in amateur theatricals." She put
her arm around Natalie's waist. "As for men, I do hate them. At
least, men like the ones Mama has been parading for my inspection over the last three years. Dimwits who are only interested in
shooting parties and horses. Or insulting bores who refuse to
discuss anything worthwhile like politics or literature with me
because I'm just a brainless female. I wouldn't consider marrying
any of them, nor do I want any part in our mother's latest plan to
make me a lady-in-waiting at court. I fully intend to decline the
honor. I'm going to Oxford and no one can stop me, not even
Mama!"

The Marchioness of Grandison, dressed as Caesar's wife, Calpurnia, for Lady Jessop's fancy dress ball, felt decidedly pleased
gazing at her reflection.

The white silk robe clung most becomingly to her voluptuous
bosom and revealed invitingly the still beautiful sculpture of her
smooth shoulders. From the soft waves of flaxen hair surround-
ing her face smoothly in a high pompadour to the tips of her
gilded kid sandals, she looked superb. Gone was the shy, sensitive girl of her early married days.

Now in her forties, Lady Louise Grandison was one of those
renowned Edwardian beauties whose classic features were repro-
duced on thousands of picture postcards, to be displayed on
pianos and mantelpieces throughout the land; a being from another world, almost a goddess.

A new hand colored card had just been issued with great success, showing Louise seated on a chaise longue with her two
daughters leaning affectionately over her, one on either side.
Both girls were breathtakingly lovely. Cordelia, the elder, so divinely fair, and Natalie in striking contrast, so dark and dainty.
The title underneath the portrait was undeniably well chosen:
"The Grandison Graces." Louise quite approved of it.

She was in an excellent mood that night. Berman, the theatrical costumier in Garrick Street, had quite outdone himself. Her
daughters, Calpurnia's humble attendants, were both to be attired
in clinging silk robes like her own. He had fashioned a diapha-
nous blue cape for Delia to match the sapphires set in a gold
filigree headband from the family jewel casket. Natalie would
wear her white robe swathed in filmy amethyst chiffon, with
combs of mother-of-pearl to restrain the dusky torrent of her hair.

At seventeen, she needed no jewels to set off her extraordinary beauty.

Every detail was in the best of taste, a criterion by which the Marchioness set great store. There was not a hint of vulgarity in the design of their revealing dresses. Yet Louise was certain that the costumes worn by the Grandisons would create quite a sensation at the ball; which was exactly what she intended.

Flora, her maid, had just opened a Morocco leather case containing a diamond-encrusted circlet to crown the pale splendor of her unbound hair, when a knock came on the bedroom door. Hurrying to answer it, Flora returned with a note. On reading it, Louise gave an exclamation of annoyance.

One guest had cried off at the last moment, and the seating at dinner before the ball would be thoroughly put out.

Places had already been set in the dining room for a party of eight. There would be herself and Arthur; Captain Charles Haversham, Natalie's beau; and Charles's sister Eleanor. Louise had tactfully invited Lieutenant Russell Gates, a fellow officer of Charlie's, to escort Nell Haversham, who was quite unfortunately plain. Delia having refused to exert her undeniable charm on any possible suitor, Louise had made up the numbers by asking Hugo Sanderson, the girl's godfather, to make up the required number.

Lady Grandison tapped an impatient foot while the maid fastened a crimson velvet train across the nape of her neck with delicate cameo brooches. Then she swept down the corridor to her husband's dressing room. Arthur's valet was just handing him the finishing touch to his costume, a laurel wreath. With his imposing figure and patrician bearing, clad in a long toga under a gold-embroidered mantle of imperial purple, Arthur made a fine Caesar. He laid the wreath down at her entry.

"Read this, Arthur," Louise demanded, holding out the letter. "It's from young Russell Gates, or rather it is written on his behalf. Apparently he fell and broke his wrist playing polo today, so he sends his regrets. It's far too late to get a substitute. My list of unattached men is so short this year. I don't know what has happened to all the eligible bachelors, even the fortune hunters."

"Perhaps they have at last surrendered to the call of duty and married, my darling," her husband replied equably. Then he murmured to his valet, "That will be all for the moment, Gaston."

His wife had picked up the laurel wreath and was rearranging its glossy leaves, pulling at them quite irritably. He took it from her, dropping a kiss on the inside of her wrist. "By the way, you are looking exquisite tonight, but I think you already know that."

She sighed, not hearing his compliment.

"What is it, my dear?" he said gently. "Something else more serious is on your mind."

Already he was well aware that her preoccupation was probably connected with the future of their daughters. She was obsessed with fears for them.

Arthur had never forgiven Louise's spinster aunt Leonora for bringing up her niece without a shred of affection, only to thrust the neglected girl into society at the unusually late age of twenty.

Totally without social graces, the shy Louise had come perilously close to accepting the proposal of a persuasive but heartless wastrel, who would have gambled away her money and betrayed her in the arms of other women.

Arthur had then only recently resigned from the navy, to take up the title so unexpectedly left vacant by the death of his elder brother. Falling headlong in love with the hapless Louise, he had saved her from making a disastrous union by marrying her himself.

Over the years that followed he had watched her blooming into an opulent beauty with great satisfaction. Only he fully understood to what extent her childhood sufferings had left her in an emotional cage of ice. And if its bars had never totally melted in the heat of his physical passion, he had learned to receive with gratitude at least the willing submission of her magnificent body. . . .

"I might as well confess, Arthur," his wife finally admitted. "I fear that there is trouble to come where Delia is concerned. We have been most tolerant of her refusal to marry, although heaven knows she has had offers enough. But now she refuses to take up the post as Princess Mary's lady-in-waiting. One might almost think there was some third alternative, other than marriage or a post at court. But of course there is none for a girl in her position."

The diamonds in her rings flashed as she clasped her fingers together in agitation. "And then I am not entirely happy about Natalie's future. Charlie Haversham is only waiting for a sign from you that he should propose to her. She is attracting so much attention, he may be beaten to the post. You must have a private word with Charlie and persuade him that tonight at the ball he should declare himself!"

Arthur's brows lifted in surprise. "But Charlie has known both our girls almost since childhood. Do you think Natalie is likely to accept him?"

"Perhaps she does not care for him yet as she should do." Louise sighed. "But it is such a desirable match. I know he has no title. Well, neither has Winston Churchill. However, like Winnie, he is the grandson of a Duke and has many excellent connections. I hear he has an eye on a fine property in Oxfordshire, not far from our own. He can well afford to buy it and a nice little house in Curzon Street, too. Natalie would be mistress of a couple of excellent establishments, both quite near to ours."

"He is a good enough chap," Arthur admitted. "Doesn't drink too much, hardly gambles, and he's been head over heels in love with Natalie ever since he left Sandhurst. No likelihood of his regiment going to India, I suppose?"

"None," replied Louise triumphantly. "I've made it my business to find out. But unless she receives a strong hint that both of us are eager for the match, I believe she will turn him down."

Arthur placed the laurel wreath securely on his head and fastened his purple cloak with a carnelian brooch. "I refuse to put parental pressure on either of my daughters to marry," he said firmly. "Natalie has time yet. I'll speak to Charlie, by all means, but she must make her own choice. You may guide her a little, tell her I agree Charlie is a most dependable fellow, but I won't have her ordered to marry any man."

Louise threw him a radiant smile. Arthur's polite deference to his beloved wife concealed a steely determination to follow his own course, once his mind was made up. She avoided confronting him directly on any issue, preferring to let the matter drop. In fact, she herself intended to exert parental pressure of the strongest kind, for Charlie was just the son-in-law she wanted.

She laid her hand on her husband's arm and together they descended the harmonious sweep of the curving marble staircase.

Grandison House was a gracious specimen of late Georgian architecture, furnished in the style of the period. Its rooms were so beautifully proportioned that the present Marquess's father had never felt it necessary to crowd them with heavy pieces of the oppressive grandeur beloved by other Victorians. The drawing room was dotted with fragile sofas and chairs, upholstered in pastel-sprigged silks to match the walls, which had been decorated with painted swags and garlands of fruit in low relief. These walls were lined with sideboards and cabinets in walnut and mahogany, inlaid with pear wood. There was a full-sized concert grand piano in the music room, and a dais at one end for a small string orchestra. Although this room often accommodated upward of fifty couples of dancers, it would be inadequate for Natalie's coming-out ball, which was to be held at Grayle Abbey later in the summer.

Throughout the ground floor the high sash windows were draped in fringed satin curtains of sage green and amber. Family portraits by Gainsborough and Reynolds adorned the walls and were lit by sparkling chandeliers, every dew drop of glass trembling slightly in the warmth of the candles.

Arthur and Louise entered the drawing room, where Charlie Haversham, slightly self-conscious in doublet and hose as Romeo, was leaning against the ornate carved mantelpiece. He was, by the standard of the day, a good-looking fellow, with his florid complexion, dark brown hair, and carefully trimmed mustache.

His sister Nell's complexion was pasty by contrast. She was seated nearby, a pallid and unconvincing shepherdess, alone on a love seat. Across the room Delia was conversing with her godfather, who looked very much at ease dressed in a painter's linen smock and velvet beret. Hugo Sanderson was a confirmed bachelor and an old friend of the Grandison family, whom the girls, out of earshot of their parents, irreverently addressed as Sandy. Without being himself gifted, he was a great admirer of artistic talent and had chosen to live in St. John's Wood, the neighborhood preferred by painters. His nature made him less strict about convention than Louise would have wished, but his genuine affection for both girls was unquestioned; and he was much in demand as a suitable escort for them on outings to art galleries, concerts, and plays.

Dinner was announced and the party moved into the dining room. Nell was looking surly, for she had expected a partner of her own age and was not very happy to walk in on Hugo's kindly arm, while her dashing brother escorted the two Grandison sisters.

As dinner progressed Louise covertly observed Delia and thought once again of her daughter's refusal to marry. Miss Bail, the governess recommended by Hugo's late sister, Mildred, had

assured Louise and Arthur that Delia was an exceptional scholar
and should be indulged in her passion for higher education. Her
parents saw no reason to forbid the girl her lessons, until she
insisted she would choose Plato and Horace as her constant companions rather than, as she said, become any man's slave. If only
Delia would accept the honor of Queen Alexandra's court appointment, thought Louise angrily, it would put an end to the
rumors that the Grandisons had failed in marrying off their eldest
daughter.

Dessert had been served when Louise roused herself from
these thoughts. "Thomas, please serve coffee here instead of in
the drawing room," she directed the footman. "That is, if you
gentlemen will oblige us by forgoing your port? Their Majesties
are expected at the ball, and it would not do to arrive after the
royal party."

"And is Princess Mary to be there, too?" asked Nell, introducing the name by design, for she was consumed with curiosity
over the rumor of Delia's selection as a lady-in-waiting by the
royal family.

Putting down her silver fruit knife with a slight clatter, Delia
rose to her feet in anger.

"I know what you are hinting at, Nell," she said vehemently.
"And I must put a stop to any such talk once and for all." She
looked around at the astounded company, color flooding into her
cheeks. "Forgive me for mentioning such a matter at the dinner
table. And, Mama, I ask your pardon for disappointing you. I
have no intention of accepting a post at court, nor could I do so
now if I wished. I am going up to Oxford in October to study for
a degree. And that is the end of the matter."

In her astonishment Louise's retort was stern and cold. "Delia,
what can you be thinking of? To refuse such an honor offered by
royalty—you must be mad. And your father would never permit
you to attend the university. It is unthinkable for a girl of your
class."

"I am sorry to contradict you, but I shall be twenty-one next
month, and I'm afraid there is nothing either of you can do to
prevent me. I hoped you might be happy to have me so near,
when you are both at the Abbey. I would very much rather go
with your blessing, of course—"

"Your father will certainly not give you an allowance," Louise
interrupted sharply, quelling Arthur with a look, for she knew her
indulgent husband might even have a word of praise to offer.

"That will make no difference," Delia replied calmly. "There is my small inheritance from Aunt Mildred, which I receive when I come of age. It will be quite sufficient to see me through four years of study. I have already passed the entrance exam and been accepted for Somerville." She turned to her father. "It was hateful having to deceive you, but I knew you would never willingly have let me apply."

"We can hardly be expected to sympathize wholeheartedly with your academic aspirations, Delia," he said dryly. "They are rather presumptuous for a young lady, and your mother is bound to be distressed by them. But she will probably come to agree that there is nothing unseemly in your intention to go up to Oxford." He braved his wife's furious stare. "I heard last year that Lady Blanche Hozier's daughter, Clementine, had passed the Higher School Certificate and was thinking of doing the same thing. Classics are your choice, too, I suppose?"

"Yes, I dare say. Encouraged by that governess of hers," Louise interjected bitterly. She rounded on Mr. Sanderson. "Hugo, this is all your fault. I trusted Mildred's judgment in recommending the woman, and I've a shrewd idea that it was she who put all these so-called advanced ideas into Delia's head. You must have known something about it, and you should have warned me." Her wrathful eyes then fell upon Natalie. "And I suppose you took part in this plot?"

Natalie, usually the last to defy her mother, answered calmly, "I did not know of Delia's plans until today. She must have worked very hard to win a place at Somerville, and I admire her for it."

"Mama, please do not be angry with either Uncle Hugo or Natalie for what you interpret as my disloyalty to the family. No one else is to blame, and no one could have persuaded me to give up my plans for the future. I dreaded telling you, but now it's out in the open." Delia pushed back her chair. "Please excuse me from attending the ball tonight. I don't think I could dance or make polite conversation just now."

She ran out of the room in a flurry of silken skirts and disappeared upstairs to the sanctuary of her bedroom.

In the ominous silence Louise sat biting her lip, barely containing her fury. Hugo busied himself with peeling a nectarine, determined not to enter the quarrel. Coffee was poured, conversation flagged, and presently Arthur drew out his slim gold pocket watch and announced that they ought to be leaving.

Audrey Ellis

* * *

From the mews behind their house in Park Lane to the elegant drive leading to the Jessops' home, not a word was spoken in the Grandison carriage. As the perfectly matched grays trotted smartly toward Hyde Park Corner, Louise delicately touched her bottle of smelling salts to her nose; it was a sign to Arthur and Natalie that she was angry rather than indisposed. The other members of the party were following them closely in a second carriage; Delia, still fuming with anger, was left behind.

Music was already drifting out from the ballroom at Lady Jessop's splendid mansion. The strains of a polka gave way to a brisk military two-step. It was well after ten o'clock, and one of the most exclusive events on London's social calendar was in full swing.

As she reached the receiving line the hand Louise laid on her husband's arm trembled visibly. The shock of Delia's scandalous defection had shaken her to the core. The poor Marchioness was noticeably on edge, another lady murmured to a friend. So unlike her, something serious must be wrong. Besides, it was unusual for the Grandisons to arrive late. Why, a few more minutes and they might have clashed with the royal party! And it was known that Lady Grandison was a stickler for the finer points of etiquette.

She was deeply wounded by Delia's outburst, and no one, not even Arthur, understood how deeply. Disturbing thoughts filled her mind, which kept harping back to that shocking disclosure at dinner. What would her friends think of Delia, a peer's daughter, at Oxford University? Such a thing was unheard of. Nell, for one, would never keep her mouth shut with such a juicy scandal to confide. Fortunately, she assured herself, she had the gift of concealing her emotions beneath a calm exterior. That evening, however, they came close to breaking the barriers of her self-control.

Her bruised spirits gradually recovered as friends greeted the Grandisons and admired their costumes. Smiling and confident, Louise explained to all who were curious that Delia, the poor dear, had been out rather too long in the park today and was overwhelmed by the heat. Taking care to reserve the supper dance and last waltz with Natalie for himself, Charlie whispered a compliment or two in her ear before wandering off to seek some boon companions in the card room. Hugo remained close to Nell, more out of pity than inclination.

The group about the Grandison family thinned at last. A gentleman they hardly knew, the merest acquaintance, was asking to introduce an old friend of his, a Russian professor named Lensky, and his protégé. Arthur graciously inclined his head and Louise allowed the foreigner, whose only concession to fancy dress was the wearing of a tasseled red fez, to kiss her hand.

He addressed her warmly. "Lady Grandison, I am honored to meet you and the illustrious Marquess. My patrons, to whom I am distantly related, have entrusted me with the enjoyable task of escorting this estimable young man on his first tour of Europe." He gestured toward his companion. "I refer, of course, to their Imperial Highnesses, the Grand Duke Constantine Voroshnikoff and the Grand Duchess Natalya. Pray allow me to present their son, Prince Andrei, to you, and to this charming young lady."

"Delighted," said Arthur heartily. "I remember the Voroshnikoffs well, as does my wife, I am sure. This is our daughter Lady Natalie."

Lensky stepped back, making way for a young man magnificently dressed as a Cossack, who swept off his gray astrakhan hat. He was tall, slender, and dark, with an air of regal bearing.

"Prince Andrei Voroshnikoff," the professor intoned proudly.

"Enchanté," the newcomer murmured, bowing over Lady Grandison's hand.

Louise was speechless. She could not tear her gaze from that noble face and the black magnetic eyes, which held hers for an instant with the proud look that had once made her the helpless slave of his father, the Grand Duke Constantine. She felt the touch of his warm, firm lips on her hand. Then to her utter dismay she saw the eagerness that glowed in those eyes as they took in the enticing form of Natalie, standing by her side.

Chapter 2

Andrei had been bored by his first experience with English society. The bals masqués in Paris, which permitted costly courtesans, ladies of the demimonde, to enter, had been far more intriguing. But, then, the sense of decorum one still found at the British court was entirely lacking from the society whose tone was set by President Loubet of France.

The weeks spent in his tutor's company in the French capital had been vastly amusing, despite his disappointment in Desirée, the trivial, empty-headed little aristocrat his parents intended him to marry. She had a cooing, monotonous voice and, he suspected, the brain of a pouter pigeon. She had not the necessary presence to wear with éclat the famous Voroshnikoff black pearls, which so became his willowy mother. However, she would bring to her husband an immense dowry, and the income derived from the Voroshnikoff estates was severely strained by his parents' luxurious style of living. It was Andrei's duty to marry a wealthy heiress, yet one whose lineage was as exalted as his own. He was quite reconciled to this fate.

But now that he had crossed the Channel and escaped the watchful eye of his future wife's guardian, he intended to make the most of his time in the other European capitals.

Vladimir Lensky was an understanding preceptor. He had received his instructions from the Grand Duke Constantine himself that Andrei was to meet everyone of consequence, and yet be denied none of the dissolute pleasures of a young man of fashion. Wherever they went, Lensky could be relied upon to have an intimate knowledge of the most titillating forms of dissipation that could be enjoyed without stirring up the adverse comment of polite society.

His discretion was absolute. Under his tutelage, Andrei had met and charmed the elite of Vienna, Rome, and then Paris. Here in London, Vladimir had considered the time was ripe to widen the boy's experience. He acquainted him with a pretty actress of the London stage whose favors were much sought after. The gift of a ruby pendant, chosen by Vladimir at Asprey's in Bond Street and hidden in a huge basket of crimson roses, had already almost persuaded her to desert her present protector and throw herself into the arms of the handsome and generous boy.

But at twenty, Andrei's heart had never been touched, nor had he ever known what it was to yearn hopelessly for an unattainable love. Older women, friends of his mother's, had not been averse to teaching the fiery and passionate youngster with the looks of a fallen angel the ways of the flesh. He tasted also the earthy love of peasant girls, who expected only a few roubles and a playful slap from the young prince afterward. These experiences he found more to his liking.

The English actress, perhaps, might be different, he thought. But all his sexual adventures so far, no matter how satisfying for the moment, had made him restless, searching for something more without knowing what it was.

It was the seeker in him that drew Andrei toward one of the late arrivals, a slender girl whose face he could only half glimpse.

Her figure, standing there so full of grace, was utter perfection. Instantly, a tremor of desire ran through him. The Prince siezed his friend's arm and asked in a low voice, "Who is that glorious creature, who has just entered?" A deep yearning took hold within him—he *must* speak with her.

"You mean the Grandisons' lovely daughter Natalie? Would you like an introduction?"

Andrei might not have insisted, but at that moment he met those incredible eyes; the irises dark blue and circled with a less determinate shade, turning them almost the color of the amethyst cloak fluttering from her shoulders. She smiled faintly, thinking that perhaps they had met, since he stared at her so piercingly. Then realizing that he was after all a stranger, the merest tinge of delicate rose stained the creamy paleness of her cheeks, and she looked away, unconsciously presenting him with a profile as perfectly sculptured as that on any Greek coin of antiquity.

Black hair poured down her slender neck in a shining, slightly curling stream to the silver girdle that circled her waist. In an instant he knew he could have spanned that waist with his fingers, and that he ached to do so; wanted to stroke that alabaster cheek, plunge his hands into that silken hair, and inhale the perfume of her flesh, which he guessed would be sweet as the crushed petals of parma violets.

"Be so kind as to present me," he said quickly, and moments later it was a fait accompli.

As he took her hand to kiss, Andrei judged Lady Grandison to have been rightly described. She was a handsome woman but cold as the arctic wastes of Siberia. Then his gaze was captured by Natalie's lovely figure in the dress that so well displayed the firm roundness of her breasts and the alluring swell of her hips beneath the tight silver belt. He drank in the serene yet mysterious regard of those violet eyes, and his heart leapt in his breast as though a great wave bore him forward. He felt a stab of longing to enfold this exquisite creature in his arms. But he could only bow, for etiquette did not permit him even to kiss the hand of a debutante.

"May I?" He reached politely for her dance program, only to find that almost all the dances were already taken. He scribbled his initials against the number before the supper dance and, more reluctantly, several dances in Nell's. He would have lingered, but suddenly the hum of conversation died down, and Lady Jessop was waiting, glowing with satisfaction at the announcement of the arrival of Their Majesties, and the guests parted, forming two long lines to receive them. Portly King Edward appeared tired and aged, and with a wave of his hand he put an end to the formalities. The band struck up a waltz by Strauss, and Natalie was whirled away in the arms of another admirer.

Vladimir, ever vigilant, knew at once of Andrei's attraction to Lady Natalie and, in a fleeting, imagined scene, envisioned himself held responsible by Constantine for introducing his charge to an eligible young girl of high birth who would put paid to his family's plans for their son. . . . But surely the young fool would not want to marry her. He assured himself he was being foolish. Why, his charge had fallen in love and out again at least ten times in the past year, he said to himself smugly. . . .

Andrei's dashing looks and air of regal breeding caused a stir among the guests, but he noticed none of their curious glances, for he could not take his eyes from Natalie.

When at last it was time for their dance together, he approached the family group and offered his arm, then led his lovely partner to the dance floor, oblivious of the cold glint in Lady Grandison's eyes. The couple swirled gracefully round the floor, enveloped in a silence that was highly charged with emotion. "How odd that I have never heard my mother speak of you," Natalie said at last. "Papa has told me that I was named for your mother, the Grand Duchess Natalya. My parents spent a wonderful summer with the Voroshnikoff family in the Crimea years ago—oh, it must have been before I was born." He said nothing, and she went on bravely: "My sister, Delia, says she can remember Mama and Papa being away for a long trip and crying because she missed them. She cried again when they got home, because they hadn't brought her a dancing bear. But she was only about three at the time. . . ."

Natalie knew she was talking wildly, for the touch of the hand that held hers was charged, as with electricity; and the fingers around her waist seemed to burn through the thin silk and caress her bare flesh. She knew nothing of savage bodily passion. Charlie's tame caresses inspired no profound desires within her. She had never been overwhelmed as she was now by physical longing, and the foreign sensations left her shaking and not a little frightened. Sensing her feelings, Andrei thought quickly how he might calm her fears.

"Your parents have so many friends and perhaps ceased to correspond with mine years ago," he said, trying to speak casually as they swayed together in the intimacy of a waltz. "But as we have this common bond of my mother's name between us, may I presume to call you Natalie? I should be honored."

She laughed at the thought of the little conspiracy and the tension between them slackened. "Indeed, you may, and I shall call you Andrei. Please tell me something about your home in Russia. I've always dreamed of riding in a troika—is it true they have arches of bells over the horses?" She smiled up at him, unaware that she was moving farther into the welcoming curve of his arm.

"Yes, quite true; and I would love to take you driving with me," he replied. "But you cannot imagine how cold it is there in winter, when the rivers are all frozen. The snow muffles every sound except the troika bells. I should have to wrap you in furs, and hold you much closer than this to keep you warm. . . ." He pressed his body against hers as they moved together in perfect accord to the music. She was taken aback by this covertly sensual gesture and the frank expression in words of his longing to hold her more closely. To strike a less intimate note, she whispered, "Is there still water flowing beneath the ice even in midwinter? I have heard it is dangerous to walk upon, for sometimes it cracks; people sink and are swept away by the swift current. . . ."

"The cruel Neva has claimed many souls in Moscow. My country is full of such savage perils, but Russia has incredible splendors, too. If I could show you the Kremlin, with its golden domes gleaming against a white winter sky . . . If only I knew the words in English to describe it!"

"I'm sure it's magnificent," she said breathlessly.

"Would you dare come there, then, with me? You would not need to fear, though it is very different, I admit, from your placid countryside. It would be my task and my delight to protect you, if only I might be permitted to do so."

As the waltz ended the other dancers were looking about them for their supper partners and heading for the sumptuous buffet in the dining hall. Nell chattered to her brother as they left the ballroom, describing in gushing terms the distinguished-looking prince from far-distant Russia. "So handsome, Charlie, he quite mesmerized me!" she quavered.

Louise was casting an anxious eye over the throng, impatient for her daughter's return, when she was invited by a gentleman-in-waiting to join the royal circle at the head table. With a gracious inclination of her head, she took Arthur's arm. But she was determined not to comply until she had found Natalie. Just as the girl was regretfully thinking she should return to her family, Andrei took her hand and, to her delight, led her out to the garden. Small tables and chairs, dimly lit by colorful paper lanterns, were invitingly set about the rim of a splashing fountain. The moon had long since risen and hung round and full above the chimney tops of Belgrave Square. As Andrei drew back a chair for her, Natalie thought fleetingly of her mother and father and, with a twinge of guilt, knew they would later reprimand her for her behavior. But when she studied the boldly handsome face framed with ebony hair, the dark, deep-set eyes above high sculpted cheekbones, and the mouth she sensed could be harshly unyielding or tenderly sensuous according to his mood, she yearned for the first time to touch and kiss a man.

As if he had read her mind, he leaned closer to her and said in a low, gentle voice, "If you felt that you desired something passionately, more passionately than anything else in the world, would you dare to risk defying society's petty rules?"

In that intimate moment the attraction between them reached a fever pitch. Her pretty lips parted slightly, his eyes gazed deep into hers, and they drew unconsciously together, both longing to savor their first kiss.

Suddenly the magic was cruelly broken by the sound of Lady Grandison's voice.

"Natalie, my dear, you must have forgotten that Charlie is waiting to take you in to supper. You will break the poor boy's heart if you tease him like this. It is most unkind of you to hide away with Prince Andrei in the garden." Her patronizing tones conveyed an unmistakable reproach. She then addressed Andrei, who had risen and become quite white and expressionless. "You, too, Prince; you're neglecting the little shepherdess who is waiting for her bold Cossack to claim her."

Louise turned and left them without glancing back, sure they would follow.

Resentment rose in Natalie's breast. To treat her like a child, and then to insult this imperious, exciting stranger—how *could* she! She struggled to restrain her fury as she took her place beside a sulky Charlie. At the other end of the table she glimpsed Nell clinging possessively to Andrei's arm as he politely held her plate, loaded with cold salmon and plovers' eggs in aspic.

Later, when they filed back into the ballroom, Andrei's anxious eyes met Natalie's, and for one breathtaking moment understanding passed between them: they would, at all costs, seek each other out again. The link that had already been forged between them was too precious to be broken.

While the Marquess and his lady were divesting themselves of their costumes, daybreak was already faintly apparent between the draped satin curtains at Park Lane. Presently Arthur, clad in silk pajamas and burgundy lounging jacket, knocked at the door of his wife's boudoir. After an important reception, he liked to watch Louise having her hair unpinned and brushed by Flora, and talk over the entertainment of the evening. He enjoyed smoking a cigar during that intimate hour together in the perfumed comfort of her dressing room.

"How did your dear Alix receive Delia's rebuff?" he inquired, as Louise removed her cameo earrings with a graceful turn of her head.

"Reasonably well," his wife admitted. "She was the first to agree that a bookish girl like Delia might be ill-suited to the post. Both George and Mary, bless them, are high-minded, conscientious, but, one must admit—a little stuffy. Delia's suffragist sympathies would not go down well there, I fancy! I must make the best of it, I suppose, and pretend in front of all my friends that I applaud her decision to remain a spinster instead of enjoying the natural occupations of womanhood: marriage, and raising children in a sound, well-provided home."

Arthur stubbed out his cigar. He gestured for Flora to leave them. "Are you sure that happiness is to be found only in the love of a good man, if such a paragon exists, for Delia?" he asked mildly. "I know how long you have looked forward to a magnificent marriage for at least one of our girls, and that Delia as the elder was your chosen candidate. I don't question your love for them both, of course; I only suggest that perhaps they may wish to follow different paths in life. . . ."

"Love? I hope I not only love them, but know my duty toward them, too!" Louise cried, pressing one white hand to her heart. "Delia has disappointed me. But she is not at Oxford yet and, like dear Clemmie, might give up the idea before the season is over. She may have second thoughts, or only stay there a matter of weeks. I believe the students are wretchedly accommodated at Somerville. We'll see how far she plans to take this independence. Remember, our girls are used to every refinement of comfort. I have not completely given up hope as far as Delia is concerned."

Arthur laughed indulgently, stroking Louise's other hand. "Dearest one, you are incorrigible. I think you will find Delia quite intransigent. But, tell me something, my love," he went on. "I hope this does not mean you will now look higher than Charlie

Haversham for Natalie. Don't try to force the child into making a great marriage. I dare say she would be unhappy."

"There you do me a wrong, Arthur," his wife declared vehemently. "I never envisaged a coronet and ermine for Natalie. She has a certain childlike quality, a volatile nature, that would be oppressed by such grandeur. Her health is not robust; it is very much governed by her emotions. I would like to see her marry well but not to be bowed down by the weight of another title. That is why Charlie will do so splendidly for her."

"The young Russian who was presented to us this evening, Prince Andrei, seemed much taken with her," Arthur said musingly, watching carefully his wife's reaction.

Maintaining her composure, she spoke coldly, "Impossible. Do you want your little daughter, with her delicate constitution and highly strung temperament, to be borne off to that awful country thousands of miles away, where civilization is still stuck fast in the Middle Ages?"

Arthur at once decided to dismiss the subject. Yet when he took in his arms the splendid body of the wife whose flesh still had the power to stir him to delight, he could not quite banish from his mind a vision of the young couple waltzing across the dance floor, completely mesmerized by the dawning adoration in their eyes.

Chapter 3

Seated at the drawing-room piano, Natalie relived in a dream her romantic introduction to Prince Andrei and their brief interlude in the moonlit garden. A frown creased the smooth forehead between her finely arched brows; memories of that magical evening were tarnished by recollections of her mother's interference.

She began to sing very softly, accompanying herself only by an occasional chord: "Drink to me only with thine eyes . . ." She sighed, deep in thought as she gently touched the ivory keys. Yesterday had marked the end of her carefree girlhood. Her relationship with Mama and Papa had always been close, but today she saw her love for them in a different light.

Suddenly Papa was overshadowed by the brilliance of Prince Andrei, and Mama had proved herself an idol with feet of clay.

Only adding more confusion to her somber thoughts was the disturbing exchange she had with Delia earlier that morning. Certain that Delia must have cried herself to sleep the night before, Natalie found her sister, already dressed in cool navy blue voile, writing a letter at her desk with such haste and vehemence that the pen nib scored deep into the paper, and ink splattered over every sentence. Seeing Natalie, Delia put down her pen and, smiling, clasped her sister's hands affectionately.

35

"Nattie, darling, don't fret." Delia's wonderful red-gold hair was hanging in a thick braid over one shoulder, and she used it as she had when they were children, to dab imaginary tears away from the other girl's eyes. "You stood up for me splendidly with Mama. I wouldn't have believed you could bring yourself to do it. And Papa, I dare say, sat on the fence as usual after I left the room. I know in his heart he is quite proud of me, but he doesn't dare to contradict Mama."

Natalie was shocked. "You make Papa sound as though he's afraid of speaking his mind to his own wife."

Delia could hardly suppress an indulgent smile. "You are so naïve, my little sister. Mama is by far the stronger of the two, and woe betide any of us who dare to thwart her. She will do her best to make my life miserable, hoping to wear me down. No doubt she says I have deceived her, gone behind her back to sit the exams." Glancing toward her half-finished letter, the girl went on. "She also blames poor Miss Bail, who sincerely thought I wanted only the kudos of knowing that I won a place at Oxford and never dreamed of taking it up. I'm writing to her to say that both she and I would do well to keep out of Mama's way for the time being. True, Papa will pity me, but he won't cross Mama, you'll see."

Delia took her sister's arm and led her to the open window. "Forget about my troubles. I am made of sterner stuff than Mama may think. Look, isn't it a wonderful day? I predict we shall soon have a troop of your admirers, including the inevitable Charlie Haversham, come calling with their bouquets." She turned to Natalie. "Now, tell me, how did you enjoy the ball? I want to know everything!"

Natalie looked away from her sister. "Actually, I danced with a complete stranger, a Russian Prince, and we sat out together," she said shyly. "Oh, Delia . . ." She faced her sister. "He's fascinating—I've never met a young man like him! He's very tall, and his dark eyes seemed to pierce right through me. And his voice is wonderful. He speaks with an unusual accent; it has almost a French intonation."

Delia was astonished, for Natalie rarely took such a fancy to a new acquaintance.

"But I'm afraid I'll never see him again," she went on, "because Mama was so horrid to him, hinting that I was already engaged. You know very well, Delia, I would never accept Charlie, no matter how much Mama wanted me to."

"You're not yet eighteen, darling. You don't have to say yes to Charlie, nor throw your bonnet over the windmill for the first Casanova who woos you with hypnotic glances and an intriguing foreign accent. Surely you know all well-bred Russians speak French at home; they think their language is fit only for serfs." Delia slipped an arm lightly around Natalie's shoulder. "But be warned," she went on. "Don't count on Papa's support if you are thinking of upsetting our dear mother's schemes. Now, do go and get dressed, darling. I must finish this letter to Miss Bail."

The last notes of Natalie's song faded. She had put on her prettiest white organdy gown with lilac ribbons. *If only he would call today,* she thought. Then, dismissing her hope with a sigh, she resumed her song, almost convinced that she was destined never again to meet the stranger who had stirred her sleeping senses so profoundly.

Unbeknownst to Natalie, the Marchioness had given strict instructions that callers were not to be admitted that morning. They might leave flowers and cards, but neither she nor her daughters would be at home to visitors.

One or two sprigs of the nobility, including Charlie, left their flowers and their compliments to the Lady Natalie.

Then came the dashing figure of Prince Andrei, in all the glory of pale gray morning dress, and carrying a huge basket of parma violets.

Louise, who was occupied in the morning room dealing with the day's batch of invitations, heard the unmistakably imperious tones of Constantine's son in the hall. He had offered his visiting card to the butler and was insisting that he wished to present his violets personally.

With slow, dignified gait Adams approached the small reception room, not relishing the task of retailing this mesage.

As he stood, tall and straight, awaiting the butler's return, Andrei became aware of a sweet soprano voice, and though just a faint strain of the lovely music drifted to him, he recognized the singer instantly. Flooded with longing to feast his eyes on Natalie again, he grew impatient. At last the servant appeared. "Please come this way, sir," Adams said in a deferential tone. But to Andrei's dismay, he was taken to the morning room and found himself confronted by Lady Grandison. She spoke sharply.

"Good morning, Prince Andrei. How kind of you to call. Are these flowers for Natalie? Charming. I am afraid she is not receiving anyone today. A headache, you know. Please leave them with me."

Extremely sensitive to her antipathy, but unable to refuse such a reasonable request, Andrei passed over his gift. "I hope I may call again on a more auspicious day. Perhaps I have given you an unfortunate first impression, for which I am heartily sorry."

"We shall no doubt run across each other at some function or other," Louise replied frostily. "Until then, *au revoir.*"

When the Prince had reluctantly taken his leave, Louise thrust the basket of violets into the arms of her maid. "Just a moment, Flora," she commanded. From deep within the bouquet, she withdrew a note. It read simply:

Natalie, *mes hommages*.
Andrei.

Tearing it into bits, Louise snapped out another order. "When you take Marcus for his walk this morning, pray dispose of these flowers; the nurses at St. George's Hospital will be glad to accept them. And clear this away." She indicated the torn pieces of paper. "Then send Adams to me."

Knowing it was wise to obey his mistress with alacrity, Adams covered the distance between Flora and the morning-room door with unusual speed and inquired, "You sent for me, milady? What may I have the pleasure of doing for you?"

"The gentleman who called just now . . . if he should come again, I wish him to be told that we are not at home. He will not be received by any member of the family. Is that perfectly clear?" The butler nodded. "Oh, and, Adams," Louise went on, "if he leaves a message, or a gift of flowers for—for either of the young ladies, it is to be brought to me."

The next day, Natalie breakfasted early and then, deciding to give up her usual promenade on horseback with Delia, joined Mama to receive callers. For the second morning in succession, her hopes rose high of seeing the Prince again. Charlie soon arrived, accompanied by Nell. There were other visitors; young gentlemen who came to make sheep's eyes at the loveliest debutante of the year, though none was as handsome as this young Russian Prince.

Perhaps she would like to hear Madame Calvé sing the title role in Messenet's *Salomé*, one of them suggested. The very first performance in England of this exotic opera was to take place the next week at Covent Garden. On the chance that Andrei might be invited to one of the many functions, Natalie was tempted to accept invitations to them all.

The Grandisons had taken a box at the opera to hear Calvé, Louise announced to the entire gathering, and she assured Charlie that Natalie would be delighted if he would escort her. The girl assented dutifully but without enthusiasm. Bitterly disappointed, she could only surmise with a sinking heart that Andrei did not care to call.

The rest of the day seemed endless, for they had no evening engagement.

The following morning, Delia, outfitted for riding, entered her sister's room. "Do ask Linnet to bring your riding clothes," Delia cajoled. "This time I won't take a refusal." Linnet, proud of being the maid chosen to come down to London from Grayle Abbey to serve the young ladies, went at once to do so.

"Oh, if it will make you happy," Natalie replied.

After a moment, her sister continued on a more intimate note: "You've pined long enough for your Prince. He obviously doesn't intend to come. Mama must have offended him to an unforgivable degree; everyone knows these Russians are insanely proud and take mortal offense over the least thing."

To Delia's amazement Natalie put her hands over her face and burst into sobs. Delia raised the weeping girl tenderly from her seat before the mirror.

"Truly, I didn't know you were so much hurt by his lack of interest. Darling, don't cry like that. Do you really want so much to see him again?"

Natalie lifted her tear-stained face. "Oh, I do, Delia. I do. I can think of nothing but Andrei. Please don't scold me for being such a little fool. I'm not used to disappointments. But I begin to realize that life is full of them, after one is grown up." She tried to smile through her tears.

"It appears to me you have grown up a great deal in the last few days; enough, at least, to lose your heart. Listen, darling, and do take my advice." Delia's voice was coaxing. "Start by drying your eyes. Here, take my handkerchief! Accept every invitation that Mama allows to come your way. This Prince moves in the same circles of society as we do ourselves. You are almost bound to run across him at some ball or reception. If it's all a misunderstanding, or something Mama has engineered, you can soon find it out." Her blue eyes gleamed wickedly. "Be brave, and when you meet, don't be afraid to speak to him. You've been introduced, after all. No one could accuse you of being forward."

Natalie was beginning to look more hopeful. "Make a start this morning," Delia suggested. "It's a lovely day again, so practically everyone we know will be driving or riding in the Row. Maybe your fascinating Andrei is already there himself, anxiously scanning the crowds for a certain young lady with dark hair and the most extraordinary pair of violet eyes!"

"You're absolutely right, Delia!" Natalie wiped away her tears. "I don't believe anyone else in the world has such an understanding sister. I feel better already. Just give me a few minutes to get dressed. I promise I won't keep you waiting."

Delia nodded and went out humming, knowing that Natalie needed a short respite to compose herself. She was in far better spirits than last night. Mama could no longer pull the strings and make her daughters dance like puppets. Both she and Natalie had the right to mold their own lives. With a confident smile, Delia stepped out into the brilliant morning sun to wait for her sister.

Cordelia and Natalie walked their horses, two superb gray geldings with manes neatly plaited, into Hyde Park under the watchful eye of the family's head groom, Jamieson. The girls looked stunning in their tailored dark blue riding dresses, and many heads turned as they rode by.

When Andrei again called upon Natalie, he was certain he was being put off when the butler informed him regretfully of her absence. Telling himself he was not really going against her ladyship's orders, and unwilling to face those piercing black eyes with an outright lie, the butler murmured that both the young ladies often went riding in the Row during the morning. After leaving an exquisite basket of orchids with the sympathetic servant, Andrei strode off, determined to hire a suitable mount for himself and join in the fashionable equestrian display.

Having inspected and found acceptable a spirited beast, he chose to ride unaccompanied and permitted Vladimir to spend the morning idly turning the pages of *The Tatler* in the lounge at the Ritz. Lensky was not a keen horseman and much preferred chatting with his fellow guests.

Andrei made three complete circuits of the Row and was beginning to feel that once more his quest for a meeting with Natalie was in vain when he caught sight of an animated group. Two young ladies reined in, with their groom at a respectful distance, to talk to one of the strollers; another girl who carried a beige silk parasol was twirling it in an exaggerated fashion to reveal the lining of countless pink chiffon ruffles.

"I seem to have lost my chaperon," she said loudly. "There is such a crush today! I only darted off to speak to a couple of Charlie's fellow officers, and we became separated in the crowd." Her voice carried loud and clear. "Natalie, my dearest love, have you seen any more of that devastatingly good-looking Russian? I could hardly get a word out of him, but he was incredibly handsome in a frightening sort of way. I adore strong, silent men, don't you? I trembled, positively trembled, when he offered me his arm. . . ."

His eager eyes scanning the group, Andrei recognized the girl with the loud voice: it was the shepherdess of the costume ball.

Then behind the golden-haired Diana in blue she was now addressing he saw another slighter figure, sitting her mount with equal grace. He glimpsed a mass of black hair, drawn back from the slender neck, the delightful tilt of the head. It was Natalie. She looked up and encountered his gaze, fixed with agonized intensity on her face.

Instinctively he spurred his horse forward, but the crowd was too thick; he could not reach them.

Just then, Nell remarked, "Why, there is Mr. Balfour with his wife, coming toward us in his carriage. It is not often one sees the Prime Minister out driving!"

Top hats and boaters were being lifted, elegant women were raising gloved hands, as the leading statesman's brougham approached, while he smiled and nodded to each salute in turn.

On opposite sides of the carriage road two women had been sitting for some time beside hooded perambulators, resting while their babies slept. During the last few minutes each had been joined by a couple of friends. At a prearranged signal between the two groups, the perambulators were uncovered, the hoods pushed back, and it was plain that they contained not sleeping infants, but piles of banners. In unison they stepped out into the road, hoisting their banners in the air, and the startled onlookers could see emblazoned on each the words VOTES FOR WOMEN. Mr. Balfour's coachman drew up sharply, pulling the horses back on their haunches. A tandem coming from the opposite direction collided with two bicyclists, who flew off into the road amid angry shouts and a welter of spinning wheels. The tandem driver lost control of the reins and shrank back in his seat, covering his mouth with panic-stricken hands. There were screams and frenzied attempts by ladies hindered by long skirts to escape the panic. A woman fainted, collapsing under the hooves of the frightened horse rearing and pawing at the air.

Dismounting at a bound, Andrei rushed to the unconscious woman's aid. He grabbed the reins and backed the frightened animal away, then helping her safely to her feet, he withdrew and merged with the crowd.

Two policemen thrust their way into the throng, smashing the banners, before arresting the unrepentant demonstrators and marching them roughly away from the scene.

Jamieson, concerned over his charges' welfare, could not restrain his outrage at the scene they witnessed.

"Bleeding suffragettes!" he cried. "Come away, young ladies, do, before the bobbies start using their truncheons."

Delia caught Natalie's rein, and the two highly bred geldings began to back off nervously. The crowd was between Natalie and Andrei, who was struggling to remount, impeded by well-wishers anxious to slap him on the back. Delia urged her sister forward, driving them further apart, oblivious of Natalie's protests. In a few moments she could no longer even see him.

The crowds became less dense as the Grandison girls cantered briskly toward Hyde Park Corner in Jamieson's wake. Natalie could hardly believe her ill luck.

Delia could think only of the courage of those dedicated combatants in the struggle to win support for their cause. "Weren't they wonderful, Natalie?" she cried as they headed home. "One can't help admiring those brave women. I wish I had the same courage of my convictions."

As the two girls entered the calm sanctuary of their own hall, Lord Grandison was preparing to leave for his club. Delia ran to him at once and began to pour out her story of the exciting incident in the park.

"They stood quite firm, Papa, all six of them, even though they were being punched and shouted at, until the police started to hustle them away. It's true they might have caused an accident if some young man hadn't quietened the horses. I wonder who he was. I must say he acted very promptly."

Natalie longed to break in and cry out, "That was my Prince!" but she kept silent while Delia went on enthusiastically: "How else can the Suffragist Movement bring its cause to the attention of the Prime Minister? He refuses to receive any deputation from its leaders."

Looking grave, Arthur handed back his leather gloves and stick to Adams. "Come into the library for a moment, my dears, before you go up to change," he invited his daughters, leading the way toward his book-lined sanctum. It was his private and solitary retreat, even more dear to him than the study, where he wrote his letters.

He could not suppress a rush of warm affection when he looked at his two girls, but the Marquess reminded himself that he had something very serious to say to both of them.

"I'm well aware, Delia," he began, "that your mother has not willingly accepted your going to Oxford. Personally, I sympathize with your ambitions, and I'm prepared to do everything in my power to persuade her to come around to my way of thinking. But if you provoke her by voicing opinions like those I have just heard from you, there's no hope of my succeeding." He frowned at his elder daughter. "She already suspects Miss Bail of being an active suffragette, and of infecting you with her own extreme views. Need I point out that these women you found so admirable might have caused great harm to innocent bystanders? Promise me that you will stick to your academic aims and not be drawn into any subversive activities that might tarnish the name of Grandison."

Delia put her arms around his neck. "Oh, Papa, I never thought of it like that. You know how I am; I say the first thing that comes into my head. Of course I promise you to be utterly discreet. And you don't know what it means to me to have your blessing."

Patting her cheek, Arthur was well satisfied with her reply. He then turned to his younger girl. "As for you, Natalie, my love, I imagine you are finding your first season something of an ordeal. I know you have attracted admirers, and that your mother is keen to see you comfortably settled. But I don't want you to enter into any engagement unless you feel certain of your affections. And somehow I do not believe you have yet met the man capable of winning your heart."

Natalie sensed that this was her father's way of admitting his lack of support for Charlie Haversham's suit. She went to lean against his shoulder, almost tempted to confide the shy awakening of her love for Andrei.

Just then the door opened and Louise came in with her adored Marcus barking excitedly at her heels.

"What a charming scene," she said lightly, holding out her hand for Arthur to kiss. Both girls noticed that her eyes were coolly watchful.

Ignoring the mild savor of conspiracy in the air, she helped herself to a supply of pink and white sugared almonds from a porcelain sweet box and sat down opposite her husband.

"Your gown has arrived from the couturier, Natalie. I must say he is most attentive. The dressmaker who brought the box is waiting to make any last-minute alterations I feel necessary. Come upstairs, my dear."

Natalie had quite forgotten her imminent presentation at court; and she now showed less interest than her vigilant mother expected.

As they went out into the hall together, Marcus following eagerly, they encountered Adams, who was carrying a basket filled with an exquisite arrangement of purple-and-white orchids.

"Oh, what beautiful flowers. Who sent them to you, Mama?" Natalie cried. Just as she spoke it occurred to her with a shock: Andrei might have chosen just such extravagant flowers for her.

Adams cast an agonized look upon his mistress. Louise was saved from having to offer any explanation by Marcus, who cordially disliked Adams and could not resist the opportunity to snap viciously at his enemy's striped trouser leg, catching the material between his teeth and worrying it unmercifully. In the ensuing fracas Adams was finally released, and the two ladies continued upstairs.

"Heavens," observed her ladyship fretfully. "Marcus has thoroughly upset Adams, and he will probably make us pay for it by serving luncheon late. It really doesn't matter who sent the flowers, darling. We have a far more important matter to attend to."

When at last the girl stood before the full-length mirror, a picture of youthful loveliness, Louise said fondly, "Quite perfect! I know you were inclined to choose the design with a fuller sleeve, but this becomes you so much better."

"Yes, Mama," Natalie agreed dutifully.

"You see?" Lady Grandison said sweetly. "You may trust your mother's judgment always to make the best choice for you."

Chapter 4

The Russian Prince and his tutor were playing chess in their luxuriously furnished suite at the Ritz. A showery day, unusual for that time of year, had deterred them from attending an afternoon performance of Longfellow's *Hiawatha* at the Albert Hall in Kensington. Part of the fun was in strolling around the Albert Memorial opposite the hall during the interval, among hundreds of singers from the cast in full Indian war paint. The project had been reluctantly postponed.

"Do you think I shall ever meet her again?" asked Andrei gloomily, toying with the ivory pawn in his hand. "Vladi, I must find a way!"

"I have heard nothing from you for more than a week but hymns of praise to the Lady Natalie," responded Vladimir, drumming his fingers irritably on the chessboard. "Can you think of nothing else? You already know my opinion. If the Grandisons do not encourage you to pay court to their daughter—which, being virtually engaged yourself, you have no right to do anyway— you can only rely on meeting her by chance. As you must both be invited to many of the same social functions, it is almost inevitable, so be more patient. And do play, Andrei, it's your move."

But the Prince procrastinated, sliding the pawn to and fro on the board without taking his hand from it. "I have been thinking," he said, paying no attention to his friend's words. "Many years ago my father told me that some flaxen-haired lady at court, whose face and figure were much admired, could not compare to a glorious creature he once met in England. She had silver-blond tresses and a perfectly shaped head set on a long, slender neck. It might have been the Marchioness of Grandison. She still has a sort of swanlike splendor. Perhaps he was too bold in his attentions to her—you know what my father is like, always so impetuous. She may have taken offense and wants now to shield her daughter from me."

"Andrei Constantinovitch! This is pure speculation. Now, do let us get on with the game." Lensky feigned annoyance, but he was struck by Andrei's words. Lady Grandison might have had good reason to fear the notorious Voroshnikoff charm. Young Andrei was as reckless as his father had once been when his desires were thwarted, the tutor thought uneasily. Vladimir would be out of favor if news reached St. Petersburg of some entanglement between the heir to the Voroshnikoff title and an English debutante, just when the alliance with Desirée was practically concluded.

A diversion was called for.

Valdimir took up the *Morning Post* and scanned the pages devoted to current entertainments.

"I suppose you'll make your move in your own good time, *mon cher*," he said lightly. "But we don't want to stay cooped up here all day, do we? As we missed this afternoon's performance at the Albert Hall, shall we go to the theater this evening? Fiona, the charming little actress I introduced you to, invited us to her opening night at the Clarence. I see it is a new piece by some Irish firebrand, and she is playing opposite Sir Michael McMahon, who is the theater's actor-manager. It's said he is the best in London. He is certainly accounted to be the most handsome, with a mane of splendid auburn hair. You've neglected poor Fiona Galbraith, dear boy. She must have been expecting you to exact payment for your ruby necklace. It is rather insulting not to do so."

Andrei agreed somewhat moodily to go. Miss Fiona Galbraith, known to her wealthy admirers as Fancy, no longer interested him. Although he had been so often turned away from the door of Grandison House by Adams, and unluckily prevented from speaking to Natalie when they had come face-to-face in Hyde Park, he still hoped that he might encounter her elsewhere. But opening night at the theater would be as likely a place as any.

As they prepared for their evening out the tutor wrote a brief note to the fascinating Fiona, begging for them both the privilege of joining her at the exclusive party in the green room that night after the play was over. There they would meet the celebrated members of the cast, including Sir Michael McMahon, the son of an excellent but impoverished Irish family. McMahon's career had followed an unusual path. He had made a distinguished debut as an actor in Dublin, and a move to the London stage enhanced his reputation. But the great roles were jealously guarded by stars of the stage who leased their own theaters and paid their own companies to act in them.

Sir Michael had some time since received an offer from a royal Duke to set him up as manager and leading man in the elegant Clarence Theatre, but there were tiresome strings attached. The Duke had a youthful mistress, for whom his ardor had cooled, with aspirations to grace the stage; could the gifted actor please take this girl under his wing and make her his leading lady? More than a little apprehensive, McMahon agreed. Such a proposition might never come again.

Miss Galbraith studied hard to perfect her craft. On stage, Michael and Fiona, who were marvelous foils one for the other, had achieved fame as consummate players of sophisticated comedy and were the darlings of the aristocracy. Offstage, Fiona had not taken long to throw herself into McMahon's arms, and the affair had only recently ended. For a while she had nursed hopes of becoming Lady McMahon, but these had been dashed by her habit of drinking to excess, and she was now a liability to Michael in his efforts to establish the respectable public image of his company. Even the slightest indulgence loosened her tongue and made her indiscreet, even to the extent of blurting out secrets of the bedroom—and Fiona frequently drank well beyond her limit.

Estranged from her leading man, Fiona openly accepted other lovers, whose chief qualification for her compliance was known to be the value of their presents, especially costly jewelry. She was fast accumulating a magnificent collection, to which Andrei's ruby pendant was the latest addition, and for which she was prepared to give full value in return.

In Park Lane Uncle Hugo was pleading with Natalie to join Delia that night at a quiet dinner party he was giving before going to the theater. His second guest was to have been Miss Bail, and he rather congratulated himself on the adroitness of his invitation, since he realized that it was no longer very tactful for that lady to call at Park Lane.

But Miss Bail had caught cold at an outdoor rally of the suffragettes in Regent's Park and was now confined to bed in her apartment, on the second floor of a shabby block of mansion flats.

"Dash it, my dear girl, I don't want to waste the ticket," he insisted, though the price of a theater seat meant little to a comparatively wealthy man. "It seems to me you're in the doldrums and need taking out of yourself," he went on. "The play will be witty enough to win a smile from you, I'll be bound; and we're invited to the green room party afterward by Sir Michael McMahon himself."

Natalie was indeed dispirited, for she had begun to doubt whether the romantic stranger had fallen headlong in love with her, as she had with him.

Certainly he had not cared enough to brave Mama's chilly reception by calling, or even by sending a note. She was being foolish, she told herself. One's heart didn't break at seventeen. And Uncle Hugo was pleading so charmingly with her. She turned her wistful violet gaze upon him.

"Yes, indeed, Sandy dear, I'd love to come to dinner at Acacia Grove," she said brightly. He patted her hand, well pleased with himself. But it was only acting on her part for Hugo's sake, to seem so gay and eager, for she was in truth desperately dejected.

The girls loved to visit Uncle Hugo's home. Easygoing bachelor that he was, Hugo had surrounded himself with a certain comfortable confusion, and with servants who, out of sheer affection, indulged his foibles. His late sister, Mildred, had ruled the household with rather an easy hand, for her nature much resembled his own. Since her death very little had altered in the spacious old house in St. John's Wood. The warmly inviting home was in a natural state of disarray—the floor littered with books and magazines waiting to be read; spectacle cases from which Hugo had lost reading glasses that he still hoped to find; pieces of Mildred's half-finished embroidery; unframed pictures; woolen comforters and shawls ready to don against a treacherous draft. Hugo was not the man to inspect his mantelpieces for dust, to query the household accounts, or to notice whether the level of port in his decanter fell overnight. It was some measure of his extremely kind heart that his home was not neglected by his servants; nor was he robbed by all and sundry.

When the time came to dress, Natalie agreed with Delia's choice for her of a gauzy white evening gown, the skirt looped up with bunches of white violets and knots of green ribbon to match the velvety leaves. It was warm again, since a morning shower of rain had lightened the heavy air, so she refused the green satin wrap that Linnet proposed and chose a white tulle cloak, collared and cuffed with delicate fronds of ostrich feathers, each sewn in place with silver bugle beads.

Delia, in hyacinth-blue satin, was equally alluring. As a compliment to Uncle Hugo, she wore around her neck the milky opal necklace set in red gold that Aunt Mildred had bequeathed to her. When he looked on his goddaughter and her little sister that night, Hugo Sanderson was a proud man. At dinner Hugo, never at a loss for conversation, did most of the talking.

"I don't keep a big staff nowadays," he admitted over his port. "I'm used to dining early like this, because it suits the servants. When Mildred was alive, we did things with a bit more style, but since she's no longer with me, God rest her dear soul, I live very simply."

Suddenly it was time to leave for the theater. "Well, I hope I have not hurried you both through your dinner," said Uncle Hugo jovially, rising from the table. "However, I am looking forward to strolling down the center aisle and making a great to-do of buying the programs, so that I may be noticed and envied as much as possible. Besides, it is pleasant to go early, to look around and greet one's friends."

A first night at the Clarence was imbued with a magic all its own. The decor was charming, with white paneled walls framed in gilded molding, crimson carpets, and curtains of pale gold satin. The gas chandeliers that Michael had rightly refused to have converted to the new electric lighting cast a pleasantly becoming glow on the smartly dressed audience. However, Uncle Hugo was not to have his wish. A dray broke down in Marylebone Road and delayed their hansom cab. So they arrived in Shaftesbury Avenue only just in time to take their places in the stalls as the house lights went down, and Natalie missed her opportunity to scan the audience before the curtains parted on the setting for act one.

The play was a wry comedy in which the worlds of servant and master were turned topsy-turvy. Natalie had never seen the famous Michael McMahon act before, but she was deeply im-

pressed by his remarkable presence and good looks, and the resonant voice that he projected with such ease.

"What a fine actor! And what a handsome fellow he is," was
Uncle Hugo's comment in the first interval. "No wonder the
ladies adore him. But tell me, my dears, can the lovely Fiona's
performance be less compelling than usual? I remember how
amusing she was as that cunning little mouse Maggie in *What
Every Woman Knows*. She received quite an ovation. I don't
think that in tonight's role she has quite the same quality."

"You are right, Sandy," Delia agreed emphatically. "Her talent
is not equal to playing the part of such a brilliant and designing
woman. She doesn't quite convince me, at any rate. Sir Michael
is worthy of a better leading lady."

At the end of act three the cast received enthusiastic applause,
and as the audience streamed out, one of the ushers escorted the
little party backstage.

In the green room, a large salon furnished with easy chairs and
low tables, there was a lavish buffet meal set out on a long mahogany
sideboard at one end. The girls hesitated at the door, for as they
arrived Fiona was making an entrance, the center of a group of
admirers. The young men who jostled one another for a place at her
side were in most cases only paying lip service to her talent and
beauty. But it was something to boast about in the club the next day,
to have had supper with Fancy Galbraith at the Clarence!

The actress was still in costume—a lavish burgundy tulle dress,
cunningly corseted, twinkling with wine-colored sequins. Stage
makeup of soft green shadows around her hazel eyes made them
seem large and alluring. Her brown hair was still dusted with gold
powder. It glinted splendidly in the light of the chandelier.

Champagne corks popped, and Fancy soon had a glass in her
hand, emptied it, and with a girlish smile held it out to be re-
filled. She was in a festive mood and had already secretly re-
stored herself from a brandy bottle she kept behind her lacquered
dressing screen. As more people entered the salon Mr. Sanderson
and his companions moved forward politely and encountered Michael, who had just come in, having hurriedly removed his
makeup and donned a fresh white dress shirt.

"Hugo, my dear fellow," Michael cried, seizing his old friend's
hand. "I do hope you were in front tonight. What did you think of the
piece? A lightweight comedy, of course, but amusing enough to
carry us through the silly season, I hope. But I forget my manners.
Please present me to these young ladies. Your nieces, Hugo?"

His voice bore little trace of his origins in County Clare, though one could discern an Irish lilt to it. Delia found him far more attractive than any of the "weeds" her mother had paraded before her; but Natalie hardly noticed his charismatic good looks, or that she and her sister were receiving the undivided attention of a man who had all London at his feet. Thoughts of another face filled her mind.

Michael was obviously enjoying the company of the two lovely girls. Delia was superb, he thought, and extremely intelligent. But Natalie's striking looks, her low musical voice, and graceful deportment held him spellbound.

Fancy was quick to notice this. She drank more wine and insisted on lighting a Balkan Sobranie cigarette in a long jade holder, although she knew Michael hated her to smoke in public. She laughed ever louder, in affected trills, tapping her most forward admirer on the cheek with a rosy fingernail, admonishing him not to be such a naughty boy.

At last she could no longer bear to be ignored by Michael. Carelessly setting down her glass so that half its contents spilled, she clapped her hands and insisted that the group of sycophants around her should join her in a toast to Michael.

He had no choice but to move closer to Fancy, giving her a look of burning reproof from his fine eyes, which told her plainly she was not behaving well.

Devoured by jealousy, and her wits fuddled with wine, Fancy became reckless. How dare Michael make it so obvious that he no longer desired her by fawning over those sickly misses, or insinuate that her conduct fell short of his exacting standards.

Just then, Fancy saw her chance to show Michael that she was not to be trifled with. Glasses were obediently raised toward Michael when she caught sight of her latest conquest, one of the last guests to arrive—Andrei, disappointed again in finding Natalie. He had been searching among the departing audience crowding the foyer, waiting for their carriages to be called.

Fancy swept across the green room to greet the Prince. "Andrei, my darling boy, how incredibly sweet of you to come. Look, Michael!" She turned to him, flung her arms outward, leaned forward, and flaunted her ripe bosom. Then she dropped her voice to a throbbing conspiratorial note. "See what this absurdly generous creature has given me? Oh, I really shouldn't accept such a gift from a stranger to these shores, unless I'm prepared to get to know him much, much better. But, what can I do? It was impossible to refuse. You Russians are so masterful!" Slowly, with studied grace, she raised the ruby pendant on its chain and dangled it between slim fingers, then allowed it to slide back into the valley between her opulent breasts. "I really must insist that after the performance tomorrow night you take me to supper at the Café Royal, Prince Andrei!" she commanded in mock imperiousness. She leaned in closely to the young man. "But you will see me home afterward, won't you?" Her slow, teasing glance made her meaning quite apparent.

Michael boiled inwardly with rage, and Andrei appeared dumbstruck. Embarrassed, he looked away, and his eyes found Natalie, standing a little apart. She was very still.

Her very gaze, so transparently hurt and disgusted, pierced him with anguish. He knew what she was thinking, and he could only stare back, silently imploring her not to believe that he could betray her. From the moment of their meeting, he had only been hers, body and soul.

One hand fluttered to her cheek. "Oh, Delia, it is so hot in here," she murmured. "Do you think we could go home?" Her sister divined at once that this was the young man who had stolen the girl's heart, and sharing her humiliating disillusionment, she answered firmly, "Of course, darling, we shall leave at once. Sandy, dear, get them to send for a cab. Natalie is not feeling well."

Andrei stepped forward. "Please wait!" he pleaded. She met his eyes, then shook her head sorrowfully. Her chin went up bravely and she moved past him so quickly that the white folds of her sleeve brushed the black broadcloth of his.

Sir Michael's shrewd eyes followed Natalie as she went out. She had pride, that girl, and spirit, as well as beauty. But if Fancy had the young man she loved in her clutches, he pitied the Lady Natalie.

While Uncle Hugo was concerned by the younger girl's sudden indisposition, Delia was deeply alarmed by it. How would she weather this turmoil of emotions? Delia could only guess at the outcome, since she herself had never fallen in love. It must be searing indeed for her little sister to feel the first stirrings of tender passion, and then to find the object of her adoration unworthy.

Chapter 5

Leaving Fancy quite out of countenance and ignoring the buzz of speculative whispers swarming around his ears, Andrei stormed out of the green room. Lensky had no choice but to shrug, throwing his eyes heavenward in wordless apology, and leave, too. He intended to berate his charge sharply for his rudeness later. But one glance at that pale, tortured face made him change his mind.

That night Andrei hardly slept at all. He blamed Vladimir for involving him with a woman who was nothing but a vulgar courtesan, and thus ruining all his chances of winning Natalie.

Consequently he had little to say to his tutor over breakfast, and rather than spend the morning with him in their suite, he went downstairs to the lounge, where he was soon buttonholed by a couple of dowagers who claimed to have met his parents many years before.

"There will be such a crush today in the Haymarket, I shall ask my coachman to take me by a different route to Kensington," one of the ladies remarked. "It is always so when Their Majesties are holding one of their 'drawing rooms.' There is nothing to equal these receptions, Prince, even at The Hermitage, I dare say."

"Yes, and the cream of the season's debutantes will be presented," the other interjected, not to be outdone. "There will be some of the loveliest girls. The Westminsters' Emily, Lillie Langtry's niece, and Lady Grandison's younger daughter, Natalie. She was voted the belle of Queen Charlotte's ball this year, and the prettiest creature to come out this season. I am astonished you have not been invited, my dear Prince, although I rather gather from Professor Lensky that your visit is quite unofficial. Or have you perhaps resorted to a diplomatic illness as far as the palace is concerned? Some court functions are boring, I quite agree."

The word *diplomatic* brought a plan instantly to Andrei's mind. Excusing himself, he left the hotel in haste. A hansom brought him swiftly to the Russian embassy.

Once inside, he had no difficulty arranging an immediate interview with Ambassador Count Benckendorff, for the Voroshnikoff family was well known to him. The Count was delighted to hear of Andrei's mission.

"I'll send a personal note to the Lord Chamberlain," he said, "and beg him to pull every possible string. I shall probably mention that you have been unwell for the last few days; otherwise, you would have sought an invitation sooner. But just at the moment when relations are, shall we say, slightly strained between our two countries, it would be to our advantage to let the polite world see that a Russian nobleman is as welcome as ever at the Court of St. James's."

Andrei was perplexed by this hint that King Edward's government was unfriendly toward the Czar, who, after all, was such a close relative to their own royal family. Or at least opposed to his Premier, the devious Count Witte. However, the Prince was too preoccupied with his personal affairs to be greatly concerned. He thought of diplomacy as a sort of formal game, where moves were always being made and countered with much theatrical sword-waving, tentative advances thwarted, and retreats glossed over. All that mattered to him was the coveted invitation card for that night's reception.

Unable to wait patiently in Count Benckendorff's office, he wandered up and down by the lake in St. James's Park, prowled around the perimeter of Green Park, and an hour later was back at the embassy. Andrei was consumed by impatience. He could think of nothing but Natalie, grudging every hour spent away from her side. He wanted her, wanted her with every nerve in his body, every fiber of his being. How painful was the knowledge that she must think him a shallow flirt, whispering words of love in her ear when he had already bought his way into a loose woman's bed. At last a messenger arrived from the Lord Chamberlain's office, and the invitation was in his hand.

With profound thanks to the Count, who was only too happy to have been of service, Andrei returned to the Ritz and, waving the crested envelope under Vladimir's nose, quite startled him by demanding, "Help me dress, there's a good fellow. Full evening regalia, and I'll wear my Order of Saint Olaf."

The Grandison carriage was stationary halfway down Constitution Hill, and the line of conveyances ahead of it stretched as far as Buckingham Palace.

The Marchioness sighed with boredom. "It will be an hour or more before we reach the entrance gates, Arthur," she said. "We should not have postponed Natalie's presentation until so near the end of the season. One wonders who all these nonentities are, that they should be paraded before Their Majesties for inspection. I wager they are not all girls of good breeding."

"You may be quite right, my love," her husband agreed soothingly. The privilege of being officially recognized by the reigning monarchs had always been reserved for daughters of the aristocracy and gentry; it was the seal of social approval for every debutante who took part. Only a lady who had herself been presented in the past might act as a sponsor for the occasion. But Arthur had heard a rumor at his club that certain unscrupulous persons charged as much as a hundred guineas to present young girls who were in no way related to them and whose antecedents were unknown to the pages of Debrett's social register. No wonder there were far more debutantes than usual this year!

Himself a picture of elegance in full court dress, Arthur beamed with pride at his lovely daughter. She was exquisite, in white satin and charmeuse, with a train lined in blush-pink tulle. Two white ostrich feathers nodded over her upswept coiffure, and her bouquet was of pink and white rosebuds. He only wished she could look slightly happier on this exciting day.

Just as well they had a hamper in the carriage, he thought, for it would be long before the time-honored ritual was completed and they could all troop in for supper.

Arthur took out his monogrammed hip flask and sipped from it discreetly. What a business it was!

He recollected the day Louise had presented their elder daughter, in whom Queen Alexandra had always taken such an interest. Delia had seemed amenable enough then. Who would have thought she would turn out so headstrong? What shocks might be in store for him with Natalie? he mused. Much as he loved all his children, his girls were dearest to him.

At last they had arrived at the palace gates. Odd, he now thought, that Natalie was so quiet, and Louise had sat tranquilly waving her feather fan in silence for the last half hour. The delicious hamper of food was quite untouched. Nerves, both of them, he supposed.

The carriage passed smoothly under a splendid wrought-iron arch, which bore King Edward's initials, into the quadrangle and under a farther archway into the inner courtyard. In the vast red-carpeted lobby there was an unending procession of guests, glittering with jewels and brocades. Natalie brightened, for she saw a friend.

"Mama, may I speak to Gwendoline Jarvis? There she is with her aunt Carrie."

Louise at once assented. Gwendoline confided that she had just become engaged. The announcement would be in tomorrow's *Times*. Her fiancé was wonderful and she felt she was the luckiest girl in the world. They were to be married almost at once, for his regiment sailed to India the following month. Mr. Jarvis was rather badly off, so a quiet wedding at his country home was planned, for which Gwendoline's wealthy aunt Carrie would bear the cost.

It was already time for Arthur and Louise to make their way forward through successive drawing rooms to the throne room. The Duchess of Devonshire, who was Mistress of the Robes, gestured with her fan to the Grandisons to take their place at her side. Louise had given Natalie an encouraging glance, but they would not see their daughter again until she was ushered in when her name was called, to bend her knee in reverence before the King, and then before the Queen.

The ceremonies took their usual lengthy course. Ambassadors who had recently presented their credentials now introduced their wives. Visiting nabobs from India and from such colorful little kingdoms as Tonga stepped forward in their order, bowed, received a royal nod, and backed the requisite three steps before melting tactfully into the throng.

From his place at the back of the room, Andrei keenly studied the eyes of nervous young women, their faces set in false smiles under the weight of jeweled bands and plumes confining hair that was fair, auburn, light brown, and dark. . . . He discovered Natalie and the anxious girl before her in line who kept looking back with anguished glances.

An official was intoning each girl's name. "Miss Gwendoline Jarvis," he recited from the card she had just handed him. The girl stepped forward, mismanaged the moment of releasing her train from one gloved hand, stepped on it, and almost fell. She sank to one knee, then rose, her face quite brilliant with shame.

"Lady Natalie Grandison." Natalie's knee was gracefully bent, her head gently inclined, and as she raised her eyes Queen Alexandra smiled. Dear Louise's second girl, so pretty in her own way, though so unlike her mother.

As the girl moved down the line of royal personages, receiving their admiring looks, her train was deftly gathered up by a page and draped over her extended left arm. She backed from the royal presence with perfect composure and followed Gwendoline, who had retreated with undignified haste.

"Oh, do you think many people noticed how clumsy I was when I curtsied?" the poor girl asked with tears in her eyes. "I didn't dare to turn around, but I am sure you managed it beautifully. I only hope Aunt Carrie doesn't tell Liam that I disgraced him today."

"Nonsense! Almost everyone stumbles. I am sure I nearly trod on the end of your train when I was giving my card to the Lord Chamberlain. Besides, you are looking so lovely, and that is all anyone remembers afterward."

In comforting her friend, Natalie forgot for a moment her own aching heart. *How lucky Gwen is,* she thought. *Her dreams are about to come true—her heart must be filled with joy.*

"You are such a comfort to me, Nattie dear." Gwendoline dabbed bravely at her eyes with a tiny square of lace. "I shan't feel nearly so jumpy in church if you are there. Promise me you'll be one of my bridesmaids! I believe Aunt Carrie intends to ask your mother this evening if you may."

Natalie was delighted to agree, and the friends were deep in conversation when a gentleman-in-waiting announced that supper was about to be served.

The two girls rose to join their parties. The buffet tables would, by tradition, be set with such delicacies as lobster, smoked trout, and quail, not to speak of sweet pastry confections and profiteroles. Champagne would flow freely.

The Marquess and Marchioness must by now have joined the monarchs, and their daughter hesitated to force her way through the throng. She moved quietly to a window and stood looking out pensively. Darkness had fallen and she saw, as in a mirror against the glass, the outline of her own shapely head. Even as she paused there, her image merged with that of another, taller figure. She turned and found the dark eyes of Prince Andrei blazing with emotion, fixed upon her.

Her first instinct was to flee, but daringly he placed his hand on her wrist, where the small shell buttons exposed a glimpse of delicate white skin.

"Don't run away," he pleaded. "Wait and hear what I have to say, at least."

"You can have nothing to say to me, Prince," she answered calmly, removing her wrist from his grasp. "We met, and we danced together once at Lady Jessop's ball. I have not seen you since, except for a moment in the park—and . . . where was it? Oh, yes, in the green room at the Clarence Theatre. But the latter occasion I would rather forget."

Andrei's mouth twisted bitterly at the mention of that fateful encounter. "It was a foolish escapade that I became involved in before we met. That woman is nothing to me, nothing, I swear it. When you refused to receive me, and didn't answer my notes, I wondered what I had done to offend you. The first time I called at Grandison House with those violets, your mother said we should be sure to meet again. But apparently I have been unlucky."

"You called, with flowers, and spoke to Mama?" Natalie faltered. "I assure you I have not received any gift, or any message from you. Indeed, I thought you had forgotten me."

He captured her gloved hand and pressed a kiss upon the palm. "Never, while I live," he replied with such heartfelt emphasis that she was unable to question his sincerity.

"One thing seems clear, my lovely Natalie," he went on, drawing her closer to him, "we are being deliberately kept apart."

"But, why?" she asked in dismay. "Mama always thinks she knows best; and I believe she has already made her own choice of a husband for me. But that doesn't explain why she would be so deceitful."

"Don't ask her, *chérie,*" Andrei implored tenderly. "Wait. She will only guess that you have learned the truth and will keep you under strict supervision. We must meet again and talk. Show your trust in me by agreeing to do this. Tomorrow, if possible. Can you arrange to come alone?"

Natalie's thoughts were in confusion, but she was certain that nothing would stop her from keeping a rendezvous with her prince.

"It will be extremely difficult. But perhaps I might express a wish to see some pictures in the summer exhibition at Burlington House. . . ." Her face lit up in anticipation. "Yes, that will do. It is quite easy to find, just opposite St. James's Church, and not far from Piccadilly Circus. I could go with Linnet, my maid. But I could not be sure what time."

"I shall be there when the exhibition opens tomorrow morning and will wait all day if necessary," he promised triumphantly.

A radiant smile trembled on Natalie's lips. Never before had she deceived her parents. But she experienced not the slightest qualm at making this promise; somehow she knew instinctively what the next move in the game must be.

"Please go now, Andrei," she insisted. "I have given you my word to be at the gallery tomorrow, but if we linger together here, it will only invite gossip." He bowed in silent acquiescence, then watched her move lightly away from him, her long satin train unfolding behind her across the gleaming parquet floor.

What a Princess she would make, he thought, dazed with happiness. But he would not expose her to her mother's suspicions by remaining at the palace and perhaps being noticed by his enemy. For he knew now that the Marchioness was indeed his adversary, determined to thwart his courtship of this beautiful girl for reasons he could not begin to imagine.

After the reception, Andrei flouted every sensible rule of prudence by electing to walk back to the Ritz across Green Park. He strode out so vigorously that a pickpocket who lurked in the shadows regretfully abandoned his first intention of setting about such a swell, to relieve him of his wallet and that glittering order he wore on his breast.

"Vladi, old fellow," Andrei greeted his sleepy tutor, who was yawning by the fire over the *Quarterly Review.* "Success at last! I managed to speak to Natalie alone for a moment, and she's agreed to meet me again tomorrow. I'm going to propose to her, and I believe she will accept. Tell me what I can do to get my father's consent. For he must be made to see that it would be quite out of the question now for me to marry Desirée."

Vladimir was aghast. He had been negligent, for he had not realized how serious were Andrei's intentions.

"Let me write to your father, *mon cher,*" he suggested smoothly. "It would be wiser not to commit yourself to Lady Natalie until we receive his permission to pay your court to her. The Grand Duke has his heart set on your marrying the young lady of his choice. He would have to be persuaded tactfully to reconsider. If we get a letter into the diplomatic bag tomorrow, Count Benckendorff will ensure that it reaches St. Petersburg in less than a week. Surely you two impetuous children can wait until the end of the month for a reply!"

"Perhaps," Andrei answered moodily. "But I must know for certain whether Natalie loves me, and I intend to find out tomorrow. Once she has promised me that she will not be dragooned into accepting some other offer to please her parents, I might be prepared to endure some delay. But I tell you, Vladi, I shall not rest happily until she is my wife."

Professor Lensky did sit down to write a carefully worded letter to his noble patron, which satisfied even Andrei in its extravagant praises of the Lady Natalie. Fortunately Andrei's diatribes had revealed that the Grandison family was against the match. But Lensky was apprehensive. He disliked the idea of taking an underhanded course. However, he knew he could put a stop to the affair instantly. He had only to drop a discreet hint to the Grandisons the very next morning, saying that the young lovers were hurrying to meet at a secret rendezvous. He dallied with the idea but finally rejected it.

The journey home to Grandison House was accomplished quickly, compared with the interminable pilgrimage toward the palace only a few hours earlier. Arthur marveled at the high spirits of his wife and daughter. The young girl seemed positively to glow, and Louise assured Natalie repeatedly that never for one moment had she feared their little nightingale's deportment would be less than perfect.

Didn't Arthur agree that Natalie's dress had been the most inspired creation? Arthur was surprised by his wife's good humor and could not know that it stemmed from a sense of thankfulness that had nothing to do with the ordeal of Natalie's presentation. At all the social gatherings they had attended during the last few days, she had dreaded coming face-to-face with Prince Andrei again. But her fears had not been realized. Perhaps he had continued his tour of Europe with Professor Lensky and she could rest more peacefully.

The girl herself tingled with renewed hope. Andrei did love her after all. His very glance had declared it, and tomorrow, no matter what the difficulties, she would see him again.

But there was one mystery that had yet to be solved. Why had Mama so cruelly deceived her . . . ?

Chapter 6

When Natalie sought out her sister the next morning in the old schoolroom, Delia was quite amazed by the change in her manner. The girl was positively radiant with suppressed excitement. Putting aside her rather odd task of braiding lengths of purple, green, and white silk cord, she rose and gave the girl a warm hug.

"You look quite a different girl today, darling Imp. I'm told you did splendidly at the palace, and it must be a great weight off your mind. Shall we celebrate this morning by going out to Gunter's for coffee and those chocolate éclairs you love?"

"Actually," Natalie said casually, "I have asked Mama's permission to visit Burlington House again. I've really not seen enough of the summer exhibition."

"What mischief are you up to, Imp?" Delia surveyed the younger girl closely. "I know what it is—you've seen that wicked Russian Prince of yours and you have a rendezvous with him!" Delia took her hand firmly. "But didn't you realize after that unfortunate scene at the Clarence what a debauched young man he is?"

"Oh, I can never conceal anything from you, Delia!" Natalie exclaimed. "But he is not what you think. It was all a terrible mistake, and he is going to explain everything to me."

"I should very much like to hear that explanation myself," commented Delia tersely. "I shall go with you and form my own opinion. You're far too inexperienced to judge whether or not you are being told the truth by a practiced Don Juan."

Natalie was admittedly relieved. "Well, so long as you don't give me away to Mama, because I must tell you she has acted very strangely. Do you know that Prince Andrei called more than once with flowers and notes, which I never received? On one occasion Mama actually spoke to him. But she led me to think that he was not sufficiently interested in me even to call."

"Well, I can only suppose it is because of her predeliction for Charlie Haversham. But, as usual, she is taking it a bit too far. Just let me tidy up here, and I'll put on a walking dress and my hat. It is much too lovely a day to bother with a carriage."

When the girls went downstairs together, with Linnet following behind, Lady Grandison emerged from the morning room.

"Ah, there you are, my dear," she said affably to Natalie. "I am coming to believe the telephone is a useful invention, after all. I have just had Adams speak to the Havershams' butler and suggest that Miss Eleanor should join you at the exhibition. She sent a message to say that she would be delighted and will be happy to return with you afterward to take luncheon with us. Nell is such a charming girl, and it is time you cultivated more friends of your own age, my love, since Delia will be leaving us soon."

Seeing that Delia was dressed to go out, she remarked coldly, "However, I see that she is willing to give up a little of the time she devotes to her studies to more frivolous activities."

"Not totally frivolous, Mama; the study of art is always educational," said Delia calmly. They emerged from the cool echoing hall into the sunlit street outside. Leaving Linnet close behind but out of earshot, the girls sheltered themselves under their open parasols for a hurried consultation as they walked down Park Lane.

"What shall I do if Nell sees Andrei? She's such a gossip; she's bound to mention it at luncheon, especially because she was very taken with him herself," whispered Natalie.

"Don't worry, my love. As it happens, it's just as well I came with you. I will undertake to keep Nell out of your way. At my prompting, she will go into raptures over some fashionable portrait. Nell will be ardently hoping to catch the eye of any gentleman of our acquaintance. Let her maid wait outside with

Linnet. Prince Andrei is bound to be waiting in the foyer, and you can vanish with him into the salon."

Pleased with her plot, Delia continued. "As soon as I have got Nell into conversation with some suitably eligible man, I will excuse myself, saying that I really must go to look for you. Then when I come face-to-face with your dashing admirer, I shall expect him to persuade me that his intentions toward you are honorable." Her twinkling eyes gave Natalie confidence.

Newspaper sellers stood at the entrance to the famous exhibition, the placards blazoning news of another Japanese victory in the northern seas against her archenemy, Russia. Natalie wondered whether this distant war, which seemed so unreal to her, could endanger any of Andrei's family if it continued to follow a disastrous course. But she could hardly comprehend that there might be any real threat. These wars never came close to home.

As she and Delia passed through the cool shade of the portico, Natalie felt a sharp stab of disappointment when she did not see the Prince right away. Then she recognized his tall figure waiting for her beyond the brass grillwork of the ticket office. Across the marble hall their eyes met, and his face lit up joyously. She touched Delia's arm and looked longingly in her beloved's direction.

Following her sister's gaze, Delia understood. "Let me wait here for Nell while you feast your eyes on an object of the very highest artistic merit!"

Linnet was hot, footsore, and disgruntled, and she was most grateful when Lady Delia put a kind hand on her arm, saying, "You need not come in with us, Linnet. Look, there are some comfortable benches outside on the terrace, where you can sit down, and I expect Miss Eleanor's maid will soon join you."

Natalie had moved forward, as if drawn by an irresistible force toward the young Russian. He bowed gravely and offered her his arm. He had their tickets ready, and they mounted the stairs, passing out of Delia's sight.

At last Natalie and Andrei were alone together in a small gallery, surrounded by massive sculptures in marble and bronze.

Taking both her little hands in his, he drew her close and spoke in low, intimate tones. "I have no right to ask you this. We have hardly met. But I loved you, Natalie, from the moment I first saw you. Until then I had pursued nothing but aimless pleasure. Now I have one unalterable goal—to marry you. Tell me that you love me, too, *chérie*. I cannot live without you."

So sudden and passionate was his declaration that words deserted her. She tried to speak but could not, and her hesitancy made Andrei dread a refusal.

"Professor Lensky has written to my father, explaining how deep my feelings are for you and begging permission for me to approach Lord Grandison," he went on pleadingly. "I dare to hope that when he knows me better, the Marquess will not lightly dismiss my request for your hand in marriage. After all, he and my own father are old friends. But you have not yet answered me. Are the words so hard to find?"

He touched her chin lightly and searched her eyes with longing. Natalie answered bravely, "I do love you, Andrei, and I will marry you. Oh, I only wish you could count on easily obtaining my parents' consent." She laid her velvet cheek for a moment against his chest.

"What objection could your parents have? The name of Voroshnikoff is one of the proudest in all Russia."

"Mama wants me to marry Charlie Haversham, and if I consent to the match, Papa would be happy because I would still be living near them. To go with you to Russia might seem to my parents like an eternal separation from them. And," she said, taking a quick breath for courage, bringing out the hateful words in a rush, "Papa's very correct in his own behavior. It would certainly predispose my father against you if he heard gossip connecting your name with Fiona Galbraith's."

"When his affections are not yet fixed, a man commits many follies," Andrei said apologetically. "I had contemplated a brief interlude with Fiona before I met you, and now I despise myself for having been drawn into such a vulgar intrigue. But I swear to you, *doragaya*, nothing has or ever will take place between us to give you a moment's anxiety. You do believe me, don't you?" He showered frantic kisses on her slender white fingers. Impulsively drawing off from his left hand a heavy gold signet ring set with a deep intaglio in chalcedony, he enfolded it in her small palm. "Keep this, until I can replace it with a circlet of the Voroshnikoff diamonds," he entreated.

Natalie did believe in him with all her heart. She longed to surrender to dawning responses she did not understand, had never experienced before; sensuous longings coursed like fire through her veins. Just then, Natalie heard her name being called, and she drew away from Andrei's possessive clasp to find her sister at her elbow.

Addressing the young man in a cool tone, Delia began, "Pardon me, Prince Andrei, I know we have not officially been introduced, but I recognize you from our encounter at the Clarence Theatre. I hope you have been able to explain the circumstances to Natalie's satisfaction, for, to put it bluntly, you seemed already involved in a rather dubious *affaire*."

Andrei stood back a pace and bowed. So frank, so noble was the beseeching glance he gave Delia, she felt herself involuntarily warming toward him. "I cannot blame you for the bad impression you must have formed at the Clarence," he admitted honestly. "Please allow me the opportunity to dispel it, for it is most important that you consider me worthy to be your sister's husband."

"I think you go too fast, sir," Delia said, halting him. "Natalie's future cannot be decided without her father's approval, and you should have spoken to him first."

"You are quite right," Andrei agreed. "I should call upon Lord Grandison, and I will do so. But I await my own father's permission, and his blessing on the match. St. Petersburg is so far away, the reply could yet take a few days to come." He turned to Natalie. "May I ask you to be discreet a little longer, my darling? And you, Lady Delia, to be our confidante?" He gave her a brilliant smile.

"We cannot discuss it now, though I should like to know you better before I encourage any further clandestine meetings," Delia said in a more friendly tone. "Come, Natalie. Eleanor will soon tire of striking admiring attitudes if no one notices her, and she will be coming to find you. The young lady in question has met you, Prince Andrei, and may gossip that we have seen you here. So please relinquish my sister if you can bear to do so for the moment." Her sincere smile belied her parental tone; she felt the Prince's intentions were genuine and good.

"Professor Lensky and I are staying at the Ritz. A message would always find me there." After one last, adoring glance at Natalie, he tactfully withdrew.

At that moment Nell joined the sisters, and the three girls strolled around the various salons, chatting amiably. Soon, much to Natalie's annoyance, Nell was off on a tangent about the trials of her heartsick brother.

"What a patient, faithful fellow Charlie is, Nattie dear," she sad, pausing by a particularly fine framed watercolor. "He demonstrates laudable restraint in trying circumstances, although he is head over heels in love with you. One must admit that it was hard for Charlie to stand back and watch you have your head turned by Prince Andrei Voroshnikoff."

Turning over a page of her catalog, Nell stole a spiteful glance at Natalie to divine whether her remarks had struck home. "We have seen nothing of the Prince since the fancy dress ball, have we?" she went on lightly. "He is probably busy breaking hearts in Vienna or Belgrade by now. . . ."

"If Charlie is suffering such tortures of jealousy, he must put his hopes to the test," Delia interrupted. "For my part, I have seen all I want to of the exhibition. We should begin walking home now or we shall be late for luncheon."

The girls joined the two servants outside and began walking toward Park Lane. Passing the Burlington Arcade, Eleanor broke away from her companions, crying, "Oh, look, there are some sweet little garnet earrings in Barnett's window. Just what I need to wear with my oyster satin. Do let us go in for a moment."

In spite of the gleam in the young lady's eyes, Delia dissuaded Eleanor, saying that Lady Grandison expected punctuality at her table, so they really had no time to spare.

Farther along Piccadilly excitement made Natalie's pulse quicken as she glanced across the road at the arcades of the Ritz Hotel. She wondered where in the vast and elegant building the Prince and his tutor were lodged. By chance she noticed two women at the gates of Green Park, adorned in large rosettes of purple, green, and white ribbon. Just the colors Delia had been weaving together that morning. They were distributing handbills to passersby, some of whom merely scanned them, laughed, and threw the crumpled papers in the gutter. Others studied the bills more closely, and Natalie saw a girl of her own age take a coin from her purse and press it into the older woman's hands. A gentleman, obviously her escort, raised his furled umbrella and flourished it angrily in the woman's face, so that she shrank back to avoid a blow.

Just as the perplexing scene was hidden from Natalie's view by the press of carriages, omnibuses, and delivery drays that crowded the busy thoroughfare, she overheard a middle-aged man saying to his wife, "More of this malicious rubbish. Votes for women, indeed! I don't know what you would do with a vote if you had one, my dear."

"Neither do I, my love," replied his companion meekly. "I've never felt the need of it."

Natalie looked over to Delia, who was carrying on a spirited conversation with Nell about the latest fashions, to ensure that Charlie's name was not again dragged into the conversation. So, Delia was secretly involved with the Suffragette Movement, thought Natalie, proud of her sister for supporting the cause she believed in. Where Natalie was tormented over defying her parents, Delia seemed to do so without a qualm. But she was also quite concerned—the issue of Oxford had already distanced mother from daughter; Lady Grandison would positively disown her if she knew of Delia's commitment to the Suffragette Movement. And as Natalie knew from experience, once her mother had set her mind on something, she would refuse to listen to another view, no matter how reasonable. . . .

Meanwhile, Charlie had met Lord Grandison, who was strolling down St. James's Street, and eagerly accepted an invitation to lunch. He had not been slow to ask whether he might now approach Natalie on the subject of their engagement.

Arthur did not pretend that he and Louise had never considered Charlie Haversham as a possible future son-in-law. Without giving too much positive encouragement, he agreed.

"By all means, ask her, my dear boy. I won't influence my little nightingale to accept you, Charlie, but I shall certainly advise her to consider your offer very carefully."

When the family, with their guests, sat down to luncheon, the conversation was somewhat stilted. Afterward, Louise suggested that Natalie play for them while they took coffee in the drawing room. After a short time, it was clearly Louise's strategy to leave the couple, for she marshaled her husband and the other girls out of the room. Charlie immediately fell to one knee and seized Natalie's hand. When he finished his well-rehearsed speech, she made no response, and he blundered on.

"Dash it! Natalie, I know I'm not worthy of you and all that sort of thing. But I'll do my best to make you happy. Your parents seem to approve, and mine would be delighted. There's a rather nice little manor house that's come on the market near Cowley. We could live there in the country and have quite a decent second home in town if you want to be close to your family during the season. I'll even resign my commission, if need be. Say yes and I'll be the happiest chap in the world."

Natalie could hardly breathe, filled as she was by a suffocating sense of panic. Instinct bade the girl to refuse outright. She hated to give Charlie any false hopes. But if she admitted that her heart was lost to another, the secret scheme would be jeopardized. Even as a refusal hovered on her lips, she realized that she must appear to be uncertain if she was to gain a respite without arousing any suspicions.

"Don't think I'm not flattered, but please give me at least a few days to consider, Charlie," she begged. "I'm very fond of you, but I'm not sure I love you. Will you trust me to give you my answer as soon as I can?"

With this he had to be satisfied, thus still hopeful but somewhat less than triumphant. Natalie went straight to the schoolroom, where she took Andrei's ring tenderly from the bosom of her dress and hid it, cushioned on a velvet pad, in her lacquered trinket box for which she alone possessed the tiny key.

No matter how bitterly disappointed her parents might be, she could never marry any man but Andrei, for they were pledged to each other, even if she could not yet wear his ring.

Downstairs in the library, Lady Grandison waited in vain for the appearance of the happy couple, hand in hand. But when Charlie came in alone, his subdued expression told Lady Grandison at once that an engagement was not as yet certain. Delicacy, however, restrained her from questioning him. Presently Charlie left with Nell, who persisted in asking bluntly ill-timed questions, so curious was she as to her brother's chances of making this desirable family connection. When at last it was clear to Nell that she would get no answers from him, she tried instead to persuade him to come into Barnett's and advise her on the choice of the garnet earrings, and possibly a bracelet to match.

Much later, Natalie tiptoed into the library. Lord Grandison, who was seated reading the *London Illustrated News*, felt a timid hand come to rest on his shoulder.

He had been absorbed in the gripping news story of the defeat of Russia's navy in the Far East. But looking up to find his pretty daughter beside him, he knew there was important business at hand closer to home.

"Papa, may I talk to you very seriously?" Natalie began. She sank down with supple grace on the fine Persian carpet at his feet and rested her clasped hands on the arm of his chair.

"You must have known what Charlie was going to ask me," she went on. "Everyone was so tactful, leaving us alone together. You do understand, don't you, that he's almost like one of my own brothers, and I find it difficult to see him in a romantic light? I had to say that I could give no immediate answer."

"Nor should you, my darling," he said, patting her arm reassuringly. "Mama is only thinking of your happiness when she advises you to make an early marriage. Her own girlhood was marred by insecurity, for she had no loving parents to guide her. No one will force you to make a decision either way. But we would certainly like to feel that we are in every sense gaining a son when you marry, rather than losing a daughter." He smoothed her hair lovingly. "I mean that our little nightingale will not be flying too far away, for we would sadly miss her song." He smiled at his own poetic fancy.

Natalie sighed. She detested the pain she would inflict on her dearest Papa, but never would she give up Andrei, not even for her father's sake.

Chapter 7

While she endured the torture of waiting to hear from Andrei that he had received a reply from St. Petersburg, Natalie could at least confide her hopes and fears in Delia, who was most comforting.

"You did quite rightly, Natalie, to give Charlie an equivocal answer," said the older girl after some thought. "Mama will imagine that you are on the verge of acceding to her wishes of your own accord, so she will not press you. Meanwhile, try to appear quite serene. My advice is to keep yourself busy with pleasant diversions. For instance, we can probably cajole Mama into letting us go to the theatrical orphanage fête in Regent's Park tomorrow. I'm sure dear old Sandy would be delighted to escort us."

Louise accorded her permission quite enthusiastically. It was the first time she had addressed more than a cold word or two to her elder daughter since the girl had revealed her foolish plans. But with time—and congratulations from Queen Alexandra and the rest of the royal family on Delia's acceptance at Oxford—her anger had cooled. Had she known that friends of the feminist movement held regular meetings in Miss Bail's chilly mansion flat, which were frequently attended by Delia, there would have been little common ground left between mother and daughter.

Some of Miss Bail's visitors were distinguished public figures, mostly radical thinkers or liberal politicians, who were completely in sympathy with the suffragist cause. All were agreed that their object was to achieve reform by peaceable means, and not to break the law. Even convinced chauvinists were becoming aware of the appalling conditions under which hordes of politically voiceless women had to work and drag out their miserable lives. But propaganda alone had done no more than force the problem on the public's attention.

The powerful opposition was unreasoning and savage; men of the highest intelligence in influential circles felt themselves sexually threatened by the female activists they so deeply resented and derided as man-haters. Now derision was no longer enough. Demonstrators who paraded with placards, or handed out tracts stating their cause, were attacked, physically abused, and prosecuted in the courts without mercy.

Delia, so far only an interested bystander on the fringes of the movement, felt a burning desire for personal freedom that embraced all the less fortunate members of her sex, and she knew that sooner or later she would be drawn into taking a more active, positive part. It seemed fortunate to Delia that her little sister was too preoccupied with her own stormy romance to have questioned how deeply the elder girl was getting involved.

Hugo Sanderson was in conversation with his gardener when a note arrived from Lady Grandison requesting his services once again as an escort. He was somewhat downcast because an altercation had arisen between himself and Lucas Fildes, the well-known miniaturist who occupied the house next door. The volatile artist had just complained most vociferously that his neighbor's laburnum tree was overhanging their common wall, and he demanded that it be cut back.

Hugo loved his laburnum tree, but then Lucas had three entries accepted for the summer exhibition that year, and he was an artist of the highest repute. His wishes should really be respected.

He took Louise's note to be in the nature of an olive branch, for he never expected an open apology from her after she had been so quick-tempered in blaming his late sister, Mildred, for Delia's ambition to take a classics degree.

Ordering his gardener to trim the offending laburnum forthwith, Hugo hurried into his study to pen a reply. He'd call for the girls promptly at two o'clock and would be obliged if he might use Lord Grandison's landau for the outing, a favor that Arthur was happy to grant.

The continuing fine weather had encouraged an enormous crowd of people to make their way to Regent's Park for the fête, both to see and be seen.

Delia was in fact looking like the proverbial English rose, in cream shantung silk. Her hair shone as brightly as liquid gold under the little cream toque piled with artificial flowers in every shade from the palest to the deepest pink. What a contrast they were, these sisters, in looks and style, thought their escort.

Natalie had a certain continental flair for dressing, Hugo decided. He felt she had made a daring but successful choice, observing how her dress of white broderie anglaise threaded with black velvet ribbon flattered her magnolia-pale skin and midnight hair.

At the entrance to the grounds, that had been given over to the fête, Hugo paused to pay for their entrance tickets and felt the usual surge of almost parental pride as masculine heads turned in admiration toward his bewitching charges. With parasols furled, since it was quite shady under the trees, they began to stroll, one on either side of him, toward a cricket pitch specially marked out for the occasion.

A team of actresses was putting up a halfhearted attempt at defending the wicket against the rather apologetic bowling of some young actors. There were many squeals of laughter and exaggerated dismay as the two batswomen collided in the middle of the pitch, teetering on their high heels. Fancy Galbraith, of course, lost her balance and collapsed in a froth of petticoats with a generous display of silk-covered ankle and calf. This sight was enough to ensure that Natalie would readily agree with Hugo's suggestion that they should seek the refreshment pavilion and partake of tea tranquilly before the thirsty mob descended upon it.

On their way the three were accosted by a group of old family friends, including Winston Churchill and his flamboyant Welsh Parliamentary colleague, David Lloyd George. The Welshman, usually at his most dashing when confronted by attractive young ladies, appeared somewhat distraught.

"You must forgive this poor fellow. I ask your pardon on his behalf," Winston remarked affably. "He has just suffered an unwarranted attack from two sturdy Valkyries intent on riding him down astride their iron-shod hobbyhorses—in other words, a pair of suffragettes who were so bold as to throw a lighted firework in his open window."

"The weather is too hot to keep them closed, and I know from experience those harpies would have smashed the glass with a brick if necessary," David grunted. "In which case I might have been severely cut, as well as having had my eyebrows singed! As it happened, I had the presence of mind to throw a vase filled with water—flowers and all—over it before the miniature Mount Etna could erupt. So no particular damage was done, except for the puddle on my study carpet."

Delia was on the verge of defending the two suffragettes; there was no restraining her once the light of battle was in her eyes, and Natalie readied herself for the confrontation. With relief she saw that another familiar figure was approaching; Sir Michael McMahon swept off his top hat in greeting as he approached the group.

"So we meet again, young ladies. A very good day to you both." He gave them his devastating smile. "Hugo certainly has all the luck. I must discover how he comes to monopolize more than his fair share of charming girls." No formal introductions were necessary, for the great actor was familiar to both the rising young politicians. Hats were raised and slight bows exchanged.

The conversation turned to less controversial topics, where Delia was at her sparkling best. But Michael observed that Natalie was not eager to participate; as he studied her more closely, he felt that the budding sensuality of her perfect figure belied the childlike innocence of her expressive face, which fascinated him beyond all reason.

"I discern that this trivial talk is of no great interest to you, Lady Natalie," Michael murmured in her ear. "Might I lure you away with the enticement of strawberries and cream, which I happen to know are quite excellent today?"

He was rewarded with the sunniest of smiles and the upward gaze of those extraordinary violet eyes.

"I shall be delighted."

Promising Hugo he would reserve a table for the whole party in the pavilion, Michael offered Natalie his arm. They walked slowly through the rose garden, where the heady perfumes of a multitude of scented blooms vied for supremacy.

"Describe to me some of your talents, for I am sure you have many," he suggested lightly. "You dance divinely, it goes without saying; I can tell that from your walk. But has Hugo persuaded you to take up your paintbrush or model in clay?"

"I have tried sketching. However, my talents, such as they are, seem to lie in other directions. I play the piano quite well—at least my family seems to enjoy it—and I love to sing. And, although I hardly dare say this to you, I get great pleasure from performing in amateur theatricals and have actually had some principal roles. Somehow all my shyness seems to leave me when I step before an audience." She turned modestly away, fearing she had been boastful.

"I should have guessed it. You have all the natural attributes of an actress. It is a pity, Lady Natalie, that your father is a Marquess. Society's gain is a loss to the stage. I can see you as Jessica to Herbert Tree's Shylock." His wonderfully resonant voice dropped to a more intimate note. "Or Ophelia to my Hamlet."

Natalie swung around, smiling, her cheeks as brilliant as the roses about her. "You're trying to turn my head, Sir Michael."

They walked on in silence, and then Natalie said, "I have just been reading a biography of Eleanora Duse. I wish I might have seen her, for Uncle Hugo did, and he considers her the greatest performer he ever beheld, finer even in many roles than Sarah Bernhardt."

"He is not mistaken," Michael answered warmly. "I, too, am a great admirer of the sublime Eleanora. I treasure some mementoes of her that I keep on display at my rooms in Albany. I have some old programs signed by her, a tiara made of paste jewels that she wore onstage, and a fan she carried in an unforgettable production of *She Stoops to Conquer*. I would love to show them to you." He paused, realizing that etiquette would not allow him to invite a young lady alone to his bachelor quarters. The invitation he could not voice hung in the air between them.

To bridge an awkward moment, Natalie said at random, "Your own leading lady, Miss Galbraith, is extremely talented. But I believe her style is quite different. She is better suited to modern comedy."

As if on cue, Fancy herself approached them, shaking her head in mock condemnation. "How naughty you are, Michael, lurking here, and wasting all your professional ability on the entertainment of one female. A host of your fanatic admirers longs to see more of you, and, don't forget, they have paid good money today for the privilege. We are here to be observed and to solicit contributions for our charitable cause. You are positively failing in your duty."

Michael was enraged by her interference. Would she never learn that he had no wish to revive their former close relationship? "The orphans have already benefited considerably from our being here today. Your antics at the wicket alone must have been worth the entrance fee!"

With a sulky pout and a shrug of her shoulders, Fancy beat a retreat, for she knew she had yet again failed to get Michael to dance attendance upon her. But she could not resist a parting shot, calling back as she went, "Tree and Irving are still besieged by autograph hunters, and the Princess of Wales has spoken to both of them."

Michael removed his top hat and bent his head, as though quite overwhelmed with sorrow. Then he raised it and chuckled, his mane of auburn hair burnished by the sunlight. "Poor Fancy, she would be distinctly put out if she knew that I was dining at Marlborough House later this week. However, time is passing, and we should go in search of tea now. There will soon not be a single table free, and your friends will blame me for being so neglectful."

But Michael was not allowed to partake of more than a sip of China tea before he was called away to award a prize to the rapturous winner of a competition for the best recitation by a child under ten.

"The question of home rule for Ireland will have to be settled one of these days," said Winston in a contemplative voice when Sir Michael had gone. "It is our shame that a family like the McMahons, of an ancient line, should be reduced to such abject poverty that a son of their name must seek his fortune on the stage."

"All the more honor to his father, I say, when he feeds his tenants rather than lining his own pockets," said Hugo with genuine feeling. "Our English absentee landlords think of nothing but wringing the last penny from their estates, as many a starving Irish peasant will testify."

Lloyd George said nothing. He was too practiced and crafty a politician to express an opinion, even in this friendly gathering, that might be quoted against him later on.

The sun was low in the sky when Hugo persuaded the Grandison sisters to leave Regent's Park.

The afternoon had been one of the most delightful Delia could remember because, for once, she had spent it in the company of two extremely intelligent young men, both of whom listened to her views and treated her as an intellectual equal. Natalie, too, found that she was enjoying herself in almost the old carefree way—her admiration for the handsome actor who had singled her out for his attention was unbounded. She felt almost guilty that she should so enjoy another man's company, but knew at once it was a harmless friendship, in no way to be compared with her passion for Andrei.

Various invitations had been delivered to the Ritz for Prince Voroshnikoff and Professor Lensky, all of which were rejected by the Prince. Unable to rest, he sought to tire himself with the most strenuous physical activity. He took a light skiff out on the river at Chiswick and rowed up the Thames as far as Mortlake and back again with savage speed.

When he returned to the hotel, exhausted but still as restless as ever, Vladimir was out. He had left a message saying that he was lunching at the German embassy with an attaché, an acquaintance from his student days in Moscow.

Andrei rang the bell and ordered cold roast duck to be sent up to the suite with a bottle of claret. He ate without appetite, then flung himself down on a sofa before the window overlooking Green Park. He dozed and was only awakened by the return of his tutor.

The Prince sat up at once and saw the other man's unhappy expression. "What have you to tell me, Vladi?"

"I have been learning some rather harsh facts about the situation at home, which is even gloomier than I supposed." He seated himself on the other side of the empty fireplace and sighed heavily. "Opinion seems to have hardened against the Czar. His recent refusal to free the serfs, as he promised, is seen in a very bad light because the notion of serfdom is particularly odious to the British. They are talking now of the Czar's reign of terror, which they say signifies a return to the Dark Ages in Russia."

"But members of the imperial family are warmly received by royalty here in England," cried Andrei. "There is no lack of good feeling between our two royal houses."

"You cannot put it on such a personal basis," Vladimir pointed out logically. "Remember, in our country the Czar *is* the government. But here, the government is not the King! Japan has a treaty of friendship with Britain. After our catastrophic naval defeat at Port Arthur, which I still find inexplicable, Balfour's ministers believe Japan is going to win the war against us. The time may soon come when Russian visitors will be considered persona non grata and asked to quit the country."

"Don't be ridiculous!" Andrei exclaimed, leaping angrily to his feet. "You are seeing phantoms where no actual dangers exist."

"Nevertheless," Vladi insisted grimly, "you must be prepared for the possibility of an outright refusal of your request to marry the Lady Natalie, and even for your father's orders to return to Russia forthwith!"

Chapter 8

Miss Caroline Jarvis was taking tea at Grandison House. She and Louise were not intimate friends; Caroline was a garrulous bore who played cards badly and had no taste in dress.

But Natalie's attendance on Caroline's niece Gwendoline as chief bridesmaid had to be discussed. Suffering Miss Jarvis's company for an hour was a small price to pay, for Natalie seemed to have regained her usual serenity in sharing her best friend's happiness, thought Louise thankfully.

What Louise did not know was that Natalie's quiet radiance came from the possession of a love letter penned by Andrei that now lay concealed, together with his signet ring, in her locked trinket box. Linnet had rather unwillingly borne a missive to the Prince in his suite at the Ritz. An answer had been forthcoming within a few minutes and was carried back to Grandison House by the young servant.

So a happy atmosphere prevailed in the great drawing room, disturbed only by the tinkle of china and silver, the chirping of some blue-and-green budgerigars in a gilded cage, and the rise and fall of Miss Jarvis's voice. Having accepted both cake and more tea, the guest now began a rambling diatribe on how Gwen's widowed father had mismanaged the family's fortune, and had been ruined by Berryman's Bank heartlessly calling in a loan, leaving two motherless girls for her to launch in society; for Gwen had a younger sister, Hetty, not yet old enough to come out.

Hoping to get back to the matter at hand, Louise broke in brightly by saying, "So it is quite decided. Both the girls will wear white muslin, with matching moiré taffeta sashes. I quite agree that straw hats with wreaths of garden flowers, and posies to match, will suit the occasion. Simple, countrified, as you say, but most becoming. Don't you agree, my love?"

Natalie was about to concur when the double doors of the drawing room burst open and a disheveled figure with torn clothing and a crushed straw boater stumbled in. Adams followed, apologizing feebly. "Beg pardon, your ladyship, but I couldn't prevent it. Lord Justin, do please take care; your nose is bleeding all over the carpet, my lord . . ." And, with an expression of acute distaste, he handed the panting youth his own unsullied handkerchief, then beat a hasty retreat.

"How did you get into this state, Justin? Have you been fighting in the street?" Louise inquired, much displeased. "And what are you doing here, away from Harrow?"

"Oh, Justin, you're hurt. Your lip is cut, and I believe your eye is swelling up," Natalie interjected, running to aid her brother.

"Back off a bit, Nattie," he said in feeble tones. "I've a frightful bump on my head where I hit it against a curbstone. If there'd been only two of those bounders, I'd have knocked them both silly, for I've a pretty useful left, you know. It was the third one who—" He sat down abruptly on a brocade-covered footstool, his color fading fast.

Now thoroughly alarmed, Louise broke in. "My poor boy, you must have been brutally attacked. Natalie, ring for Adams, and we shall have dear Justin taken upstairs to bed at once. I must send for the doctor. This is quite likely to get him expelled," Louise added dolefully.

In the face of this impending family crisis, Miss Jarvis reluctantly hoisted her rotund form from her chair.

"It is all arranged, then. I shall call for dear Natalie promptly at nine o'clock next Saturday and bring her home safely to you early in the evening!" So saying, she took her leave, with several backward glances at the chaotic scene in the room behind her.

When Justin was stripped of his ruined clothes, it became

evident that he had been involved in more than a mere street brawl; the boy had been cruelly thrashed, for scarlet welts on his back were beginning to turn purple and black.

He seemed only semiconscious; the doctor diagnosed a concussion and said the lad had best be allowed to sleep.

When he awoke, his natural color returned to his cheeks, but Louise found her son most unwilling to communicate his troubles, and he turned his fair head away from her on the pillow, answering her questions only in gruff monosyllables.

"Could Natalie sit with me for a bit, Mama?" he blurted out at last. Knowing what a great rapport there was between these two of her children, Louise agreed.

"Nattie, dear, it isn't fair, and I don't expect anyone else but you to understand," he said when she was by his side. "I told Julian I would cut and run for it, but he said I just had to take it like a man, and remember that I am a Grandison. The beatings, I mean. But why should I, from another boy, just because he's a fag master, and I'm only his lowly fag? I come at once when he shouts for me, black his boots, stoke up the fire, and make his toast. He takes a delight in whacking me, I know he does. . . ."

"Who does, darling?" Natalie knew of the odious system that put a first-year student into the power of an older lad who was sometimes both vicious and sadistic. But she was not aware that Justin had been particularly unlucky in having been assigned to this boy as a fag.

"That rotter, Victor Berryman. He says his grandfather ran up against Papa years ago, and he despises him as a pious hypocrite and a loathsome toady to the King. His grandfather's some sort of banking bigwig. Just because I'm a Grandison, he intends to whack me whenever he feels like it, and that's pretty often!

"Today, I had about enough of it. And I knew it was no good going to Julian again. Gosh, I feel rotten, and my head aches like fury. But I suddenly got the bit between my teeth, Nattie, and I walked out, down the hill into town, and set off for home. I knew I must find my way as far as the Edgware Road, and then keep going straight till I got to Marble Arch."

"But it's twelve miles or more from Harrow! Did you walk all the way?" asked Natalie in amazement.

"No. At first I had a stroke of luck. I offered a florin to a chap who was driving a delivery van for the Great Western Railway. I knew he'd be going back to Paddington Station eventually, and he had only a few more calls to make. But when we left Kilburn and got to Praed Street, he couldn't take me any farther, so I climbed down. Almost at once some fellows started to call out rotten names. So I squared up to one of them and hit him on the nose, made his claret flow, I can tell you. Then the others all went for me. I don't exactly remember what happened next, but I must have landed in the road, because I was nearly run over by a costermonger's barrow. He was a decent chap, helped me up, and wanted to send for the rozzers—policemen, that is. But I said no, thanks, I'm in enough trouble as it is."

Justin's color was getting higher, and when Natalie laid a cool hand on his forehead, she knew he was running a fever. So she drew the linen blind, then urged her brother to try to go to sleep again.

Upon hearing of the incident, Arthur was left with a sense of unease at the mention of Victor's grandfather James Berryman. Lord Grandison had not thought of the family since that unpleasant incident at Nicholls's place in Norfolk, and the unpalatable news of Francis Berryman's suicide just before he and Louise left for their trip to St. Petersburg eighteen years before. Their paths had never crossed. He was unaware of how fiercely the wealthy banker cursed the fact that the Marquess of Grandison had no Achilles' heel, where the sharp arrow of scandal might strike and bring him down. But Berryman was willing to watch and wait for his opportunity—for the long anticipated chance to disgrace the Grandison name.

Arthur drove out to Harrow for a private interview with the boy's housemaster. The school term was drawing to a close. Justin would be excused from attending for the last couple of weeks, and would go down to Grayle Abbey by train later, together with Julian.

The Marchioness had no occasion to remark about the coincidence of hearing twice in one afternoon the name of Berryman. She had listened with only scant attention to Miss Jarvis's boring account of her brother's misfortunes. She hardly remembered the woman mentioning the "thieves" at Berryman's bank as the cause of his downfall. When Arthur returned with the tale of Justin's victimization, she cut him short, saying, "It is a horrid story, and I don't wish to hear it. Only be sure that our son's housemaster understands he should oversee more closely the welfare of the boys in his charge."

* * *

While Natalie helped her brother back to good health, she received two more precious notes, elegantly written in French, from Andrei. The poetry of his words moved her to the depths of her ardent young soul.

Delia, meanwhile, made daily visits to the ailing Miss Bail's bedside. A letter from Miss Maitland, the principal of Somerville, had regretfully informed her that, as the number of students who could be accommodated on the premises was limited, Delia was to be designated a home student, which meant she must live with relatives or friends who were within walking distance of the college.

Fortunately, rooms were available with Miss Bail's sister, Bessie Bradleigh, whose husband was the chief clerk of a highly respected firm of Oxford solicitors. They resided in Woodstock Road, in a house that Mr. Bradleigh had bought as a newly wedded husband expecting a quiver full of children; but none had arrived to occupy the many bedrooms. Now, years later, not only was the house too large for its owners, but the upkeep proved quite beyond Mr. Bradleigh's means. They took in his wife's bedridden aunt, an ancient lady who snoozed away her days in a room on the top floor, and who paid well for the privilege of keeping the maids running up constantly to answer her bell. And now the idea of sheltering a girl of such high rank at least for a year under their roof was most agreeable, especially to Mrs. Bradleigh, who would act as chaperon when required, and could boast among her friends about the Lady Cordelia to her heart's content.

Gwen's wedding was a social event that Delia had regretfully to miss, for a weekend trip to Oxford with Miss Bail had been arranged with her parents' permission before the date was set. Now convalescent, the ex-governess hoped to regain her health completely, spending a few days sitting quietly on the back veranda at her sister's house and allowing herself to be coddled. This was just the chance to introduce Delia, and arrange in a genteel manner the terms for which she would receive full board.

The village of Dartley lay just over the Kent and Surrey borders. It was a pretty drive out from town, lasting only a couple of hours, through the hilly country beyond Streatham Vale. Rather daunted by the prospect of making the journey alone with Miss Jarvis and her insufferable monologues, Natalie was surprised when the runaway from school elected to accompany her to the wedding. In the back of the carriage, brother and sister were compelled to endure the old lady's endless talk about trivial matters.

Eventually Miss Jarvis directed a skillful probe in Natalie's direction. "I might have suggested that you should travel down with Sir Michael McMahon. But fine gentleman that he is, and sufficiently respectable to be received by royalty, it would not have been proper. An actor, when all is said and done! And hardly old enough to be considered an unimpeachable escort, like dear Mr. Sanderson—to whom, I may say, I would willingly confide the care of any daughter of my own."

This was said with a piercing look, for she wondered whether Natalie might disclose that Uncle Hugo was not as trustworthy as Lady Grandison supposed.

To her chagrin the girl ignored Miss Jarvis's innuendo and exclaimed impulsively, "Why, I met Sir Michael only the other day at a theatrical garden party. He is quite charming, and I'm delighted to have the opportunity to further the acquaintance. I had no idea that Gwen or her father knew him."

"Quite the contrary! He is a friend of the bridegroom," Miss Jarvis declared. "The Hallorans, who are Protestants, of course, reside in Belfast. But Liam did attend the university at Dublin before deciding to go into the army. That is where he met Sir Michael, and although their paths have diverged since, they have corresponded and met from time to time. Not the sort of person I would have chosen as Liam's best man, though . . ." She shook her head sorrowfully.

The carriage soon drew up in the semicircular drive outside Orchard House, a double-fronted house facing the village green behind a dignified entrance framed by stone pillars. The orchard for which the house was named could immediately be seen to one side of the formal gardens, its ancient cherry trees already heavy with fruit.

Inside the house excitement had reached fever pitch. The little bridesmaid, who had already been arrayed in her finery and forbidden to spoil her pretty white dress, welcomed young Justin with cries of surprised pleasure, much to Natalie's amusement. She knew she could happily leave her brother to the company of young Hetty Jarvis.

The bridegroom and his best man were nowhere in evidence.

Liam had stayed overnight, as custom demanded, elsewhere, at the Rose and Crown. Several village women Mrs. Halloran had brought in to arrange the vases and lay the trestle tables on the terrace outside were busily employed putting the finishing touches to their work. The tiered wedding cake, which had proved beyond the artistry of the village baker and had been delivered by a pastry cook from Beckenham, was ready to be set in place. The grand piano had been pushed near the open French windows in the drawing room so that a small orchestra, including two violins and flute, could entertain guests during the wedding breakfast. In expectation of seeing the day continue perfectly fair, as Mrs. Halloran assured the party from London it would, the terrace had been carefully swept and was ready for dancing.

Natalie went upstairs at once to see the bride. Gwendoline was already dressed in white satin, wearing her late mother's lace veil, and was almost in tears because her flustered maid could not fix it becomingly under a coronet of wax orange blossoms. However, her expression brightened at the sight of her friend.

Natalie put the awkward veil to rights before swiftly changing into her muslin dress, which was laid out on Gwen's bed. The fit was perfect; the creamy sash fell in soft folds from its neatly tied bow and her leghorn straw hat wreathed in blue love-in-a-mist looked splendid against her glossy raven-black braids. In the precious few moments they were alone together, Gwen began to question her friend with timid curiosity.

"Do you know what the great secret is, which no one will reveal before your wedding day, Natalie? What happens, I mean, on one's wedding night? Delia is rather a worldly person, and I thought she might have found it out and passed it on to you. Papa said I must be sure to ask Aunt Carrie, but she took an instant dislike to Liam's mother and went up to London in a huff, saying she washed her hands of the whole affair. . . ." Her voice trembled into silence. She had not intended to ask such an intimate question even of her dearest friend, but there was no one else to advise her.

"Darling, I'm afraid I don't know," Natalie had to admit, "and I'm sure Delia doesn't either. At least, we've never spoken of it." A surge of passionate emotion swept through her at the thought of her own impending physical union with Andrei. What would it be like? Yet the prospect did not fill her with shame.

"If Liam loves you as much as you do him, I am sure you

need not be afraid. It can't be anything so terrible, after all." She spoke shyly, but with deep conviction.

At that moment the maid appeared with a tray of refreshments, closely followed by Miss Jarvis, flourishing the bride's bouquet and leading Mrs. Halloran, who had only been permitted to take charge of the chief bridesmaid's posy.

"Come, my dears!" cried Miss Jarvis. "You are already five minutes late for the church!"

It was most important that the older ladies should be seated in the correct pews at the front of the congregation. As Miss Jarvis's carriage was the only one available, it was pressed into service to transport first herself and Mrs. Halloran, and then the bridesmaids, to the church.

Finally the carriage returned for the third time to the lych-gate bearing the bride and her proud father. Mr. Jarvis tenderly escorted Gwendoline onto the porch.

As Natalie smoothed the rich folds of the satin skirt and spread wide the voluminous lace veil, she sensed that her friend's confidence was wavering.

"Don't worry, darling," she whispered. "You look lovely. Remember, this is your great day, and Liam is waiting for you!" She was not aware of the tall figure of Sir Michael McMahon standing next to the bridegroom, and both men's faces turned toward the processional.

The bride and groom had eyes only for each other. But the best man's gaze stayed with Natalie, whose light step made her appear almost to float up the aisle on the way to the altar.

After the register was signed, the happy couple triumphantly left the church amid a shower of rice and confetti. The guests drifted in laughing groups toward Orchard House, then gathered on the terrace for the feast to come. Champagne flowed freely, and soon well-filled plates of food were passed around. The cake was cut, toasts drunk, and speeches made. The orchestra struggled through Liam's regimental march, and Miss Jarvis helped Gwendoline change into her going-away outfit.

While the guests thronged about the departing couple's hired carriage, the terrace was cleared and made ready for dancing. A number of ladies were hoping for the privilege of being partnered by the famous Sir Michael McMahon, and the village squire had already invited Natalie to dance the polka with him.

While she revolved sedately around the floor in a waltz with Mr. Jarvis, indulged in a hectic galop with Justin, and gave the squire his promised polka, Michael's eyes seemed frequently to be turned in her direction. As soon as he judged it politic he approached the breathless girl and invited her to walk with him in the gardens to escape the noisy throng of wedding guests.

"How is it that you are able to spare a whole day from the theater?" Natalie asked him as they skirted an ornamental pond where fat silver and gold fish swam languidly below the surface.

"My understudy is only too happy to play my part at the matinée, and will be delighted if I'm also absent from the evening's performance. To tell you the truth, I am not much enamored of the piece," he went on, his deep, vibrant voice sinking to a more confidential tone. "It is no great sacrifice and very well rewarded if, in return, I have the honor of standing up for my old friend Liam. Not to mention this opportunity to enjoy your company, and to make the acquaintance of your young brother, whom, by the way, I like extremely."

Natalie's dark lashes dropped shyly at these compliments. "But I can't help thinking of your audience," she persisted gently. "I should have been most disappointed if you had not been appearing the night I saw the play."

"You are too tender-hearted," he replied lightly. "I am already sufficiently a slave to the dictates of an insatiable public. Would you begrudge me one day of respite, Lady Natalie?"

He laid his hand with a dramatic gesture on his heart.

She moved away with a quick laugh. "You are teasing me, I think!" He hastened to catch up with her and, by design, led her toward a rustic gate that separated the closely manicured lawns they had been treading from the rough grass of the orchard. He leaned for a moment on the gate, regarding his companion.

"The cherries are ripe, I believe," he remarked in a conspiratorial tone.

"Oh, I know." Natalie's eyes were still full of mirth.

The girl passed through the gate into the orchard, flouting convention by removing her hat, then impatiently pulling off her lace gloves. Suddenly Natalie caught sight of a swing, suspended from the stoutest bough of a gnarled old tree at the far end of the orchard. "Oh, Michael, a swing! I can't resist it!" she cried and ran ahead.

He followed her at a slower pace. *Yes,* he thought, *she is still just a child, a beautiful child, probably wildly in love with that Russian of hers. I still remember the agonized glance she gave him in the green room. How much older I must seem. Our worlds are so far apart.*

She took a seat on the sun-bleached swing, and he was behind her, holding the ropes, drawing her up close to him for one dizzying second. He pushed her from him with almost savage strength, and she swung high, still laughing, and began to sing in a voice that surprised him by its expressive sweetness:

> *Quand nous en serons au temps des cerises*
> *Et gai rossignol et merle moqueur*
> *Seront tous en fête*
> *Les belles auront la folie en tête*
> *Et les amoureux du soleil au coeur.*
> *Quand nous en serons au temps des cerises*
> *Sifflera bien mieux le merle moqueur.*

At the end of the first verse of this plaintive old song, Michael caught the ropes again and drew Natalie back to him, holding her soft, pliant frame pressed against the hardness of his own body. "How sweetly you sing. I, too, love cherry time," he said, trying to keep his voice steady. "I like to think of lovers going out to pick baskets full of fruit, the sunshine filling their hearts, the blackbirds singing . . ."

He reached up and plucked two dark red clusters of cherries on twin stalks and looped them over her ears. Then he placed his hands lightly around her waist. "There, Mam'selle, you have a pair of precious earrings to wear, brighter than rubies, ravishingly pretty, and good to eat, too." He paused, at a loss for words to this young woman who was entering his heart. "It has been a perfect day, hasn't it?"

Natalie closed her eyes, allowing herself to relax in his undemanding embrace. "Almost perfect," she breathed. And it would have been completely so, if only Andrei had been there with her in that enchanted orchard.

The journey home to London allowed Natalie to drift into a delicious reverie.

After voicing her many complaints about the ceremony and the reception, Miss Jarvis thankfully fell into a sound slumber.

When he was sure the owner of the carriage was fast asleep, Justin commented in a whisper, "I say, Natalie, Gwen's little sister, Hetty, is getting remarkably pretty. Did you notice? By the way, I talked a good deal with Sir Michael McMahon. I must say, he's a spiffing fellow. I believe if he were to take the part, I could even manage to sit through *Macbeth*, and I usually jib at Shakespeare. . . ."

His remarks ended in a yawn. The golden head nodded and came to rest against her shoulder. But Natalie remained wakeful all the way back to Park Lane, her mind teeming with the memories of the delicious, unfamiliar sensations that had filled her when Michael's strong hands grasped her waist and she had allowed herself to lean back against him. She had never had such feelings before, and knew somehow they were associated with the timid questions Gwen had asked about the perplexing secrets of the wedding night. Natalie remained as mystified as ever and was determined to tackle Delia on the subject as soon as her sister got back from Oxford.

As it happened, Delia knew no more than she. Young ladies were carefully shielded from any reference to physical intimacy. So the details remained mistily clouded in Delia's mind, too. Her knowledge of the subject was as scant as that of her younger sister.

Chapter 9

"Coffee for both of us, and pistachio ice creams, please."
Convention demanded that the two sisters should be chaperoned
as they sat in Gunter's, and they received a few frosty glances
from some older society ladies. "Pay no attention to those inquisitive dowagers in the corner," Delia said. "It will soon be com-
monplace for girls like ourselves to visit Gunter's on our own."

The coffee arrived on a silver tray. "I hear that Sir Michael
McMahon seems to have put the bridegroom in the shade at his own
wedding! I think Sir Michael admires you, and I sincerely hope you
enjoyed flirting with him, even if ever so mildly." Her teasing failed
to evoke even a smile. "No more news from Andrei?"

Natalie stirred her coffee absently. "No, nothing since his last
note, which Linnet brought to me. She was so nervous of being
caught out, she refused to go to the Ritz again. I shall have to call
myself, I suppose, if this uncertainty becomes intolerable."

In her enthusiasm to support every young woman's fight to
mold her own life, Delia knew she had encouraged the impetuous
Natalie to pursue a romantic dream. Now she was afraid she led
her sister astray, for the couple were too much in love to be less
than reckless. Exactly what perils might be involved remained a
mystery to Delia. She knew only that it was not wise for such
lovers to be alone together. And she distrusted the passionate

nature of the young Prince and dimly discerned that if thwarted, it might lead him to cause Natalie some frightful harm.

"This charade had gone on far too long, darling," she said gently. "I imagined it would only be a matter of days before Andrei could approach Papa. You can't leave Charlie hanging on like this. It's not fair to him."

Natalie put down her silver spoon, leaving her ice cream untasted. "Charlie is coming to dinner tonight, and I suppose Mama will make some excuse to leave me alone with him afterward. I have tried to explain delicately to her on several occasions that he could never be more than a brother to me. But she always cuts me short, saying that I shall feel quite differently about him when we are on our honeymoon. You know that once she has made up her mind about something she cannot bear to be contradicted."

Delia sighed, accepting that for a girl of Natalie's age, a mother's decisions were final.

Mr. Sanderson was also drinking coffee, on his terrace, trying to reassure himself that the laburnum tree did not really look much hacked about, when his butler, Gleason, came through the French doors, bearing a note.

"There is a young gentleman to see you, sir. May I show him out here, and shall I bring a second cup?"

Breaking the wax seal and unfolding the stiff paper, Hugo read that it came from Prince Andrei Voroshnikoff, who urgently begged the privilege of a few words with him. Of course, he would not refuse to grant such a reasonable request, and he nodded an affable assent to Gleason.

Prince Andrei politely refused both the offer of a chair and any refreshment. He strode up and down the terrace in an agitated manner, and Hugo noticed up that there were dark shadows under his piercing black eyes, as though the boy had spent a sleepless night. But he decided to make no comment.

"I know you will think this something of an imposition, but it is most important that I should have a private interview with your goddaughter, Lady Natalie, but for reasons I do not understand, Lady Grandison refuses to receive me. My intentions are quite honorable, I promise you, or I would not ask you to allow us to meet under your roof—"

"First things first, old fellow," Hugo interrupted, sufficiently startled to put down his cup and get to his feet. "It is Lady

Cordelia who is my goddaughter, but her sister is equally dear to me. I don't question your motives, which I am sure are above suspicion," he went on kindly. "But I do not see how you can ask me to let her meet you here, if her parents would not permit it at Grandison House."

"Our future lives and happiness depend upon it," the Prince implored. "There would be no impropriety, I assure you. If there were only some legitimate reason for the young lady to visit you, I would ask for but a few minutes of her time."

Hugo found himself in an awkward situation. But the young man was obviously sincere. "Well, it might be possible," he agreed reluctantly. "Lucas Fildes, my neighbor, has often spoken to me of requesting Natalie to sit for him. I suppose I might call on her mother this afternoon and suggest that the girls should drive over tomorrow morning to meet him." He paused. "Of course, I cannot guarantee that Lady Natalie will wish to have a conversation alone with you," he went on warningly. "That will be for her to decide. I presume you have met her by chance, or I fear by some clandestine arrangement, as you are so confident on the subject."

Before he could say another word, Andrei had clasped his hand and shook it fervently.

"I can never thank you enough, Mr. Sanderson. You have a great heart. Until tomorrow morning, then. I shall call again, promptly at eleven." He bowed with military precision and withdrew, leaving poor Hugo with grave doubts about his indulgence.

His mind filled with wild plans, Andrei rushed back to the Ritz, where he found his tutor peaceably reading *Baedeker's Guide to Venice,* the Contessa Pavarini's palazzo in that great city being the next stop on their tour. "I wish you would let me see my father's letter!" he said immediately, for he knew a missive had arrived that morning from the Russian embassy.

"The letter was addressed to me, Andrei. There is no secret about the contents. Your father asks me to convey to you his unequivocal refusal to consider breaking off the match with Desirée. He will not hear of your marrying the Lady Natalie and forbids you to mention this absurd idea to her parents. You had better make up your mind to it, *mon cher.* The sooner we leave for Italy, the better."

"Once and for all, Vladi, understand that I wish to marry Natalie in all honor, with the consent of our parents; but since it is unreasonably withheld, I intend to elope with her." Still smarting from the castigation he had received in the Grand Duke Constantine's letter for letting his charge drift into such an entanglement, Lensky saw with mounting dismay that Andrei would not easily be deterred from making good his threat.

He played his trump card. "Don't force me to call on Lord Grandison and tell him of your rash intentions. I do not know myself the cause of your father's deep-rooted objections, but that is only half the difficulty. The lady's parents obviously find your suit unacceptable. Let us leave immediately, tonight!"

"Tshort Vosmee!" cried Andrei, snatching up the guidebook and throwing it violently to the floor. "The devil take it! You are asking me to tear the soul from my body. This is the love of my life, and my father calmly insists that I should sacrifice it on the altar of blind, filial obedience, just because he has set his mind on that infernal French marriage. Do you really expect me to meekly pack my bags and go, never to see Natalie again?"

He began to prowl around the room, as restless as a wild and hungry jungle cat and, to judge from the glitter in his eye, as dangerous. Then he paused, poured himself a glass of neat vodka, and tossed it down. A pulse throbbed spasmodically in his cheek, but Vladimir dared not comment. He could not tell what was running through Andrei's mind.

Then the Prince seemed to waver and he murmured in low, distraught tones, "How can I fight both her father and mine? Impossible!" His voice broke. "You are right, I must give her up. But I cannot leave without explaining to her that I am in despair, and that my sufferings will exceed hers. I owe it to her to tell her in my own words and say farewell. I shall be ready to go tomorrow evening, not before."

Vladimir should have suspected such a prompt capitulation. But the easy way out of any dilemma always seemed best to the indolent tutor, and with huge relief he patted the young man affably on the back. "Believe me, Andrei, we'll have a splendid time in Italy—soon all this will be forgotten."

Professor Lensky was quite unaware that the Grand Duke Constantine had blanched when he received the missive pleading Andrei's cause and flung it from him in horror. Having never communicated with Louise privately since the fateful days of their illicit intrigue so many years before, or seen a portrait of her younger daughter, Constantine had not been forced to acknowledge to himself until that moment that this was his child. But he had always surmised it to be possible and even, deep in his soul, hoped it might be so.

Lady Grandison was flattered by Hugo's invitation to her daughters to meet the celebrated artist, and Delia was happy to accompany the younger girl. A visit to Uncle Hugo was always a pleasure.

They had just turned into Cumberland Place when she tapped the coachman on his shoulder.

"Grimes, please let me off at Alexandra Mansions before you take my sister to St. John's Wood," she requested.

"Are you not coming with me to Sandy's house, then? Surely not another drama reading at Miss Bail's flat? It's rather odd to hold one at such an hour."

Delia smiled. The political meetings she attended were variously described for the benefit of her parents as poetry or drama readings, a fiction also believed to be true by Natalie.

Delia was silently debating whether she should reveal the true purpose of her visit. She was going to take part in the planning of a new campaign for the Suffragette Movement. But, unsure that they would agree on the wisdom of actively championing the cause of votes for women, Delia kept this from her sister. As the landau drew up outside Alexandra Mansions, Delia stepped out with directions to the coachman to call for her later.

Hugo was taken aback when he hurried forward to meet his charming guests to find only Natalie at his doorstep with apologies from Delia, who was calling on Miss Bail. He desired nothing more than to get the encounter over with as quickly as possible, without actually breaking his promise to Andrei.

Natalie was quite bewildered to find herself being ushered toward Hugo's garden room, a small, informal apartment at the back of the house. "A friend wishes to speak to you for a moment, my dear. He is in here," Hugo said fussily, throwing open the door. He immediately withdrew, mopping his brow with a silk handkerchief.

Natalie caught a glimpse of an elegant dark-haired figure in profile, outlined against the sunlight filtering in through the open windows. Then Andrei, who had been looking out into the garden, turned toward her, and with a cry of delight she ran to him, the pleated folds of her chartreuse silk skirt and the creamy ribbons on her hat fluttering behind her.

"Oh, ma petite fleur, que tu es belle!" he declared exultantly, and they stood for a moment, hands clasped, gazing into each other's eyes. She was indeed lovely as a little flower, quite distractingly lovely, dressed all in that tender shade between the palest yellow and green, with her skin of gardenia and rose and her eyes like dark violets.

"I love you, Andrei, oh, so much," she whispered. With a sigh he gathered her close. He rained kisses on her smooth forehead then on the soft yielding mouth. Desire almost overcame him, and breathing fast, he held her away. "Listen to me, *ma bien aimée,"* he told her. "I have some bad news. My father will not give his blessing to our union. So I cannot come in all honor to Lord Grandison, as I had hoped, to ask for your hand. Ah, do not cry, my beloved. These parents of ours are old, Natalie, they do not remember what it is like to be young, to love as we do. Tell me, for God's sake, that you will never give me up."

She saw him through a haze of tears. "Never, Andrei, never."

"Trust me, then; that is all you have to do. Tomorrow Vladi and I should leave for Venice on the *Orient Express.* I have taken out a special license; you and I will be married at the Russian Orthodox church in Bayswater—and *we* shall use the train tickets! Vladi will be left behind, and when he discovers what has happened, it will be too late. We shall be married. No, wait, don't speak now, there's more." He pressed one finger to her lips.

"The Voroshnikoff yacht is awaiting my uncle Dmitri's arrival in harbor at Venice, to take him on a tour of the Greek islands. I shall send a wire from Paris to the captain that there is a change of plans. I shall be using the yacht instead, for a wedding trip with my bride." Andrei's face flushed with excitement. "We shall honeymoon in Greece," he went on, "then sail through the Dardanelles to the Black sea. When we reach our family estates in the Crimea, my parents will certainly fall in love with you at first sight. Just let my father see what a jewel I have won and he will relent."

Hugo, hovering uncertainly in the hall, heard snatches of this incredible conversation. He never imagined that his fond indulgence toward the romantic impulses of young people had led him to connive at an elopement. Reluctantly he decided that he must call upon Lord Grandison that very day and unburden his conscience.

Within the garden room Natalie agreed to Andrei's plan amid feverish kisses and caresses. Once he had gained his point, the Prince was eager to depart; there was a great deal to do if his scheme was to succeed, and time was of the essence.

* * *

In the carriage going home with Delia, Natalie was in a torment of indecision. Should she confide that she had just promised to elope with Andrei? But the elder girl was clearly preoccupied. Emily Pankhurst had been an unexpected guest at the meeting, and Delia was fired with an excitement of her own. Natalie could not find the right words to broach the subject, so she kept her news to herself, hoping to find Delia more approachable later.

While the landau was making its roundabout journey, Hugo reached Park Lane and found Lord Grandison enjoying his first glass from a new case of very dry sherry. One glance at Hugo's anxious face made Arthur pour a second glass for his friend and wave aside the footman.

"My dear fellow, I'm here on a most unpleasant errand," the older man began, sinking down into a leather-backed chair. "I have been an utter fool, and I shall be fortunate if you and Louise can ever forgive me—"

"Hugo, my old friend, you are surely exaggerating. Do get your breath and take a sip of sherry before you try to explain," interrupted Lord Grandison with kindly concern. He had never seen Hugo so distressed.

"I agreed to let Prince Andrei Voroshnikoff meet Natalie at my house without her mother's knowledge, but I did not realize that he actually intended to propose to her. Worse still, he persuaded her to elope with him."

"Good God! Did I hear you aright?" Arthur leapt up, knocking his own glass unheeded to the carpet. "Natalie agreed to elope with that Russian? You cannot be serious. Why, they have only met, as far as I know, on one occasion. Where is she now?"

"On the way home from St. John's Wood," said Hugo miserably. "The carriage had to pick up Delia from Miss Bail's flat, and that is how I arrived before her."

"Delia at Miss Bail's? These daughters of mine will be the death of me. I shall have to tell Louise at once." At that moment the lady herself entered the library.

"I'm afraid there's a scandal brewing, my dear," Arthur began, moving forward to take her hand. "It concerns Natalie, sad to say. Apparently she considers herself engaged to that young Russian, the Voroshnikoffs' boy. I can't imagine where they've been seeing each other, but from what Hugo tells me, they were hatching some scheme to marry without our knowledge when they met at his house this morning."

Louise swayed, turning suddenly pale. She clutched Arthur's arm with a convulsive grip.

Hugo, anxious to complete his confession and be absolved, went on. "We bumped into him in the green room at the Clarence one evening, not long after Lady Jessop's party. But Natalie didn't speak to him then, I swear, for the poor girl felt most unwell and wanted to leave soon after."

"Oh, keep quiet, Hugo," said Louise, waving him to silence. "Where was Delia while all this was happening? Surely she is not party to such an insane plot."

All three were transfixed by the sound of voices in the hall. The Grandison carriage had just arrived home.

Louise swept out of the room and seized Natalie by the wrist, forcing her upstairs, before the girl could utter a word of protest.

"I think you had better leave, Hugo," said Arthur tersely. "After all, it is a family affair. I must say you are not without blame, but I shall deal with my daughters firmly, for I see I have been too lenient in the past."

Delia was astonished to see Uncle Hugo pass her without a word of greeting. While she stood bereft of speech her father issued an abrupt summons. "Delia, come into the library at once; I want a word with you." Perhaps he had found out about the meetings. Well, she was determined to defend her principles, even against Papa, if need be. Chin up and ready for battle, she followed her father into the library and closed the door.

"Delia, what is this I hear about an intrigue between your sister and the Voroshnikoff boy? Have you encouraged her infatuation with him?"

"Not exactly, Papa," Delia countered, "although I truly believe that she does love Prince Andrei." She was about to go on when he cut her off sharply.

"That is nonsense, and I will not give it credit for an instant. Answer me truthfully. Were you aware that these two intended to meet this morning and plan to run off together? If Hugo had not done his duty, we should have known nothing of it, and in all probability we could not have prevented it."

"Papa, stop. Natalie has told me that she and Prince Andrei are in love, and they cannot understand why you refuse to receive him. He has been awaiting a letter from his own father, to show you how warmly Natalie would be welcomed by his family. I had no idea they were meeting today, and certainly not to discuss an elopement." She rose and approached him anxiously.

"But you see how impossible this marriage would be?" Her father spoke more kindly now. "You will use all your influence, won't you, to persuade your sister to give up any idea of it?" He drew her nearer to him still and held her fast.

"You favor Charlie only because you and Mama are on such friendly terms with the Haversham family," Delia replied trenchantly. "Why should Natalie not marry where her heart dictates?"

Lord Grandison stroked back the hair, so like his wife's in color but tinged with the ruddy hues of molten gold, from Delia's forehead. "You think yourself infinitely more sophisticated than your little sister, because you are older," he told her lovingly. "But in effect, you have led the same sheltered existence and know little more than she does how cruel life can be. Oh, yes, the young man seems charming enough, seen against the background of our own society, but can you imagine our little nightingale in Russia? I have stayed with his parents in St. Petersburg. Let me tell you how it was. Come, sit down."

Seating himself opposite his spirited daughter, Arthur spoke carefully. "I have seen Andrei's father order a *moujik,* a peasant no more culpable than one of our own tenants convicted of poaching a rabbit or two, to be given a hundred lashes. The man died, quite predictably, as an example to others. In St. Petersburg he admitted to me that the poor freeze to death by the thousand every winter. When a drought makes the harvest fail, and the markets are empty, the starving line the city streets. If they demonstrate against injustice, the people are sabered down in the streets by mounted guardsmen. No one dares go out to help the victims, who bleed to death before they receive any help. . . ."

"Oh, don't go on, Papa, I can't bear it." Delia's voice was piteous, and she turned her head away.

"I must make you understand," he insisted, cupping her chin with his hand and forcing her to look at him. "There is no safety for people in our class in Russia, however much they delude themselves. They are always in danger from an anarchist's bomb or a revolutionary's bullet. Oh, I know that before Natalie was born, our dear Queen, who was Princess of Wales then, reassured us that we ran no risk in visiting the Voroshnikoffs. But it was not true. Hatred of the great landowners was already running riot, even in those days. Serfdom is officially abolished, but slavery is still the lot of millions reigned over by the Czar. Much as I enjoyed my old friend Constantine's company, I would not wish my daughter to be crushed under the mighty weight of the responsibility he and his kind have to bear.

"Agitators are at work, urging the peasants to slaughter their masters. Czar Nicholas will not listen to the grievances of his people, but one day there will come such a bloodbath that he or his successor will be forced to hear. When that day comes, however far in the future, do you want your sister to be among those to have her jewels snatched from her neck, to be subjected to unspeakable horrors by the mob, then brutally slain? Because our own monarchy is closely related to the imperial family, I and my fellow peers dare not openly criticize, but we know that sooner or later, this holocaust is bound to come."

There was an anguished silence between father and daughter.

"I only wanted Natalie to be happy," Delia said at last. "I did not see why she should be persuaded by you both into making a marriage against her wishes. But perhaps Mama is wiser than I realized. And yet, Andrei seems such a noble young man, I can hardly believe he would be capable of the kind of cruelty you tell me you have seen with your own eyes."

"There are enlightened men of good family, and I have met a few, such as Prince Dolgorukoff, for instance," Arthur agreed. "Perhaps youngsters like Constantine's son, Andrei, may also have liberal views. But by the time they are old enough to exercise any political influence, I fear it will be too late. Promise me, Delia, that you will do all you can to dissuade Natalie from the hopeless pursuit of this ridiculous fantasy. I shall have to send her down to Grayle at once, and I'm afraid it falls to me to make it quite clear to Prince Andrei that his attentions are unwelcome. I know I can speak for your mother as well in saying this."

Delia replied uncertainly. "Let me think about all you've said, Papa." She rose. "If there are such terrible dangers to be faced, you would have to force her to relinquish him, even if it meant banishment to Grayle for a time. Poor Imp, please let me go with her. . . ."

"Can I feel sure that you will exert a good influence? I wonder. It might be better to send Justin with her. Oh—and her maid. Which reminds me; Is Linnet implicated in all this?"

Delia knew that if Linnet's part in aiding the affair were revealed, she would instantly be dismissed.

"It was I who acted as their go-between," she replied with downcast eyes. Shocked at her words, Arthur turned away. "Well,

I'm afraid that changes matters," he said at last. "I would not have believed such deceit possible of either of you, and I think for the time being you would be better apart. Besides, Natalie must understand that she is in disgrace." He cleared his throat, quite choked by emotion. "Now, luncheon has been delayed quite long enough," he went on briskly. "We have been keeping the servants waiting. I will tell Adams to serve it at once, for I am of the opinion that your mother and sister will not be joining us."

He offered Delia his arm, and they went out together; but at the door she hesitated, turning troubled eyes toward him.

"Mama will explain all this to Natalie, I suppose?" she asked doubtfully. "Just as you have to me. Oh, she must do so!"

Arthur shook his head. "The poor child is certainly in no state to believe anyone who tries to reason with her. She would only think it a fabrication. Let us hope Natalie will soon get over her infatuation with this young man, and her resentment against us for separating them. Thank heaven you have never given us such anxiety. And I know that level head of yours. You'll think over all I have said?"

Denied the opportunity of speaking to Natalie, Delia did think long and hard about her sister's plight, and she concluded that although her parents had mismanaged the affair, they had been in the right. And her own newfound sophistication, she began to realize, went only skin deep. No matter how profound her academic knowledge, she still had much to learn of life in the great world beyond.

Upstairs in her mother's boudoir, Natalie had been subjected to a searching inquisition into her conduct and had finally admitted both her clandestine meetings with Prince Andrei and their secret betrothal.

"Please, Mama, say that you understand," the girl begged. "I never wanted to deceive you, but although I dared not speak of it, I know that Andrei sent me flowers and messages, which you must have intercepted. What have you against him?"

"Perhaps his parents, whom you tell me are also quite set against the match, understand as we do how unsuitable it would be." Her voice dropped persuasively. "Believe me, Papa and I did speak of Prince Andrei's obvious admiration for you after Lady Jessop's ball. Do not think that we came to the decision that he should be discouraged without some heart-searching," she went on. "You must know that Papa and I were thinking only of your best interests. It was just this sort of foolish impetuous nonsense that we wished to protect you against. Why, at your age, lacking parents to guide me, I myself became seriously entangled with quite the wrong sort of man! It is fortunate that Hugo had the good sense to warn us in time to prevent you from ruining your life—for I assume there has been no intimacy between you and young Voroshnikoff?"

"Indeed, there has!" Natalie insisted. "This morning he kissed me, several times—as he had every right to do, because we were to be married tomorrow." Despite her fury, Louise could almost pity her younger daughter in the purity of her innocence.

"So you have never before this morning been alone with the young man?" Louise asked in gentler tones. "Remember, such folly would be sufficient to destroy your reputation," she warned. "No gentleman would dream of marrying a girl whose behavior had been the least bit questionable. Such a faux pas could not be overlooked, even by a fond and indulgent suitor like Charlie Haversham."

"Charlie! How dare you mention his name to me in the same breath as Prince Andrei's?" cried Natalie, approaching her mother with a challenging step and such rage in her eyes that the older woman almost drew back.

"Don't take that tone with me, my child," Louise reproved. "Your father and I think only of your future happiness. I assure you life in that foreign land is very different from the cherished existence you have here, whatever highly colored pictures your Prince has painted."

As though she had not heard one word, Natalie insisted, "I will marry him. Do not try to prevent me, Mama, I implore you."

"Indeed, you will not. There is no question of your being allowed to embroil yourself any further in this scandalous affair. Papa will order our private railway coach to take you down to Grayle at once. I shall tell Linnet to pack your things." Louise left the room, deftly removing the key from the lock and turning it on the other side of the door.

Lord Grandison soon penned a vitriolic note to Prince Andrei Voroshnikoff, forbidding him any further contact with Lady Natalie. He intimated that his daughter was to be sent instantly to the country, and he advised—indeed, he insisted—that Andrei should leave England's shores within the day.

Chapter 10

Natalie had never suffered humiliation and despair to equal that of her trip to Grayle Abbey the next day. She was hurried to Paddington Station with Lord Grandison and Justin by closed carriage, their servants following with the luggage.

Disheartened by her father's coldness, and in complete turmoil about the failure of Andrei's plans, the unhappy girl sat staring out of the window as the fields and woods slipped past in all their summer panoply of green and gold. Her father had little to say to her, and Linnet, of course, sat with Lord Grandison's valet in the compartment reserved for them.

Justin knew nothing of the drama that had taken place at Grandison House; he and his father were engrossed in happy conversation about school, cricket, plans for the summer holiday . . . He was unaware that curious callers at the mansion in Park Lane would be told that he and Natalie were suffering from a fever, which necessitated this sudden trip to the Abbey. Two such callers, however, chanced to meet on that hectic morning of departure at the Grandison home—Caroline Jarvis and Nell Haversham. No sooner were the two acquainted than they already decided to visit Grayle Abbey at the earliest possible occasion to ferret out any whiff of scandal that might have caused the prettiest debutante of the year to be banished to rustic seclusion.

* * *

Natalie, along with Delia, usually looked forward to the long summer days spent at Grayle. Their parents appeared at intervals, for Lord Grandison liked to call on all his tenant farmers and occasionally read the lesson in church. During their absence the girls took to short skirts and romped with the boys, hair flying loose, for all the world like village children. But this year, without Delia's sunny presence, and only Justin for company, her beloved Abbey seemed more akin to a dreary prison.

Any sense of guilt that Natalie might have felt for disobeying her mother was outweighed by the conviction that she had been cruelly treated. Bitter anger boiled deep within her. She would certainly never recapture the childish confidence in her parents that had illumined her first seventeen years. It had vanished forever.

The events of one evening had stripped away most of her illusions. She remembered her stunned surprise when Mama had been so unkind, so unfair, to Delia. And Papa, that cherished hero, had meekly acquiesced. Then only hours later, at the fancy dress ball, she had been deliberately humiliated by their mother before Andrei with those fabrications suggesting an engagement between herself and Charlie Haversham.

To prevaricate did not come easily to Natalie. But now, in desperation, she made up her mind to tell any lie, use any weapon, if it would help bring about her heart's desire.

The country seat of the Grandison family was much larger than the elegantly proportioned house in Park Lane. It had originally been a monastery, built in the fifteenth century to the design of some inspired master builder, of tawny ochre stone. Little remained of the early abbey, but, fortunately, the many additions made over the years had been carried out in stone of the same rich hue, which glowed in the sunlight like golden honey. Indeed, Grayle Abbey was often spoken of as "Golden Grayle."

One caught sight of its stately outlines from afar, across undulating parkland where herds of deer kept the grass close-cropped. Each of its soaring turrets was topped with a delicate fretwork of stone, so that the mansion seemed to nestle like a crown in folds of emerald velvet.

Its central façade was enhanced by a profusion of oriel windows, and niches with scalloped canopies sheltering statues of venerable churchmen and saints. Crenellated towers stood guard at the ends of both east and west wings, providing vast bedrooms with commanding views over much of the estate.

From as far back as Natalie could remember, summers at Grayle had been idyllic—and she had only happy memories of life at their country home. But now she spent hours gazing in misery from the windows of her tower room in the west wing. Exile did nothing to quench Natalie's passion. No matter where she turned, Andrei's image haunted her, and his fervent pledges of love echoed in her ears.

Papa's stay at the Abbey had been disappointingly brief, and he had hardly said a word to her while he was there. Now she was completely cut off. No letter came for her, nor was she permitted to send any; and when she rode about the estate on her little bay mare, Gypsy, a groom was always close behind her. When she grew tired of the confines of her own room, Natalie would read in the library, lush and elegant with its thick carpet and leather chairs. But her mind would wander and she'd instantly forget all that she had tried to read. *I might as well be guarded by jailers*, she would think to herself, casting aside her book.

Soon harvest time approached, and Julian joined Justin at Grayle Abbey to take part in the festivities. But to Natalie's heavy heart, this celebration only marked the passing of time since she had been parted from her lover. Natalie's eyes began to seem enormous in the pallor of her face, which appeared daily to grow thinner. Then at last, when she was quite ill with longing, came the news she had so eagerly awaited.

One morning curiosity among the servants was rife when a letter arrived, addressed to Linnet, from Italy. The envelope was inscribed with a flowing masculine hand, and several of the footmen exclaimed, admiring the unusual stamp. The housekeeper was in half a mind to open the letter herself when Linnet, blushing and protesting at the teasing she had endured, rose from the breakfast table and ran off to the butler's pantry to open the envelope. There was another sealed letter inside, enclosed by a single sheet of paper folded around it, addressed to herself. The note, from Prince Andrei, implored her to say that the missive was from a waiter at the Ritz whom she had met in the park on her day off, and who was now enjoying a brief holiday at home in Venice with his family. The enclosure was for Lady Natalie. The Prince concluded with his sincere thanks and extravagant promises of a substantial reward for her efforts.

Natalie's eyes filled with tears of relief when she saw Andrei's letter. He wrote that he was on the point of leaving Venice and returning to England. His tutor would join him in London later, but here was the ideal opportunity for Andrei to visit Oxford alone, in the role of an interested tourist—and he would be installed at the Angel Hotel by the time she received this letter. He was traveling incognito as Mr. Constantine and would await word from her as to where they might meet. She was to be cautious, but he hoped that she was as eager as he for them to be reunited.

The young Prince concluded by expressing his complete confidence that her love would not have been diminished by their parting. *"L'absence pour l'amour est comme le vent pour les flammes. Il étaint le petit el allume le grand,"* he wrote. Truly, the girl thought, if her love had been a weak flame, absence might indeed have extinguished it. But it burned in her heart more strongly than ever. Natalie turned to her maid and inquired breathlessly, "If I write a very important letter, would you post it for me, Linnet?"

"A letter to His Russian Highness?" Linnet faltered. "Oh, milady, you know I'm forbidden to send any letters for you."

"But you will do it, all the same!" Natalie's pale cheeks began to glow with hope.

Defenseless against the persuasive charm of her adored mistress, the girl agreed.

On the same day, Natalie received a formal and businesslike note from her mother, the first communication of any kind from either of her parents since her exile, announcing the arrival of Miss Caroline Jarvis and Nell Haversham as visitors to Grayle. Heartened by the news she was receiving about Natalie's good behavior from the housekeeper, Louise saw no reason why the two ladies should not visit the girl; besides, Nell would be an apt reminder that Charlie Haversham still patiently awaited her reply.

She preferred solitude to the intrusion of visitors, but Natalie penned a submissive yes to her mother's inquiry—if she appeared no more subdued than any other girl recuperating from an illness, Mama might let slip the vigilance with which she was guarded, allowing her the opportunity to escape when the time came.

The visitors arrived from the station by carriage, complaining that they should really have brought their maids; even an overnight stay required so many changes of dress. Their hostess received them with grave politeness.

At luncheon Natalie apologized for the absence of her brothers, who were taking part in a cricket match at Banbury that day. But the two guests seemed not to notice as they gazed in awe at the splendor that surrounded them—particularly Miss Jarvis, who was actually reduced to silence by the carved furniture, the famous portraits, the superb food. Nell surveyed her young hostess closely. "You certainly have lost weight, Natalie dear, to an extent that is quite unbecoming," she remarked. "Such a pity that you had to leave London at the height of the season. But even the best parties have been overshadowed, I fear, by the shocking political news. Isn't that so, Miss Jarvis?"

"I don't know what you are speaking of, my dear," said the older woman vaguely.

"I'm afraid the newspapers are not delivered unless my parents are at Grayle. What are the events you find so shocking, Nell?" Natalie enquired.

"Why, the terrible rift between our own government and Russia!" the other girl cried in mock surprise. "Surely you have heard something of it, even here? There was the most frightful cartoon in *Punch* showing the Russian bear twisting our English lion's tail. The Japanese Emperor is shown as a little monkey jumping up and down in the background, wearing a silly grin. Of course, the Russians think we ought to break our treaty with Japan and come in on their side in this ridiculous war, which, it seems, they are in danger of losing. Underneath the picture it says, 'Velly funny. Foreign devils fight each other while we win war!'

"I shouldn't be surprised if we did end up fighting the Russians over this," she continued gleefully. "You know how we Britons love to defend the cause of the underdog. There are so few of the Japanese, and they are so backward. Why should they allow a powerful nation like Russia to drive them from Manchuria? The Czar already has limitless lands he doesn't know what to do with. My papa has explained all this to me, and I am surprised, Natalie, that Lord Grandison has obviously never spoken of it to you. But, then, you have not seen your parents recently, have you? Perhaps they do not think you are old enough to be interested in politics."

Natalie did not permit herself to give Nell the pleasure of

seeing how hurtful she found these jibes. Nell went on complacently: "It must be most embarrassing for our Muscovite visitors, such as Prince Andrei Voroshnikoff. I believe he is in Italy at the moment, although he has been invited to Lord Dunmeath's shoot, or so Charlie tells me. But, then, of course, he need not return to Britain if the situation becomes too tense. He can always go to France and stay with the Comte de Paris. After all, it's open knowledge he is engaged to the Comte's niece, Desirée something-or-other. A rather dowdy girl, but terribly rich."

Natalie was toying with a delicate glass of pale Rhine wine. Involuntarily her grip tightened so that the stem snapped and a few drops of blood flowed from her cut fingers.

Miss Jarvis did not notice this little mishap, so intent was she on steadily consuming the medallions of veal with tiny artichoke hearts on her plate, but Nell jumped up in alarm.

"Look, Natalie, you have hurt yourself. Your nerves are really in a frightful state."

Natalie staunched the flow of blood with a small cambric handkerchief, fighting to regain her self-control.

"Obviously it isn't within our power to restore your good spirits," Nell went on. "Perhaps a gentleman might be more successful. Maybe I can persuade Charlie to come down to see how the improvements are progressing on his new property at Abingdon. Conventions are less important in the country. If you two were engaged, I believe he could drive over every day without any impropriety."

This was the last straw. Natalie threw down her napkin and rose in anger. "Once and for all, Nell," she said furiously, "let me tell you that there is no question of an engagement between myself and your brother. If he labors under the misconception that I am still considering his proposal, please go immediately and tell him that I refuse it."

Nell was furious enough to call for the carriage to take her and her chaperon away to the station forthwith. But she was overruled by Miss Jarvis and forced to stay the night, since the older lady protested that she was much too exhausted to make the return journey that evening. Nell remained sulky for the rest of the day and retired to her bedroom, claiming a headache.

Natalie was compelled to spend all afternoon sitting on the terrace with Miss Jarvis, who, try as she might, was unable to get the girl to reveal any clues to her withdrawal from London society. Eventually she gave up, and while she rambled on, Natalie was lost in her own anxieties. She had been indiscreet. Nell was bound to carry back to town a tale that would be a rude shock to Mama's hopes of an alliance with the Haversham family. It might also revive her parents' fears that she had not quite relinquished all thoughts of Andrei. The girl wished she had held her tongue. But how could she have sat idly by and accepted Nell's words? It *had* to be a lie, this foolish talk of Andrei's engagement to Desirée. But she could not quite rid herself of a pinprick of suspicion. Might he, after all, merely be playing a game with her affections?

Louise felt positively faint when Nell confronted her in the Grandisons' drawing room with the news of Natalie's outburst. She got rid of the girl as soon as politeness allowed and hurried to find Arthur in the library. "I should have foreseen this, and stopped that foolish, tactless girl from going down to Grayle," she murmured.

"Well, my dear, I always told you you were backing a loser there," her husband reminded her gently. "A fellow like Charlie had little chance with such a starry-eyed dreamer as Natalie. Nothing romantic about him." Arthur contemplated the glowing tip of his cigar for a moment. "I have to admit, you were probably right in your notion that we should get Natalie settled," he went on, "although, to my mind, she is still far too young. Only seventeen! Thank God we were able to prevent her from making an irreparable mistake—especially now with diplomatic relations so strained since those mad Russians began sinking our ships at sea."

The furor had not yet subsided since the Vladivostok squadron of the Czar's navy had sunk a British ship, the *Knight Commander*, mistaking it for a Japanese vessel. The tension between the two governments was due mainly to the Czar's almost insane suspicion that Britain was somehow aiding Japan in the war, now seen to be dragging toward a disastrous conclusion for Russia. The imperial fleet had been beaten not only at Port Arthur, but at every subsequent engagement, by the forces of Nippon. The loss of face was shaming and the repercussions of this catastrophe were to be incalculable. . . .

But, returning to the matter at hand, Lord Grandison was

painfully reminded of the unhappiness the period of exile must have caused his darling songbird. "We can look to the future now," he continued thankfully. "There are other young men in the running. We shall soon find a husband for her, just as much to your taste as Charlie Haversham. Although I know his mother is your greatest friend.

Telling herself that her husband was probably right, Louise dismissed her lingering fears. In spite of her crowded engagement diary, a date was set several weeks ahead for their traditional exodus from town to Grayle Abbey.

Natalie was not left to brood over Nell's innuendos about Andrei's engagement for long, for she received a wire from Delia, who would be taking up residence at Mrs. Bradleigh's the next day. She expressed the hope that her sister' and brothers would drive over from the Abbey to visit her immediately, and Natalie soon deduced that it must have something to do with Delia's twenty-first birthday, now only a few days off.

Returning triumphant from a visit to the solicitor's office, Delia found her mother ready to pounce, demanding the reason for her daughter's imminent departure. All the luggage she was sending in advance was waiting in the hall, clearly labeled with the address in Woodstock Road.

"I have been trying to speak to you for ages, Mama," Delia said firmly. "But you are always busy. I believe I'll be able to get on with my reading much better once I have settled in at Oxford. I have Greek responsions to get through in December, worse luck. My tutor thinks the tranquil surroundings in Oxford will encourage me to work hard. Mrs. Bradleigh is expecting me tomorrow, and I have sent a wire to Natalie suggesting that she and the boys should drive over. I'm longing for a sight of them all."

Louise was distinctly annoyed and said coldly, "I have left it rather late to propose, but I had thought of inviting Hugo, and perhaps a few other old family friends, to dinner. Nothing elaborate, of course; one would not wish to draw attention to the way you have retired from society and immersed yourself in these most unladylike studies."

"Well, it is all to the good, then, that you have left it too late to arrange any sort of jollification for my birthday. I hope you and Papa had not planned to give me any special present either. I couldn't accept it, knowing how much you both resent what I am going to do." Delia had just received an advance on the handsome sum of money she had inherited from Aunt Mildred. It was more than sufficient to pay her way quite comfortably.

Louise took her daughter's arm, leading her to the morning room. "Listen to me, Delia. Natalie's conduct has been closely supervised at the Abbey, and I have made certain that she can receive no news there from Prince Voroshnikoff, nor can she communicate with him. She never goes out unattended. Now you tell me you have calmly invited her to visit you in Oxford, where I have no idea what mischief she may get into. I insist that you give me your solemn promise never again to act as go-between for Natalie and that unsuitable young man."

"You have my word, Mama." Delia's face clouded. "Papa convinced me, as you very well know, how heedless I was to encourage Natalie in that direction. I think you were mistaken in imagining she would accept Charlie. But I never wished her to be embroiled in a love affair that could only end miserably. Some of the blame is mine. Truly, don't you think she has now been punished enough? It's time we should put all these unhappy events behind us. After all, she can't be kept a captive at the Abbey forever."

Despite her fears, Louise had to be satisfied with Delia's positive undertaking not to conspire with her sister to meet Prince Andrei again, should he return to England.

That night at Grayle Abbey Natalie lay wakeful in the big four-poster bed, her cheek pressed to the feather pillow beneath which Andrei's letter lay concealed. The girl's body was afire with eagerness for their reunion. Her reply, cautiously addressed to Mr. Constantine, and promising to arrange a rendezvous in the near future, was awaiting him at the Angel Hotel. Perhaps her lover had already received it!

Chapter 11

The excuse to go to Oxford came at just the right time, and Natalie was counting on her sister as an ally; perhaps she would suggest some practical plan to accomplish the elopement. The only doubt clouding her perfect confidence in a happy future with Andrei was concerned with Nell's spiteful rumor about the French heiress Desirée. Well, there was sure to be some simple explanation.

After a night during which she slept little, for sheer excitement, Natalie was up early and dressed with extra care, although the likelihood of her coming face-to-face with her Prince that day was slight. A rendezvous would have to be arranged. But she could hardly wait for the others to be ready, and her face was radiant as she stepped lightly into the old-fashioned wagonette.

The housekeeper came out into the drive to see the conveyance depart. She was a little uneasy because Lord Julian insisted that he should drive. But a reliable groom was to be seated next to him, in case of an accident, and the man was waiting by the horse's head while Julian took the whip. The young Viscount was proud of his driving, and although there was a threatened spill at the crossroads near Bampton, the party arrived in record time. When they turned into the gravel drive at the house in Woodstock

Road, the boys were too busy admiring the enormous monkey puzzle tree that dominated the front garden and speculating on whether they should climb it to notice the speed with which Nattie flew to her elder sister's arms.

Natalie's figure had been refined to an almost ethereal grace; but Delia was relieved that the violet eyes had not entirely lost their sparkle, and a faint rose color showed in her cheeks.

Mrs. Bradleigh watched their reunion from the lobby, which led through inner glass doors to a tiled hallway in which many pots of aspidistras flourished. She was a good-hearted soul who wore a habitually apologetic air because her husband and his relatives so patently blamed her for being childless. But just now she was in seventh heaven. The Lady Cordelia Grandison, daughter of a Marquess, and her sister, here in her home!

Mrs. Bradleigh hovered in the background while Delia showed Natalie the apartments upstairs that were to be her sitting room and bedroom. The former was large and airy, with two sash windows looking out onto the road. It was light, but not particularly welcoming, being furnished in a rather gloomy style with prim upright chairs, a workmanlike table, and a leather-topped desk. There were shelves on either side of the fireplace, some already filled with the books Delia had been unpacking. The curtains were of severe green serge, and the horsehair sofa was uncomfortably upholstered in drab brown leather. But Delia had already flung a big cashmere shawl over it, and she added a few cushions, covered in cut velvet in cheery colors. She had filled a brass vase with armfuls of yellow and apricot-tinged gladioli, carefully laying away the dried pampas grass plumes that had been placed there by her landlady.

"Why, it is splendid, Delia!" exclaimed Natalie with enthusiasm, looking around as she removed her veil, then unpinned the shady hat it had held in place for their drive.

Delia flung open the door to the next room. "This is the one I like best. Isn't it charming?" she declared as they stepped in.

It was indeed pretty. The architect had provided it with a whole wall of casement windows, and deep window seats, possibly intended as toy boxes for the children who had never come to bless the Bradleighs. Even the wallpaper, a little faded now, was primly striped in pink alternating with white, sprigged with rosebuds. The starched dimity curtains blew inward from the open windows, which gave a fine view of the garden full of dahlias and daisies. At the far end of the lawn, trees much older than the house itself formed a solid backdrop and were as dense as if the property stood on the edge of a forest, rather than in the heart of a city of dreaming spires.

"I dare say Nell would think it 'deevie,'" Delia admitted shyly. "It is not by any means 'divine,' but I do rather like it. Now that you have seen the extent of my domain, darling, shall we go downstairs to tea?"

"I shall have a tray sent up to you," interjected Mrs. Bradleigh, beaming. "I believe you two young ladies have not met for several weeks and must have a lot to say, I'm sure, over the cup that cheers without inebriating."

As soon as the girls were alone Delia inquired seriously, "You do not blame me, Imp, that I did not write to you? Mama flatly refused to allow it, and so I gave way. You see, it was so near my birthday, and after that she could not stop me from coming to live here, or from sending a telegram suggesting that you and the boys should visit me. Yes, I paid for my own railway ticket— second class, if you please—and had myself driven here from the station in a fly. The cabby was very kind, helping me up with my valise. The large pieces of luggage had been sent ahead and were delivered by dray only an hour after I arrived. But I'm running on, because I am somewhat embarrassed." She paused, aware that she was making too much of her first long journey alone. And she was still apprehensive about Natalie's mood.

"Come, let's sit down together," she went on. "I'm quite tired from all that unpacking and putting away, since I did so little for myself at home." She beckoned her sister to the bed, and they both sank down upon it. After a moment, Delia spoke. "Don't pine, darling, for what can never be. Oh, it is all my fault that you have had to suffer so much, because I encouraged you to meet Prince Andrei again. Papa made me see everything in quite a different light, for he knows so much more about the world than we do. I realized how impossible it would have been, the dangers you would have risked. Thank God you're only seventeen; you'll soon forget. Maybe you have already done so . . ."

Upon hearing her words, Natalie felt as though she were sinking, sinking down through the soft mattress into a dark pool of despair. She realized Delia was on the enemy's side, and despite the pity in that other fair young face, it would be useless to attempt winning her back.

She had never before deceived Delia, but she drew a deep breath, then said quite steadily, "I suppose I shall get over it. But it was very hard to be sent down here in such a hurry. Linnet forgot to pack my books and my music, and most of my new frocks. May I borrow something to read from you, darling? Or have you brought nothing but your stuffy old tomes in Latin and Greek?"

"Take the latest novel by Elinor Glyn. It's next door, on the top shelf. The plot is rather daring. Miss Bail would certainly not approve of our dipping into it at all. It might shock you!"

"Most of our books at Grayle are positively antique. I should enjoy reading a new novel." Deliberately she rose from the bed, quite unable to look Delia in the face, and passed back into the sitting room.

As she searched the shelves diligently for the book, Natalie congratulated herself; she had lied to her sister without a qualm. "Of course, you didn't trouble to pack any sheet music, did you?" she went on. "Even if Mrs. Bradleigh had an instrument, you have never been fond of the piano."

The other girl followed her, smiling indulgently. "No, I have nothing of the kind. But it is easy enough to buy in Oxford; in fact, I believe there is an excellent music store next to Ellistons, in the High."

Delia had played straight into Natalie's hands. "Why, of course, I remember it now," she said innocently. "I might send Linnet to get me some Chopin waltzes and nocturnes while we have the chance to talk. Oh, but I have no money."

"Don't worry, dearest Imp. I can easily run to such an insignificant gift for you." Delia moved to the desk and opened the top drawer, taking out a well-filled leather purse. "I'm sure half a crown will do, but I had better give Linnet a sovereign to be sure."

"What a kind sister I have! Linnet will bring you the change." Natalie seated herself, took a sheet of paper from the writing stand, and scribbled out her requirements. "I think I will just go down and send her off on the errand at once," she said, rising and taking the money on her way to the door. The sound of servants' voices led Natalie to the kitchen, where Linnet was sitting comfortably at the scrubbed pine table, watching the cook slice some runner beans. She nodded to them and beckoned the maid out into the hall.

"Now, please, Linnet, don't argue, but do as I say," she whispered urgently. "Go at once to the Angel Hotel. The policeman in Cornmarket Street will direct you. Ask for Mr. Constantine and say I will call on him there within the next few days. You can hand in my order on the way back at the music shop next to Ellistons. But hurry!"

"Lawks, Lady Natalie! Oh, don't make me lose my place," Linnet beseeched fearfully.

"Silly girl, there is no danger of that. When you return, just say the pieces I wanted were out of stock. You have put in an order on my behalf and it can be collected in a couple of days."

Over tea Delia tried to probe delicately into her sister's state of mind, for she knew Natalie well enough not to be entirely satisfied that she had recovered from her thwarted romance so quickly. Although she was as affectionate as ever, there now seemed a certain distance between them. Delia wanted above all to do something positive to rekindle their previous loving relationship. An occasion soon offered itself.

Over supper, to which the ravenous brothers returned from an afternoon of exploring, Natalie deliberately spoke with a wistful air of the joys of living in Oxford.

"I wish I might stay here with you, Delia, even for a little while," she said diffidently.

"Then, why don't you?" Her sister's face lit up. "I will ask Mrs. Bradleigh's permission." Julian and Justin, it so happened, had already hatched a scheme to prevail upon Delia to let them stay a couple of nights later, when the annual fair took place in St. Giles. So it was arranged that on the following day the groom would drive Natalie over to Oxford, with a small valise containing her necessities for a night, and that the two girls would manage very well indeed without a maid for such a short visit.

Mrs. Ponder, the housekeeper at Grayle, thought the proposal an excellent one, since Mrs. Bradleigh was an ideal chaperon and would relieve her of any responsibility.

Natalie took long to decide what she would wear, and which simple dresses to have packed. She was quite determined to slip out somehow and see Andrei without anyone else's knowledge. She could hardly contain her impatience and insisted that the groom should make an early start, so they arrived at Stonelea well before midday. She was greeted with a kiss by Delia, who ran out at once to the front gate.

Mrs. and Miss Olivia Chalfont, who lived next door, were peeping out of their drawing-room window and admired them both; the blond girl in pale blue spotted lawn, with her skirt caught up in ruches; and the dark beauty in primrose yellow voile, with fine tucking from neck to hem and billowy angel sleeves. The neighbors hurried out to wish Lady Cordelia good morning and to ensure that they received an introduction to her exquisite visitor.

Natalie's valise was soon unpacked, her white nightgown and robe laid away in a drawer. The girls sat down together on the sofa in Delia's salon, as she had decided to call it.

"Are you sure you don't hate me, darling, for siding with Mama and Papa?" she asked wistfully. "I feel so much to blame, not just for the heartache I know you've suffered, but because of the way you've been punished by our parents. Of course, I had no idea you were going to meet Andrei at Uncle Hugo's. But they are right, you know. If you married him and there was some sort of revolution in Russia, it might have put you in dreadful danger."

"Let's not talk of it, darling," Natalie said firmly. "I've quite, quite recovered from my silliness. Now, please tell me more about Somerville, and your tutor, and whether you shall like her, and whether you feel certain of passing those wretched exams in December."

All the time Delia was busily describing her first impressions of student life, Natalie was planning how she could escape, but she had come up with no solutions by the time the lunch gong was sounded and Mr. Eustace Bradleigh strolled through the front door. This was customary on a Saturday, for one o'clock signaled the end of the working week for him. His status as chief clerk excused him from returning to the office for the rest of the day. He came in looking more solemn than usual and went straight to his wife, with only a passing nod to each of the Grandison girls.

"Bad news, I'm afraid, my dear!" he said portentously, accepting her meek kiss on his cheek.

The news was certainly sufficiently grave: Miss Bail's neighbor had just telephoned him from London to say that the poor lady was seriously ill. Apparently, while they were taking tea together, she had begun coughing. Then, without warning she had a severe hemorrhage from the lungs. The doctor, who came at once, thought it was consumption, and he had immediately called for a second opinion from a physician in Harley Street. The consultation seemed to have confirmed his diagnosis.

During her recent convalescence in Woodstock Road, Miss Bail had overcome a lifetime of dislike and forced herself to confide certain fears to her brother-in-law. She had extracted from him the telephone number of his office, saying quite rightly that a telegram of an alarming nature would throw her sister into hysterics, and if her premonition about her health proved true, she would rather reveal it to the more phlegmatic Mr. Bradleigh in the first instance.

"Please take me up to poor Martha at once," Mrs. Bradleigh entreated wildly. "Get out the timetable, dearest, and see when the next train is leaving."

"I don't think I should be of any use if I went with you, my love," he demurred. "Forgive me for mentioning it in front of these young ladies, but Martha and I do not get on, and the sight of me will only do her harm. Besides, illness is women's business, and you are quite friendly with that overpowering neighbor of hers. Between the two of you, you'll sort out what is to be done, and the good lady has already undertaken to arrange for a bed in some suitable hospital where Martha can be cared for."

At the sound of the word *hospital,* Mrs. Bradleigh turned quite faint. To enter one, stricken with the dreaded tuberculosis, was equal to a death sentence.

Delia now stepped in and announced that she would accompany Mrs. Bradleigh up to town. Indeed, it was her absolute duty to go to the aid of her former governess.

"But your sister, dear . . . she cannot be left here unchaperoned," faltered Mrs. Bradleigh.

"Poor Natalie!" agreed Delia sadly. "Perhaps you had better return to Grayle."

"No, no, that will not be necessary," interrupted Mr. Bradleigh, addressing his wife. "Your Aunt Bella is upstairs, is she not? An adequate chaperon, in my opinion. Lady Delia should return tomorrow, when you have made all the arrangements. Martha's neighbor insists on helping, you know. The two of you can easily take charge. In the meantime, if Lady Natalie can amuse herself for the afternoon, I am playing in the finals of the bowls championship at the Parish Club. Then I must attend the churchwardens' meeting. What if I were to order a cold collation to be served at seven o'clock, my dear?" He turned politely to

Natalie. "You could join me for that, and then I would be proud to escort you to the organ recital at St. Margaret's afterward. . . ."

Delia was rather taken aback when the younger girl accepted with charming deference, saying she would call on Miss Chalfont next door, explain the circumstances, and persuade her that they might stroll down to the music store together.

In the rush to catch the earliest possible train, Delia neglected to question Natalie's decision to stay on at Stonelea without her. Mrs. Bradleigh ate hurriedly, then went off with Delia in attendance, crying out confused instructions to her husband and the domestic staff to the very last moment.

No sooner was their conveyance out of sight than Natalie wished Mr. Bradleigh good luck in his bowls tournament and promised to amuse herself until his return at seven o'clock. There was no need to introduce her to Miss Chalfont formally, she said, for the young lady had spoken to her in the most friendly manner that morning.

She took up her parasol and gloves and set off without even pausing at the gate next door, inwardly astounded at her own temerity.

Although Miss Chalfont often walked into town alone, demure in her white serge costume and boater, without attracting as much as one glance on the way, it was not so with Natalie. Many heads turned, and a few audible comments were made about her charms, so that she was flushed as any rose by the time she reached the lobby of the Angel Hotel. Before she could strike the bell at the reception desk, she was all but brushed aside by an officious courier, resplendent in a dark blue uniform, ready to address a small group of people who had obviously been waiting for his arrival.

"Are we all assembled for the afternoon visit, ladies and gentlemen?" he began in a businesslike manner. Equipped with camera apparatus and guidebooks, the tourists gathered obediently around him. "As ever, you will find that Thomas Cook always offers the best tours. We shall start with a rare architectural treat, University College, founded in 1249, and the oldest of Oxford's temples of academe . . ." The last in the long line of inquisitive tourists was a young man who lagged at the back of the crowd.

Natalie instantly recognized her lover's tall figure. Her eyes feasted upon his proud bearing, his air of elegant indolence, and the arrogant tilt to his dark head.

"Andrei . . ." she called faintly.

He swung around and was at her side in a couple of paces, his disdainful expression vanishing. A joyful smile lit up his finely chiseled features. "My princess! You don't know how I've longed for this moment. I thought you would never come." Impetuously he seized both her hands. There was a ripple of interest among onlookers at the rapturous greeting of this handsome couple.

Conscious that they were now the cynosure of many eyes, Andrei spoke quietly. "Where can we go to be alone? I have so much to say to you. Shall we walk into the town together?" he suggested with mounting impatience. His gaze implored her to hint at some retreat where he could enfold her in his embrace and shower her trembling lips with kisses.

"I have to collect some pieces of music. But perhaps afterward you would like to return with me to Woodstock Road, where my sister has taken rooms. I should hardly have known how to introduce you, but as it happens, Delia and her landlady have had to go to London. News arrived only just now that a close relative of Mrs. Bradleigh's who used to be Delia's governess has suddenly been taken ill. It is such a pity, for I've come to stay the weekend, and now I'm left quite on my own for a few hours . . ." Her voice trailed into silence.

It was obvious what a golden opportunity she was shyly offering.

"Forget your errand," he begged, unwilling to sacrifice even a few precious minutes of his time alone with her.

"Shall we walk there, then?" she proposed. "It is really not very far." As she took his arm Natalie's thoughts were in wild confusion. What would the servants think if she invited a strange young man into the house? But the weeks of enforced separation had made her bold beyond belief. She would worry about the consequences later.

"I dared not mention my good news when I wrote," the Prince began excitedly as they walked rapidly along the thoroughfare of St. Giles. "At first I was in despair when my plan to go to Venice and take over our yacht failed. You remember it was to wait for my uncle Dmitri to arrive, because he, too, had been invited to join the Contessa Pavarini's house party before starting his cruise of the Greek islands." Before Natalie could reply, Andrei continued: "He gets bored easily and would soon have cajoled whichever guests he found most congenial to join him on the yacht for the journey as far as Piraeus, if not for the rest of the trip. But Dmitri was quite prepared to remain in Venice when he found me, plunged in gloom, staying at the palazzo. I was almost suicidal at the thought that I might have lost you forever."

"Are you suggesting that Count Dmitri could possibly help us? And why should he wish to do so if he knows that your father is against our marriage?" Natalie asked diffidently.

Andrei flashed her a quick smile, twirling his silver-headed cane with a nonchalant air. "Because there has always been a feud between my father and Dmitri, who is my mother's youngest brother. He's rather a black sheep. But he is more closely related to the imperial family than my father, and he is a great favorite with the Czar. The Czarina, who dislikes most of her husband's friends, has a fondness for my uncle. I must say, he is such a charmer that few women can resist him. When he saw the photograph in *The Tatler* of you in your presentation gown, he declared you a raving beauty and was not surprised I wanted to marry you."

He took her small gloved fingers and tenderly kissed them. Her eyes were wide with adoration, although she did not yet comprehend where all this was leading.

"Dmitri could well understand that I refused to have some dull little French heiress foisted on me as my bride," Andrei went on. But Natalie stopped in her tracks.

"Then there was some truth in the rumor that Nell Haversham repeated to me." Natalie faltered, drawing away from him. "I refused to believe it, but she told me an alliance had already been arranged for you in France."

Andrei had the grace to look guilty. "The girl is only fifteen, and there would have been no question of announcing our engagement yet," he excused himself. "The possibility was spoken of between my father and her guardian some time ago, and I did meet her in Paris. But I swear I gave her no encouragement, nor did she seem greatly taken with me. There is absolutely no commitment on either side, I promise you."

Although this was something less than the truth, Andrei refused to let the slightest seed of doubt take root in his beloved's heart. He needed her trust in him to be absolute.

"You do believe me, don't you?" he inquired reproachfully. She nodded in acceptance of his explanation.

"Forget all that, then! Let me tell you more about my plans for our future together." Possessively he tucked her hand once more into the crook of his arm as they resumed their way along the Woodstock Road.

"My uncle Dmitri could not be persuaded to give up his Greek odyssey entirely," Andrei continued. "But he has undertaken to curtail it, and within a couple of weeks he will be back in Russia. He intends to go straight to the Czar's summer palace at Tsarskoe Selo and tell him the whole story. He will explain that I am bringing you by the fast steamboat passage through the Kiel Canal to St. Petersburg, and that we shall have been married on board ship. As soon as we arrive I shall take you to the palace and place you under the Czarina's protection. Dmitri can always persuade Their Imperial Majesties to approve any cause he champions. The Czar will command my father to accept you as my wife."

The girl was quite overcome by this lofty speech. "I can hardly believe that the Emperor will concern himself with our fate," she said doubtfully. "But if you are certain of it, darling, that would solve all our difficulties."

"I have worked out every detail," Andrei asserted proudly. "We need say no more about that wretched fiasco in London weeks ago! This time good fortune is on my side. It was easy to deceive Vladi, as he was ill with some wretched fever. I made him believe that I was bored in Venice, and he was easily convinced that I merely intended to pass through London on my way to Lord Dunmeath's shooting lodge in Argyle. The old laird was once a great crony of my father's. I had promised, before I met you, to join the shoot for as long as possible, before having to return home. Vladimir must be well by now and will arrive in Scotland in a day or two," Andrei went on, delighted with his scheme. "Of course, he has no idea I have been in Oxford. I must be at the lodge when he gets there. If he asks whether I lingered at all in London . . . well, I shall tell him I couldn't resist renewing my acquaintance with the fascinating Fiona. Oh, don't look so startled, my charming Natalie. Since I gave you my pledge, I have not seen her at all, and do not intend to. . . ."

Full of confidence, he pulled her around to face him. "You trust me, I hope, *mon amour?*"

Natalie's heart thudded uncomfortably at the mere mention of Fiona Galbraith's name. She could not quite forget the humiliating scene at the Clarence Theatre, but it would be unworthy of her love to question Andrei's word now. She frowned, but he did not even notice, so keen was he to outline his stratagem.

"To allay Vladi's suspicions, and so that he will inform my father I have bowed to his wishes, I must stay perhaps as long as two weeks at Dunmeath's lodge. But you should be ready to leave Grayle and join me at a moment's notice. I'll contrive some quarrel with another guest, accuse him of appropriating the birds I have shot for his own bag, perhaps. Duels have been fought for less! Then Vladi and I will leave precipitately, however strongly the poor fellow protests against it, and go straight to the Ritz in London. I will send a wire to Linnet, that fetching little maid of yours . . . is that how you call a pretty girl—fetching? But not as beautiful as the stars, like you, my dearest one." His voice dropped to a more intimate note. "How exquisite you are in that pale dress with your ravishing little straw hat."

He paused and bent his dark head so close to hers that she half feared, half hoped, he might kiss her.

"Let your maid explain away the telegram by saying her admirer from Italy is back in London," he continued, withdrawing to a more conventional distance and walking on. "But that will be my signal. You must order a groom to drive you both to Oxford. Say you are visiting your sister, and when you arrive, dismiss the carriage. As soon as possible, make some excuse, go to the station, and take the first train to London. I'll be waiting at Paddington all afternoon, meeting every train. . . . How furious Vladi will be! But when I explain that Uncle Dmitri has won the Czar's approval for our marriage, I don't think he will put any obstacle in our way. If he tries, I shall tell him to go to the devil! We shall embark at Harwich and I'll engage a private stewardess for you on board, if by any chance Linnet refuses to accompany you. Within four days we'll be in St. Petersburg!"

Having reached this triumphant conclusion of his recital, Andrei paused, patently expecting some admiring comment.

But Natalie was quite bereft of speech. "What a brilliant idea," she managed to say at last as they reached Mrs. Bradleigh's gate.

Cook and the house parlor maid were taking their afternoon rest, and the kitchen maid Elsie, who had just been summoned by the old lady who dwelt on the top floor, did not hear Natalie ringing the bell several times. At last she rather timidly tried the handle of the door and found it unlocked. The hall was deserted and there was no sound of a footstep on the stairs.

"I can't imagine where the servants are. But I suppose you had better come in," she said hesitantly. "It would hardly be conventional, but at least we can talk in Delia's sitting room without being overheard."

Etiquette demanded that if she were to be unchaperoned in a room with a young man, the door must be left open. But when Andrei had passed before her with a graceful bow, she deliberately closed it, feeling herself starting to blush as she held his gaze with her own soft violet eyes. She knew that this one significant gesture revealed her total submission to his will. She would sacrifice her reputation and the respect of her entire family, if need be, to follow Andrei wherever he led her.

Hurriedly stripping off his gloves and casting aside his hat and cane, he gathered her fiercely to him. They clung together like survivors of a shipwreck, almost unable to believe that they had both weathered a violent storm, clinging to the same spar, and were now in sight of land.

At last he said, "Come and sit down, *ma bien aimée*, and let me look at you." As they sat on the sofa her intuition told her that this was a moment of decision from which no retreat could be made. He cupped her chin with both of his strong, steady hands, smiling tenderly at her shy dismay, and turned the delicate oval of her face up to his. Their eyes, so dark and eloquent, met and locked. As his fingers stroked the nape of her neck, an uncontrollable shudder of anguished anticipation ran through her.

"Are you afraid of me, that you draw away?" he chided.

"No, no . . ." she breathed, struggling a little in spite of herself, caught fast by his hands, like a butterfly that has winged its way into a spider's web and only then begins to sense danger. His hands slid behind her head, and his fingers stole upward, tracing its shape under the crown of lustrous hair. A feverish, trembling pleasure invaded her as he unpinned the coquettish little hat and laid it aside. He laughed again, exultantly, running his supple fingers down to encompass her pulsing throat in a caressing gesture. Then he began to draw the tortoiseshell combs from her smooth-coiled hair until it fell in a curling torrent to her waist.

"My princess, you are beauty incarnate. I shall always worship you," he whispered, first kissing the tips of her fingers, then taking hold of her arm, bare to the wrist below its billowing angel sleeve. He pushed up the gauzy material until he could kiss the soft skin inside her elbow.

As he bent his head the thick black locks springing back from his temple were so close that Natalie could not resist brushing them with her lips. The clean, virile scent of his body was in her nostrils. Andrei's close-shaven skin was as pale as marble. A casual observer might have taken the young man to be delicate, even effete. But like some lithe animal on the prowl, whose muscles flow powerfully beneath its satin hide, his strength was merely concealed by grace. He held her quite powerless to move with one hand, while, with the other, he slowly opened the tiny shell buttons fastening the front of her gown.

"What is this?" he exclaimed in wonderment. "Ah, my ring!" he cried as she drew from between her breasts the thin gold chain on which she wore his signet. Pressed against the soft flesh of her swelling bosom by her ribboned camisole, it had left the slightest of red marks on the snowy flesh.

"My love, have you worn it so all this time?" His voice was husky with emotion, so deeply was he touched.

"Since they sent me to Grayle, when I contrived to take it with me, I have worn it day and night."

He snapped the fine chain impatiently and cradled the ring in his palm. "What are the words of your marriage ceremony? I have heard them and I thought them so beautiful. 'With this ring I thee wed!' Is that what the bridegroom must say?" He took her left hand and began to slide the ring onto the third finger as he spoke.

He pulled her closer. "With my body I thee worship, with all my worldly goods I thee endow."

The metal band slid home painfully as in his eagerness he pushed it with one swift movement onto her slim finger.

Never, never, he vowed, would he wed any girl other than the graceful princess of his dreams, who yielded at this very moment to his embrace. He would make her his and never let her go.

All his innate nobility forbade it. The instincts, the training of his class, bade him to respect and preserve the sanctity of her untouched maidenhood. Yet his brain teemed to bursting point with reasons, arguments, in his justification.

This girl he venerated and had sworn to marry. But his blood had run hot for her these many weeks past. And he would do her no wrong, worship her none the less, if he were to take her now and not wait for the Archbishop's hand raised in blessing. Moreover, from the moment he deflowered her, there would be no going back, no denial, he told himself. She *must* then be allowed to wed him, and that was the most powerful argument of all. A trick of fate had brought them together, and if all his nobility pleaded for him to respect her innocence, all his sensuality urged him to possess her while he might. Let the Grand Duke and the Marquess pursue some secret feud for which he cared nothing, or private quarrel between the Grand Duchess Natalya and Natalie's mother, the implacable Marchioness. For he could think of no other more sinister reason why he and his beloved should not wed.

As he raised his head from the fragrant hollow of the girl's slender throat, he saw through the half-open door Delia's bed, spread with its smooth unsullied coverlet. Thin curtains moved softly in the light breeze; for she had flung her windows open to the sweet scents of the garden that morning. The tempting sight swept away his final scruples. He rose, lifting Natalie easily in his arms, carried her into the bedroom, and laid her down on the smooth, cool cover. Her lips parted to protest, but his own insistent mouth came down on hers, quieting them.

Gently, irresistibly, he pressed his tongue between those petal-soft lips, between the pearly even teeth, until it met her own, surprised, darting away, and then replying to his tender advances.

And gently he slid one hand beneath her pliant body, arching it up to his while he released it from the fragile cocoon of her dress, then her transparent lacy camisole, and slipped both layers of clothing down to release the twin globes of her rounded alabaster breasts, so daintily pink-tipped that he moaned with ecstatic delight as he stroked and caressed them. He felt her struggle defensively for a moment and then yield to his touch as wild thrills of response shot through her. Now he had bared all the upper part of her body, the bodice pushed back from her shoulders, and buried his face in her sweet flesh, his hands still caressing, sliding down to her thighs, stripping away the rest of her clothing, until she wore nothing but her embroidered silk stockings, held around her slender legs above the knee with ruched and ribboned satin garters.

The erotic sensation of seeing her thus clad, so maidenly and yet as provocative as some practiced priestess of the demimonde, overwhelmed all his last warning thoughts of restraint, of care.

His palms measured her waist, the fingers almost meeting, then slid up over her ribs to explore again the curves of her bosom.

As the buds of her nipples hardened she felt the same delicious sensation in the downy pit of her firm, girlishly rounded stomach; a warm, melting throb of desire that caused her instinctively to part her thighs and to arch her supple back higher to press her breasts against him, to seek an ever closer contact between his hard body and her soft one.

Her eyes were half closed, and she saw him only through a fringe of heavy lashes as he raised himself to slip off his own clothes. She barely saw his naked body, the surprising shape of his maleness; then she was feeling only his deft hands, his fingers making open the way ahead. Then came the thrust of his entry. But so expertly, so gradually did he first caress the sweet sheath offered to his sword that she felt no distress, only a sort of fierce pleasure in being wounded, conquered, conceding her defeat and thus being made one with him. A moment came of piercing sensation that transcended pain. The spasm forced a cry from her, astonished, exultant. Slowly, slowly, their rapture faded.

They loved again, and this time Natalie sobbed in ecstacy at the pleasure bestowed on her with the caresses of his hands, his lips, all the riches of his splendid body. Still entwined, they drifted into exhausted slumber.

Later that afternoon Natalie awoke. She lay on her back, one arm flung up over her head, her eyes still half closed. When consciousness of her abandonment dawned on her, she started up, pressing one arm across her breasts to shield them from his gaze. He murmured, then turned away from her, still sleeping. Quietly the girl rose, as shy as a naked nymph, put on her white nightdress and robe, and then took up her silver-backed hairbrush from the dressing table and drew it through her cloud of night-black hair. Andrei had awakened and was watching her with a melancholy gaze. Leaving her for the time being, as he knew he must shortly do, would be pure torment for him.

"Come back to bed, my lovely bride," he whispered invitingly. At that moment there was a knock on the door of Delia's sitting room. Putting a finger to her lips and shaking her head at Andrei, Natalie moved lightly to answer the persistent knocking.

"Come in!" she called courageously.

The maid, surprised to see Natalie in her robe, held a tray set with a silver tea service, cucumber sandwiches, and slices of caraway-seed cake, an offering from Cook to tide Natalie over until the evening meal.

"I have a terrible headache. I had to lie down, I'm afraid," she explained. "Tell Mr. Bradleigh how sorry I am, but I really cannot join him at table, and I won't be able to go to the recital tonight." Leaving the tray of food, the maid regretfully passed the news on to Mr. Bradleigh, who was disappointed; he had been complacently anticipating the buzz of envious admiration that would greet his appearance that night with such a gorgeous young creature on his arm.

As the shadows lengthened on the grass the lovers lay sated by their joy, talking in whispers, while Andrei caressed again and again the smooth contours of Natalie's body. She was not ashamed, but she felt bound to confide. "I have been wicked, I suppose. I hope that my family will forgive me in time. Do you have brothers or sisters, Andrei?"

"I had an elder brother in the Preobrazhensky Guards. He was killed horse racing. Broke his neck falling at an awkward fence. When I became a cavalry officer, I promised my mother I would not race. The cavalry are such daredevils. But in the case of Vassily, I think it was to impress a woman. And my sisters . . . One died as an infant of diphtheria. The other of an illness that was never diagnosed, but in two days she was dead. She was only eleven, and I was a child of nine. She was so pretty, very much like my mother. Her name was Tatiana, and I have never forgotten her. I am the only one left. Poor *Mamushka,* she would gladly have exchanged all her diamond tiaras, her ropes of black pearls, for the lives of her lost children."

Natalie pressed herself against his lean, hard body, letting her fingers play possessively with the hair that tumbled around one of his ears, nipping the lobe between rosy polished nails, then tracing the sleek musculature of his shoulder, down to the elbow, savoring the touch of his flesh.

"Tell me where we shall live, my darling. Tell me more about Russia. Describe it to me. Will your family understand me if I speak only French? Oh, there is so much for me to learn. . . ."

But Andrei did not wish to waste even one more moment of their precious interlude together on conversation. When he released her, the shadows had grown long in the garden, had become hardly perceptible, and the blue sky was fading into an amethyst haze. A light evening dew was falling, so gentle that it rested on each blade of grass with a pearly sheen. The blackbirds were making a great fuss about settling down for the night in the elm trees at the end of the lawn. Far away in the woods beyond Christchurch Meadow, a nightingale was preening herself, balancing on a hawthorn twig, ready to serenade the moon when it rose. Natalie shivered and crept to shut the window.

Mr. Bradleigh had resigned himself to going out alone. This was still, he reminded himself, one rare evening of freedom from Mrs. Bradleigh's stolid company. He accepted the verger's invitation to go home with him and "take a jar" after the recital.

So at an hour much later than usual, he stumbled up the drive and, with difficulty, negotiated putting his key in the lock, then quite forgot to insert it on the other side of the front door to make his castle secure. He slid the lower bolt and proceeded upstairs with an uncertain tread. He fell asleep in his shirtsleeves, across the matrimonial four-poster, crushing the neatly folded nightshirt that had been laid on his pillow, and he did not stir when, just before dawn the next morning, Andrei ran lightly down the stairs and let himself out of the house.

Natalie lay facedown in tears on Delia's sofa. Her body ached from its unaccustomed use. It would be at least two weeks before she saw her lover again.

But the young Prince strode at express speed all the way back to his hotel, in a high state of exaltation, impatient to put his ambitious plan into operation and sublimely confident of its success.

Chapter 12

On the morning that news of Miss Bail's illness arrived in Oxford, Lord and Lady Grandison went driving together in Hyde Park. They returned about noon, much too early for luncheon, but the parade around Rotten Row that usually took more than an hour had been accomplished in forty minutes. None of their fashionable friends were to be seen, and the famous Grandison grays had not been held up once by the press of other carriages.

"London is a desert!" Louise complained, sipping an aperitif, which Adams had just served to her in the morning room.

"Of course," Arthur replied placidly. "The season is over, and has been for weeks. I suggested that after our jaunt to Trouville, which turned out to be such a bore, we should go straight down to Grayle. And here we are still, at the end of another week. The boys are surprised we have not joined them there already, my love. Did I tell you I had a letter from Julian this morning? If I read his scrawl correctly, the weather continues to be splendiferous, dry and extremely hot. He says that Justin's cricket has improved, since he has shown him how to keep a straight bat before the wicket. We could leave tomorrow or, at the latest, on Monday. Shall I tell Adams to make the necessary arrangements?"

His wife did not answer immediately. She touched the enormous pear-shaped diamond dangling from her left ear and appeared to secure the small gold screw that held the earring in place. She knew she was responsible for postponing, to an unreasonable point, their annual departure for Grayle Abbey. Of course, she longed to see Delia and her boys, but she positively dreaded her next encounter with Natalie. Suppose the girl still languished for love of Prince Andrei, still blamed her mother for coming between them, even hated her? Natalie's blood tie with the secret love of her own youth made her especially dear to Louise. She did not believe she could bear to see hatred in the eloquent glance of those wonderful eyes. For she could never justify herself, never explain how necessary her action had been to protect her beloved child from frightful harm.

Mrs. Ponder wrote every week, saying that Natalie gave no trouble. She was quiet, biddable, and apparently resigned. True, she did little justice to the magnificent fare placed daily before her, and had lost some of the sweet roundness of her figure. But apart from a certain listlessness, she did not seem ill.

Both parents had been reasonably satisfied with these reports, until they heard from an indignant Nell of Natalie's most uncharacteristic outburst at the dinner table. It was so unlike her, for she never flared up in anger. Louise was prepared to put it down to Nell's habit of rubbing people the wrong way. But from the moment the story was recounted to Arthur, he had been increasingly anxious to depart for Oxfordshire.

His wife knew he was watching her closely, waiting for a reply. "Come, my dear, surely you agree with me. People will wonder what on earth we are doing here, when all our friends went abroad, or to the country, weeks ago. Besides, it's our duty to spend some time with the children. We should not punish the boys by depriving them of our presence because Natalie has been in disgrace."

This was an argument he knew would instantly appeal to Louise. She set great store by doing the right thing, and by sustaining the image of the Grandisons as perfect examples of how the nobility should behave. It was now certainly the right thing to do to go to Grayle Abbey. Any further delay would cause speculation, even gossip.

"Very well, Arthur, I absolutely agree," she said with unaccustomed meekness. "Flora will pack for me, but I shall take sufficient wardrobe for only a few days, and I advise you to do the same. You know dear Alix expects us soon at Sandringham for a private visit. His Majesty is in poor health at the moment, and that always makes him irritable. It would be a kindness to her to go, and we really have no option; it is in the nature of the royal command."

There was a very special relationship between Louise and the Queen, who, as each year passed, grew deafer and more handicapped by painful arthritis. The King, for his part, had always found Arthur's company congenial; so the Grandisons were more frequently invited than most to join the royal pair when they were resting out of the public eye.

Neither parent had the least idea that Delia was returning to London that day on an errand of mercy. Leaving Mrs. Bradleigh to attend to all the invalid's immediate needs, Delia went straight to Mr. Sanderson's house by cab, and finding him not at home, she sat down and drank some tea while waiting for him.

Her godfather was attending a matinée at the Clarence, for the Irish piece had failed to please the public and was to be taken off the boards. Uncle Hugo, such an admirer of Sir Michael McMahon, wanted to see him in the leading role again and returned to Acacia Grove with the news that the theater would soon begin a short season of Shakespeare's tragedies.

Having heard of Miss Bail's illness, he insisted that Delia should stay the night in St. John's Wood. Tuberculosis was known to be contagious, so he firmly overruled his goddaughter's plan to return to the mansion flat and sit with the sick woman until the ambulance arrived to take her away. Mrs. Bradleigh had decided to accompany her sister to the private sanatorium in Epping where a room was already reserved for her. So Sandy allowed the girl to make only a brief visit, which left her more alarmed than ever, for she could see the first ravages of serious illness in her dear friend's face. How suddenly it had come upon her, thought Delia, as she sat huddled forlornly in the corner of her compartment during the journey back to Oxford.

But without the final diagnosis, there was still hope. Having seen her sister comfortably installed, Mrs. Bradleigh was to come home the next day, and she might bring better news.

Delia was hardly aware that Natalie was very subdued and thoughtful. Absorbed in her own fears for Miss Bail, she was almost thankful that the visit was over so soon, and somehow the long, intimate chat she had meant to have with Natalie about her blighted love affair never took place. Even the simple family celebration Mrs. Bradleigh had offered to arrange for Lady Cordelia's coming of age was canceled.

The arrival of their master and mistress threw the servants at Grayle Abbey into quite a panic of activity. Linen was aired, parquet floors were polished with mops by footmen in carpet "slippers" who skated solemnly to and fro over the gleaming wooden floors. Hothouses were stripped of flowers and fruit, so that hardly a ripe nectarine or a Malmaison carnation in full bloom was left. The home farm yielded up vast amounts of poultry, butter, cream, flitches of bacon, and whole cured hams. Gamekeepers bore their tributes, furred and feathered, to the great house, along with flat baskets of newly caught trout, perch, and pike, still quivering in their mantles of silver scales.

While the senior members of the staff lined up at the doors to bow and curtsy respectfully, Natalie and the boys awaited their parents in the drawing room. Louise entered with a flourish, holding her head high. The boys were embraced and complimented on having grown so tall.

There was nothing about Natalie's dutiful kiss to disappoint either parent; but it seemed as though shutters had been closed behind the luminous purple-blue eyes. This lack of warmth cut both Louise and Arthur to the quick, but it hurt him most. Although he knew Louise was right to forbid the ill-fated match, at that moment he might have overcome his fears, his prejudices, to give his little nightingale her heart's desire.

Their visit was to last at least a week, and Louise wasted no time, determined to find out Natalie's true state of mind. She began by questioning Linnet but learned nothing except that the Lady Natalie had received no letters and had gone out very little.

Louise then made a ceremonial visit to Oxford to sound out Delia. She charmed Mrs. Bradleigh and made pleasant conversation. Alone with her daughter, she gave her limited approval to Delia's living quarters at Stonelea; although the sycophantic Mrs. Bradleigh was no more to her taste than the prickly Miss Bail had been, she seemed respectable and anxious to please. Delia would be reasonably well accommodated while she indulged her academic follies at Somerville.

But when Mama came to inquire about Natalie, Delia shook her head and would offer no help. The younger girl was not as candidly confiding as before. They had talked of this and that, but nothing intimate.

When summoned to her mother's presence, Natalie offered an apology for deceiving her parents, then changed the subject. Yes, she would like to go abroad with them that autumn. Yes, she would require some new dresses for the cooler weather. And would it be possible to have some of her afternoon gowns altered, since her waist was smaller by a full inch? With a sigh, Louise realized that Natalie had no intention of confiding in her.

Arthur had no better success. He often heard his songbird play and sing, but here at Grayle Abbey, she seemed always to choose sad music. He vaguely understood the heartbreaking words when she sang the old French ballad about cherry time, with its plaintive middle stanza:

> Quand vous en serez au temps des cerises
> Si vous avez peur des chagrins d'amour
> Evitez les belles . . .

Were there no cheerful songs for a young girl to choose, who has recovered from being crossed in love? Why sing only of fearing its pain? Yet there seemed an air of increased maturity, of almost triumphant serenity, about her that supported her claim to have accepted her parents' wise decision. He longed to whisk Natalie away with them to Sandringham, but the party there was exclusively middle-aged, and even at its most informal, royal society was hedged about with dull, boring etiquette. Abandoning this idea, Arthur busied himself with plans to rent a villa on Lake Como. He would row on the lake with Natalie and take the cablecar up to the summit of Monte Bré with her, to enjoy the breathtaking view.

Once when they were out riding, he dared to ask, "Have you put your sorrows all behind you, darling? There is nothing Mama and I wish for more than to know your heart is mended. Time does heal most wounds, my little nightingale, but I believe yours went deep, and I hope it has left no painful scar. . . ."

Natalie gave back his troubled gaze with innocent eyes. "Of course, Papa. I needed some time alone at the Abbey without being constantly catechized by Mama on my feelings. Sending me here was a wise decision, although at first it seemed a harsh one. Please let us never speak about my—my infatuation for Prince Andrei again."

How easy it was to playact, Natalie thought; she, whom they believed so artless, could make those who loved her believe anything she wished. It was as though she suddenly possessed enormous power, and that her parents had become puppets on strings to dance at her direction. She felt all at once older than Delia, for she had been initiated into the mysteries of womanhood, while her sister remained in ignorance.

At last the boys went back to school, with many rough hugs and kisses, and exhortations to their little sister to write often.

Their anxhieties almost completely assuaged, Louise and Arthur left the Abbey to join the royal house party at Sandringham.

Upon their departure, Natalie experienced all the joy of a prisoner released from bondage. The mornings were cold and the skies were flamboyantly blue. Every tree in the long alleys that crisscrossed the local woodlands was turning golden or flame. She rode fast and hard early each morning, with her groom scarcely able to keep up, the skirt of her habit streaming out behind horse and rider. It gave her an almost savage pleasure that she, always considered to be the most naïve of creatures, had duped her parents and even Delia with ease.

Natalie hoped each day might be the one to bring Andrei's message, but none came. She rarely glanced at the newspaper, but when she did, it troubled her that so many headlines spoke of mighty Russia in disparaging tones: "The Czar's Navy Impotent Under Attack," sneered the *Morning Post*. The incredible announcement that Russian ships had attacked a British fishing fleet in error, and the peremptory demand by King Edward's government that an abject apology must be made forthwith, foretold that war loomed ominously near. Gradually Natalie became plagued by doubts.

Her lover's first plan of a hasty wedding seemed, in retrospect, impossibly optimistic. The success of this second scheme depended on her getting clean away to London without arousing any suspicion at Grayle. The flaw in the whole plan seemed to lie in her doubtful power to make Linnet keep silent for as long as was needed. Even a handsome present from the Prince of twenty guineas might not be sufficient to keep her quiet.

The faint roses in Natalie's cheeks faded and were replaced by the pallor of her first heartsick days at Grayle.

Lady Augustus Haversham was bored with life in London out of season, and, moreover, she was deprived of her husband's company while he attended Lord Dunmeath's shoot. She had sent

Nell off with Miss Jarvis to the Grand Hotel at Eastbourne. One of her dearest friends, Louise Grandison, had just returned to town from royal Sandringham. If it were not for her, Lady Augustus would have felt lonely indeed. One morning she received news from her husband so sensational that she called for her carriage at once and set out toward Park Lane and Grandison House, without even having her hair fully dressed.

Louise was still in bed, and her husband was taking a brisk constitutional in the park. He could not tear his thoughts from the tragic death of those wretched fishermen whose boats had been summarily sunk by the Russian Baltic fleet, under the delusion that their harmless vessels were Japanese gunboats. Russia must apologize soon, or war would be declared. And time was running out. . . .

The house had the forlorn air of an establishment about to be closed for the winter, with many of the corridors encumbered with trunks brought down from the attics. The departure for Como was imminent, and some of the servants had gone ahead to see that the villa would be just as their master liked it, well aired and heated, on his arrival. Lady Augustus was admitted without question by Adams and hurried upstairs still clasping the now crumpled letter in her hand. When Flora answered an agitated and peremptory knock at Lady Grandison's bedroom door, she burst in.

"Louise, you must hear this," she began at once. "Augustus writes to me that Prince Andrei Voronshnikoff is one of his fellow guests."

"I had no idea the boy was back in this country," Louise said uneasily. "I imagined he was staying in Venice."

"Well, it seems that the events of the season were being discussed, and several gentlemen declared Natalie to have been the prettiest girl to come out this year. Augustus mentioned, just in passing, that we had great hopes, which you and Arthur shared, of welcoming her into the Haversham family as Charlie's bride. Apparently this Russian firebrand leapt up and insisted that my poor Gus should retract, since the girl was already engaged to him and could not possibly marry Charlie! The tutor, a Professor Lensky, tried to restrain the young madman, but nothing would keep him quiet."

Louise, her hand pressed to her cheek, tried feebly to interrupt. "But, Julia, that is impossible . . ." she managed to get out.

The other woman went on quickly: "You have by no means heard the worst of it. Augustus quite properly contradicted the impudent fellow, and he practically called him a liar to his face. We both know you and Arthur refused to consider such an alliance. However, what does the fool do but strike my husband in the face and challenge him to a duel! At this, Dunmeath interfered, said that he forbade it, and asked the Prince to leave his house at once—which he refused to do, until he had obtained satisfaction."

"Oh, my God," faltered Louise. "Surely Augustus did not let himself be stung into taking part in such folly."

"He was not compelled to do so. Lensky hauled his charge off upstairs to cool his temper overnight. Early next morning a wire came from Count Benckendorff, their ambassador, calling on them to leave the country at once. Do you know how serious the situation is between ourselves and the Russians, my dear? There will be war before the week's out if Lord Balfour does not receive an official apology for that outrageous incident in the North Sea." Lady Augustus paused to take a breath. "They probably traveled down on the same train that brought this letter. I dare say they're in their suite at the Ritz, packing all those mountains of luggage Russians cannot travel without, and will leave tonight. But had the Voroshnikoff boy any right to insist that he is engaged to Natalie? I thought you had long since put paid to any such ideas." She trembled with suspicious indignation.

"Yes, we had." But Louise's voice was uncertain. Now Andrei was here in London, perhaps consulting timetables, making reservations on some train or steamship, scheming to carry her daughter away forever. She hastily decided her only recourse was to go to the Ritz and insist on an interview with Prince Andrei to stop the scandal of his false assertions being spread further.

As she dressed in haste Louise was in torment. If only she could consult Arthur. But she knew the task had to be hers alone.

Her first inquiries at the hotel confirmed that Prince Andrei was in the suite alone; Professor Lensky had just gone out. After being announced, she was respectfully escorted upstairs by a bellboy, dreading the encounter to come. "Enter!" an impatient voice called at the boy's knock. The Prince awaited her, his face alight with pitiful eagerness. Could she have changed her mind? Was she about to give her blessing?

But as he bowed over her hand he sensed that her opposition was even more determined. Yet for a moment her heart almost played her false. He was so like Constantine, with his proud stance and arrogant grace. "I have not come to hold out any false hopes," she said, laying aside her gloves and moving over to the window. She was as pale as death.

"I did not think so," he said after a moment. "But with or without your consent, I shall marry Natalie. I consider her already to be my wife, my Princess."

"That can never be. There is a reason, greater than any prejudice that my husband and I have against her going to Russia, which would condemn you both to be eternally unhappy."

"Name it! I do not believe you!"

"Can you not accept my sworn word that it would be so? Ah, I see you will not. But I had hoped never to admit this shame to any living soul. For it is my shame that stands between you and Natalie." Like a mournful shadow in the dove-gray gown she wore, she bent her head, the halo of egret's feathers on her hat floating iridescent above her silvery hair.

The Prince felt sick with apprehension. "For God's sake, tell me!" he cried.

She spun around sharply. "Did you never suspect? There is a certain likeness between you. Oh, I know I've always said that Natalie resembles my aunt Leonora. Hardly, for even when young, the woman was coarse of feature, ugly as sin. You are far more like your father than she, but there is something there... the way she holds her head, the arch of the brows. She does resemble him..."

Understanding began to dawn. Andrei leaned over the desk, gripping the polished edge with moist palms. "Are you telling me that Natalie is my father's child?" he ground out in rough, uncertain tones.

"Thank you for making it unnecessary to speak the words. Until now, I have been fortunate. Arthur, my husband, never thought of it, and few of our friends remembered what the Grand Duke Constantine looked like. Besides, I was above suspicion." Her voice was strained. "Such scandals have never touched the family. And they must not do so now.... But that is of lesser importance. You are your parents' heir, their only living son. You must carry on your name, have children. I have heard it said the

Voroshnikoff pearls bring tears to the wearer. That is just a superstition, of course. But you know what the risks would be for Natalie!"

"Yes, Natalie is my half sister. I realize the frightful possibilities. Our children might be abnormal!" He began to wander restlessly about the room under the gaze of Louise's brimming eyes.

Suddenly he turned on her, and she felt the lightning flash of his hatred flicker between them. "How did this happen?" he asked in icy disgust. "Were you and my father lovers, long ago, here in London?"

"No, I am at least innocent of that. We fell desperately in love, I admit. But I refused him a dozen times, begged him— yes, Andrei, *begged* him—not to tempt me further. I was weak, but somehow, at God knows what cost, I kept faith with my marriage vows. When your parents returned to Russia, I was guiltless. But that visit we paid to them later in St. Petersburg, which you do not even remember, for you were a small child in petticoats . . . it was then that he contrived to make me his mistress."

She started up, clasping her hands together and nervously wringing them as if to wash away the stain of adultery. "How cleverly your father played on his knowledge of Arthur's career in the navy," she went on bitterly. "It was nothing but a stratagem to get him invited to various naval occasions, so that my husband was often absent from your home for days at a time. Natalya suspected nothing. She thought that your father was jealous of Arthur, imagined that she had a *tendresse* for him, and took advantage of every excuse to keep them apart."

The Prince looked at Louise with utter contempt. "So you deceived my mother, too. You are both heartless and unchaste— and careless into the bargain, or you would not have borne a daughter who has no right to the name of Grandison. What would your husband call it—sailing under false colors? If only I had known; or we had never met!"

"You must see now that you cannot marry Natalie. But can we keep the reason from her? Is there some way to spare my darling this shameful knowledge? Even then, she is headstrong. Some madness might drive her to insist on a union that you would always know to be incestuous—as your father knows already, or he would not have been adamant in forbidding it."

He looked at her wonderingly. "You do have some heart. You love her, I believe."

"Of course I love her!" cried Louise, the tears spilling over. "Perhaps I am overbearing, too certain that I know what is best for my children. It is a fault Arthur charges me with, but not with lack of affection. If you, too, love her as much as I feel sure you do, there is a way that will save her from all but a momentary anguish."

He loosened his cravat, for he had all the sensations of suffocating. "I must have time to think, to decide what to do," he pleaded vainly, like a condemned prisoner who already knows his fate.

"There is no time," Louise broke in. "I know your ambassador has ordered you to quit the country before war is declared. If you had any false hopes of taking Natalie with you, you must forget them after what I have told you."

"My anguish will never cease," Andrei said bleakly. "To give her up now is unbearable. But I see I must bear it, for her sake."

"You do not believe me now, but you will forget. Or almost, as I had almost forgotten your father, until that night I saw you, so like him, at the ball. There is a way, the only way, to spare her the worst suffering. Write to her now, saying that you are compelled to return to Russia at once, and bidding her good-bye, as though there had been nothing but a lighthearted flirtation between you."

Andrei paled. "Dear God, that is impossible. I have already taken her maidenhood, made her my wife. Yes, you are right to look on me with horror. But there would have been no harm done, would not now be, if it had not been for *your* sin!" His gaze cut her like a sword, and his fist closed convulsively. For a moment she thought he would strike her.

She bowed her head. "Yes, my sin. But your father's, too. He would not be denied, he would have me no matter what the cost. It is worse than I thought. My poor little girl."

Andrei flung himself into a chair at the desk. "Tell me what to say. I cannot find the words to dismiss her. Wait, I know how it must be."

He began to write, his pen driving angry grooves into the paper. At last he signed the page, then held it out.

She read:

My dear, enchanting little Natalie,

So our idyllic summer has come to an end, without the further meeting I had hoped for so much. I thank you for your exquisite generosity, for all that has passed between us, and wish it might have been repeated. Events force me to return to Russia, as you must know if you read reports of the crisis that has blown up out of all proportion to its cause! A few fishing boats, after all, is that of so great account? And I fear I've spent too long in London, hanging around stage doors, attending green room parties. You know I find it hard to resist the attraction of certain pretty actresses, such as F.G. Attractions more fleeting than that of the dancers of the Imperial Ballet, perhaps, although my little friends of the Maryanski Theatre, to whom I shall shortly offer my homage, are no more enchanting than you. Adieu, lovely Natalie. Do not think too badly of me for being so light-minded, but nothing could have come of our flirtation, could it? Your mama has probably warned you that it is as hard to fix Russians in an affection as it would be to catch a will-o'-the-wisp. If, when you are married, you come to St. Petersburg, you must not forget that you have promised to ride with me by moonlight in a troika . . . Andrei.

"It will serve the purpose." Her voice broke. "Oh, but it will make her so unhappy."

"Say no more. If you do, I shall tear it up and steal her away from you, no matter how you try to prevent me. *Je suis au bout de mes forces.*"

"Forgive me. But how dare I ask that of you? Address the envelope, and I will post it. Do you leave tonight?"

"My tutor, Lensky, is fetching our papers from the embassy, and the tickets. Do not look so agitated, Lady Grandison. By midnight I shall be beyond doing more harm to Natalie. I shall never see her again." Then a frightful thought struck him. He started to his feet. *"Moi Bosze!* Dear God, you don't think she will be driven to do something foolish—to take her own life?"

"No, no, Andrei. At the same time that Natalie receives your letter, my housekeeper at Grayle will have instructions to bring her up to London. She won't be left alone for a moment."

He sank back into the chair, his face contorted by pain.

Louise touched his arm timidly. He closed his eyes, rigid under her touch, and she thought how similar he was to the martyred saint in the icon Constantine had given her. A drop of blood appeared on his bitten lip. She turned away, slipping the letter into her muff.

But she did not send it that day. She wrote to Mrs. Ponder, saying that this letter would shortly arrive and was to be given to Lady Natalie. Andrei would be well beyond reach by then. She allowed two full days to elapse, and on the third, she posted it.

It did not occur to Louise that the child would be too proud to acknowledge that she had been so mistaken about the Prince's sincerity. But she dared offer no consolation until it was asked for, for Natalie must not suppose that she knew anything of the letter and had insisted that it should be written.

But Lady Grandison's plan to keep Natalie under careful observation until she had time to recover from the first brutal shock went sadly awry. The footman who was entrusted to post Andrei's letter was also given the errand of sending the telegram to Mrs. Ponder, ordering her to accompany Natalie up to town.

Flora, always eager to avoid the thankless chore of taking Marcus for a walk, had prevailed upon the young man to give her ladyship's lapdog an airing. The letter was duly posted, and as John turned in to Mount Street, dragging the reluctant Marcus at his heels, he came face-to-face with another servant exercising his master's Doberman Pinscher. Marcus flew at the larger dog and sank his needle-sharp teeth into the Doberman's hind leg. In an instant the vicious animal had ripped a fatal gash in his small attacker's throat.

John sped home with the pathetic bundle of fur in his arms, already aware that he was more than likely to lose his place over the incident. The telegram Louise had promised Andrei to send was never dispatched.

Chapter 13

In Oxfordshire the weather was moving into a sullen mood. Lord Grandison's tenant farmers were of the opinion that they were now paying for the extraordinary summer of 1904, such a succession of golden days as could not be equaled in living memory. Now each morning began with a pall of fog low over hedge and path, field and furrow, stable and sty. Rain fell stubbornly during all the hours of daylight from lowering skies, and when a jaundiced gibbous moon rose, it was often obscured by a frosty veil. Even the countless log fires, stoked every hour or two by an army of servants, quite failed to keep the Abbey warm.

As day succeeded disappointing day Natalie anxiously awaited word from Andrei. Time was of the essence. The thought of Como, pretty as a colored postcard, would beckon her parents home soon to prepare for their Italian sojourn, and she would be summoned to join them.

Then, amazingly, on a morning that began like any of the other gray mornings, a letter arrived propped against the silver coffeepot on her breakfast tray, addressed to her in Andrei's flowing hand. She delayed opening it, suddenly apprehensive when she should have been overjoyed. Posted in London the previous afternoon! Her spirits rose. At last she brought herself to open the flap and slide out the sheet of notepaper it contained. The early light was so pallid that she rose from her bed and took it over to the window to read. The words jumbled and danced crazily before her eyes without making sense. Calming herself, she read it slowly again from the beginning. Odd that he wrote in English. He had never done that before. Her mind played with this thought, unwilling to accept what her eyes had taken in.

She could no longer deny the meaning of Andrei's words. All lies—his talk of the appeal by Uncle Dmitri to the Czar, the romantic journey by steamship to St. Petersburg, the wedding in the great cathedral, the palaces, the Voroshnikoff pearls. The proud head she had drawn lovingly to her naked breasts would never rest there again.

But that could *not* be true. Her thoughts somersaulted. There must be some explanation. The letter was a cruel hoax; he had not written it. Or he had been forced to write it—at pistol point, perhaps. She held back the sobs that welled up within her, willing herself to think clearly. She knew she had to see Andrei once, to hear the truth from his own lips. He might not as yet have left London. But she needed Delia's help.

She took a few sips of coffee, leaving the rest of her breakfast untouched, and hurriedly dressed in a plain outfit of leaf-brown surah silk, which came to her hand first from the wardrobe. She ran downstairs, hat in hand, and pinned it in place, while a maid fetched Mrs. Ponder from the stillroom, where she had been busy with the autumnal brewing of sweet syrups and cough cures.

"I quite forgot to tell you, Mrs. Ponder," Natalie said brightly, adjusting the tilt of her hat in a mirror to avoid the woman's eyes. "Lady Delia and I have a fitting today with the dressmaker for the blouses and skirts we ordered. Foolish of me to forget . . . One of the grooms could drive me to Oxford in the wagonette. I'd like to leave as soon as possible, so please tell Linnet to put on her cloak."

Mrs. Ponder was perturbed. "It's Linnet's day off, milady. Would you take one of the other maids?"

"Certainly not. I shan't really need a maid. I shall be lunching with Mrs. Bradleigh, and I'll be back well before dark." She dared not ask Mrs. Ponder for money, for there would be no need; even the dressmaker's bill would be sent to her father.

The housekeeper saw no harm in Lady Natalie visiting her sister, and went to summon the groom. Minutes later they were off, Natalie clutching the crumpled letter in her pocket.

The trip seemed interminable, and when at last she arrived at Stonelea, the maid informed her that Delia was out; Mrs. Bradleigh herself was sitting upstairs with Aunt Bella. Waiting in Delia's salon, Natalie fought back a wave of bitter disappointment. Presently she noticed that the top drawer of the desk was not quite closed; Delia's stout leather purse was just visible. She told herself her sister would understand as she plucked a half guinea and some small change from it. Slipping from the room onto the landing, she could hear no sound of activity in the hall below. She glided downstairs, let herself noiselessly out of the house, and set off for the railway station, clutching the coins in her hand.

Thus began a nightmare such as Natalie had never experienced before in all her sheltered young life. The journey to London dragged on; with each stop the train made, she felt more like screaming. Images of her lover and their brief affair churned in her mind. Surely Andrei had not written that cruel and heartless letter, she tried to convince herself, her head throbbing.

When the train arrived in Paddington Station, Natalie was overcome with nausea, for she had eaten nothing that day. Entering the stuffy station tearoom, she bought some food and sank down next to a blowsy woman in tawdry finery. Wearily she laid her hat and purse on the table and tried to eat, but could not. Faintness overcame her, and she was forced to close her eyes for a moment. When she recovered sufficiently to look around, the woman had vanished, along with Natalie's hat and purse. Only the two pennies she had received in change at the counter were still clutched in her hand. A cab was out of the question.

Darkness had fallen when, after stumbling through the drizzle, she climbed aboard a waiting omnibus outside the Great Western Hotel. Hoping that she had enough money to pay the fare as far as Piccadilly, she sat wedged against a scrawny girl clutching a hemp bag of vegetables. The conductor pushed past her to argue with a navvy who had traveled farther than his fare allowed, and the man spat indignantly when he was forced to alight, the spittal staining Natalie's skirt. She, who had never entered an omnibus before, hardly noticed: *Just let me get there in time*, she pleaded inwardly. It seemed an age before they had passed Marble Arch and Hyde Park Corner.

At last they arrived at the stately arcades of the Ritz. Smoothing her loose strands of hair, Natalie approached the porter's desk. Sensing her distress, he attended to her immediately. "Yes, miss?" he inquired politely.

"Prince Andrei Voroshnikoff and Professor Lensky. Are they still staying here?"

The man consulted the register. "Both of them left here several days ago, miss. Left the country, I believe, for I've no forwarding address other than"—he consulted a neatly written book that he took from under the desk—"St. Petersburg, miss. Would you care to have it?"

"No . . . no, thank you." She turned away. A page stepped forward. "Call a hansom for you, ma'am?" Natalie shook her head, for she had no money left, and hurried out into the street, unable to restrain the tears that rolled down her cheeks. She wandered blindly along Piccadilly toward the circus, where dozens of theater lights beckoned. Fancy Galbraith at the Clarence. Maybe she knew where Andrei had gone. At least it was somewhere to go, but she felt so faint, so feverish.

Natalie paused by the streetlamp, leaning against it for support. She was unaware that standing there, hatless, and resting with unconscious supple grace, she was asking to be accosted. After less than a minute, a man approached her and thrust his face so close to hers that she smelled the sour beer on his breath.

"How much?" he asked brutally. She made no reply. "Got a place near here, have you? You'd better. And I hope it's clean. Skinny, but not bad, with them dark eyes and black hair. Frenchy, are you? Tell you what, give me something special, you know what I mean, and I'll make it five bob." Natalie, uncomprehending, still did not answer. The man caught her shoulder and, as she started back, ripped the lapel of her costume away from the white flesh. "Cat got your tongue? Not good enough for you, eh? Impudent hussy, wasting my time . . ." He pushed her violently, so that she tripped and half fell on the edge of the pavement.

On her knees, Natalie leaned forward, retching into the gutter. Her hair tumbled down to her waist, and she wiped her face with it, panting and sobbing. A woman passing on her husband's arm said crossly, "See that horrid creature, James! Drunk, I suppose. It's a disgrace. The lower orders should be banned from the west end streets, I do declare."

"Hush, my love, don't look at her," a man's voice soothed the self-righteous lady.

Presently the spasm passed. Natalie rose and staggered on,

from one pool of light to the next. It was not far to the circus now.

She threaded her way across it, through the menace of horse-drawn buses and hackney carriages, until she reached Shaftesbury Avenue. At last she could see the lights of the Clarence Theatre. The foyer was plastered with photographs of Sir Michael McMahon, more handsome than ever with darkened skin and hair, the epitome of the hot-tempered Moor in Shakespeare's *Othello*, and Fiona Galbraith, in elaborate draperies and jewels with a fine display of white bosom, as Desdemona.

Natalie stole along a side alley toward the humble, ill-lit entrance to the pit and the gallery. At the stage door she pleaded with the doorkeeper, who regarded her doubtfully. "Miss Galbraith, is it? Well, I'm not supposed to let anyone past. But it's still an hour to the performance. Go on in, and I'll say I never saw yer." The crimson carpet and golden wall coverings were clearly for the front of the house only. The stairs and corridor were made of unadorned stone. Barely able to see where she walked, Natalie made her way down the hall, clinging to one wall. At last there was a door that bore Miss Galbraith's name, with a gold star above it. The girl knocked weakly and, when no answer came, leaned her forehead against it, trying with hands that shook uncontrollably to rearrange her dress into some semblance of order. When at last she knocked again, a sulky voice answered. It seemed impossibly hard to turn the handle, but she achieved it, and then she was blinking in the light of twin gas lamps that brilliantly illuminated the actress's makeup mirror.

Fancy had come in early, as she often did, to fortify herself with a glass or two of neat gin before the performance. She sat in a loose cotton wrapper at her dressing table and poured a second tot of gin into a tumbler with a practiced hand.

"What do you want, bursting in here?" she asked rudely. This visitor had taken her by surprise, for Fiona drank strictly in solitude, before the arrival of dressers and fellow actors, hoping to keep her addiction from Michael. He was disappointed with her performance as Desdemona, and she knew it. Already he was apprehensive of the critics' reaction when they transferred to the Brady Theater on Broadway for a season of Shakespeare in New York. She had promised Michael, in a fit of penitence, to drink no more gin until after the run, but as usual, she had failed to keep her promises.

"State your business and be quick about it, or I'll send for the doorkeeper. Stagestruck, are you? Is that it? We've no need to employ amateurs." The pale girl did not reply. "Nothing to say for yourself. Are you dumb, then?"

"Forgive me for disturbing you, Miss Galbraith," Natalie murmured, swaying unsteadily. "But I believe you are acquainted with Prince Andrei Voroshnikoff. Could you tell me whether he has left the country yet, or when he plans to do so? He spoke of having seen you recently, in a letter. . . ."

She produced the crumpled sheet from her pocket as though it might be some sort of passport to Fiona's good graces.

The actress rose, eyes agleam with curiosity, and snatched it. Suddenly she recognized the bedraggled girl who stood before her, although she had seen her only twice, and then she had been elegantly clad and beautiful, and as remote as an angel. But she remembered that Andrei, whose generosity she had been eager to repay, had suddenly dropped out of her life after that party in the green room. She had caught the poignant look between those two, the Prince and Milady Grandison. This was the girl to blame, and the same society miss in front of whom Michael had humiliated her at the garden party in Regent's Park. So the Prince had been forced to leave England. A pity. The rascal had gone too far with this silly debutante and had dragged in Fancy's own name as an excuse for jilting her. His air of nobility must have been only a façade. She had never seen that desirable young stud again, more the pity, or earned the price of the ruby pendant. But now she saw her chance to get her own back for the disappointing fiasco. At that moment a flash of gold caught Fiona's eye in the lamplight—Andrei's signet ring of gold and engraved Chalcedony hanging on a ribbon around Natalie's neck.

"Andrei? Yes, I have been entertaining him at my house," she went on with mendacious candor. "Such a demanding fellow. So intense in his emotions. But exhausting; I was almost glad to wave him good-bye when the time came." She took a deep swallow of gin and then continued. "An actress in my position has such admirers who swear eternal constancy, threaten to kill themselves if dismissed. But one must not take too much notice of it. These hot-blooded Russians, for instance, tell such extravagant lies, that one learns to ignore their oaths of lifelong devotion."

Natalie lost her head. "I don't believe a word of it. Andrei would not have sworn devotion to a coarse, drunken woman like you. He would not have touched you!" She snatched back the letter from her tormentor and, in doing so, knocked the glass in Fiona's unsteady grip. Gin dribbled down the other woman's flimsy wrapper and satin corset.

With a shriek of rage, Fiona flung the glass from her to smash against the mirror-fronted wardrobe. Seizing Natalie by the hair, she launched into a tirade of hysterical abuse at the top of her voice in tones that would have reached from the wings of the stage to the back of the gallery. Suddenly Michael McMahon appeared in the doorway. He saw Fancy step back and deal her opponent, whom she held at arm's length by her magnificent black tresses, a stinging blow on the side of her face. The exhausted young woman in torn clothing, with terrified violet eyes in an ashen face, looked toward him in agonized entreaty, her knees buckling under her.

He caught the girl as she slid sideways, just in time to prevent her shapely head from striking the mahogany base of Fancy's velvet chaise longue. Fiona was leaning for support against the dressing table, flushed purple with fury, but the shock of discovery sobered her. *Damn Michael for coming in early,* she thought.

"One of the stuck-up Grandison bitches. She insulted me. Can't come here insulting me!" she whined uneasily in her own justification.

Michael ignored her, instinctively gathering the frail, unconscious figure to his chest. Of course he knew this girl . . . had thought about her more than once as summer faded into autumn and longed to know what had led her to this miserable state. He had never seen such despair as in that expressive face just before merciful blankness had blotted out all suffering.

Instinctively he cradled her in his arms. That proud young girl, he thought, whose aristocratic presence at his green-room reception had so dismayed Fancy's latest admirer. A vision rose before him of the same debutante at the garden party who had bent her pretty head to drink in the perfume of a rose, no sweeter than that of her own body. Their second encounter, at Liam's wedding. The laughter, the backward look of a beckoning nymph, as she sped through the long orchard grass to the swing. And his own undeniable longing, sophisticate though he was, as he pressed her body intimately against his own, his hands enclosing hers on the ropes. He could hardly believe that this poor wounded creature in the stained and torn dress could be the same girl, and he was stabbed by angry pity, for he knew not what disaster had brought her so low. Laying her down on the velvet couch, he stripped off his evening cape of black broadcloth lined with red satin.

"I'll not go on tonight, Fancy," he said abruptly, breaking into her catalog of complaints, which were fading in hiccoughing sobs of self-pity. "Tell John Gaunt this is his opportunity. It's not often an understudy gets the chance to appear in my place. Say I expect him to rise to the occasion, and heaven help you if you dare to mention this young lady's name."

He wrapped Natalie's unconscious form in the cloak, and she moaned but did not come to her senses, although her eyelids fluttered a little. He gathered her up in his arms and strode out of Fancy's dressing room, leaving the door swinging open behind him. At the foot of the stairs he turned in to the doorkeeper's office.

"Whistle me up a cab quickly, George. Be discreet about it, though. Wait. Is Mr. Gaunt in yet?"

"Yes, Sir Michael. He's passed me by this instant." The doorkeeper was peering over his shoulder to see what the actor's burden was. But a brisk nod from Michael hurried him on his way out into the alley. A hansom drew up behind the theater in Rupert Street with a jingle of harness just as Natalie sighed and began to open her eyes. Before she could speak or even realize what was happening, he had her inside and hidden from curious view.

"Just try to rest," he advised her. She knew nothing of the short journey that followed, and she did not really come to herself until the iron gate creaked open, as the top-hatted doorman admitted their conveyance to the quiet sanctuary of Albany.

Michael had rented a spacious, rambling apartment there for several years. His man, Leon, a dark and saturnine Irishman who was totally devoted to his master, kept it impeccably clean and tidy and would permit no female servant to invade this masculine stronghold. Very few friends had ever penetrated this private retreat of Michael's, and even those found his home rather different from what they had expected.

The style of furnishing was less cluttered and florid than fashion demanded. Faded Oriental carpets in shades of pomegranate and rose with the silky sheen of age were spread on the parquet floors. A great white bearskin rug lay before the fire, where a low brass fender, well polished and shining, surrounded the fireplace set with willow-patterned tiles. The mahogany mantelpiece was topped by a Chinese mirror framed in lacquer, with a few invitations carelessly propped against it. Books covered the walls, and elegant display cabinets stood in between the crowded shelves, filled with Michael's collection of theatrical memorabilia. The atmosphere was restful, and expressive of a man whose tastes were subtle and refined.

Leon asked no questions as Michael deposited his visitor tenderly on the sofa. Michael slid down beside Natalie and put his arm behind her head. He asked Leon not to turn up the gas; her face was bathed only in firelight. He studied the aristocratic flare of the delicate nostrils, the harmony of her pure profile. There were dark smudges beneath the closed eyes, a bruise where Fiona had struck her, and an angry scratch beneath her collarbone where the brown dress had been ripped away. As she stirred he saw the heavy signet ring on its ribbon slip out from the valley between her breasts, now more sensuously rounded than he had remembered. In one hand she still grasped convulsively a twisted sheet of paper. Loosening her fingers, he took the letter, hesitated, then read it by the gleam of firelight. It was there, by the fire, reading the tragic letter, that Michael understood, his heart filling with pity. Laying aside the paper, he stroked her cheek lightly, saying gently, "Natalie, my dear child, try to sit up. Do you think you could swallow a little brandy?"

Her eyes opened. "No, please, only some water," she murmured. He was startled by the impact of those dark pools of amethyst that seemed to draw his soul down into their shining depths.

"Very well." He fetched water for her from the sideboard. She drank a few sips. "How pale you are, and your hands are icy. Don't try to talk yet, to explain anything." After a moment's thought, he tugged the bellpull to summon Leon, and requested him to bring a cup of hot consommé with a little Madeira. When it came, he fed Natalie gravely with a spoon, and she managed to swallow some of it valiantly. Then she began to look about her in bewilderment.

"Where is this place, for I don't remember coming here?" she asked finally. "Oh, it must be your home. I see the mementos of Eleanora Duse you once mentioned in that cabinet." She sat up in alarm. "But shouldn't you be at the theater?"

"My understudy will play tonight. It is a sort of baptism by fire, you know, for I shall expect him to go on for me sometimes when we are in New York. Now, we must try to sort out your troubles, my little one," he went on. "You were in sorry straits when I walked in on your disagreement with Fancy, who can be a positive virago when crossed. What happened between you?"

"I thought she might tell me where I could find a friend who is about to leave the country," Natalie replied awkwardly. "I must reach him somehow."

"Prince Andrei Voroshnikoff?" She shrank from his searching look. "Pardon me, but I read the letter you were holding. I had to know what caused you such distress, and whether, as I judged, you had run off from home on some impulse. A most ill-advised one, if I may say so." The kind intonation of that wonderful voice robbed his remark of any offense.

"If you have read the letter, you must have guessed my predicament," Natalie said reluctantly. "Prince Andrei and I were to be married. Indeed, we are married, in all but name. I was merely waiting for the signal to meet him here in London. For I have been staying at Grayle Abbey most of the summer, you know. My parents did not want me to have any further opportunity of meeting the Prince." Her voice rose in agitation. "But why, why do they not want me to be happy? I cannot live without him, or he without me!"

"I would say that this letter proves otherwise. It was little short of criminal to deceive a young lady, especially one like yourself with such high connections and untainted reputation, and then—quite frankly—to jilt you. For that is what he has done, isn't it?"

She joined her hands in her lap and looked down, not wishing him to witness her anguish; she was driven at last to admit that this was the truth.

"If he has, I no longer have any wish to live!" the girl burst out, her self-control deserting her. She rose and went over to the window. In the foggy darkness a haze of light seemed to waver around the streetlamps in the deserted inner courtyard of Albany.

Michael came to her and laid his hands on her slim shoulders, turning her to meet his gaze, and stroking back her fragrant, unbound hair.

"You say you are already Prince Andrei's wife. Do you mean that this marriage, which it seems now will never take place, has already been consummated?" Delicacy made it impossible for him to put the question more bluntly.

But she answered resolutely without any trace of shame. "Yes."

He cast about in his mind for a way to voice his fears without frightening or offending her. "Could there be the slightest possibility that you are . . ." He paused. "Could there be ruinous consequences? I mean, excuse me for this frankness, do you think you might be with child?"

Natalie drew away to stare at him blankly. A great tide of color washed through her cheeks, and then receded. "I don't know," she said in a small voice. "If so, I might as well be dead. For my life is ruined, in any case. . . ."

"Perhaps I ought to have taken you straight to your parents. But I considered you were hardly in a state to face them immediately, and that here in peace and quiet, you could confide in me. And together we might hit on some quite believable explanation for your presence in town."

"You mean that I must accept Andrei's desertion . . . forget that I loved him and banish all thought of him from my mind?" she asked in wonderment. "I cannot do that."

"One does not die of a broken heart at your age, my poor darling. But you must be protected from the effects of your overgenerous folly toward a young man who has proved, to say the least, unworthy." Mentally he heaped coals of fire on Andrei's head, but it would have served no purpose to voice the vile epithets in his mind.

"Protected—how? I don't care whether my parents disown me, or what becomes of me," she protested recklessly.

"You say that from your lack of experience, little one." He lifted her easily and carried her back to the fire, where they sank down together on the soft fur rug. "Besides, they wouldn't permit such a scandal. You should be packed off to the Continent in the care of some trustworthy servant, the baby would be taken from you at birth, and you would know nothing of its future. But after that, your parents would perhaps not risk allowing you to marry. A discerning bridegroom would guess he had been fobbed off with a bride who was no virgin. Excuse me again for speaking so directly. But you could well be forced to lead an arid spinster's existence all your days."

He drew her up so that they knelt face-to-face in the firelight. He loomed so large over her that she had to lift her chin to meet his eyes. A sudden inspiration had set him aflame. "I could offer another solution," he said carefully. "Marry me, Natalie. I know I

am much older than you, but at least I am not under an obligation
to any other woman. My family is not of the same degree as
yours, but my title is ancient and honorable, and my profession
has made me wealthy. You see, in trying to convince you, I have
just realized that I am quite eligible!"

He tried to smile, but even in his own ears the touch of humor
rang hollow. "Take my name and sail with me next week to
America," he went on persuasively. "Let the press call it, if they
will, an impulsive elopement. It will be surmised that your banishment to Grayle was really on my account. And if there is to be
a child"—he paused significantly—"I shall love it as my own.
For I am coming to believe, Natalie, that your happiness is rather
precious to me."

She started back violently, shaking her head. "Don't, Michael,
don't. It would be terribly wrong. You offer me so much: a
chance to survive without dishonor, even a dazzling future as
your wife. But, you see, I have nothing to give you in return.
Nothing. I could never truly be your wife. It would all be a
sham."

"You will do as I say, Natalie." His expression was suddenly
steely, his mouth stern. "In your circles, I know, there exists the
idiotic custom of keeping girls in ignorance of the basic facts of
life. But that excuse will not save you from the consequences.
Far from it. I have shown you a way out—the only way. You
must marry me."

There was a tense silence between them. A coal burned
through in the fireplace and collapsed in a shower of embers.
Finally she swayed forward in defeat.

"I am too unhappy to be properly grateful," she said. "I only
hope you will not come to regret your generosity."

He laughed, but it was almost a snarl. "Generous? To wed a
girl so widely acclaimed as the most beautiful ever to grace London's social scene, the daughter of a peer? Other men will envy
me." More gently he went on. "I promise I will ask nothing of
you until you are ready to give it," he said quietly. "I would never
force myself on you, I swear it. And if the time does not come,
then that will be my misfortune, not your fault."

Michael spoke sincerely. *But, God help me,* he thought, *if she
never comes to care for me. For I love her. And yet I have just
sworn not to touch her unless she offers herself to me of her own
free will. . . .*

Slightly less distraught, Natalie swallowed a little more of the hot soup. She was amazed to see how much like her usual self she now seemed in the mirror as she pinned up her hair. But at the door she faltered. "I can't do it, Michael."

Still in a masterful mood, he swept her on. "Nonsense, my dear, of course you can. I believe there is a talented actress hidden in your small frame. Let her emerge, and just follow my prompting. If you hesitate, I'll carry the dialogue along!"

On the way to Park Lane he rehearsed her carefully on what to say if she were questioned. Fortunately Lord Grandison was absent. But her ladyship was at dinner with Mr. Sanderson. Secretly her nerves were already strained to the utmost by her nagging fears about Natalie. She was stunned when Adams interrupted the dessert to hand her Michael's card. The note penciled on the back brought Lady Grandison to her feet and into the hall in an anxious whirl of pleated satin skirts.

Before she could voice any of the outraged inquiries that rose in her throat at the sight of Natalie, so unsuitably dressed, Michael turned upon her all the batteries of his remarkable charm. This stagestruck girl, bored with the country, had taken it into her foolish head to journey up to London on her own, quite heedless of the dangers involved, just to see him as Othello before the whole company departed for New York. Of course, he had lost no time in restoring the erring daughter to her mother's care.

"Have her put to bed, Lady Grandison," Sir Michael drawled, tossing back his mane of chestnut hair and gazing down at the bewildered Marchioness from his great height. "Postpone your scolding until tomorrow, I implore. Then would you be so kind as to offer me some refreshment?" Those expressive eyes of his were narrowed now, telling her that he had something else to impart.

Louise adroitly dismissed Mr. Sanderson and had Natalie led away, then commanded a glass of port, some Bath Oliver biscuits, and a portion of Stilton cheese to be provided on a tray in the morning room.

When they were alone together, she impatiently watched Michael consume a fragment of cheese, furious that this total stranger knew more than he had yet disclosed of Natalie's shame.

"Your explanation simply will not hold water, Sir Michael," Louise announced at last. "I intended to have Natalie brought up from Grayle tomorrow by my housekeeper, since we are leaving for Italy in a day or two. I surmise she has embroiled you in some ridiculous attempt to run off with a totally unsuitable young man. I really must thank you for so splendidly covering up her foolishness. But the matter ends there, I think."

"I am afraid it does not, Lady Grandison." Michael rose, throwing down the damask napkin that he had just touched to his lips. "I must be frank. Natalie trusts me as a friend. She confessed to me that she has been *more* than indiscreet with her lover, Andrei Voroshnikoff. She is not well. We must even fear that her . . . indiscretion . . . may bear fruit . . ." He paused, studying her distressed face minutely. "I see this is no surprise to you, my lady. There must be some very good reason why, faced with such a monumental scandal, you still refuse permission for your daughter to marry the Prince. What other future is there for her if she is to avoid complete disgrace? Not to speak of the slur on the good name of Grandison."

"Accept that the reason exists," Louise begged him. "Don't ask to know more."

"I'm afraid I must, Lady Grandison. I understand this is a family matter, but I'm quite mystified by your harshness, and far from convinced that it is necessary. This note that Natalie received, jilting her in the cruelest terms, did not seem quite in the writer's character. You had better take charge of it." He handed the creased and twisted sheet of paper to her ladyship. "Frankly, I see your hand rather than that of Price Andrei in this disgraceful letter."

"I could convince you utterly," Louise said in a low, colorless voice, crushing the paper nervously in her hand. "To do so would be to admit my own shame. Do you force me to it?"

"I am obliged to do so. There is a possible solution, but I would not for the world insist that she accept it, if she could instead have her heart's desire."

"Andrei is her half brother. You can guess the rest. But Natalie must never know it. Oh, promise me that you will keep my secret?" Her voice broke piteously.

Michael could hardly believe his ears. But suddenly it all made sense to him. He even understood the courage of the young Prince, who had taken the greater burden of suffering on himself, to spare his beloved from knowledge even more painful than mere renunciation. "Obviously your husband knows nothing of this?" Lady Grandison bowed her beautiful, flaxen-fair head in assent. "Well, then, you must help me, before a single eyebrow can be raised. I shall take her to America with me when I sail for New York on the *Majestic* next week. She has already agreed to this marriage of convenience, for, on her part, she says, it can be no more than that." He laughed, but the sound was bleak. Then he went on.

"Make it easy for me to carry her off. You can safely leave all the wedding arrangements to me. Let us hope nothing comes of our fears, but if Natalie is delivered of a child too soon after our wedding, you and Lord Grandison must share the general assumption that it is mine, born prematurely. It might even be the case. Any other possibility is unthinkable. Are we agreed?"

She was too dazed by these disclosures to reply. "If need be, after the ship has sailed," Michael continued calmly, "use Andrei's letter to persuade your husband that his daughter was led astray by a heartless seducer, even if that is not quite true. It will be an easier pill for him to swallow than to think her a light-minded little flirt. Reassure him. Tell him that I solemnly vowed to you to cherish Natalie until death us do part."

"This is very chivalrous of you, Sir Michael, but why in heaven's name are you suggesting that you should marry a girl you hardly know, in such dubious circumstances?"

"It is true we have met only on a few occasions. But I have often thought about her, and when she came to me in such distress, I realized how deeply concerned I felt. The truth is that I seem to have lost my heart to her."

Louise could not doubt his sincerity. Much as she longed to go to Natalie and comfort her, she dared not say too much, for fear of disclosing her own guilty part in the tragic affair. Seated by the girl's bedside, she only murmured in a shocked whisper that, having heard Sir Michael's story, she knew recriminations were useless and would do all she could to ensure that a quiet wedding with Michael took place without Papa's knowledge. He could not be expected to give his consent. Lady Grandison stood in silence, while tears of remorse for Natalie's suffering slipped down her cheeks.

Lord Grandison was not entirely convinced by his wife's explanation that Natalie had come up to town unchaperoned, merely to see some actor perform on the stage. Yet he could not imagine such folly to be in any way connected with her previous entanglement. That Russian had left the country, as he had taken pains to find out. But he saw that this poor child had, as Louise explained, suffered a severe fright when assaulted and robbed of all her money, and needed several days to recover before they could set out for Italy. He sent off reassuring messages to Delia and Mrs. Ponder. The thought that plans were afoot for her to elope with a new admirer never entered his head, since he had no knowledge of the true part played by Michael in Natalie's rescue, or indeed of any urgent need for her to be wed. The trunks were ordered back to the attic, and tickets were reissued for a later date. In fact, the day after, the *Majestic* was due to sail to New York, with Sir Michael McMahon's name already on the passenger list.

Chapter 14

Michael revealed his wedding plans to Lady Grandison over tea at Claridge's. He would marry Natalie on the morning of their departure for New York, at the Church of All Saints, in Marylebone Road. Louise remarked, with a heavy heart, that it could not be too soon, since she had been unable to convince her husband to delay their own departure for Lake Como longer than the day following. The shock would seriously upset him; she despaired of reconciling her enraged spouse to the discovery of yet another intrigue by his younger daughter. But, as Michael told her quite tersely, that was her affair. The girl herself was being kept in bed, suffering from a severe chill and—though Lady Grandison avoided mentioning it—a kind of stunned withdrawal from reality. Her mother hoped this worrying symptom would gradually disappear, and she saw no reason to report it to Michael.

The famous actor-manager had scant opportunity to reflect on the impulse that had prompted him to offer this pampered little aristocrat, who had been so cruelly used by fate, the shelter of his name. His motives, he had already confessed to himself, were not entirely altruistic. The time had come when he ought to marry, if only to put an end to Fancy's pretensions, and those of other pretty actresses who pestered him in the same way. A wife as highly born as the Lady Natalie would promote the respected, even exalted, image he was striving to achieve for his company. Michael dismissed from his mind the dangers of the game he was playing, and the misery to which he was self-condemned in falling fathoms deep in love with Natalie if she remained forever indifferent to him.

The most difficult of his problems Michael postponed until the last moment. Fancy had frequently attempted to lure him into her dressing room for a tête-à-tête, or waylay him backstage, but he had so far evaded her. "I've not breathed a word about your little visitor," she murmured as they bowed together to the third curtain call after their last performance of the season at the Clarence. "But I'm curious. How do you intend to keep my mouth shut on a more permanent basis?"

He kissed her hand with a flourish, urging her forward to take the plaudits of an entranced audience on her own. "I'll tell you after the end-of-run dinner at Romano's. Let me see you home."

Fancy enjoyed making much of the fact that she refused all other offers of escort that night. Her leading man was to have the privilege, she protested flirtatiously. But as soon as the key turned in the lock of her own house, her mood changed.

"What is going on, Michael?" she demanded fretfully. "That Grandison girl obviously made a fool of herself with Voroshnikoff, and he has shown her a clean pair of heels. Got more involved than he intended, I suppose. Well, I've said nothing to anyone of the exhibition she gave in front of me, for which I hope you're duly grateful. But it's a prime piece of gossip. I just might let something slip out about it, unless you've a very good reason to persuade me I should not."

"The best," he replied tranquilly, discarding his cloak. "I intend to marry her myself. Consequently you will say nothing about her visit to the theater, or her involvement with the Prince. No one else is aware of it, so if the slightest rumor were to reach my ears, I should know at once whom to blame. Your contract with me could easily be canceled. And there are certain rumors about your intemperate habits, my dear, which would preclude your getting a new one elsewhere, if I chose to make them public." He paused.

Fancy stood as if petrified, her ostrich-feather boa gradually slipping from her shoulders, unregarded, to the carpet. "You do fully understand, I hope?" Michael concluded with a touch of menace in his quietly controlled voice. "I'm sure I may count on your absolute discretion. No hysterics, please. They will not move me, although I perceive from your expression that you are about to try their power to do so. There has never been a question of my taking you as my wife, not at least since you began to welcome an unending succession of lovers to your bed, on those nights when you are not too gin-sodden to receive them." He checked himself. "I'm sorry to have spoken so harshly. I realize you take my marriage to Natalie as a personal affront. But at least you will be able to triumph over the rest of the company, to tell them that you shared our secret from the start!"

Fancy pouted and tossed her head, then finally agreed to Michael's demands. He bid her good night, relieved to have survived this unpleasant interview without the threatened fit of hysterics. But moments after his departure, her lips contorted into an ugly sneer as she glared at herself in the mirror.

"How does she catch them, I wonder?" she muttered. "First my randy young Russian, and now Michael! A wanton by nature, for all her fine manners. I'll put her in her place yet, make her an outcast from decent society..." She meant every word of her threat. For with the perversity of her sex, now that Michael was irretrievably lost to her, Fancy desired him with all her insatiably greedy heart.

Michael had not seen Natalie from the time Flora led the girl away, still wrapped in a borrowed cloak, until she joined him at the altar in the small, unfashionable church he had deliberately chosen, where no one was likely to seek them out. Much to his distress, Natalie seemed in a daze. She made her vows in an expressionless voice, and the cheek on which Michael bestowed a formal kiss at the end of the ceremony was as cold as the hand she placed in his.

Michael's servant and the vicar's housemaid acted as their witnesses, while Lady Grandison kept watch impatiently outside the church in the carriage that was to take the newlyweds straight to the railway terminus.

She was preoccupied with thoughts of the unpleasant task of breaking the news to Arthur, and how much of the truth she would be forced to divulge. After the ceremony, her farewell to

Natalie was so hurried that the bridegroom was quite shocked. But nothing seemed to touch the girl's emotions.

"Good-bye, Mama," she said quietly and turned away from the carriage to pass under the great arched entry at King's Cross Station.

Afterward, as the train steamed toward Liverpool, Natalie hardly spoke again. It was as though she had retreated within herself, like a wounded animal whose instinct drives it to huddle deep inside a dark cave for protection. Understanding her need, he ceased trying to engage her in conversation, but meanwhile counseled himself to be patient. He was more than a little alarmed by her lethargic state, but was determined to reawaken in his bride the lovely, confident girl with whom he had fallen in love. For he now realized he did love her, whatever shadow lay across her future, and consequently his own.

The train reached its destination, and they gathered together their belongings. Before they left their private compartment, he took her gently in his arms. "I have seen how bravely you can rise to an occasion, as you did that night I first laid eyes on you." He scanned her impassive face with a searching look. "You walked past the lover who did not deserve you with your head held high. Can you mount the gangway with me now as proudly?"

She looked into his eyes as if drawing strength from them, and gathered around her the rich sable furs that had been his wedding gift. No one who saw them embark on the *Majestic* would have guessed that the smiling, gracious bride was not head over heels in love with her adoring husband. But when they had run the gauntlet of press reporters, photographers, and curious fellow passengers, and were alone together, she relapsed into the same stony-faced silence.

Several days passed before Natalie could leave the splendidly appointed stateroom Michael had provided for her on their voyage. There was every excuse. It was a rough crossing, as always at that time of year, and the mountainous waves of the hungry Atlantic tossed even the mighty *Majestic* from side to side. However, she was not troubled by *mal de mer*, as far as Michael and their stewardess could judge. But she ate almost nothing, and was certainly not fit to appear in public. When he came to sit by her bedside, as he did for hours at a time, Michael found her lying forlornly quiescent, looking more fragile with each passing day.

He could afford to wait, he told himself repeatedly. He understood that Andrei had awakened in Natalie a deeply passionate nature, and though she might shrink with loathing at this moment from the thought of permitting the same amorous intimacies to another man, he believed that would pass. Experienced as he was in the seduction of women, he was confident of eventually wooing this sweetly enticing little creature he had married into willing surrender. Until then, he would be patient.

However, this unsatisfactory state of affairs could not continue indefinitely. When he took a dozen turns around the boat deck, as he did each morning and afternoon in spite of the bitter cold and driving rain, he was acknowledged by the smiles and raised hats of other first-class passengers eager to meet him. The official list, mentioning "Sir Michael and Lady Natalie McMahon," had aroused such curiosity that complete strangers accosted him, desiring to make his bride's acquaintance and offer their congratulations. Since sympathy did nothing to improve her condition, Michael decided to try another tack.

"Get out an evening gown, my lady's jewel case, gloves, shoes—whatever she needs to wear," he told the stewardess. Turning to the startled girl, he ordered, in a tone that brooked no refusal, "Natalie, we are dining with the captain, who requests you to honor him tonight. I have accepted on your behalf. If you fail to appear, the latest *on-dit* will be that I beat my wife, or keep her handcuffed to the bedpost." His voice was brusque, but his eyes begged her to end his misery and make some attempt to take her proper place in society.

The vehemence of his appeal pierced her apathy, and she nodded in acceptance. She chose a dress of delicate shimmering green, embroidered with crystal beads, and an old-fashioned necklace of green peridots and amber, a gift from her mother on her seventeenth birthday. Camellias, with a few of their glossy dark leaves, were pinned in her hair, and she clasped matching bracelets from the same *parure* around the wrists of her long white kid gloves.

Michael's hand rested for a moment on her smooth shoulder. "Delectable, adorable Natalie; in that dress you are springtime incarnate . . ." Before he knew it, the gesture became a caress, a demand. She shrank away with a gasp, a hardly perceptive shudder. Over her head he nodded to the stewardess to leave them, cursing himself inwardly for his lack of control.

Natalie was the first to speak. "Forgive me, Michael. I didn't mean to insult you, God knows. It is enough to make you angry, when I act as though your touch is repulsive to me. I realized at once it wasn't pure chivalry that made you offer to marry me. You are just a little in love with me, I think." She paused, peeping nervously through her lashes at his face, which was now implacably stern. Then she went on, almost in a whisper. "It was just an impossible dream that could never come true, my affair with Andrei. I think I always knew it, but I couldn't bear to admit, even to myself, that fairy stories like ours sometimes end sadly. But I made myself believe it would last, and now I can't give it up!" Her voice broke. "I can't accept that it's all over and in the past. I'll never be able to forget him."

"You will, my darling. Believe me, you will. Until then, let me help you show a brave face to the world. It's the quickest way to pick up the threads of your life again."

Michael offered her his arm. He seemed so sure that there was still a happy future ahead for her, no matter how long and dark the tunnel through which she was traveling. She laid her hand on his elbow and they went down together to dine at the captain's table, undeniably the handsomest couple on board, and the cynosure of all eyes.

Their arrival in New York was greeted by the press in force, and a suite on the twelfth floor at the Waldorf Astoria was engaged to be their temporary home for the duration of the Shakespeare season.

Natalie's health was still Michael's most serious concern, for she was clearly not well, though whether from her recent shattering emotional experience or from the pregnancy he feared, he could not tell. But even if she sometimes had to conceal moments of faintness and nausea, she insisted on accompanying Michael each time he set out for the Brady Theater. Soon *Othello* was completely booked, and tickets were disappearing fast for the production of *Romeo and Juliet* that was to follow.

Natalie's enthusiasm was at least as great as Michael's to see the stage sets that had traveled with them in the hold of the *Majestic*. She watched enthralled while he supervised their reconstruction. The papers were full of articles about the idol of the London stage and his romantic runaway bride. Natalie was New York's darling. She was as much pursued by journalists as was her husband.

Returning one afternoon from a business meeting with the

famous "Diamond Jim" Brady, Michael came into their suite at the Waldorf to find her standing by a window, studying the view below. He joined her, following her gaze up Park Avenue toward Central Park.

"Isn't it amazing, Michael?" She turned to him almost gaily. "Have you noticed that everyone seems in such a hurry? And the traffic moves much more quickly than in London. Our little Irish maid, Noreen, told me today about the historic occasion when a multimillionaire, John Jacob Astor, came hurtling down the street at the wheel of a surrey with a steam-driven engine under the seat. The whole thing caught fire, just outside this very hotel."

"Shocking, my dear. How hazardous." He looked down at her quizzically. "I'm glad to find you taking an interest in what goes on around you again. Dare I hope it's a sign you're feeling better?"

She drew away from him, the hunted look returning to those luminous eyes. "Give me time, Michael. Please give me time!"

Michael bit his lip, cursing himself for assuming too easy a victory. "Of course, little one, all the time you need." He could hardly conceal the heat of his desire. He had sensed Natalie's passionate nature from the start, and his was no less so. But now the temptation of her nearness and the knowledge of his rights as a husband over her body were driving him almost to madness. . . .

"You must begin to wish you had never met me," she said in a low voice, approaching him timidly. "Poor Michael, I have been a dreadful disappointment to you, haven't I?"

"No. You were perfectly frank with me, promising me nothing. But I confess I thought you might have ceased to find me repulsive by now . . . in spite of your . . . delicate condition."

She chose to ignore the hint, the possibility of which would account for her capricious moods.

"It was not only discovering that the man I loved did not love me," she said simply. "All on the same day I learned how vile life is for most women. Not the protected, petted existence I led as a peer's daughter. The life millions of women lead, doing battle just to stay alive. How could I have been so blind, so uncaring? Delia is far more aware than I of the real world outside our charmed circle. But I don't believe even she really knows how wretched, unfair, and degrading life is for girls who are poor."

Michael thought of those Irish estates, where every woman— beautiful or not—starved to death if the potato crop failed, for there was no one with money enough to pay for their virtue if they tried to sell it. After a moment, he spoke solemnly. "Don't grieve for what you cannot alter. Thank God, here in the New World, there's at least work and food. Not equality for all, of course, but not the yawning void between rich and poor we know at home."

Natalie was glad to assent, relieved that the moment of threatened intimacy had passed. But still she could think only of Andrei: to feel again the warm pressure of his hand as he enclosed her own, holding the gold signet ring that was to be her wedding band. She sensed his presence, as though he were nearby, imploring her not to cast him utterly from her heart.

Invitations were flooding in from the Astors, the Vanderbilts, the Waldorfs, the Stuyvesant Fishes, the Fricks, the Roosevelts. Plans were afoot for a gala ball to be held in the hotel's Empire Room, Ava Astor had eight hundred names of the *crème de la crème* on her list, and the McMahons were to be guests of honor. The magnificence with which New York entertained them was ostentatious and, frankly, occasionally vulgar. But for her husband's sake, Natalie appeared to enjoy every dinner, dance, and reception.

Michael was constantly amazed by the facility with which his young wife could assume the part of a happy bride. But at times he saw that it was still only a mask, and when she let it slip, sorrow often stared out at him from her still face. However, he persisted in filling her mind with novel experiences, not only because he believed it would hasten her recovery, but because he soon found he could not bear to let her out of his sight.

Just before Michael had left London, the middle-aged actress who was to have played Emilia, Desdemona's maid, told him regretfully that she did not wish to leave England and had accepted a place with the well-known Compton Comedy Company.

So he was obliged to engage a replacement in New York. Natalie enjoyed the auditions. She took the script and helped the nervous applicants by reading the necessary cues. When her husband was doubtful about the final choice, she performed with both the actresses vying for the role in the bedroom scene that precedes Desdemona's murder by Othello, abandoning the script and playing it from memory.

Michael was astounded by the strength and projection of Natalie's voice, her flowing movements and mobile changes of expression. Her despair melted away as soon as she stepped onto the stage. He left his seat in the fifth row of the stalls and moved to the back of the theater, where she was still clearly audible. Why, Natalie was perfect in the role, he thought, as adept as though she had trodden the boards professionally for years.

His choice for Emilia fell on an Englishwoman, widow of an actor who had emigrated many years before. With her plain face and ample figure, Michael decided, she would complement Fiona's Desdemona perfectly, and he could see her later making a good nurse to Fancy's Juliet. But how much lovelier, more heart-rending in her portrayal of both these characters Natalie would be . . .

He put the wistful thought from him, for much as it warmed Michael's heart to see Natalie become daily more absorbed in the production, there was a fly in the ointment. He was apprehensive of Fancy's arrival. Knowing her jealousy of old, he could picture her spite when she saw that Natalie, without any intention of setting herself up as a rival, had become one. Obviously his bride was usurping much of the public interest and adulation that would otherwise have been poured out at the feet of the well-known actress, who would soon arrive on another great liner, the *Celtic*, along with the rest of the cast.

News of Michael's marriage had thrown the McMahon company into a turmoil of speculation. Fancy queened it over them, claiming she had known all the time of the actor's secret meetings and correspondence with the Grandison girl.

Released from Michael's supervision during the voyage, and distinctly worried, Fancy drank more than her usual allowance of wine, and a great deal more gin than she had consumed for a long time. Uncertain about her position and jealous of Michael's lovely young bride, she lost all self-control over her drinking and arrived at the Waldorf, where a suite awaited her on one of the lower floors, in an alcoholic haze.

Consoled by finding a magnificent basket of flowers from Michael with a welcoming message, Fancy pulled herself together. At once she ordered a bottle of rye whiskey from room service. Further exhilarated by seeing her enormous wardrobe trunk of expensive new outfits unpacked by an admiring maid, she changed her dress. When she descended, it was to receive a group of admirers clamoring for her autograph. She leapt into a cab and directed it to the Brady Theater, where she had been told by the desk clerk her leading man was busy with auditions.

Outside the theater she stopped to study the posters. Her name was in satisfyingly large letters, but she made up her mind as a matter of principle to ask that it should be printed larger still.

Inside the lights had just been dimmed and silence reigned while a new backdrop was lowered into place. Michael had insisted that Natalie should sit beside him, and the two of them were alone together in a sea of empty seats. He was still spellbound by the memory of her voice, its accents so rich and pure, speaking the sad farewell to life of the innocent Desdemona:

> Kill me tomorrow, let me live tonight! '
> But half an hour, but while I say one prayer . . .

"I have never heard those lines rendered with more feeling," he said in all honesty, taking her hand.

"Poor Desdemona, she hardly had time to be afraid. She never guessed she was going to die." Natalie glanced behind them, but they could not be overheard. "I wanted to die, Michael," she whispered. "You must have guessed that if I'd had enough courage, I would have attempted to take my own life. But I wasn't brave enough. It's easier to go on living, isn't it? Even if it means suffering every waking moment, dreaming such terrible things."

Michael sat immobile, uncertain how to reply. He resisted the impulse to turn toward her, not daring to risk breaking the spell of the moment. At least she was giving him all her confidence as a friend, if not as a lover.

"Is it more bearable now?" His voice spoke volumes of his own love.

"I believe it is. Because you understand, you don't judge or condemn. And you don't ask the impossible . . ."

"The lovebirds!" Fancy trilled sweetly. "Michael, darling, here I am."

Surprised, Michael rose as Fiona Galbraith came sweeping down the center aisle, her trailing skirts brushing the seats on either side. Together he and Natalie moved out to greet her.

"Congratulations, you sly thing," Fiona said archly, holding out a gloved hand at arm's length, thus compelling Natalie to take it. "If he had not confided all to me, I would never have guessed that my worldly-wise Michael had fallen victim to the charms of a debutante. Only a little younger and you might have been his daughter!"

Michael knew at once *...t alcohol had made her truculent, and this gross and unflattering distortion of the facts h. him quivering with rage. Natalie stepped in. "I believe the ι ι zen years or so between us will not prove an insurmountable ba 'ier to our happiness. But, thank you for wishing us well, Fiona," 2 replied serenely.

Her husband's lips twitched. His anger evaporated and he could not repress a brief admiring smile. At that moment he was called to the stage.

Fancy's claws were out and she was furious when Michael only bowed to her. Offering Natalie his arm, he asked her to come with him to inspect some draperies that were to be brought in on one side of the set.

The respectful words of welcome that greeted the celebrated leading lady did not quite drown the flattering comments Natalie was receiving on her splendid rendition of Desdemona as the couple strolled toward the stage.

The impudent little hussy, thought Fiona, masquerading as a languid lady of title, and aspiring to her place on the stage, as well as in Michael's bed! She was mortified but concealed her ire when later he joined her and said there was no need to concern herself with rehearsals until the following morning.

Determined to be tactful, Michael asked his publicity director to accompany Fancy back to the Waldorf. He suggested a press conference should be held later in the day when she was rested, at which time he would join his leading lady for the benefit of the photographers.

Fancy's outrage knew no bounds. She was aware that she was being given a private signal to cease drinking. He wanted her fit and radiant, witty and adorable, for the press.

The maid who came in answer to her persistent ringing offered a pot of coffee, but was summarily dismissed. Be damned to Michael, Fancy thought, and she spent the afternoon pacing her boudoir angrily, and frequently helping herself to nips from the whiskey bottle.

Michael had invited Fiona to come to his suite at five. Despite her tipsy condition, she was elegantly clad in a green velvet skirt, high-heeled buttoned leather boots, and a frilled lace blouse; in all, a stunning picture. Jewels glittered at her neck and wrists. She felt ready for anything, even to cross swords with that damned interloper Natalie.

But Fancy's confidence began to evaporate as soon as she entered the McMahon suite. Michael was writing at his desk and Natalie was seated by the fire in a gilt chair, with the tea trolley, laden with gold-rimmed china, drawn close by her side. She was occupied with some embroidery, just choosing a new thread from a skein of silk. In her dress of oyster-gray velvet, with a panel of Mechlin lace frills from neck to hem, she looked as dainty and fresh as the model for an old Chelsea china figure.

Fancy eyed her with loathing and compressed her full lips. Perhaps it was the contrast between her slightly overblown beauty and the budding rose that was his wife, or the scent of her breath, when she embraced him, where eau de cologne had not quite effaced the fumes of whiskey, but Michael let a grimace of revulsion and contempt betray him as he offered her a chair.

"This is too bad of you, Fancy," he said coldly, retreating toward the fireplace. "What a pity you could not tear yourself away from the bottle long enough to meet the press in a tolerable state of sobriety!" The words were no sooner spoken than he wished them unsaid, knowing the storm they would invite.

"Please, Michael, don't," Natalie broke in, genuinely pitying the actress for being so fiercely reproved.

Fancy's fury was instantly unleashed, and the object of it was not her critic, but her defender, Natalie. "Damn you for a pious hypocrite, you highborn whore!" she cried. In an instant Fancy had snatched up the sharp embroidery scissors that lay shining on a side table. As she leapt toward Natalie with maniacal strength, Michael stepped forward to protect his wife; the dagger-sharp blades completely pierced his hand, slicing through a vein, which immediately began to ooze dark, viscous blood. Michael reeled, drawing out the weapon with a groan of agony. Natalie ran to him, trembling and speechless with shock. Her husband stumbled against her, dragging her down with him to the floor, his whole weight falling across her. She cried out in pain.

Fancy, aghast at her own act, ran sobbing from the room. The elevator door was opening, and surprised faces seemed to stare accusingly into hers. She rushed for the stairs and, hesitating at the top of the flight, lurched forward unsteadily and caught her heel in the first brass stair rail. She pitched forward, and then she was turning over and over, gaining momentum, the screams choking in her throat as the breath was knocked from her body. She hurtled to the bottom and lay still.

A waiter rushed forward, then drew back as he saw her head lying at an unnatural angle against the skirting board.

Michael staggered to his feet, trying to gather Natalie to his breast with his unwounded arm. He scooped her up and carried her toward the bed, half tripping on her long skirt. He laid her down as gently as possible. There was blood on her petticoat, blood, he felt suddenly sure, that had not come from his wound. He fumbled to remove the telephone receiver from its hook.

"Clerk? Is this the desk clerk? Get the house doctor to my suite at once. It's Michael McMahon. My wife is ill! She's hurt herself!" he gasped out. There was a horrified silence and a crackling on the open line.

"That's terrible, sir..." the clerk stammered. "I'll get the doctor to you as soon as possible. But there's been an accident; a guest has fallen down the stairs. A lady, sir. I'm afraid she's dead."

TRANSATLANTIC MAILBAG

From Lady Cordelia Grandison to Lady Natalie McMahon

Woodstock Road, Oxford

My dearest Natalie,

It was brave of you to write so frankly and tell me the truth about your awful experiences of the last few months. My poor little sister, how you must have suffered! And not the least of your problem was fearing to confide in me. I should have known, have understood, that you are not the sort of shallow, light-minded girl who falls out of love as easily as you seemed to do. Forgive me, darling, for misjudging you. Why do you beg me not to be angry with you for foolishly trusting a man who proved to be unworthy, and finding yourself in such a horrible dilemma? It is really Mama—no, it's the system that decrees the manner in which girls like ourselves are reared that is to blame.

You are right to decide that Papa should never know the full extent of your surrender to Andrei. However, darling,

my heart aches to think of the way you were robbed of
your innocence and compelled to face the shock of marriage in such painful circumstances to a comparative
stranger. Thank God Michael seems to be a gentleman in
the truest sense of the word. You were lucky to fall into the
hands of "a very parfait gentil knight," so eager to win
you.

Something in your letter, I must admit, disturbs me. It
seems to me that you have accepted this marriage with
reservations. Surely, darling, if you will forgive me for
saying this and accept it as a most loving remonstrance, it
is unfair to Michael? I don't seek to advise you on the
intimacies of marriage, since you now know more of them
than I do, but it seems a poor beginning to a relationship
that I hope and pray will presently be unclouded by regrets.
Please reassure me if you can, Nattie dear, that you have
put the past behind you. Of course, I need hardly say that
you are the envy of every young woman in Oxford, and
probably in London, too. Sir Michael McMahon seems to
be the idol of pretty well every female I meet.

Write to me again soon, darling, with all your impressions of New York.

Your loving sister,
Delia

From Lady Natalie McMahon to Lady Cordelia Grandison.

Waldorf Astoria Hotel, New York

My dearest Delia,
Your letter relieved my mind considerably. So you do
not blame me too terribly for having been idiotically foolish and dishonest into the bargain toward you and our parents. Poor Papa, I can only hope he finds it in his heart to
forgive me. I know Mama already has, for, in a way,
Delia, she was unexpectedly kind and not at all censorious.
I do wish Papa would write to me. I know Michael has sent
him a quite beautiful letter apologizing for not having
asked his permission to marry me in a conventional manner, and promising all sorts of wonderful things for me in
the future. Undying devotion, a permanent home in Lon-

don if I wish, a marriage settlement for myself and my
children (as if that mattered!), etc.

My health, which Michael considered gave him cause
for alarm, is steadily improving. New York is fascinating
and, I am glad to say, holds no poignant memories. Oh,
Delia, don't remind me that I owe everything to Michael
and that I repay him very ill for his unselfish and chivalrous act in marrying me. I try *in every way except one* to be
a good wife, and in public, at least, I believe I succeed. He
tells me how proud he is of me.

At the moment he is in terrible distress. You may have
read of the cause in the newspapers before you receive this
letter. His leading lady, Fiona Galbraith (you remember we
saw her on the opening night of the Irish piece at the Clarence?), suffered a fatal accident the very day of her arrival.
She fell down a staircase here in the hotel and broke her
neck. Between ourselves, she was not quite sober when it
happened. I disliked her, but she did not deserve such a
horrible fate.

Michael's performance as Othello has been acclaimed,
but Fiona's understudy, Maude Edmunds, is quite unknown
and not truly equal to the part of Desdemona. Some book-
ings have been canceled and the money for the tickets had
to be returned. Americans are quick to express their disap-
proval if they feel they are defrauded, or "taken for
suckers," as I heard one of them say at the box office. I go
every day to the theater. Michael finds it helpful in coach-
ing Maude, and then I sit in the stage box at the evening
performance. People here stare so and comment loudly on
my gown or my jewels as though I were deaf and could not
hear them. But it is worse for me to hear them disparage
poor Maude's performance.

The social scene is all glitter and tasteless display of
wealth, an endless competition among the best families in
vying to spend the largest sums possible on entertaining us.
Truly, I have never heard money mentioned so often. My
Irish maid, Noreen, tells me they don't go to church in
New York to worship Almighty God, but the so-called
"Almighty Dollar."

Please write soon, dearest Delia. I miss you, Mama,

Papa, and the boys extremely, and long to hear more about your career at Oxford.

                              Your loving sister,
                              Natalie

P.S. Michael has asked if I wish Linnet to be sent out to me. I think not—she would only remind me of what might have been. But please tell her I wish her well.

From Lady Cordelia Grandison to Lady Natalie McMahon.

                              Woodstock Road, Oxford

My dearest sister,

What is this I read in the press? I should never have seen it, but Mrs. Bradleigh takes the *Daily Mirror* and scrutinizes it, I swear, from cover to cover. *You*, my little sister, have taken New York by storm in the part of Desdemona! The most beautiful actress and the most affecting performance ever seen on the stage of the Brady Theater, apparently. All New York at your feet, from the critic of the *Herald Tribune* to the program sellers who show the audience to their seats. But I thought you were indisposed, with Michael seriously worried over your health, and you still moping over your lost love. Obviously I was wrong. This is a change for the better, indeed. But where did you find the confidence to appear on the *professional* stage? I know you always had the knack of learning a part quickly if you had to, but to step into a leading role in a Shakespearean tragedy at such short notice . . . I'm lost in admiration.

I don't know how Papa will take it. He was obviously favorably impressed by Michael's background, and his father's distinguished career in the Indian army. But the thought of one of his own daughters actually treading the boards and being paid for it will take some getting used to, as my friend Margaret Douglas would put it. Meg is a "fresher" at Somerville this year like me, but she's living in college, lucky girl. She insists on introducing me to some of the men, too. Has loads of relatives "up" at the moment, including a cousin at Trinity Hall. I've tried to explain that I'd rather not meet anyone, but I can probably avoid it, as I must go down to London, if only to visit Miss Bail. She seems very little improved, and her letters sound lonely.

Let me end on a serious note, darling. Is your marriage to Michael still just one of convenience? I fear it is, and that way disaster lies. Please, Nattie, dear, *forget Andrei.* And don't be cross with me for interfering. I do so want you to be happy.

All my love,
Delia

From Lady Natalie McMahon to Lady Cordelia Grandison

Waldorf Astoria Hotel, New York

My dearest sister,

I know you sincerely want me to be happy. I know your advice is good. The only trouble is, I can't take it. Do you think I have not tried, and failed, to forget Andrei a thousand times? Michael's patience will not last forever, and already I fear it is wearing thin. Our partnership onstage is perfect. Sometimes I feel it is I who love Michael, not Desdemona who loves Othello. But it is just an illusion. When the curtain falls, it fades. I would not blame him, Delia, if he refused to wait any longer to take what is, after all, by every law of God and man, already him. But if he possesses me against my will and I shrink from him in disgust, I don't think I could bear it, and I know he could not. Oh, Delia, I do try so hard to forget Andrei—to believe that it's over, and we'll never meet again. I can only hope that the day will come soon when I can go to Michael joyfully and say, "Love me, I'm truly yours." Pray for it, Delia, as I do, with all my heart.

Natalie

BOOK TWO
1905
The Eagle, the Daffodil,
and the Unicorn

Chapter 15

Delia moored her punt on the shady side of the Cherwell, under the low-hanging branches of a willow tree. She often tied up there, knowing she was almost hidden from view. Although her mass of bright hair was partially concealed by a wide-brimmed straw hat, it was impossible to quite obscure its splendor, as richly golden as sheaved corn. If noticed, it was apt to provoke admiring comments from fellow students, strolling in Christchurch Meadow, which bordered the other bank of the river. Sometimes even a shouted invitation to join a band of impudent "townies" who also enjoyed using the riverside walk.

Delia preferred studying in the open air. As she had chosen to read for an honors degree in Classics and not merely for a pass, there was no need to worry about the formidable Moderations exam, looming ahead in July. She had another year to wait for that ordeal. But the syllabus was a daunting one. Divinity, Greek, Latin, Logic, and Archaeology. Her linen bag was full of books, tidily spiked with markers; including a volume of odes by Horace which she read for pleasure. After a few minutes, she put it away.

Stretching out more comfortably on the cushions with which the hired punt was provided, Delia applied herself to her Greek lexicon. But her mind wandered. Among her most pressing prob-

lems, and there were several, Delia now had to include Mr.
Bradleigh, the master of Stonelea in Woodstock Road. Lately he
had begun contriving excuses to be alone with Delia whenever
his wife was busy upstairs with Aunt Bella, whose health had
recently taken a downward turn.

Delia did not welcome these attentions and tried to head them
off. She also feared that the lecherous Eustace Bradleigh would
be beside himself with rage if he knew how much his wife had
blabbed to her lodger of their lack of money. He seemed to imagine Delia thought him very comfortably placed financially, and
rather a fine fellow when it came to a flirtation.

Only last night Eustace had caught up with her as she descended the stairs and pushed past, brushing far more intimately
than was necessary against the enticing curves of her bosom. His
excuse was that he wished only to precede the young lady and
open the dining room door for her. But the feverish glitter in his
eyes betrayed the real motive.

She could leave, of course. There were other places to be
found, though few were as conveniently situated so close to the
college. But her weekly contribution to the household budget was
important, and now there was this other anxiety on account of
Mrs. Bradleigh's sister.

Dear Miss Bail was no better for her lengthy stay at the nursing home in Epping. She spoke longingly of going to Switzerland, where her recovery would be swift and complete. But she
could certainly not run to the fees in a Swiss sanatorium; it was
out of the question.

Delia had secretly consulted the matron of the home, and was
already in touch with a doctor who would receive the poor lady in
his care. By subletting Miss Bail's mansion flat in London, adding this sum to the slender contribution the Bradleighs could afford, and sacrificing half her own small income, the project was
just feasible. Miss Bail need never know; she could be told that
Aunt Bella had been unexpectedly generous, or that her brother-
in-law had been rewarded by his employers with a handsome
increase in salary.

It was only for a few months, perhaps. But in the meantime,
could Delia support herself on half the money that had seemed
little enough during the first year at Somerville?

She leaned over the side of the punt idly scooping up handfuls
of water and allowing them to cascade in a shower of shining

drops. She could not ask her parents for a penny, remembering only too well the proud declaration of independence she had made, and her mother's assertion that Papa would not give her an allowance at Oxford. A worried frown creased her forehead.

Sandy was not to be thought of, either. He had been kind enough when his sister Mildred's will had left him nothing but her share of the quaint old house in St. John's Wood, and she had left to Delia all the capital that produced her modest income. It might be possible to write to New York and, without any feeling of false shame, request a contribution from Natalie. . . .

She looked up to see impatient hands parting the willow boughs and felt the prow of a boat bumping the side of the punt. It was brilliant dark-haired Margaret Douglas, leaning out recklessly and shaking her own craft to the laughing remonstrations of the two young men rowing it.

"Delia, what a swot you are!" the other girl remarked, reproachfully. "For a moment I thought you had a fascinating companion—that second-year man from Brasenose, young Lord Hurst, who tells everyone he adores you. You have nothing here but a bag of books. How boring! We decadents, however, will soon be enjoying tea and fresh scones at Mrs. Tovey's farmhouse." There was a hint of jarring malice in her laughter.

Meg Douglas had seemed at first a kindred spirit and a true friend to Delia, but lately she was always sparring and teasing. Delia envied Meg her phenomenal memory, which made light of their studies, and even more her rooms in the college itself. Although she was rather inconveniently accommodated at West Hall, on the far side of the lawns, and had to walk a considerable distance to the main building.

"My dear girl, it's like being in prison . . . certainly worse than the most closely guarded boarding school," Meg had complained. "You are so much better off. Mrs. Bradleigh is obviously wax in your hands; living in her home means you can do exactly as you like—go out or invite friends of both sexes to tea in your rooms . . . men, if you feel like it. My cousin, for instance. I could come for coffee with Piers and his friend Clive, and Mrs. Bradleigh would not dream of protesting. Whereas, in college, Miss Maitland wouldn't let them set foot in the drawing room after dinner. . . ."

"You mean Piers Douglas? Oh, I thought he was your brother!" exclaimed Delia.

"Well, as good as one—a first cousin. I may have let our principal assume we are brother and sister, since, thank goodness, our surnames are the same. After all, one must think of a first cousin like a brother. I mean, one could never marry him." She looked away for a moment. Delia had not, even during the halcyon days of her unclouded friendship with Meg, enjoyed entertaining Piers Douglas at Woodstock Road. Nor had she liked Clive Berryman, another second-year man who was his crony, and the inference that together they would form a sociable foursome.

Clive was the epitome of the kind of Magdalen man who prided himself on being a "blood," and he followed all the unwritten rules to the last unspoken word. Piers was of quite a different character. He gloried in being one of the "hearties"—those who rode with the local hunts whenever possible and participated in every sport even though they excelled at none. He was often fined and had to pay a "sconce" for making remarks that were deemed to be unmannerly at table, because he was still too much of a schoolboy to keep up the elegant standards of conversation required. Piers, who was beginning to cast frank glances of admiration in Delia's direction, was, at least, an honest, warmhearted fellow. But Clive was, at best, she had decided, a cold fish who cared little for anyone but his urbane, well-tailored self.

"I don't think you will succeed in persuading an earnest student like Delia to join us," he said now in his irritatingly sarcastic drawl.

"Do come with us, Delia!" It was Piers who entreated.

"Clive is right; we're wasting our time. Farewell, Delia dear..."

Meg let drop the curtain of willow boughs. As their boat drifted by she quietly unloosed the slack knot of Delia's mooring, knowing the punt would edge slowly out into the stream.

Delia would have been amazed to know that Meg was wildly jealous of her. The girl nursed a secret passion for Piers and permitted him many small intimacies under the guise of "sisterly affection." She had grown up with her cousin in one of those large, rambling households where several branches of the same family existed in reasonable harmony. But propriety could not safely be ignored. After being caught once in a passionate embrace with her, Piers had kept his distance; marriage, he knew, was an impossibility for himself and his cousin. He now turned his attention, and his affections, to Delia.

Deeply engrossed in her books, Delia did not notice the punt nosing its way out through the reeds, drawn by the insidious current into the main thoroughfare of the river. With a start she realized she was adrift and reached for the punt pole. Her sudden movement almost overturned the craft, and her bag, still containing a couple of books, fell into the water. There was the grinding bump of a violent collision with a skiff being rowed fast in the opposite direction; just before her bag sank from view, an oar, quickly maneuvered, slid neatly through the loops and lifted it, dripping, into the air.

"What the devil do you think you're doing, madam?" the rower cried angrily, transferring his sodden trophy to the cushions of the punt with a skillful hand and splashing Delia's white linen skirt. She glimpsed a Panama hat, worn rakishly askew, the glint of pince-nez glasses on a high-bridged nose, and a square chin, deeply indented and now thrust aggressively toward her. The man spoke with stern authority, but she was too confused to frame an apology, or even place him in the Oxford hierarchy.

Moving the punt back to the right side of the river, he went on angrily. "You are a menace, young woman. *Never* lean over so far on one side. In another moment you'd have been in the water yourself, and I should have been put to the trouble of fishing you out, as well as your belongings."

"Thank you, sir, for rescuing my books. I'm sorry to have given you a fright," she said, trying to conceal her affront at being offered such elementary advice.

"A fright! Impudence. Ye gods! What are these females coming to?" He set himself manfully to both oars, sculling away at a great rate.

But that was not to be the end of the encounter. When Delia had punted upriver again to the boathouse near St. Hilda's College, she found herself second in line to the bad-tempered oarsman who had been so rude. He leapt ashore, moving with athletic ease. He was tall, of slender build, with an exceptionally alert stance, and when he took off his Panama and shook back his light brown hair, he seemed about ten years her senior, and not middle-aged, as she had first believed. The next moment, he was looking straight at her, holding the pince-nez in his hand, and she found that his eyes were an unusually bright hazel, with rings of green and gold around the irises. A scar ran through his right eyebrow, giving his face a rather quizzical expression.

"Well, madam, I see you had no further dangerous incidents," he said in amusement. "May I offer you my hand to disembark?" There was a noticeable Welsh lilt in his voice.

Ignoring the hand, Delia stepped lightly ashore, with the ruined bag of books under one arm. "Thank you, sir, I can manage." Her firm chin was lifted, her soft, rosy lips compressed.

He laughed with a lightning change of mood. "I see that you can. Forgive a cantankerous, quick-tempered fellow, will you? It is only that these days so many confounded youngsters who haven't the least idea of how to handle a boat get in my way. They put a great strain on my patience—never my strongest point! Let me carry that sopping bag before it does more harm to your skirt."

Delia relinquished the uncomfortable burden, and they began, somehow by mutual accord, to stroll toward Magdalen Bridge.

"May I introduce myself?" her companion asked affably. "William Prynne, a rather odd sort of don—tutor and lecturer at Magdalen College. And you are Miss . . . ?"

"Grandison," Delia replied awkwardly, feeling it unnecessary to mention her title. He paused when they came to the bridge with its three gray stone arches.

"I always stop here and pay my respects to our famous college tower," he remarked, contemplating the other side of the river, where undergraduates lolled at their ease on green lawns sloping right to the brink. "The glass houses there, in the Botanic garden, reflect the afternoon sun in such a marvelous way and lead the eye naturally to the tower itself, so solid and yet delicate, that it looks poised as if to soar upward. A medieval miracle in stone. Do you know that King James the First said of it that it is the most absolute building in Oxford?"

Delia looked mystified. "I don't quite know what he meant by that. But it seems to me like the stem of a growing plant, and that its cluster of smaller towers encloses a bud, which is just about to open into a magnificent flower. But you'll probably think that rather fanciful."

"Not at all. Other perceptive people have made the same comment." Dr. Prynne turned his piercing eyes on Delia so keenly that she looked away, then moved on hastily.

"You will have made a tour of the colleges, I suppose?" he questioned.

"Certainly. Last summer." She recalled her tour with Miss Bail, which now seemed ages ago. "A very dear mentor devoted several days to taking me around them."

"Aha! A very dear mentor. Well, I will not presume to follow in his footsteps. But have you attended any concerts at Balliol, or the Sheldonian Theatre, with him?"

"No, I have not had the opportunity. I am an indifferent performer on the piano, although my sister is exceptionally gifted. But I love to hear good music."

"We are about to do so. Listen." The bells in the tower above them began to peal harmoniously, marking the passing of the hour. "All ten bells chime at six in the morning each day, and they make such a din that the building itself seems to shake. As it is close to my rooms, I wish they were quieter. But now, at this time of the afternoon, it's one of the sweetest sounds on earth." Suddenly the air was filled with a positive symphony as clocks near and far melodiously chimed the hour. "Oxford is a city of rare beauty, you know," he went on, "not merely, as our critics assert, a citadel of port and prejudice!

"I would like to show you our deer park," he continued, "a favored haunt of mine. It lies behind the college, and I believe its informality would please you. We are exceptionally fortunate in having over a hundred acres of grounds—more than any other college, in fact. But I dare say you will want to hurry home and change. Perhaps on another occasion." They were passing Rose Lane, and Dr. Prynne halted outside the porter's lodge, in the shade of the Muniment Tower and the old St. John's Hospital buildings. "I should really offer to escort you farther, if only to carry this gruesome object . . ."

"No, no!" Delia interrupted hastily. "I should have explained that I am a student at Somerville. But I have lodgings quite near the college, at a house called Stonelea, in the Woodstock Road. Truly, it is not far to walk, just along the High, then Cornmarket and St. Giles . . ."

"Very well. I bow to your independence."

"Thank you, Dr. Prynne, for coming with me this far, but I couldn't trespass further on your kindness," Delia said, holding out her hand for her property.

He took the offered hand and clasped it in a strong grip, then reluctantly gave up possession of the bag. "I'm sure we shall meet again," he said positively, then passed, a tall figure with a quick, nervous tread, into the shadow of the lodge.

All the way home Delia took herself to task for acting so naïvely, as though she did not know how to make conversation with an older man.

At Stonelea a letter from her father awaited her, as well as a substantial missive from America.

Lord Grandison proposed visiting Oxford and staying overnight at the Clarendon Hotel, en route for a week's trout fishing with a friend in Hampshire. He mentioned in passing that he had been prevailed upon by his wife to give Linnet a dowry, for she was shortly to marry Dick Bates, the carrier at Grayle village. It was usual for him on such an occasion to make estate servants a substantial present of money, especially those who were personal attendants on members of the family. Lord Grandison wrote:

> But I still do not feel entirely sure the little minx was not involved in Natalie's romance with her Russian Prince. Somehow, I never got to the bottom of the affair. And I am not entirely sure she is happy with that actor. I long for her return, which seems to be unduly delayed . . .

Delia also was haunted by fears that Natalie's relationship with the famous Sir Michael McMahon was far from idyllic. Natalie's letters were filled with reports of the company's success on the New York stage, of her own growing confidence as an actress, and of the parts she was currently studying. After triumphantly completing his Shakespeare season with a magnificent *Macbeth*, Michael extended his lease of the Brady Theater to present a series of Restoration comedies. But, while proud of their sweeping theatrical success in America, the young bride was obviously homesick. Although she wrote at length, her concluding sentence was far from reassuring:

> Michael has been persuaded by a wealthy and charming Irish widow, Mrs. Maeve O'Malley, to appear at several charity galas; they often dine together after the performance at Rector's in order to discuss the details—or so I am given to understand.

Natalie said nothing of lying awake in the great double bed, with its satin canopy, listening for Michael's return, and the sound of his dressing room door discreetly closing in the early hours of the morning. Not even to Delia could she confide the heartache caused to her by Michael's growing involvement with the extravagantly lovely red-haired Maeve. Nevertheless, Delia knew all was not well in her little sister's outwardly glamorous and enviable life.

After an unexciting evening meal at the Bradleighs' table, Delia mentioned her meeting with the eccentric Dr. Prynne. Eustace Bradleigh's reaction took her by surprise.

"I am only too well acquainted with the gentleman," he said vehemently. "Some say he is a genius, and the world will be startled by the experiments he is carrying out in the Daubeny Laboratory. But I have another word for him—madman. He is at the moment engaged in litigation with my principal, Mr. Archibald, on account of that infernal machine he rides." Mr. Bradleigh thrust his folded napkin most emphatically through its silver holder. "Have I mentioned Mr. Archibald to you, Lady Delia? Our senior partner, no less. His offices adjoin some former coach houses in Catte Street, now rented out as garages to Prynne and the owner of an electric brougham, on condition that no noise of a disturbing nature is to be made. The other gentleman respects this agreement, but not Dr. Prynne. On several occasions Mr. Archibald's clients have been alarmed during a conference by the starting up of his engine and then he goes roaring off down the street most dangerously on his motorcycle, as he calls it, frightening the horses, giving ladies palpitations! I have written him a strong letter already, on instructions, and have received a quite uncompromising reply. He says he makes as little noise as possible but insists we must all accustom ourselves to the march of progress, which includes machines propelled by petrol engines. He will be lucky not to be sued for creating a nuisance!"

Delia had a vision of the tall and curiously dashing figure of William Prynne, in cap and goggles, thundering down the street astride his mechanical steed, and she began to laugh. But she subdued her mirth when she caught Mr. Bradleigh's outraged and offended glare.

"Does his wife do nothing to prevent him from risking his life in this way?" Delia inquired mildly.

"I believe him to be a bachelor; but he's a Welshman, and they even say he's a socialist, which perhaps accounts for some of his peculiarities."

At one moment she felt elated knowing that William was a free man. But the next few words brought her back to earth. A tremendous chasm yawned between the daughter of an aristocratic family and a man who held socialist views.

"Shall we take coffee on the veranda, my love?" Mrs. Bradleigh was inquiring timidly, anxious to divert dear Eustace's annoyance.

Delia returned to her room, where her studies awaited her. Hardly had she turned up the gas lamp over her desk and spread out her books when she heard Mr. Bradleigh's unmistakable tread rapidly mounting the staircase. Then he gave a peremptory rap on her door. She was quite startled and paused before saying uncertainly: "What is it?"

He came into the room, clutching a sealed envelope. "This has just been brought around by a servant. Who, I ask myself, would have the effrontery to address you in such terms?" It was inscribed "Miss Grandison, By Hand" in a sharp, sloping script that disclosed the writer to be swift and impatient. She tore it open; obviously Mr. Bradleigh intended to wait and see who her correspondent was. The letter was a brief invitation to attend the next Sunday evening's concert at Balliol College, in the company of Dr. Prynne, who would call for her at 7:00 P.M. The program was to be Beethoven's *Pathétique* sonata and some Chopin nocturnes, concluding with selections by the college choir. He signed himself "Yours cordially, Wm. Prynne."

"It is only a note, asking leave to escort me to a concert, from the gentleman we were discussing at dinner," Delia said reluctantly. "There is no discourtesy intended. I simply failed to mention my title."

Mr. Bradleigh seized her wrist recklessly. "You will not accept, I hope! Without a chaperon? I wonder that he dares to suggest it."

"Of course I shall accept," said Delia. "Why not? I'm sure he will see me safely home."

"I forbid it!" Mr. Bradleigh trembled with rage. "You will not appear in public alone with an unmarried man who is certainly *not* old enough to be your father, as I am. Well, at least I am considerably older than is Dr. Prynne." He clutched her arm, drawing her toward him in an agitated manner. "A certain intimate relationship I see no harm in, if it is sufficiently discreet. Eh, Lady Delia? Between these four walls, let us say. Nothing to offend the public eye, to cause gossip. I have known you long enough to judge that you have a passionate nature . . ."

Before she had grasped his intention he forced her down on the sofa, frantically tearing her dress from her shoulders to expose her rounded breasts. One hand slid hotly behind her neck, pulling her face closer. Using all her strength, Delia struggled free and struck him hard across the mouth. He shrank away, whining with pain.

"Never do that again, Mr. Bradleigh, or I shall leave this house immediately and tell your wife why I am going. Need I remind you that *you* are a married man? You disgust me."

"I thought you favored me." He fingered the cut her topaz ring had made on the edge of his lower lip. "The way your eyes seek me out, hinting, enticing . . ."

"That is pure fantasy on your part, because you wished it to be so. Now, please leave my room, and don't try to enter it again on any specious excuse."

Mr. Bradleigh crept out, leaving Delia to pen a quick, coolly worded reply accepting Dr. Prynne's invitation to the concert. It could be delivered by the kitchen maid, Elsie, in the morning. But first she washed her hands, her neck, and her burning cheeks, for she felt defiled by the other man's moist, sweaty touch.

Later, when all the lights were extinguished, Eustace Bradleigh sidled past her closed door, then up another flight of stairs to the second story, where Elsie slept alone in a small room. He flung himself savagely on the unwilling girl and slapped her hard into submission, using, with great satisfaction, fiercer blows than the one he had received from Delia.

Chapter 16

The next day, Delia tried to decide what to wear for the Sunday concert, choosing at last a cream georgette gown with tasseled handkerchief points to the skirt, a long string of coral beads, and two glorious pink silk roses for her hair.

There was a divinity lecture that day, given by an enlightened don who allowed female students to attend. Many others closed the doors of their lecture rooms to girls. It was boring and failed to hold her attention, which kept straying back to the encounter on the river. Had she appeared very stupid and careless? She did not know how her mooring could have become untied. A suspicion rose in her mind of Meg Douglas, who so enjoyed teasing and playing tricks, but she thrust it from her as unworthy.

Meeting Elsie on the stairs at Stonelea, Delia checked to make sure her note of acceptance had been delivered safely to Dr. Prynne. *Poor dear,* Delia thought as she continued on her way. *She must be overworked, for she looks so pale.*

She could not get out of her head her conversation with the eccentric don, and she thought of a dozen witty and intelligent remarks she might have made. After a game of doubles at lawn tennis the following day, her partner asked Delia if she had seen the notice on the board in the library.

"We've all been wondering when the second-years were going to give their summer dance, but they've kept it remarkably secret until now," the girl observed, fitting her racket into its wooden press. "Usually, it's before the end of June, but this year it won't be until July. A bit of a nuisance, really, for so many of the best men go down earlier. We'll be hard put to it to find partners. Have you anyone tremendously handsome and eligible in mind? Rupert Hurst, or perhaps that dandified fellow one sees about with Meg Douglas and her brother—or is it her cousin, Piers? Clive Berryman . . ."

"I don't think I'd care for either of them as my escort. I suppose I must ask someone, to make up the right number," Delia said uneasily.

"Of course. It's not as though Miss Maitland had a 'little book' of desirable males. There are plenty of undergrads dying to be asked, but then they're so young, and most of them are positively crass, don't you agree?"

"Well, I'll think about going," promised Delia, who had hitherto given no thought all that term to the rare social events that were organized for female students.

"And what will you wear?" one of their opponents asked Delia. "A Paris creation, no doubt!" There was an edge to her voice. Delia's clothes had such quality and style as to be noticed and envied by most students to an extent she never realized.

"Probably the dress I'll be wearing to the concert at Balliol on Sunday. It's not cut low enough for a ball, but this will just be an informal dance, I hope."

"Lucky girl to be invited to the concert!" commented her companion. "May I ask who is taking you?"

Delia answered calmly, "Dr. William Prynne. One of the Magdalen dons."

"An old family friend, I presume."

A devil danced for a moment in Delia's sparkling blue eyes. "No, I only met him for the first time yesterday, on the river."

She marched off happily, holding her racket under her arm and a string bag of tennis balls over her shoulder. What a meal for the gossips! *Let them get their teeth into that!* she thought triumphantly.

Like a man with a sore tooth who could not resist prodding it, Eustace Bradleigh insisted on introducing the name of the reckless motorcyclist into every mealtime conversation, and the next morning at the breakfast table was no exception.

"The man is highly thought of in some quarters, I know," he said grudgingly. "But those dubious experiments he's dabbling in at the Daubeny Laboratory smack more of a stage magician's tricks than anything genuinely scientific. Causing materials to glow in the dark without heat, I've heard. He claims they give off rays that can pass through flesh. I'm told he went over during the last long vacation to consult with those cranks in Paris, Pierre Curie and that mad Polish wife of his. And all at the university's expense. Wasting the young gentlemen's time, stuffing their heads full of nonsense about invisible rays, instead of getting down to their syllabus. It amazes me the vice chancellor allows it."

"Where is the Daubeny Laboratory, my love?" Mrs. Bradleigh questioned soothingly. "I have never heard of it."

"Next to the old physic gardens of Magdalen College, my dear," snapped Eustace. "All the years we've lived here, and I have to tell you that! They used to grow herbs there to make medicines, but since those huge glass houses were built, it's the fashion to call it the Botanic garden instead—"

"Oh, yes, Dr. Prynne pointed them out to me," Delia interrupted. "He has offered to show me the deer park, and I shall certainly request a tour of the glass houses as well."

"Well, my advice is to be a little standoffish where he's concerned. After all, the man is not a gentleman, only the son of some obscure Welsh medical doctor in a poor mining village. If his behavior is rough and ready—and I know it to be so—what can one expect?"

Delia sliced the top off her boiled egg with a steady hand, but she felt an inner resentment fast turning to loathing for the truculent little clerk who dared to speak of a distinguished tutor in such sneering terms.

"Mr. David Lloyd George is the nephew of a poor Welsh shoemaker, I believe," she said with deceptive mildness. "Yet he has risen to the very height of his profession, and he is not the less well thought of even among titled politicians. I have met him and found him very charming and good-mannered."

Mr. Bradleigh responded with a grunt of disparagement. For Delia life in the same house as Eustace Bradleigh was becoming intolerable. Yet other girls envied her, especially Margaret Douglas.

* * *

"You don't know how lucky you are to live at Stonelea." Meg sighed. "To be completely *free* of all the conventions here. And it's so dull here, in the College. Some of the other girls are so provincial; they speak as though Oxford were a great city, and sipping tea in the drawing room a great event!"

"But I don't seem to join in the social life of the college at all," Delia complained. "Please encourage me, Meg. Don't put me off."

"What an innocent you are. Don't you realize that the other girls say they find you snobbish, when really they are envious of you?" Meg rummaged in her desk drawer for a silver case, from which she took out a cigarette, which she lit before continuing. "Of course they envy you, your title, your wealth, and especially your beauty. When you move in your accustomed circle—your charmed and rarefied circle—it includes many other girls equally wealthy and well connected, though few, I dare say, as lovely. When you appear on the scene, what chance have they of being noticed? Oh, they pretend their claws are not out to scratch you, but they hurt you in the only way they can—by ignoring you." She paused to inhale deeply from her cigarette.

"Meg, stop! I simply don't believe it." Delia's eyes were growing moist. "Yes, I do," she said after a moment. "So many little remarks I've heard, mostly made behind my back, but intended for my ears all the same." She was kneeling on the window seat of Meg's room in West Hall and she sank back, clasping her knees with her arms. "Do you think that is why Miss Maitland designated me a home student?" she asked forlornly. "There are so few, and the others are special cases, like poor little Laura Boscawen, who is delicate. But are you sure, Meg? Most students speak of men in such disparaging terms, as though being noticed by them were the last thing that mattered. Debutantes, when they do the London season, are quite frankly in search of husbands. They think of nothing else, and they make no secret of it. I wanted so much to come to Oxford to get away from that sort of thing."

"Miss Maitland may have thought you would have trouble fitting in," Meg said shrewdly. "I don't believe she meant you to suffer for it, and if you explain to her how much you feel you are missing of the social side of being a Somervillian, I believe she'll accommodate you in the college for your second year."

Meg was regarding herself in the mirror over the mantelpiece, trying the effect of tucking a rose from the vase on her desk behind her ear. "I believe she might do the same for Laura Boscawen," she went on. "Obviously it is her mama who has persuaded the girl that she is sickly. Haven't you noticed how she has blossomed since being away from the influence of her family? I am really getting very fond of Laura. She writes such splendid poetry."

"Meg, do you mind if I ask you something rather personal?" Delia rested her pretty round chin on one knee. "We were such good friends at first, but lately you tease me all the time, and it isn't just in fun. It couldn't be for the same reason you say the others dislike me, as your family is part of the charmed circle you mentioned just now."

"I'm just the most inconsequential creature in the world. Pay no heed to my fads and fripperies!"

Meg had no intention of confiding the secret of her blighted romance with Piers, or the fit of angry pique she had experienced when struck by his transparent admiration of Delia. She would go much further than stealthily untying a rival's mooring rope when jealousy pricked her.

"Let's talk about something really important," she went on hastily. "The second-years have at last decided to honor custom and give a dance. Shall you have someone down from London as your escort, or will you make do with one of my handsome admirers, Piers or Clive Berryman?"

Meg was cautiously flying a kite to see which way the wind blew. "I'm not sure yet. Ask me again after next Sunday." Seeing Meg's obvious interest, Delia went on: "But certainly neither of those two. Forgive me for being frank, Meg, but I've nothing in common with Piers, and, for some reason, Clive positively repels me."

Meg was well satisfied with this answer. Piers was, so far at least, safe with Delia. As for the urbane Clive, on their ride out to take tea in the country he had given Meg certain meaning looks, a lingering touch of the hand when he helped her down from the gig. While she still considered herself in love with Piers, the volatile Miss Douglas was intrigued by his friend. She judged that Clive never acted impetuously. If he began courting her, he had something serious in mind. And Meg was quite capable of renewing her close friendship with Delia, once she was convinced that Lord Grandison's lovely daughter had no intention of poaching on her preserves and posed no threat to her future plans.

"I shall not fail to ask you after next Sunday," she said, smiling. "Remember, I will countenance nothing less than a belted Earl, and . . . I insist that you introduce me as your dearest friend!"

Delia laughed, wondering uneasily how much of a sensation it would create if the partner she had in mind deigned to accept. He was by far the most fascinating man she had ever met. He had a quick temper. How would he react to the revelation that she was a young lady of title? Once over that hurdle, she could not long conceal that she was also a passionate believer in the rights of women. Sooner or later she would have to reveal her fervent beliefs. And she had little hope he shared them.

Delia appeared at the dining table on Sunday in her filmy evening gown. Having eaten with a healthy appetite her roast beef, Yorkshire pudding, and a pastry-topped plum pie at luncheon, Delia was not really hungry. She toyed with the thinly sliced ham and cucumber salad placed before her by Mrs. Bradleigh, who presided over the dishes on the sideboard.

The master of the house kept glancing in the direction of his paying guest as she sat on the heavy mahogany chair. His eyes were drawn by the soft drapery of cream georgette over a sheath of matching satin, which faithfully outlined the girl's firm breasts and narrow waist, the swell of her hips, and the long line from thigh to knee.

"How pretty you look, my dear," Mrs. Bradleigh said admiringly. "That color is so becoming to you. Don't you agree, Eustace, my love?"

"Yes, indeed," her spouse muttered. The meal ended in silence. "Bring me a cup of coffee. This ham is so salty, my throat is quite sore. Speak to Cook about it," Eustace grumbled.

The doorbell sounded, having been most vigorously pushed.

"I'll go," Eustace said at once and rushed out of the dining room. He opened the front door cautiously, preventing Dr. Prynne from entering. When the distinguished lecturer wished him a cordial good evening, he stood aside, frowning. Delia's swansdown-edged wrap lay on a chair. When she came forward, he snatched it up and laid it around her shoulders with a possessive hand.

William bowed, his eyes narrowed behind the severe pince-nez glasses, and Delia had an instant impression that in formal evening dress he cut an extremely elegant figure. With his waving light brown hair loose about his brow, and not controlled by even a trace of macassar oil, he had a slightly unconventional air.

William offered her his arm, and as she laid her hand on it, she felt a warm throb of delight. But Eustace could not resist voicing his censure. "I must tell you, sir, that I was extremely shocked to see that you addressed Lady Cordelia, the daughter of a Marquess, as *Miss* Grandison. I presume no insult was intended, however rude it appeared."

"It was quite an understandable mistake, and I am not in the least offended," Delia interposed boldly. "Shall we go, Dr. Prynne? I should hate to be late for the concert."

When they reached the gate, William turned to face her, his expression stern. "Why did you not correct my mistake, Lady Cordelia?" he said icily. "Grandison. I must assume you are one of Lord Grandison's daughters. No wonder that jumped-up office boy, whom I recognized from an unpleasant interview in his employer's office, took me to task. I realize I have transgressed the rules of etiquette. As you are a young lady of title, I should have provided a chaperon for the evening."

"Please, Dr. Prynne, it really does not matter. I never gave the conventions a thought, only my pleasure that you had seen fit to invite me."

Suddenly he flung back his head and laughed. "Shades of my Methodist upbringing! Compromising the daughter of a peer of the realm! What would my father say, the chapel elders, my sisters and cousins?"

"I'm truly sorry Mr. Bradleigh was so insolent," Delia said. "It was all my fault. I should have explained who I was when we met. But is it of any consequence?"

They were sauntering down St. Giles, and the scent of lime trees was sweet in their nostrils. "Yes," he said gravely. "I think we shall find that it is."

They walked along in silence until Delia summoned up the courage to say tremulously, "You probably believe all men are equal, Dr. Prynne. I agree. And so are all women, for that matter. Can't you remember only that you are a teacher, and I am a student? If there is any difference between us, it is not a matter of rank, but of intellect, in which you are far my superior."

"And age. Yes, I am better than you by more than a decade of experience!" he said with a rueful chuckle. "To tell the truth, I am a little taken aback at having had the temerity to invite you. Here I was imagining that I had made the acquaintance of a rather awkward and gauche little duckling who would feel flattered to attend a Balliol concert; and I find instead I have netted a glittering swan, with a coronet atop her graceful head, like a Princess in a fairy tale."

"Please don't feel you have to flatter me, Dr. Prynne," Delia said earnestly. "And thank you for taking such good care of me the other day, instead of blaming me for nearly upsetting your boat. I must apologize on Mr. Bradleigh's behalf. His wife is kindness itself, but he's not a pleasant man. He presumes to suppose he has some sort of responsibility for my behavior, which I assure you he has not."

"Let's forget him, then. The mistake about your title was quite accidental on both our parts, and I was not disturbed by that strutting cockerel, even when he crowed his loudest."

Other couples were moving in the same direction and converging on Balliol College. The ladies, looking like pale butterflies in their evening dresses, seemed to float in the twilight, skirts billowing and frothing around them in the slight breeze that had come up.

Their escorts were mostly in academic dress, some in their gowns trimmed with rich scarlet or blue silk lining to the hoods, edged with white fur.

"Let's talk about something else," he said in practical tones. "Poor Horace, for example. I believe it was his book of odes that suffered a dousing in the river. Part of your syllabus, I suppose?"

The steps of the great hall were crowded with undergraduates wearing gowns over dark evening dress. As they took their seats in the front row, Delia was unconscious of the radiant picture she made as William had relieved her of her light wrap, the chandeliers above them gilding the rich aureole of her hair and casting a mellow sheen over the exquisite molding of her shoulders and half-revealed arms.

As usual, the hall was packed. There was a muted round of applause as the pianist took his place. Then he began playing, and it was all perfection. William's eyes never left Delia as she sat, so utterly absorbed that she seemed hardly to breathe.

During the interval he left her for a few minutes. It gave her just time to acknowledge how much she was enjoying the evening and to anticipate a delightful conclusion. Already the girl's heart was beating a little faster at the thought of the walk home with William under a full moon; but to her vexation she found herself being directed toward a waiting carriage.

William offered Delia his hand. "May I help you in?" he asked courteously. "The coachman has his orders to drop you off at Stonelea, and I've told him to accompany you to the door, then make sure the bell is answered before taking his leave. Good night, and many thanks for your delightful company, Lady Cordelia." His voice was perfectly level, yet he bent a little toward her and his eyes seemed to search hers.

"But . . . but I thought we should . . . walk home together," Delia stammered. "Oh, of course, it is in the opposite direction to Magdalen, quite the other end of the High Street. But it is such a lovely night, and it is really not far."

Her pleading voice, low as it was, sounded strident in her own ears. "When shall we meet again?" she heard herself say, to her amazement.

"I think we shall not do so. It would really be imprudent, since we belong to such different worlds." Only the Welsh lilt in his speech gave the slightest hint of emotion to his dismissal. He bowed curtly, then strode away, his feet ringing sharply on the cobblestones of the street.

Chapter 17

Talk at the college was all about the forthcoming dance and the vexed question of suitable partners. Piers approached Delia during an encounter at Benson's bookshop in the High Street. She was replacing her volume of Horace, which had proved unreadable even after she had laboriously dried the pages.

"I say, Delia, I've been wanting to ask you," he began, fixing her with a beseeching look, "may I take you to the dance? Your shindig at Somerville, I mean. It would be an honor. Dash it, I'd be terribly grateful if you said yes."

It was a challenge the girl couldn't resist. "I'm so sorry, Piers," she replied swiftly. "I already have a partner for the dance. Dr. Prynne. He's a tutor at Magdalen, you know." Now she knew she would have to approach Dr. Prynne and renew the offer of friendship he had spurned. How humiliating if he refused.

By a question here and there among girls following the honors course in mathematics, she had elicited that William Prynne was near the peak of his profession. Indeed, he had aroused a good deal of jealousy among colleagues very much his senior for this reason.

Certainly he was generally considered eccentric, but rumors

were rife among the male undergraduates that he was on the verge of announcing the results of some revolutionary experiments, and that he was collaborating with the Curies at the Sorbonne on the uses of their recently discovered new elements, polonium and radium.

More delicate inquiries as to his marital status, only possible because Laura Boscawen's family lived near to his in Wales, confirmed he was a bachelor with, as Laura put it, "a parcel of pretty sisters and cousins." She did not know the family well but considered it to be relatively poor and undistinguished. The father was a physician who, upon the death of his wife, moved to the village of Criccieth, not far from the Boscawens. He was known to be a devout chapel-goer, and teetotaler.

In spite of Delia's preoccupation with William Prynne, she welcomed the diversion of her father's visit, which she had been looking forward to ever since receiving his letter.

Lord Grandison intended to stay only one night at the Clarendon and he expected Delia to dine with him and spend the evening there. She noticed at once that he seemed rather distracted and did not look quite himself.

"How is Mama?" she asked over dessert.

"As well as can be expected," he said with a sigh. "You think perhaps that Mama does not love you as tenderly as I do," he went on. "There you do her less than justice. She finds it hard to express her affection—always has, even toward me. She misses you more than you realize, and she still feels you have chosen a direction in life that you had no right to, given your station and the natural responsibilities of our class. . . ."

"Stuff and nonsense, Papa!" cried Delia, startled into annoyance. "Forgive me for speaking so sharply, but if I feel any responsibility, it is to spread the gospel of enlightenment about the education and emancipation of women. I know I sound as though I'm riding a ridiculous hobbyhorse; all my friends tell me so. But Mama's ideas of duty are not mine. And I find it hard to believe that with all the frivolous activities of her set she finds time to miss me."

"Believe me, she does. And she is constantly uneasy about Natalie. Judging from the girl's letters, I can't rid myself of a suspicion that her husband does not seem to have won her heart, even yet. If the company remains in America much longer, I shall write a strong letter myself to Sir Michael, insisting that Natalie at least should come home."

"Please don't take a high-handed attitude, Papa," Delia begged. "He's quite within his rights to make a decision about extending the season, and Natalie told me they've received a magnificent offer to appear in San Francisco. Suppose he decides to accept?"

Arthur did not reply, only placed his cup neatly in its saucer and, after a silent moment, went on. "Tell me, may we expect you to join the family at Grayle this summer?"

"I will come for a week or two while the boys are at home," she agreed. "But I also plan to go to Switzerland. There is a middle-aged lady who would act as my companion, and one of the other girls at Somerville, Laura Boscawen, is keen to go, too." For the supposedly delicate Laura was delighted to make up the party.

She did not say that Miss Bail was the lady she had in mind. Or that she intended to carry off her former governess on the excuse of a short holiday, install her in the sanatorium, and spend a few days seeing that she was comfortably settled before returning to England. Soon, thankfully, the conversation shifted to Justin and his studies at Harrow.

"He has not fitted in at school as well as Julian did," Arthur said. "Perhaps it is just that he resents having to live in the shadow of a successful elder brother, but he has the oddest ideas for a youngster. I would not be surprised if he suddenly informed me he wanted to change his religion, become a liberal, or even a socialist!"

Delia was startled. Why, Dr. Prynne was almost certainly a liberal, although surely a university don could not even secretly embrace socialist principles. Suddenly she was aware of the gap that yawned between her family and William's, and that there might be valid, if misguided, reasons why he had felt it better not to pursue their friendship. Illogically she felt angry with her father, defensive and admiring toward William Prynne. She would have it out with him, force him to admit that his motive for dropping her was ridiculous, and not worthy of his intellectual superiority.

She lay awake for hours that night. When the hall clock chimed two, she got up and sat before her mirror, the gas lamp showing flushed cheeks, feverish eyes, a tumble of corn-gold curls lying in heavy ringlets about her shoulders. "Delia, my girl, you're a fool," she whispered to her reflection. "You are no more able to put this impossible man out of your mind than poor little

Nattie was able to forget her Prince." It came to her that the Grandison girls were ill-fated to be offered suitable matches by the dozen, yet to yearn after men who were, for one quite good reason or another, unacceptable to their parents.

Somerville College was playing a hockey match with St. Hilda's, and Delia had been inveigled by Meg into accompanying the team to cheer them on.

Burdened with hockey sticks, towels, and other sporting paraphernalia, the party decided to take the tram, a prosaic means of transport that trundled through the town drawn by two sturdy horses. Delia was trying to banish William from her thoughts and concentrate on the delightful possibilities of her own team winning the match, but her mind kept turning back to this unusual man. Suddenly, as though thinking of him had conjured up his physical presence, a motorcycle appeared around the corner ahead of the tram, with a bespectacled figure crouched behind the handlebars. The rider, intending to turn right and pass them in the other direction, skidded, and the narrow front tire of his motorcycle became caught in the tram line. Both horses reared and he was almost crushed under their massive hooves. The tram driver was struggling to rein them in with a squealing of brakes when the motorcyclist just managed to avoid disaster by heading for the gutter. By the time the tram had come to rest, the handlebars of the bike were askew and the tire hopelessly ripped.

Amid cries of concern, the cyclist rose stiffly, ripping off his hat and goggles and shaking his fist at the startled and dumbfounded tram driver.

Recognition and relief simultaneously brought Delia to her feet. She climbed down and ran toward the still irate William, who was berating the tram driver.

"Didn't you see me coming? Taking up the whole road with that great juggernaut of yours! By Jove! My wheel will take some straightening, and I'm not sure if the whole frame isn't twisted. Well, I suppose I was lucky to get off so lightly myself." He flexed his left wrist, grasping it gingerly with his other hand and wincing. "Not entirely scot-free, but I was probably somewhat to blame," he admitted with a magnanimous grin.

"Sorry, sir, hope there isn't too much damage," the driver muttered, relieved that the accident had not been serious.

Delia hovered in the background, unable to resist a smile at

William's lightning-fast change of mood, which she already had cause to know well. "Why, Dr. Prynne, I never thought our next meeting would take place under such unusual circumstances," she said sweetly, stepping forward. "May I help you take your damaged steed to the garage, wherever that may be?" He stared at her, nonplussed.

"In Catte Street, as you very well know from Mr. Bradleigh," William said gloomily. "I shall have to push it all the way. Would you care to walk alongside me on the pavement?"

They set off under the indignant gaze of Meg, who was being carried northward in the tram.

"We seem fated to meet in rather odd places and conditions, Lady Cordelia," was William's rueful comment as he glanced up at his companion's cool, composed young face. "This time it is you who have me at a disadvantage, I admit."

"Please call me Delia. I feel that my title is like a thorn in your flesh and has caused you to decide that we could never be friends, although I suppose it is presumptuous of me to imagine that a distinguished scholar like you would wish to be friendly with a mere student, particularly a female student."

"You are very direct. And extremely articulate when it comes to making your point. I like that." His voice dropped. "You are right, Delia. Why shouldn't we be friends?" A frankly boyish grin illumined his features. Then he chuckled. "What a comical figure I must look."

She took advantage of his good humor and, bravely, invited him to be her partner at the Somerville dance.

"What on earth do you want with a clumsy oaf like me?" he inquired in apparent astonishment. "I assure you I have two left feet on the dance floor, and I am hardly accomplished in the art of polite conversation with young ladies and their swains."

"You are probably too modest about your prowess on the dance floor. Don't make it a reason to refuse." She raised her hyacinth eyes to his, and he gazed down into those deep blue pools, all resistance vanquished.

"I accept, of course. Indeed, I am flattered. Perhaps I may be able to reciprocate even before the date of the dance. Didn't we discuss a visit to Magdalen College? I believe I was going to give you a tour of the grounds. Shall we say Thursday afternoon, if you have no lectures? Ah, now, let me think. I'm giving a demonstration in the Daubeny, so may I suggest a rendezvous for tea at Ellistons in the High at about four o'clock?"

Time yawned interminably before her. Just a couple of days, but they felt like months, before she would see him again. To be with him was delight. To be far from him was desolation.

Responses she had never known before shook her with a sensuous trembling every time she remembered the touch of his hand on her arm, the glance of his piercing hazel eyes. Something deep within her stirred and came to life. She stared at her reflection, bare-shouldered in the revealing ribboned camisole before the mirror, and dropped her eyes, ashamed of their expression, liquid with yearning.

Why this man, and this man alone? she asked herself. She was twenty-two years old, and never before had she felt these pinpricks of desire. He was not of her world, not even of her generation. But his experience, his maturity, and his erudition only excited her more. Those young men who had declared themselves to be her slaves who had physically cast themselves at her feet, she thought of with contempt. But a secret fire burned in her veins at the thought of giving herself to William Prynne. . . .

The fashionable hour for afternoon tea found the best-frequented tea shop in Oxford crowded. Delia glanced about, as she stood by the cash register among a bower of potted ferns and palms, and could not at first see William. Then a tall gentleman at one of the best window tables rose, bowed, and came toward her. She felt her throat swell with emotion as William greeted her. Oxford was not London, of course, but she was conscious of many eyes on her and was glad she had dressed so simply, all in white.

A deceptive simplicity, though, for the gown had been created for her in Paris. The silken sheath, veiled in muslin scalloped and embellished with broderie anglaise, looked as though Delia's glorious body had been poured into it. The hat, a confection of the same material, seemed to float above, rather than rest on Delia's burnished chignon, which she had twisted into a figure eight low on her neck.

Soon he was escorting her along the High toward Magdalen College, telling her far more of its long and fascinating history than Miss Bail had managed to extract from her guidebook. He led the way through a passage that brought them into a formal garden bordering a gracious Palladian edifice illumined with many tall sash windows.

"This is the New Building, where most of the dons, other than myself, live. A non sequitur, since it was built early in the eighteenth century. Here we are on the edge of the grove, with our famous elms and the herd of deer I promised you."

The sight before them was an enchantment to the eye. Contrasting with the clipped greensward of the quadrangles, the undisciplined water meadows spread in a harmony of undulating knolls and dimpled valleys to the banks of the meandering Cherwell, where that river seemed to hesitate and take its wandering course at ease. Butterflies and bees were busy along Addison's Walk, which curved along the bank of the river.

"Shall we go down to the meadow?" William suggested. "There's a comfortable old log I often sit on when I need to think. It's good for a scientist to leave his experiments behind in the lab and worship the wonders of creation for a change."

Delia was startled by the revelation of this sensitive side to William's nature. As they walked in silent amity through the meadows, the grass catching at her trailing skirts, she wondered what accident had left his forehead scarred, then realized how much there was to learn about this man at her side.

As though William sensed her unspoken thoughts, he said abruptly, "I know little enough about you, except that you are Lord Grandison's daughter, and presumably had to fight some family opposition to become a student at Somerville. But you know nothing about me. I am not so ancient as I appear behind these gig-lamps of mine. I, too, am a fighter. In fact, it was when defending a principle I hold dear that a policeman's truncheon knocked me unconscious and left me with this ugly pucker over my right brow. Not to speak of damaging my eyesight. Ah, well, I was no Adonis beforehand, though I was a sportsman of some merit. But I was lucky enough not to be left groping in eternal semidarkness . . ."

He swung around to face her, running his hand through his hair nervously. "I don't know why I confide my early vicissitudes to you," he said jerkily. "It is not often I allow myself the luxury of bemoaning my fate. All this happened when I was a youth of seventeen, an impractical idealist who had not yet learned that a few sharpshooters among the ranks of the workers cannot succeed against the big guns of the industrialists."

"But what exactly did happen?" Delia asked, her heart filling with compassion.

He spoke without meeting her gaze. "You may find it a harrowing tale, my dear, softhearted Delia."

They had reached the riverbank. "I lived in Merthyr Tydfil then," he began. "My father, a poor doctor, was working for a mining company. He did his best for the men, I suppose, but he hated his employers, the despair of his patients, and the squalor they lived in. I had just won my scholarship to Oxford when the men became desperate and began to demonstrate against the mine owners at the pit head. My father told me to stay at home, but I joined them at the gate and carried one of their banners. The police had orders to disperse us, and I was . . . unlucky." His deep musical voice changed key. "Shortly thereafter, my mother died. A distant relative of my father's, Dr. Hughes, heard of our loss and he wrote, offering him a partnership in Criccieth. It was already a growing practice, too much for the men, as I came to call him, especially since he was more concerned with the saving of souls than of bodies. He had a friend in the same village, a wonderful preacher who had also just moved into the district, with a newly built chapel to preach from. Richard George, a man of great faith and great probity."

William's harsh expression softened at the thought of his first meeting with the inspired minister of God. "I was embittered by all I'd been through and intended to give up my scholarship. I'd wanted to help the working men, so unfairly treated, and now this, too, was rendered impossible. But it was Mr. George who brought me out of my despair, and—though I'm no chapelgoer yet—he inspired me to go on with my schooling."

They were passing into the shadow of a spreading beech tree, where the ground was piled deep with soft beech mast that deadened the sound of their feet. Drawing Delia on toward the riverbank, William continued: "Besides restoring my confidence, he introduced me to a good friend—his nephew, David Lloyd George, who was older than I by quite a few years. He'd just qualified in the law, left the office over at Portmadoc, and put up his own plate in Criccieth. Poor, with a widowed mother, he never doubted he had a dazzling future—not as a lawyer, but as a politician."

"Why, I've met Mr. Lloyd George!" cried Delia. "He's the coming man in the Liberal Party, isn't he?"

"A future Prime Minister," William said slowly. "I know it. Already at forty-two he's a member of the Cabinet. But I'll never forget what his friendship meant to me when I was still a youngster and he was just at the beginning of his career."

He took Delia's hand and gestured toward the fallen elm trunk that rested on a carpet of buttercups. "Shall we sit down for a while?" he suggested, shaking out a spotless linen handkerchief and gravely dusting off a place where she could sit. "May I request a favor? William's as bad a mouthful as Cordelia. Please call me Will. That's what my sisters call me at home."

As Delia seated herself, in a billow of white muslin, he stood back, his eyes caressing her. Delia bent her head in assent. She looked up and said in a soft, hesitant tone, "I should like that, Will."

Chapter 18

They sat together for over an hour, Delia listening intently to Will's stories of his boyhood and hearing how the difficult years soon gave way to the awards and accolades of his outstanding scholarship. He finished simply by saying, "You must inspire confidences, Delia. I've never spoken so openly to anyone before of my youthful struggles, my faults and failings. But I must admit that my sympathies are always with the underdog. In a political battle your father would be on one side, and I on the other. Socialism is a splendid idea. 'To each according to his need; from each according to his ability.' Why should the masses meekly accept that their destiny is, as the hymn tells them, 'the rich man in his castle, the poor man at his gate; God made them high or lowly, and ordered their estate'? What a monstrous aspersion to cast on the sublime nature of our creator!"

"I don't deny that. I begin to realize myself that it is unjust," Delia said slowly. She raised her head, and her blue eyes held a questioning appeal. "Was that why you decided at the concert we shouldn't meet again? But you yourself have risen in the world, accepted academic titles that make you the equal of any peer of the realm."

He shrugged. "There you have a point," he acknowledged

with the merest of smiles. "In any event, fate seems to have decided that we should meet again, and when you look at me like that, I can't resist you, my dear Delia."

The next day, after a night of sleepless slumber, Delia awoke to a world that was thrilling and new. She had never before known the delight of sharing the company of somebody like William Prynne. She was filled with pride, thinking of the man who had overcome the poverty of his youth and the physical disability inflicted on him by a brutal attack. And his towering intellect had triumphed over the snobs of the Oxford establishment. Now if he would only love her, nothing else mattered.

She lay in bed, luxuriating in the warm, flower-scented air that wafted in from the garden outside.

She did not even have to wait for the dance to see him again. He had asked her to take tea with him in the country that afternoon.

He arrived promptly, dressed informally in tweeds and carrying a long ash stick in his hand. His first words were hardly loverlike.

"I hope you're wearing stout shoes, my dear girl, for, if you agree, we'll tramp out to Headington instead of driving. On a pleasantly cool day like this, I'm sure you won't find it too tiring. What do you say?"

"I like walking," she replied equably, looking down at the smart little boots buttoned over slender ankles. "How do you do, William?" she went on, eyes dancing.

"Dammit! I forgot to ask how you did. Any now I'm swearing, which only shows how unaccustomed I am to escorting ladies, and how I gained my reputation as a rough, unpolished fellow in this tight, polite little world of ours. By the way, you look delightful, something I also failed to mention."

The walk to Headington was quite a bit farther than Delia had expected, but she lengthened her stride to match William's, and she felt the need to rest only during the last mile. He lifted her up to perch her on the crossbar of a stile and then leaned against it, crooking the handle of his stick to gather a clump of vivid blue speedwell that grew by the path, saying abruptly, "Not to be compared with your eyes. They are more azure than the bluest of flowers." Then, after a pause, he disclosed some exciting news.

"Did I mention to you the strangest thing about the new element discovered by my friends, Monsieur and Madame Curie? They named it radium, and even a small quantity in a darkened room emanates a faint blue light." He laughed. "Marie Curie is an absolute genius, but so typically feminine. A few years ago she said to me, 'When we isolate our radium, I hope it is a beautiful color. *Je veux que ça soit belle.*' Those words were spoken by the foremost scientist of the modern world."

"Yet she is a woman," Delia dared to comment.

"An exceptional case," he protested. Delia sensed that this was not the moment to air her views of feminine suffrage. But he was smiling at her gaily.

"I realize I have shrugged off my black mood. It must be your influence," he continued. "Shall we walk on?" He held out a strong hand to help her descend. "The truth is, I'm in a devilish state of depression. My experiments have reached a stalemate. Some process has been incorrectly carried out, but which one? I shall have to start again at the beginning, and that's very trying to an impatient chap like myself." He swung his walking stick to decapitate some nettles that barred their way. "You see, I'm on the track of something that I can honestly say will open up totally new fields to science. I have to produce irrefutable evidence before I can publish my findings. But I'm so near my goal! Well, let's forget it for the time being. Ah, this is Headington, and a very pretty little village it is. Let's take a rest here at the Fox and Duck."

While Will went inside the pub to order some ginger beer, Delia saw a group of familiar faces; Meg, Piers, Clive, and Laura Boscawen were heading toward the door.

Suddenly Meg spotted Delia and broke away from the group to confront her friend. "I had no idea you would go out alone with Dr. Prynne! What can you be thinking of?"

"It is entirely my business," Delia answered frostily. "And certainly none of yours."

At that moment Laura joined them, murmuring in piteous tones, "Come away, Meg. Please don't quarrel with Delia on account of anything I have said."

Delia gave her a questioning look, but before Laura could go on, Meg flounced off, remarking loudly as she went, "That Welsh wizard has turned her head. Who would have believed it of our prim and proper Delia?"

* * *

When she curled up in bed that night, Delia went over and over the unhappy incident in her mind. Perhaps to her friends she was "prim and proper," as Meg had said, but she longed to explore new feelings with Will, and—most of all—she longed to tell him that, with each passing day, she was growing to love him more. . . . Then she found her eyes full of tears and she drifted to sleep, clutching a damp handkerchief.

The moon was full on the evening of the dance. Rain threatened intermittently, and there was some uncertainty among the organizing committee about the outdoor decorations. However, the night, if cool, was fine. The girls, in their pale frocks, drifted about on the lawns like moths aflutter on the arms of their partners, laughing, fanning themselves, and yielding on this one occasion, at least, to a sort of frenetic gaiety.

Delia waited in the hall longer than most for the arrival of her partner. When at last Will appeared, her heart lurched in her breast. His tall, spare figure showed to great advantage in his well-cut tailcoat.

"I'm late, I know," he confided, straightening the white dress tie over his starched shirtfront. "Couldn't find my gold studs, and this confounded rag around my neck wouldn't make a presentable bow. I threw it out of the window, but a couple of freshmen passing by in the quad brought it back. One of them tied it correctly in a trice. It'll be all over the college tomorrow! Shall we dance?"

Disappointment enveloped Delia as Will led her to the dance floor. She knew she turned heads as they mingled with the other dancing couples, yet Will seemed not to notice how lovely she looked. But as they danced he drew her nearer, and his proximity filled her with an irresistible yearning to know more of his touch. A current of awareness was running between them, and she knew it was his lack of convention that so appealed to her. It was all she could do not to press her soft breasts against the hard chest so enticingly close. Her golden lashes fluttered, resting almost on her cheeks, then raised to take in the strong, clean lines of his firm mouth.

At last he said, almost casually, "I neglected to say that you are looking quite exquisite. Forgive me. Those milky opals, with their tantalizing sudden flashes of fire, are perfectly in tune with your beauty, Delia. They become you. There are hidden fires in your nature, too, I believe. Tell me that I am not wrong."

Delia caught her breath. Suddenly the whole room shimmered, the music soared. She thought, *I'm in love . . . in love with this strange, changeable, arrogant man . . .* "You are not wrong. . . ." she said softly, close to his ear.

The music ceased. Delia and Will stood face-to-face, alone, her hands lightly clasped in his. "You won't dance with anyone else, I hope."

"No one else has asked me—as yet," she said calmly, although her heart was racing. "I have given them little opportunity."

He tightened his grip on her hands. "But can I take it you grant my request?"

She nodded, color rising in her cheeks, daring at last to meet his intense look with her own.

Another dance began. As they glided around the floor she murmured in his ear, "Will, what lies you tell!"

"What do you mean?" he retorted sharply.

"Why, that you are an oaf on the dance floor," she explained. "In fact, you are an extremely accomplished dancer."

"Only when you are my partner. . . ." He swept her off into a lively polka, not pausing until she was quite breathless and insisted on sitting down.

They strolled outside, and he pulled out a chair for her at one of the tables, each set for six guests. He then went off in search of refreshments from the buffet table.

Seeing her alone, Meg joined her and then beckoned Piers, Clive, and an uncharacteristically silent Laura to take the other vacant seats. As Will reappeared Clive said deliberately, "May I have the pleasure of the next dance, Delia? Your company has been monopolized so far."

"I must stake my claim, too. You'll save the one after that for me?" insisted Piers.

"Lady Cordelia has promised me every dance, I'm afraid." Will's voice was decisive as he put down two dishes of sherry trifle on the table. "I'm sadly in need of practice, and she is taking pity on such an indifferent performer."

"Surely that is open to misconstruction, Dr. Prynne," Meg interjected silkily. "What would your fiancée, Miss Hughes, have to say if she knew that you were showing another young lady such marked attentions?"

There was a stony silence. Delia sat rigid in her chair, waiting for Will to speak, to deny Meg's assertion. But he said nothing to break the tense silence.

"Charmian Hughes is a lovely creature, I believe," Laura added hastily. "My mother has met her. But perhaps I am mistaken and there is no engagement? I remember my mother describing the fine betrothal ring you gave Charmian, and how proud she is to wear it."

"Mrs. Boscawen is perfectly correct. I did give her that ring." Will's voice was as cold and hard as flint. He turned his head slightly, and Delia met the full force of his stare. For a moment she looked deep into the compelling greenish-gold eyes, which neither denied his admission nor attempted to justify his behavior toward her.

She rose, saying with perfect composure, "I believe I will sit with Miss Maitland for a while. In case you decide to leave early, I'll say good night, Dr. Prynne."

Ignoring the others, she walked back into the drawing room, not seeing the expression of hopeless anguish that distorted Will's features before he, too, turned away and strode off rapidly in the direction of the gatehouse.

Chapter 19

Delia had no intention of sitting with Miss Maitland. Wrapped in her cloak, she ran as fast as she could away from the college.

As she let herself quietly in at the side door of Stonelea and crept upstairs, a slow anger began to build in Delia's heart. William Prynne had said nothing to suggest he was in love with her. But he had admired her so frankly and had openly sought her company. A deliberate deception on his part.

She turned restlessly in her bed for hours and then woke late, disturbed by the sound of voices in the hall. In a flash she remembered the events of the previous night. A dull ache settled in her heart. The romantic interlude with Will was over, and she never, never wanted to see him again.

The voices downstairs sounded familiar. Delia dressed hurriedly and was just pinning up her hair when a knock came at her door.

"Beg pardon, milady, but I've brought up your breakfast. Madam thought you would like it in bed. And there's a Miss Boscawen from the college to see you. Shall I ask her to wait in the drawing room?"

"No, thank you. Ask Miss Boscawen to come up, and bring a second cup. I hope there's plenty of coffee." She was composedly beginning her breakfast when Laura entered meekly.

"Do forgive me, Delia. How could I have been so tactless?" Laura began before the other girl could speak. "I should have had a word with you privately, especially as we are hoping to go to Switzerland together. I do hope I have not spoiled everything. . . ." She was close to tears. "Truly, Meg forced me to say what I did. She felt you ought to know about Miss Hughes, since Dr. Prynne was so very attentive to you, and that it should be mentioned in front of him—"

"What a storm in a teacup," Delia interrupted her. "Don't apologize, please. By the way, will you join me with some coffee?" Laura's habit of asking pardon for everything she said or did was not to be encouraged.

But the other girl persisted. "My mother has always told me that Dr. Hughes had two boys who died very young. Only Charmian survived. It must have been lonely for her. When Dr. Prynne joined the practice, she made William her hero and adopted his sisters as her own. Even if my mother was mistaken about the ring, there is certainly a close bond between that girl and our fascinating professor."

With great difficulty Delia steered her guest away from such reminiscences, assuring her that there had been no romantic attachment between herself and the tutor from Magdalen.

The conversation now turned to their tour together in Switzerland. Laura agreed with every one of Delia's plans, relieved that she had not ruined her chances of going on this wonderful trip with such an aristocratic companion.

It was not until the following day that Delia completed all her tasks, including writing a letter to Miss Bail and conferring with the travel agents. A chance encounter with Meg left the two girls more or less reconciled.

"I was very much at fault, dearest," Meg confessed, with every appearance of penitence. "Afterward, both Piers and Clive gave me a terrible tongue-lashing for daring to expose Dr. Prynne's duplicity in such an ungenteel way. They said I had made use of Laura, who knows no better. But, very much worse, I forced them to witness your distress, which was cruel of me. Can you believe I had your best interests at heart and forgive me?"

"Let's forget the whole incident," Delia answered obliquely. "The entire affair was blown up out of proportion to its importance. Don't think of it again. I assure you, I shall not!"

But Delia's pillow was wet with angry tears on that night, and for many nights afterward, yearning for the man who had so abruptly and shamefully walked out of her life.

After a leisurely couple of weeks spent journeying slowly via Basel to Bern and Interlaken, it was agreed that Miss Bail should be comfortably installed in a pension, while the two girls traveled on to make a steamer trip on the Lake of Lucerne. Laura was not surprised, on their return, to be told by Delia that the ex-governess had decided to take up residence in the bracing air of some mountain resort for the rest of the year, and she was quite exhilarated by the daring prospect of traveling back to England without a chaperon.

After counting her Swiss francs and setting aside a substantial sum for any possible emergency, Delia had decided they might stay their last night in the fashionable Drei Könige Hotel in Basel.

While they were packing, Laura confided: "I've so enjoyed our travels together, Delia. I will look back on this experience with fond memories in the years to come. I suppose what I'm trying to say is—well, I believe I will elect to be more cautious of Meg Douglas's influence in the future. Now that I know what a good-hearted and responsible person you are, it makes me even more ashamed of behaving so badly to you concerning Dr. Prynne. Oh, I know I'm explaining this very poorly, but I believe you really cared for him, Delia, and in spite of everything, I know he cared for you." She clasped her hands in agitation, twisting the little chain bracelet she wore. "There was a sort of magical aura around the two of you, as if you were meant for each other. Why did I let Meg persuade me to say anything to spoil it?"

"You didn't spoil it, Laura." Delia's voice was trembling. "I should be grateful to you for opening my eyes to the truth, although I wasn't at the time." She swallowed painfully. "It's all over, and I've quite put it behind me." But neither girl entirely believed this brave assertion.

On the morning of their departure Laura announced, "I dare say I'm homesick. I want very much to see Mama and all my friends. Is that childish of me?"

"No, quite natural!" Delia took the girl's arm. She had grown quite fond of Laura, particularly after their talk the night before.

* * *

The arrival at Victoria Station was pandemonium, for the Channel crossing had been bad, the steamer delayed in port at Calais for several hours, and the train timetables thrown into confusion. Delia was not expecting anyone to meet them, and both girls were amazed to see Mrs. Boscawen, wearing a most fetching new gown and hat, waiting at the barrier. Laura wept and threw herself into her mother's arms. In the babble of other passengers' greetings they could hear nothing. So, signaling the porter, who was trundling their luggage to bring it directly to the Grosvenor Hotel, Mrs. Boscawen led the way and settled them all in the lounge for tea.

Her reason for being in London, she soon explained, was that her husband, a wealthy wine merchant, had decided to attend some sales, and he had brought her with him for a treat. He had returned already to Wales but had allowed his wife to stay on for a day or two so that she might meet Laura, whose company they had sadly missed, and invite her charming companion to visit them in Portmadoc.

"How kind," murmured Delia, her heart racing as she thought of Criccieth, William's home, so temptingly near to Portmadoc.

"What other news is there I have forgotten, Laura dear?" Mrs. Boscawen prattled on. "So much happens, even in a couple of weeks! Ah, yes, a sad event. You remember only recently I wrote to you of my meeting that dear creature Charmian Hughes at a sewing bee? I thought it odd that she had been so long engaged to an Oxford don who was certainly in a position to marry when there was no impediment to the wedding."

The two girls sat as if turned to stone, Laura not daring to look at Delia's still face. "The reason was really not far to seek. It seems that since she suffered from rheumatic fever as a child, poor Charmian had a weak heart. She could never have married. Both the doctors knew this, and so did William Prynne and his sister Anna. But the girl was kept in ignorance, and the engagement was a delusion that made her happy and hopeful to the last. She died only a week ago, poor thing, just from the excitement of welcoming her William, as she used to call him, home from Oxford. I went to the funeral. She was buried with his ring on her finger, Anna told me. It was William's wish that it should be so. He has gone mountain climbing, they say, quite alone. But perhaps when he returns, we should invite him to dinner."

She stirred her tea vigorously, surprised that neither her daughter nor the other girl made any comment. The chatter of other returned travelers rose about them, until Delia broke the awkward silence.

"Since I am not expected at Grayle Abbey until my brothers leave school in July, and you have suggested it, may I accept your kind invitation?"

Chapter 20

Mrs. Boscawen could hardly believe her good fortune. She was to have the honor of sheltering a young lady of title under her roof! At once she was in a flutter of excitement. The rooms that had been reserved only for the day at the Grosvenor, so that the travelers might rest after their tiring journey, were taken also for the night. Mrs. Boscawen was longing to share with her daughter all the delightful stories of the girls' trip, and they gossiped together until after midnight.

Delia, curled up alone in bed next door, was at once elated and fearful. Perhaps Will did love her but had not felt free to tell her so—bound by a mockery of an engagement to a girl whose days were numbered, and for whom he felt no more than pity. He had deceived her, one must allow, but his motives were not ignoble. All was not lost, after all. Delia's lips curved into a sleepy smile as she burrowed into the soft pillow, imagining how she would introduce William to her parents, and whether he would shock them with his eccentricities, though he knew very well how to appear the suave gentleman when he wished.

The knowledge that every mile carried her closer to him made the tedious continuation of their journey by train easier for Delia

to bear. The sound of her companions' gentle, singsong Welsh
voices frequently lulled her almost to sleep. Occasionally a fragment of conversation roused her interest and she leaned forward,
elbows on the linen-covered armrests, listening intently, although
her eyes were still fixed on the open book before her.

"They're saying in Criccieth that Miss Anna has shed precious
few tears over Charmian's death," Mrs. Boscawen murmured,
leaning closer to Laura. "Gossip, that's all it is, I'm sure. But the
duties the two girls were supposed to share all fell to her, especially toward the end. And both doctors were doting on the poor
invalid, God rest her, while neither one of them noticed Anna
laboring away keeping house, taking messages, sending out the
bills. And Anna's too old to marry now, more's the pity. A spinster she'll be to the end of her days, at the doctors' beck and call,
and both the dear men too deeply involved with their patients
even to be grateful!"

"That's just hearsay, Mama," Laura said quite sharply, amazed
at her own presumption.

"Well, my love, such stories go around when a very young
person dies," her mother returned placidly. "We must remember
the Lord's word; in the midst of life we are in death. By the time
William Prynne gets back from his mountain climbing, he'll be
over the worst of his sorrow, or so we must hope. Goodness,
Laura, we're passing Harlech Castle, and that means we are close
to home. Put your hat straight, dear."

Delia was quite embarrassed to find how much trouble had
been taken to make her comfortable and entertain her on a grand
scale at Tanglyn, a spacious old house just outside Portmadoc on
the Beddgelert road. She was delighted to find Mr. Boscawen
both kind and exceptionally cultivated. He obviously preferred
the pursuit of his literary tastes to the conduct of his wine business, though he offered to give his guest a tour of the cellars and
bottling premises if she so desired.

Each day Delia sat gracefully among Mrs. Boscawen's potted
aspidistras and ferns, allowing herself to be questioned and admired by a stream of callers. The girl knew how much pleasure
her presence conferred. And although the room was over-
crowded, dark, and rather stuffy, she tried to give the appearance
of enjoying these sessions as much as the visitors did. When she
could escape, she often wandered with Laura into the library,

which was stocked with a fine selection of books, some on the most erudite subjects.

"Papa loves books, and these were all chosen by him," Laura volunteered. "I believe he would have wished to attend some university, if he had not been compelled to enter the family business. He is extremely well informed, you know, and not only on the subject of wine. But the love of learning is quite a natural trait on his side of the family. I owe my education to my aunt Dilys, Papa's sister, to whom I am eternally grateful. I was lucky she was so fond of me, for I would never have qualified to take a place at Somerville if she had not brought me on so splendidly."

Laura ran her fingers over the leather bindings of a fine set of Shakespeare's plays. "It was Papa who insisted that I should have my chance. He had faith in my intellectual powers, and having been deprived of the scholastic life himself, he was determined I should not be held back from it by Mama's qualms about my health. I'm not really less hardy than you are, Delia. I'm — smallundersized, some unkind critic might say. But Dr. Hughes has always insisted that I'm wiry, and he laughs at Mama's fears. He's a wonderful doctor, and if anyone could have saved Charmian, he would have done so. It's only owing to his devotion that she lived so long."

She moved to the door, remarking casually over her shoulder, "It's such a pretty old house, where the two doctors live. And you'll want to visit Criccieth, even if only to see the castle. Shall we drive over there tomorrow? We could take the pony and trap. I suppose my mother will be too busy, but someone should offer condolences on behalf of our family. And maybe William will have returned from his mountaineering," she concluded. With a conspiratorial smile, she left the room.

Secretly seething with excitement, Delia forced herself to run her eye calmly along the packed shelves. She noticed a volume of Elizabeth Barrett Browning's sonnets. Taking it down, she opened it to her favorite, which began:

> How do I love thee? Let me count the ways.
> I love thee to the depth and breadth and height
> My soul can reach, when feeling out of sight,
> For the ends of Being and ideal Grace.

She read on to the end, lingering over the last few lines:

> I love thee with the breath,
> Smiles, tears, of all my life!—and if God choose,
> I shall but love thee better after death.

She carried the book upstairs and laid it on the nightstand by her bed, to read again later, when the house was asleep.

The girls set out next morning in the trap, with a sturdy Welsh pony between the shafts.

"Criccieth is very different from Portmadoc," Laura remarked rather smugly as they approached the center of the village. "Such a sleepy little place."

The rutted surface of the streets made the trap sway dangerously, for there were no smooth paving stones here. Squat houses on either side gave the place rather a mournful aspect, their windows beetle-browed with overhanging eaves and closely curtained or shuttered like blind eyes. No whitewashed façades, intersected by oak beams, no thatched roofs as were to be found in villages near Oxford. Only dark gray stone and darker slate. The whole effect was slightly forbidding in aspect.

The property belonging to the two doctors was larger than most, the result of having joined two cottages together many years previously. An extension had been added at one side, with a glassed porch, and stables behind that. A polished brass plate fixed to the railings beside the gate announced that a surgery was held each morning between the hours of nine and eleven by Dr. Hughes, and another at six o'clock in the evening by Dr. Prynne, Sundays excepted.

As the girls walked up the path to the door, Delia noticed that the garden was denuded of flowers, probably all heaped in great bunches on the raw earth of Charmian's grave. At that moment she wanted to turn back. She should not have had the effrontery to seek Will out in this way. But the passion that consumed her demanded to know whether she had been right to imagine he loved her in return. If she might only have that precious knowledge, she would wait for him, no matter how long, with all the patience she could summon.

Laura's knock was answered by a charming young woman, very slender, in half mourning, who was clearly William

Prynne's sister. She had the same high-bridged nose, and the same cleft chin, although her eyes were milder. She greeted Laura affectionately, and she introduced herself to Delia as Olwen, the married sister Will had mentioned in Oxford. In fact, she explained, both she and her husband, Howel Griffiths, were expected for dinner that evening at Tanglyn. "So I'll have an advantage over the other guests, Lady Delia," she said lightly. "I have met you already. Please do come in, and I'll call Anna. Father and Dr. Hughes are both out on their rounds, and Will has gone off to the castle, but I'm sure they'll be happy to hear you came over to see us."

Delia's first impression of Anna was so chilling that she felt a shiver go down her spine. If Will's features were austere, Anna's seemed carved from marble. Her sandy coloring missed the charm of either brother or sister. While handing around a plate of rich, fatty Cree Cakes, which politeness demanded the guests must accept, she challenged Laura openly on her motive for calling on "this grieving household," as she put it.

"We always knew the marriage would never take place," Anna acknowledged, drawing a dark knitted shawl close around her thin shoulders. "That's why we kept the betrothal private. It was one of those ridiculous childhood games. When she was a little thing, Charmian was always pestering William not to marry anyone else until she grew up, and, quite in fun, he promised not to. No one else took it seriously. But once Charmian turned twenty-one, she insisted on having an engagement ring to show off, and she wanted plans made for the wedding. Knowing how weak her heart was, and not wishing to cross her in anything, William indulged her fancies, as he always did. She hung on to life longer than anyone expected, even her own father. Just sheer determination, he said afterward. But it wasn't fair to Will, Olwen, and well you know it. Where else could he look for a wife, bound to her as he was?"

Delia was surprised to hear such intimate matters aired before a stranger, and so, it seemed, was Olwen.

"Lady Delia can hardly be interested in our family sorrows," Olwen broke in, giving Anna a warning frown. "Neither is Laura, for that matter."

"That's as may be. But we must hope he'll stop fretting and remember that life is for the living. He must look about him for a healthy girl who'll devote herself to his comfort, in the good old-fashioned way. Not someone with a head full of notions about higher education." She gave Laura a significant glare.

"Anna, I'm surprised at you." Olwen cut her short. "Charmian is hardly cold in her grave, and you're playing matchmaker for Will. Let his grief go by first."

"His affection for her was only that of a brother, Olwen." Anna's tone was curt. "He's wasted the best years of his youth unwed. What girl could be expected to deal with the quirks and oddities of a bachelor four years past thirty? He's left it late enough, I say. But that doesn't mean he should fall prey to the first female who fancies her chances with him, who might be totally unsuitable." Her gaze lingered pointedly on Laura.

Olwen rose, now quite vexed at Anna's unfeeling remarks. "You should get out more, Anna, meet new friends," she said sharply. "The world doesn't revolve around Criccieth, you know, and there are other young men in it beside our William."

"And who's to do the work that's needed here?" Anna asked angrily. "Will you ride over on your bicycle more often and help me with the accounts? Or perhaps my dear brother-in-law would take the books into his office and deal with them there?"

Olwen appeared not to hear this, making much of ushering the two other girls to the door. "Please forgive Anna," she begged. "She's obsessed with the importance of William marrying and having children to carry on the family name. He's the only boy, of course. And she has had a hard time coping on her own. I should have helped her more; I see that now. You will forget those silly remarks, won't you? They must have sounded quite spiteful to you both." She lifted the latch, which creaked in protest.

"Will finds it hard to be in the house with Anna just now, I'm afraid," she went on. "As soon as he got home from the mountains, she began to speak in the most dictatorial way about his future. Father was furious, and Dr. Hughes was terribly hurt. I thought he might have gone out with his painting gear, but apparently he left it behind, and goodness knows what he's doing. Just brooding, I suppose. Have you seen any of his watercolors, Laura? They're framed and hung in Da's consulting rooms. Will does such beautiful work; he might have made a career as an artist. But today Anna says he took none of his paraphernalia, not even a packet of sandwiches."

William's artistic talent was another aspect of this singular man that Delia hadn't known, and which thrilled and intrigued her.

As they drove off, Laura's mouth trembled and the corners turned up reluctantly. "I can't help laughing," she confessed, "although it's so sad, and one ought to feel miserable. But Anna clearly thought that I had hopes of attracting Will Prynne's attention, and she never even glanced in your direction, Delia." She shook the reins and drove off briskly, turning the trap toward the sea.

"I believe I should call by for a chat with Betsy, my dear old Nanny," she said presently. "My mother finally persuaded her to retire when I went to Oxford. We'll go on a bit, and I'll drop you off at the beginning of the slope leading to the castle; you can climb the rest of the way. Feast your eyes on the view for the next quarter of an hour. I won't spend more than a few minutes with Betsy. Then I'll drive back, and if you're nowhere in sight on the path down, I'll come and join you."

Delia was happy to acquiesce, understanding Laura's tactful way of giving her an opportunity to meet Will without an observer. As she began to run up the slope, which was steeper than it appeared from a distance, her heart thudded unevenly. Above her loomed the great keep of the castle, still almost intact. She reached it, panting, out of breath. It was breezy up there at the cliff's edge. Her hair was loosened, and she tore off the confining ribbon, letting its golden masses spread out into a billowing cloud on her shoulders. As young as she appeared in her navy skirt and white linen blouse, she was all woman at that moment: lips moist, eyes sparkling. She looked around but saw no one.

Beyond the keep was a staircase leading to the battlements facing the bay, and at the top of the stairs she found an archway. She swayed back against the thick stone wall, suddenly giddy. Sunspots whirled before her eyes. Then through the arch she became aware of a tall, spare figure leaning against the crumbling parapet. She started forward, stumbling. A stone slipped under her foot and rolled toward him.

The man turned. His expression told her nothing, but those eyes caught and held her own. As if in a dream, she moved toward him. Was there pain in his face, or merely reproach? He did not seem surprised to see her.

"Delia, you should not have come," he said unemotionally.

She drew still nearer, silent. A fitful breeze lifted his hair, and

he turned his head away, as though he could not endure her beseeching gaze. Far below, in the silence between them, the waves
twice made their whispered advance and retreat on the bleached
sand of the headland shore.

"Why not?" she asked softly. "Laura invited me. And I have
become fond of her since we traveled abroad together. Did you
know that we have just returned from a trip to Switzerland?"
Delia was struggling to keep her voice steady.

"I have heard so. But that is not the reason you came to Portmadoc. You wanted to know why I treated you so unchivalrously,
without a word of explanation or apology."

"You did not owe me anything." Delia's chin was lifted
proudly, her eyes blazing with a steady blue fire. "I admit that I
was hurt. But that was my own fault, for presuming that a few
compliments meant more than you apparently intended. Later, I
heard the tragic reason why you have never chosen to tell me of
your engagement." She paused, uncertain how to go on. "How
you must have suffered in your loss," she faltered. "Please accept
my sympathy."

"Delia, we are playing with words." William was forced to
look at her now. "You must know that my promise to marry
Charmian was no true engagement. But it had to be honored as
long as she lived. It is ironic, though, that I hurried back to
Wales, unable to trust my own determination not to see or communicate with you again, to find her mortally ill. Thank God I
was with her at the end, for she was terribly afraid."

"But couldn't you have confided in me, Will? I would have
understood that for the time being, at least, we could be no more
than friends." Delia's eyes still implored an answer.

"We *are* no more than friends," he said forcefully. "My first
instinct was right. As soon as I knew who you were, I realized
that there could never be any other relationship between us. We
live in different worlds, Delia. Almost in different galaxies." His
voice dropped to a somber note as he whispered the last words.

Delia laid both hands on Will's arm where it rested on the
parapet, seeing the fist tighten convulsively. His muscles were
iron-hard under the soft woolen sleeve.

"What does that matter? If you feel for me even a fraction of
what I feel for you, surely we can find a bridge between us."

"There is no bridge. I despise your world for its hypocrisy and
the calm assumption by men of your class of their natural superi-

ority over the poor devils my father has spent a lifetime tending. He is just a shabby country doctor, more at home speaking Welsh to his humble patients in their own stinking hovels. Telling them that good air and good food might cure them when he knows how helpless they are to follow his advice."

"I acknowledge that inequalities exist. I'd be a fool to deny them. But we two alone cannot set the world to rights. Nor can my father. If it matters to you, Will, he would admire you. I am certain of it. An Oxford don since you were twenty-five; one of the youngest men ever to achieve such a distinction!"

"I see you have carried out some research, and have your arguments ready," he said sharply, drawing away from her touch. "But it is hopeless, I tell you."

Suddenly he seized both her wrists in the powerful grip of his right hand, making her helpless even to shrink away. "Look at me closely," he ground out. "Disfigured by this ugly scar. Condemned to peer through these wretched spectacles of mine since my eighteenth year." Then, with a shrug, he said, "Hardly the athletic Adonis your parents would expect! They will certainly object that I am already past the age for a bachelor to make a good husband!" he went on scathingly. "And what can you say of my character? Subject to unreasonable rages. My income? A few hundred pounds a year, and the use of some tolerable rooms. Your father will expect a suitor to offer twice as many thousands, a fine establishment, and a handsome marriage settlement into the bargain. My lineage? My escutcheon? I have neither. Do you think I paint too lurid a picture of my unsuitability to wed the Lady Cordelia Grandison? The only marvel is that you would yourself consider it," he concluded bitterly, releasing her wrists.

Delia had shaken her head violently at each of William's self-denigrations.

"I don't want to hear any more of this, Will. Please stop!" she protested. "Only tell me whether you love me. At the Somerville dance I thought you did. It was in your eyes when you looked at me, in your voice when you spoke. Was I wrong? Don't you love me at all?"

Again, more timidly, she stretched out to touch him. Gravely Will detached her imploring hand from his sleeve, his eyes all the time devouring every line of her lovely face.

"Truly, Delia, I am unable to give you the answer you want, or the future that your breeding, your beauty, and not least your brave spirit deserve. It was a misfortune for us both that fate threw us together a second time, and that, to my eternal shame, I found your company irresistible. Blame me. If I have made you unhappy, I ask your pardon. Just accept that whatever there was between us, Delia, is over."

"But I refuse to accept it." A few tears trickled down her cheeks.

Will took her trembling hands and tenderly kissed the inside of each soft palm; and then she was in his arms. He enfolded her, raining kisses now on the wide brow, the thick silky eyelashes, the rosy curve of her cheek, and then the soft moistness of her lips.

"It seems, my Delia, that you will not take no for an answer," he said shakily at last, holding her away from him. "Can you wait a little longer? I need time to think. My heart is bruised by that poor child's death, although it is true I did not love her; it's you I love."

Delia's face was glorious. This was what she had been longing to hear. . . . "You have said you love me. That's enough. Of course I will wait, as long as you wish. We could hardly announce our engagement immediately."

"Our engagement?" He caught a long strand of her hair and toyed with it gently as he spoke. "You are determined, then, my headstrong love. Give me the rest of the summer vacation to put this possibility of our marrying more in perspective. Please keep our secret until then. I'll write to you, so that when you return to Oxford, there'll be a letter waiting. Can you be patient for so long?"

At the Boscawens' dinner table that night, Delia was placed next to Olwen's husband, a pleasant fellow who spoke admiringly of Will's scholarship, of Anna's selfless dedication, and pityingly of Charmian. Over coffee in the drawing room Olwen complimented Delia generously on the excellent effect her friendship had had on Laura, who was blossoming at last into a radiant, confident girl.

"You look quite lovely, if I may say so," said Delia, returning the warmth of the young woman's smile. "I could never wear that subtle shade of green; but with your eyes and hair, it is the perfect choice." She felt strongly drawn toward this charming new friend.

* * *

"I should be happy to receive you in my house at any time, if you cared to come," were Olwen Griffiths's parting words when she left that night. For Delia was off to Grayle Abbey in the morning.

"But you'll stay with us again, won't you?" cried Laura, echoed by the heartiest of invitations from both Mr. and Mrs. Boscawen.

"I hope to visit you all again someday, and before very long!"

As the train pulled out of Portmadoc station Delia echoed that wish sincerely in her heart.

The returning traveler was struck anew by golden Grayle, in all its gleaming, opulent beauty. Walking through the Abbey's palatial halls, Delia saw clearly their sharp contrast with the low, cramped rooms of William's home. The vehemence with which Will had spoken of their differences stemmed directly from his distaste at the thought of coming humbly to meet her wealthy, high-born family. Her aristocratic background, which she had previously accepted as both natural and fitting, now became almost loathsome to her. It was unfair, of course, to blame Papa for raising an almost insurmountable barrier of wealth and title between herself and the man she loved. But for the first time in her life Delia found it a distinct disadvantage to be one of the much envied Grandison girls. Thoughts of William filled her with a sense of longing. But, she reminded herself severely, he needed time to think about the future, if indeed there was any future for them together. She had been wrong to go to Wales and try to force the issue. Now she must possess her soul with what patience she could muster while her fate rested in the balance.

Chapter 21

It was a chilly day with a hint of autumn in the air when Delia returned to Oxford. Her first impulse was to call at Somerville College in case the letter she expected from Will was waiting for her there. But the porter at the lodge only shrugged and said, "No, miss, I'm quite certain. There's nothing waiting to be collected." Swallowing her disappointment, Delia went on to Stonelea. But again she found no letter from Will. She was sure there had been some error; that he had not written at all was inconceivable . . .

Delia questioned Mrs. Bradleigh, who was delighted to see her and triumphantly produced some unimportant missives and a letter from Natalie. After unpacking her books, she sat down at her desk to read it, trying not to give way to her chagrin. Michael had accepted the offer of a short season in San Francisco, Natalie wrote. She adored the town, the fresh breezes, and their little house, perched on the side of a precipitous hill with a stupendous view of the bay. Michael's *Othello* had been rapturously received. All sorts of New York problems had been left behind on Fifth Avenue! This was a new start for them both!

* * *

The days dragged on until a week had passed with no word from Will. A note from Laura Boscawen, due herself to return to college any day now, was the final straw for Delia.

> W.P. went off to Oxford yesterday, Olwen told me. Looking very bronzed and fit from his climbing, and from a week on the Riviera, where he met Mr. Churchill recovering from some illness! He's put Charmian quite out of his mind, she thinks . . .

So, Will had returned to Oxford without making any effort to get in touch with her. He must have decided that they had no prospect of happiness together after all, and his silence was perhaps the kindest way he knew of indicating his feelings.

Delia, always so healthy and energetic, felt suddenly listless, and she was afflicted with such fierce headaches that she was quite prostrated.

Later that afternoon, when she was dozing in a half-feverish reverie, there was the sound of a sharp argument on the landing. A door banged on the second floor, and Delia thought she heard hysterical crying. Disturbed by the commotion, she got up, bathed her eyes, and went down the hall. Mrs. Bradleigh was holding an agitated conversation with Cook.

"She admitted it. No better than she should be, I'm afraid. I would not have thought it of Elsie, always so timid and meek, and especially seeing where she came from."

"That type needs watching, mam; still waters run deep, I always say. But what better can you expect from a charity brat? Still, the impudence, refusing to tell you who it was. Shall I try and get it out of her?"

"What is the matter? Was it Elsie I heard crying?" Delia asked, looking from one to the other of two flushed faces, both oddly conspiratorial and self-righteous.

"Nothing for you to be concerned about, Delia dear!" Mrs. Bradleigh came forward quickly. "That will do, Cook," she said, glancing at the other woman.

Cook retreated, muttering in sullen tones, "Just as you say, mam."

"How is the headache?" her landlady inquired. "A little better, I hope?"

Admitting that it was indeed better, and still perplexed by the scene she had just witnessed, she went back to her room.

Delia felt well enough the next day for an interview with Miss Maitland, to discuss the possibility of her being accommodated in Somerville. Looking very neat in a tailored green cashmere suit, and pulling on spotless white kid gloves, Delia set out for the college.

The interview went well. A room on Meg's floor in West Hall was empty, and it had the advantage of being particularly well furnished, as the previous occupant had left behind some luxurious items. Delia felt she would be comfortable in it, and her spirits rose a little.

Coming out of West Hall, she fell into step with her tennis partner of the previous term, and the other girl suggested they might walk down to the Cadena Café for coffee. They were not the only people seeking refreshment at the Cadena. Drawing back politely to let others enter the door in their turn, they came face-to-face with a portly and impressive figure whom Delia recognized at once from the Balliol concert—it was Dr. Herbert Warren, Chancellor of the College.

Raising his hat to the lovely young woman, he spoke most affably. "Come along, then, Prynne, since this young lady yields her place to us!" he said in jocular tones.

Delia started, seeing William standing just behind Mr. Warren. He came forward and opened the door wide as the older man vanished inside the café's portals. He gazed down at Delia with an expression of such desolate suffering that she felt cut to the quick by it. There was no option, however; she had to pass by, quite close to him, saying, "Thank you. Excuse me, please!" in a remote tone, as though he were a stranger.

When Delia left the café, she was fighting for composure. Will was clearly watching her as she made her way gracefully through the crowd, with no hint of the anguish she felt inwardly. She was little consoled by finding Margaret Douglas on the doorstep of Stonelea, waiting to offer her a bouquet of pink asters.

"Congrats, dear girl! I knew Miss Maitland would find a place for you!" she drawled, quite ready to curry favor with her titled friend if it might pay dividends.

When Elsie answered the bell for the two girls, she was

clearly unwell; she looked pale and upset, with dark circles under her tear-swollen eyes.

"I am worried about that girl Elsie," Delia observed later, when she was arranging her flowers in a vase.

Meg surveyed her pityingly with dark, penetrating eyes. "Delia, my darling, you are so naïve. The girl is in trouble, I don't doubt, of the usual sort that afflicts servants. She is, to put it vulgarly, in the family way and will have to be got rid of before it becomes more noticeable."

She reached over her friend's arm and pushed the stiff flower heads into place. "There, that's better. Only last year my mother had to dismiss her own personal maid without a recommendation and for the same reason. She was just turned out, with a month's wages, I suppose. I never did hear what became of her."

Delia was speechless. What on earth could a servant do in such dreadful circumstances? She would have to return to her family, in the most dire disgrace. As for the man responsible, he probably went scot-free.

"What a charming hat. May I try it on?" Meg had already abandoned the subject of Elsie's dilemma as uninteresting. She tried without success to get Delia to confide in her on many topics, foremost being the mysteries of her romance with William Prynne. But Delia would reveal nothing and was secretly pleased when Meg gave up her inquiries and rose to take her leave.

"I must begin at once to remedy my neglect of Ovid and Pliny." The Scottish girl sighed. "We have Moderations ahead of us, remember. The exams seem far away now, but next June will soon come around."

When Meg had gone, Delia curled up on the sofa to await the luncheon gong.

What is the matter with me? she wondered. *I have what I always wanted. A room in the college, just like other students. My academic work is not unsatisfactory. And I've helped to set Miss Bail on the road to recovery.* But remembering William's agonized glance at her earlier that day, she knew she wanted, more than anything else in the world, to make William love her. Delia closed her eyes and surrendered to a wave of self-pity, but it was not in her nature to do this for long. *There are those who suffer far more than I do,* she told herself, and rising to go to luncheon, she silently vowed to help young Elsie out of her predicament. For, if she didn't, who else would?

Mr. Bradleigh was absent from the table, and Delia took the opportunity to prepare Mrs. Bradleigh for her own imminent departure. The lady became tearful at once, for she had begun to think of the young lady almost as her own child. "I don't know what Eustace will say," she moaned.

So anxious was Delia to settle down to her studies that she was quite surprised to find it was teatime when Elsie brought in her tray and set it down with a great clatter. The maid backed toward the door, murmuring apologies.

"Do stay a moment, Elsie," Delia said calmly. "I've been wanting to speak to you all day." Elsie wiped her damp hands on the corner of her apron. Delia closed the door and pointed to a comfortable chair. "Sit down, please," she said in such a gentle manner that the girl knew she need not fear to sit in the presence of her ladyship.

"You are in some sort of trouble, I know. I couldn't help overhearing a few words Mrs. Bradleigh had with Cook. What is it?"

"The usual sort, for a girl like me," Elsie replied dully. "I'm three months on in the family way, and I can't pretend I'm not. Fainting, you see, and bringing up me breakfast into the kitchen sink. Cook knew weeks ago, and now she's spoken to the mistress, and I'll be sent back to the workhouse, I suppose."

"The workhouse—is that where you came from? How old are you, Elsie?"

"I'm fourteen, just a few months past. That's the age they send us out to work, if we're strong and someone will take us."

"Are you an orphan, then? You have no parents who would take you in, perhaps even look after your baby?"

"Gawd, no, miss—milady, I mean. My mum was put in the workhouse younger than me, for the same reason. Only thirteen, she was. She's never been out since, though I believe she could have found someone to marry her, for she used to be pretty, as well as I can tell from a distance. We're not let to meet, you know. It isn't allowed."

Delia had the sensation of standing on the edge of an abyss—the abyss of her own ignorance, for there was something wicked and vile that she was about to learn, and she did not entirely want to hear it.

"You mean, your mother had a love child by some man who

would not marry her?" she questioned hesitantly. "And at the age
of thirteen she was judged a moral reprobate and virtually impris-
oned for the rest of her life?"

"Don't know about reprobates and that. And I wasn't exactly
a love child. It was her own dad who forced her to it; she told me
all about it the only time we ever got to have a chat. She did say,
but no one listened. Hated him, she did. Like I hate the man what
did this to me. But it's no use complaining, 'cos who cares. It's
my fault, Cook's forever telling me. I've made me bed and must
lie on it."

Elsie began to weep—silently at first, but soon she was covering her face with her apron and shaking, with long, wrenching
sobs.

"Who was it, then? Is it some boy who might be induced to
marry you, if he could afford it, and give the baby a name?
Perhaps I could persuade him." Even as she spoke Delia knew
how feeble was this hope, but if she could earn the money or sell
some of her possessions . . . it would be the least she could do to
help this child.

Elsie got up, sniffing and red-eyed. "No, there's nothing to be
done, miss. When I get clumsy-like, and not fit to be seen about
the house, they'll take me away. I'll be lectured and preached at,
and put to scrub as long as I'm able. After the babe comes, I
won't see it again. Then it'll be the workhouse laundry for me,
most likely, for the rest of me natural life."

"But that's monstrous and needlessly cruel! Oh, I can't believe
such things really happen! I'll do better than that for you, Elsie,
and your baby. You can count on it. Try not to worry too much,
and keep cheerful. Moping will do you harm. I'll think of a plan,
I promise you."

Elsie's jaw dropped slackly, leaving her mouth agape. But
Delia thought she saw a flicker of hope in the girl's dim, red-
rimmed eyes as the dejected scullery maid nodded before slipping
out of the room.

Delia sat on by the desk, her head bowed. She had made up
her mind to fight for the rights of women with all her strength,
and if she could not have the love of her life, she would take
no other husband. She would give everything of her heart, her
mind, and her strong young body to the cause of women's
suffrage.

* * *

The organizer at the headquarters of the Oxford branch of Suffrage for Women regarded her eager young visitor with some surprise. "Do I understand, Lady Cordelia, that you attended some of those very interesting meetings held at the home of Miss Bail last year? One of which, you tell me, was addressed by Mrs. Pankhurst herself?"

"Yes, that is so," Delia answered swiftly, taken aback by her interrogator's air of disbelief. "You see, Miss Bail was my governess for many years, and it was she who encouraged me to come up to Oxford rather than pursue the usual social round."

"Ah, now I understand." The woman's aggressive tone softened. "So you wish to become a member here . . . May I ask you to take this leaflet, which describes our aims and activities? If you feel yourself in sympathy with them, please attend our next meeting. We're holding a public discussion, and sending out handbills, toward the end of the month. Perhaps you will distribute some of the bills yourself, and be sure to get there early!" Delia promised to do so and emerged fired with enthusiasm.

A visit to the bank made it clear that she had already totally committed her income, and she knew some other course of action would be needed in her determination to save Elsie. She thought fleetingly of William's fight to help the miners in his hometown, and she could not completely banish the thought from her mind, even when she stood in the jeweler's shop, holding the black velvet case containing her opal necklace, waiting to see the manager.

"Do you really wish to sell the necklace?" the man asked smoothly. "That would certainly be a pity, madam. It is quite unique. But, unfortunately, we have little call for such pieces."

"I inherited this from my godmother." Delia ran the ribbon of jewels, flashing sulkily in the gaslight, through her fingers. "I had been hoping to pledge it—pawn it, I suppose I mean. Then I could redeem it later."

"I'm afraid we do not offer that facility," the man said regretfully. "I could offer you one hundred pounds."

"I'll accept it," Delia said swiftly. Somehow it assuaged her growing sense of guilt to provide for this one victim of a callous society by selling her dearest possession.

A full twenty-four hours passed before Delia could waylay Elsie on the stairs and impart the good news. Having explained

that she had just received an unexpected gift of a hundred pounds
for which she had no immediate use, the Lady Cordelia was
instantly believed. What was less believable to Elsie's mind was
that this sum was hers to draw on when she became unable to
work. That she might lodge respectably and give birth to her
baby in comparative comfort had been a dream beyond belief.
Her gratitude was almost pitiable as she caught Delia's hand and
tried to kiss it, succeeding only in drenching it with tears.

Late that night Delia sat up reading. Presently she heard a
timid knocking on her study door. She got up, put on her heavy
satin robe, and went to answer it. Elsie slipped in without invitation, scrawny and pale as a ghost in a tattered cotton wrapper.

"It's secret, what I've come to show you, and I'd decided not
to, for the master would kill me if he knew. But now that you're
going to help me, out of the kindness of your heart, I've made up
me mind that one good turn deserves another."

"Sit down and explain what sort of good turn you can do for
me." Delia drew the pathetic little figure down beside her on the
sofa.

"I wanted to give you this. It's yours, anyway, seeing as it
came addressed to the Lady Cordelia Grandison." Elsie produced
a crumpled piece of notepaper. "He opened your letter, see. The
master, I mean," Elsie gabbled on. "I saw the post come, and the
writing, and I guessed it was from *him*. Him what took you to
the concert and made the master so jealous. I hid at the top of the
basement stairs and looked through the glass pane in the door. I
saw him read it, then twist it up like it is now. He went into the
study with it, and later, when I was in to empty his wastebasket,
there was the pieces of the envelope all torn up. But not the letter.
Found it in the drawer where he keeps his stamps, pushed to the
back."

Delia smoothed out the paper, trying in vain to decipher the
letter by wavering candlelight. The soft golden glow brightened
and steadied, and William's nervous, spiky handwriting leapt to
her eyes. She read slowly, almost voraciously. The writer had
begun in Welsh and underneath that continued in English:

Melyn cariadigyd, which means "my lovely golden
sweetheart." I have thought very long and seriously about
our future, and whether we have any hope of being happy
together. There are drawbacks enough to daunt two spirits

less ardent and courageous than ours. But my dearest, together we are capable of conquering all difficulties—that is, if you are still prepared to put up for a lifetime with such an unreasonable, ill-tempered, self-centered man as I know myself to be. I am prepared to admit that I do not think I can live at all without you. Will you marry me, Delia? I shall do my best to assure your parents that you are not entirely throwing yourself away. Accordingly, I lay my heart at your feet.

Please give me your answer as soon as you receive this letter. If, of course, you have come to your senses sufficiently to realize what a poor match I would make, ignore it. Do not trouble to reply.

Ever your devoted,
Wm.

Chapter 22

A great tide of happiness rose within Delia, washing away all the searing humiliation of believing herself jilted. Her heart raced and she went to the open window for some air. The hour of midnight sounded from the clock towers of Oxford. This was the beginning of a new and wonderful day.

It was Delia's first impulse to dress at once and run through the quiet moon-washed streets of the town to rouse William; her second urge was to hammer on the door of the bedroom where Eustace and Bessie Bradleigh slept peacefully and demand to know why Mr. Bradleigh had purloined her letter. But already she knew that thwarted desire and jealousy must have prompted the spiteful act which had nearly ruined her life.

She turned to Elsie, who was sitting slumped awkwardly in her corner. Delia's eyes were soft as blue velvet. "I can never thank you enough. I'll make it up to you, Elsie, you'll see. Now, go to bed, and don't worry that you may be blamed if Mr. Bradleigh finds the letter gone. I'll never allow that man to terrorize you again."

Elsie heaved a great sigh. "That's a weight off me mind. I was worrying something chronic. But I shan't anymore—not if you'll stand up for me, milady." She slipped out the door with the ghost of a timid smile.

249

Delia extinguished the lamp and stretched out on the sofa. She lay there, planning how best to approach Will and explain that her apparent rebuff had been engineered by his enemy. At last she hit on a plan that satisfied her, and she slept fitfully as the light in the quiet little salon grew stronger and the dawn chorus in the trees outside greeted a momentous day in her life.

Delia approached the porter's lodge at Magdalen College the next morning. The young lady claimed she had a message for Dr. Prynne and wished to deliver it personally at his lodgings. She remained outwardly quite unconcerned as she rang the bell, despite her inner trembling. Will's servant answered the door wearing a baize apron. It was early for callers, and Jenkin, the little Welshman who had served Dr. Prynne since he had moved into rooms in the college, was most curious about the lovely vision in green who asked that her message be delivered to Dr. Prynne. She wished him to know that she could be found by the river's edge in the deer park if he cared to seek her there.

With a smile and a graceful inclination of her head that set the feather in her hat aquiver, Delia turned away and began strolling toward the open meadow beyond the college buildings.

At the river's edge Delia sat down on the log where Will had first asked her to use his name. Gray and silver ripples mingled and danced on the gently moving water. She had not long to wait. Impatient footsteps sounded near, then nearer. William came toward her with a look gradually turning to cautious delight.

"Delia. My letter. There is an answer, after all?" His voice trembled with emotion. "I had ceased to hope." He took her hands and raised them tenderly to his breast.

"I only just received your letter, Will." Her voice was trembling, too. "It was put away, by mistake, and forgotten." Her head dropped shyly and her lips sought his fingers, clasping her own.

"To find you sitting here on the same log where I first let you guess that I loved you. . . . Golden girl, my golden girl." He lifted her chin so that her eyes must meet his as she came to her feet. "What is your answer, then? Will you have me, after all?"

She began to laugh a little shakily. "I'm rather a poor bargain myself. One of those ardent and all too articulate feminists you detest. Strong-minded, self-willed, and very different from the sort of meek, adoring little Welsh girl your father and sisters would pick out for you. . . ."

He stopped her protests with a kiss, which left her breathless. "We have chosen each other. Nothing else matters. I will strive for your sake to seem worthy in the eyes of the Grandison family. No doubt you'll be greeted with awed wonder by mine. Only, if I may ask one favor, may we postpone the announcement for a while? Charmian's death is so recent . . ."

"Of course. Let us leave it until Christmas . . . just a precious secret between our two selves." *Perhaps Natalie will be home by then,* thought Delia. What joy it would give Delia to meet her darling sister with this happy news. As they slowly made their way through the meadow, every leaf and blade of grass was gilded now with morning light. Will's firm body was pressed against her hip, brushing her breast as he reached over her shoulder, the better to encircle her waist. On the promise that he would escort her to a concert at the Sheldonian Theatre within a few days, she unwillingly allowed him to take leave of her.

"I have just one more series of experiments to finish," he promised. "Afterward, we can meet every day if you wish. But, until then, we must act circumspectly." He immediately demonstrated the impossibility of doing so by kissing her ardently in the quadrangle arch, oblivious of any passerby who might observe them.

Her face flushed with happiness, Delia ran most of the way home.

Elsie was busy polishing the brass door knocker at Stonelea. Delia paused on the step, beaming with joy. "I've just seen Dr. Prynne and put everything right between us. Thank you for giving me his letter, Elsie. You're a brave girl. The master hasn't been after you about it, has he?"

A subtle change, almost a hardening, took place on the girl's face. "No, milady. He's done me enough harm already . . ."

The truth struck Delia like a blow. Remembering the night he had come into her room and made advances on her before leaving in a rage, it was now startlingly clear that Eustace was responsible for Elsie's condition. She knew she would have to confront the culprit directly and force him to admit his guilt. Delia watched carefully for her chance.

That evening, when Mr. Bradleigh disappeared into his study, she paused in the hall, then entered without knocking.

Eustace looked up, saying, "Who is it? Have you brought me my evening toddy, my dear?" Seeing that it was not his wife, his look of pleased surprise changed to one of alarm when he noticed

Delia's implacable expression. She closed the door calmly behind her and came forward into the ring of lamplight. "Ah, Lady Delia," he said uneasily. "You wish to consult me about something?"

"Not at all—I came to warn you," she said sharply. He cringed at the knife-edge of her voice. "I know about Elsie's condition, and that you are responsible. Your wife has not yet mentioned it to you, but she soon will. However, I'm sure you already suspect that the girl is with child, as a result of your sneaking up to her bedroom and making use of her poor little body to slake your own passions."

"The girl is to blame. She suggested it—" Eustace began feebly.

"In the same way that I suggested I wished to submit to you, I suppose," Delia interrupted coldly. "She says you struck her, threatened to throw her out of the house if she struggled, and used her vilely, on repeated occasions. I believe her, and so will Mrs. Bradleigh, when I have occasion to tell her of it." Delia was improvising wildly.

"For Christ's sake, don't do that!" Eustace pushed back his chair, startled out of his spurious refinement. "There's no need to cause trouble, is there?" he whined. "Not over a chance-got slut from the workhouse . . ."

"She is a human being, for all that, and was a virgin, a decent girl, before you stole her innocence," Delia said forcefully, determined to hide the sick horror that nearly overwhelmed her. "When your wife mentions that Elsie is in trouble, and speaks of sending her to the authorities to dispose of, say that there is no hurry. As long as she can work, you wish her to stay. You would get no other slave so cheaply. I shall make arrangements to have her cared for when the time comes, which will not be until after I have left here. And do not dare to abuse her or to interfere again between myself and Dr. Prynne. I found the letter he sent, and which you purloined. Yes, you start and shake as if you had the palsy. I looked in your desk. I rifled it, in fact. If it comes to my knowledge that you have spoken ill of Dr. Prynne or myself, I will tell him of your disgusting behavior, and he will undoubtedly thrash you as you deserve. Say that you understand me, Mr. Bradleigh, for your company is loathsome to me, and I don't wish to prolong this conversation."

There was an agonized silence, during which Eustace clutched his chest and drew a sobbing breath.

"I do understand, milady, and . . . and I beg you won't ruin me," he said at last in a shaky voice.

"Good night, then." She swirled her skirt around with a dry, angry whir on the carpet, and then stormed out of the study. But halfway upstairs she paused. She hoped Will would feel as she did, that something must be done to save women from the vile fate to which society condemned so many, unheard and unpitied, like hardened prostitutes.

Later, it struck her that the act that had taken place between Eustace and the terrified kitchen maid Elsie would also be the culmination of her own wedding night with William Prynne. But he circumstances would be so different; the love and tenderness between them was of such rare delicacy. Yet his eager kiss had bruised her lip only that morning. A faint sense of foreboding— realization that physical love must be something more than the mystical union girls like herself were led to understand—clouded her anticipation. And, strangely, it stirred still further the mael- strom of erotic sensation and emotion caused by the thought of her initiation into the mysteries of marriage.

Suspecting that Will had no flair for arranging a meeting in complete privacy without flouting convention, Delia put her own mind to the problem. She went in search of Laura and told her friend in the strictest confidence that she and Will were to be married, but their engagement, for the time being, was to be a secret.

Laura was delighted, and quite shamelessly suggested that they should call on Will in his rooms together, on the principle that one girl would chaperon the other. Laura could occupy her- self happily for many hours making charcoal sketches from the windows of Will's study while the lovers met privately in another room.

They began the long walk to the High immediately. Like any other girl in love, Delia desired to know every detail of Will's past life and his achievements.

Laura had little to relate, since she considered anything to do with science dry as dust and uninteresting. She did remember that old Dr. Prynne had been active in campaigning with Lloyd George for charitable causes, and she went on at some length about the stories she had heard of the men who worked in the local slate quarries, struggling for their rights.

"What else do you remember?" Delia prompted. "How did Will look in those days?"

"Very distinguished. Half the girls in Portmadoc were in love with him, but he took not the slightest notice of females, other than to treat them politely, as he did his sisters. I was only a child then; I believe he was self-conscious because of his reading glasses and that scar on his forehead. But, in a way, they made him more attractive, such an unusual-looking young man."

They were approaching the Carfax by this time, and another five minutes walk would bring them in sight of Magdalen Bridge. "Another thing I recall," Laura went on. "Hearing my mother tell Da what a devoted son William Prynne was. My papa reckoned the fellowship and his lecture fees might together amount to no more than five hundred a year. But even then he was carrying out experiments in his spare time, frequently working fifteen hours a day, old Dr. Prynne suspected. Yet William sent home more than half his salary."

Jenkin's nerve was considerably shaken by answering the doorbell to find this time not one, but two young ladies on the doorstep. He admitted them rather hastily, imagining that the dean's lady, who had been paying a call opposite and was just leaving, might turn around at any moment and see the unlikely sight of a pair of girls, quite unchaperoned, bearding the bachelor don in his private apartment.

William himself was delighted, as he said with a twinkle in his eye, to welcome an old family friend, Miss Boscawen, and her companion, the lovely Lady Cordelia.

Laura settled down at once to making a sketch of the quad, seated in the drawing room, while Delia and Will went into his cheerful cluttered study. A canary chirped happily in a birdcage by the window. Books were piled everywhere, as well as lining the walls, on the desk, upon chairs, even on the floor. A beautiful mahogany box stood open on the windowsill, revealing a fine brass microscope lying on top of scientific journals piled so high, they threatened to tip it over.

On the wall nearest the window, Delia noticed at once that pride of place had been given to a plainly framed draftsman's print, an exploded drawing of a motorcycle engine with the legend PANTHER—TWO-STROKE ENGINE DESIGN. His goggles were draped over one corner of the frame.

"Don't blame Jenkin for this muddle," Will said apologetically, drawing Delia close. "I only let him in once a week or so to tidy up for me. Even that is purgatory. The idiot sorts my papers, and I cannot find anything I need afterward." She had taken off her jacket and unpinned her hat. He ran his hand caressingly over her burnished hair. "What gave you the splendid idea of bringing little Laura Boscawen with you?"

"She is the only person who knows the truth about us, although it is bound to become public knowledge if we are often seen together outside your rooms." Delia looked remorseful. "Would that be so terrible? The announcement need not be made just yet, but I could not bear to live so near you and not see you every day—at least, nearly every day."

"You go too fast, *cariad*. Before we speak of any precipitate announcement, how do you imagine we shall live? I think you should know a great deal more about me, and consider the hard facts," William began seriously. "My salary as official fellow here is three hundred a year, and as science tutor I receive a further two-fifty, making a princely total of five-fifty a year. I dare say you are in the habit of spending as much on dress alone. Marriage for the younger dons is frowned upon, and not permitted at all without a college order—a formality, in your case, for the dean would only be bewildered to guess how I had won such a prize as yourself."

Delia looked mildly offended. "What slaves we are to the age-old customs of this university. Any woman you chose for your wife would be acceptable, even to the chancellor, I'm sure. For I suspect you have never been easily pleased by girls, Will. As for my dress allowance, I can't say what my clothes cost, for Papa used to pay all my bills. But since I've been at Somerville, I have paid my own way, and I have such a tiny income that I have not bought one new frock. Those I had were more than enough and will last me for years yet, I dare say."

"You always look enchanting, my darling, though I am no expert on what ladies should wear. Which brings me to another moot point. Am I of good character where women are concerned? Your father is bound to ask this question."

"Now you are being ridiculous, Will. The story of your engagement does you nothing but credit. Papa will understand and commend your conduct—"

"But I am no saint, either," Will broke in. "In my youth there were a few episodes of which I should perhaps be ashamed. There was in particular a lady in Oxford, whom I will not name to you, since you will meet her socially. I have always been discreet; one owes that to a woman who is overkind." He laughed suddenly. "What a prig I must sound. But are you shocked?"

"Why should I be? I am glad you are not without experience —so long as I am certain these old flames are now extinct. Heavens, I feel quite agitated; but it is only because I love you so much that I feel jealous and have such a ridiculous desire to put my arms around your neck ... like this ... hold you close, and never let you go."

There was silence in the study for a long minute while they kissed and Will murmured words of endearment into her ear, then returned to fasten his lips firmly to hers. At last she released him with a happy sigh.

"The next question is, where shall we live?" Will went on thoughtfully. "So certain was I of your acceptance that I spent my first few days back in Oxford looking at houses—both suitable and wildly impossible. I decided on one, which is indeed wildly impossible, as the perfect setting for you. Even the name is charming; at least I thought so. Sundial House. It is out at Folly Bridge, and it is to be had very reasonably. Rather far out, larger than we need, and quite impractical. You will love it, Delia, as I do, when you see it. The house is old, tall, and built of a rosy brick in a sort of castellated Venetian style mixed with Gothic. Every room has a pleasant vista of woodland or water, or both. It stands on an island between two rivers, close to a lock. It is not, as one might expect, damp, and the garden is very private. There is a greenhouse with some sturdy vines planted outside, which are led inside through a hole in one pane of glass, roofing it with its grapes every summer. Also, there is a coach house, able to accommodate my motorcycle, a small motor car, since that will provide a convenient form of transport for both of us; and that will still leave a goodish space vacant for me to fit up an excellent laboratory..." He paused, out of breath.

"You see, I was so sure you would have me. You may imagine how wounding to my self-esteem was the shock when you did not reply to my letter. Thank God a miracle has happened, and I have not lost you, after all!" He took Delia in his arms and bent his long legs to sink into an armchair, cradling her in his lap. "You don't ask where the money will come from to buy this white elephant of a house, which only an eccentric like myself, and the woman who condescends to love him, would consider?"

Delia shook her head.

"I have been awarded a prize, known as the Kimberlake Award, for a paper on the nature of the nucleus. To be exact, the title is: 'Energy Contained in the Nucleus of a Radioactive Atom.' That will sound like gibberish to you, I suppose. However, I am to receive one thousand pounds. More than enough to pay for the house. We shall be able to furnish all the rooms on the ground floor, and possibly two bedrooms upstairs, for a start."

Will was extremely persuasive. If Delia liked it as much as he did, he intended to buy the property at once.

Delicious vistas opened before her. With Laura as a willing and indulgent chaperon, they would visit the house at Folly Bridge, choose the colors for redecoration, prowl sale rooms to pick out furniture, order curtains to be made. She would tackle her studies with renewed vigor. Whether her own parents and William's father would welcome the marriage seemed quite unimportant.

Eventually the patient Laura knocked on the folding doors to announce that she was expected for lunch by her landlady promptly at one.

There were reasons for Delia to feel relieved when the discussion about their future had to end for the moment. Neither of them doubted that, as the daughter of a Marquess, she would be judged a suitable wife for any don. But if she were to appear in public as a fully fledged member of the Oxford branch of Suffrage for Women, her acceptance by the university authorities might be seriously jeopardized. Will knew nothing as yet of her intention, and she suspected his sympathy with the cause was, at best, halfhearted. Delia hoped to follow her convictions. But she realized, with a sinking heart, that they might cost her dearly. She might sacrifice the assent to their marriage, which Will was taking as a foregone conclusion.

Nor had she mentioned Elsie's condition, and that she had sold her opal necklace to provide funds for the girl's support. She could not see her lover accepting a maid with an illegitimate baby at her breast as the sole domestic servant in their future home. He would want to keep Jenkin, with some capable older woman, perhaps one who lived locally and came in daily to cook and do the rest of the housework. Besides, the girl's shame would be talked about, for in such a small community there would be no concealing it. The ideal solution would be to send Elsie away from Oxford to some other town where, hopefully, she could start a new and happier life.

These considerations acted a little to dim Delia's state of euphoria. Nevertheless she felt her cup of happiness filled to the brim. All that was lacking was the presence of Natalie. And even that joy was now promised to her. Before her next meeting with Will, when he escorted her to the Sheldonian, the joyful news arrived that Natalie and Michael had taken the train back from San Francisco to New York, and they expected to arrive, by the first available sailing, in England well before Christmas.

Chapter 23

Meg insisted that Delia should give a cocoa party to celebrate her installation in West Hall. These gatherings often continued until a late hour, long after all the milk and cocoa powder had been used up and the fire had gone out. With their hair down, and wearing dressing gowns over their petticoats, the students discussed every aspect of education, and they set the world to rights among themselves.

After the last guest had departed, Meg lingered on. "That was great fun. Aren't you glad to get away from the stultifying company in Woodstock Road?" she questioned, gathering up some china mugs and plates.

"Very glad, indeed, although I have grown quite fond of Mrs. Bradleigh. Her husband is a most unpleasant man, and I intend to avoid meeting him in the future."

"Didn't he cause a great deal of trouble between yourself and Dr. Prynne?" Meg insinuated, making herself busy with the tray. "Laura tells us his fiancée has died, poor girl. If he is as struck with you as we all supposed, it will be much easier for him to renew the acquaintance now that you're living in college. You are so thick with Laura these days (and the silly little creature goes about looking as though she were guarding some great secret), I am forced to wonder!" Meg cried.

Delia took the tray from Meg's grasp and put it down on a table. "Let's not behave like hysterical schoolgirls. Laura's mother is an old family friend of the Prynnes. Not a close connection, but sufficiently so to justify her daughter visiting William now and again. She admires him, but she is a little intimidated by his manner. You know how shy she is. I enjoy his company extremely, far more than I do that of younger men." She paused significantly. "If I go with her, she gains confidence, we chaperon each other, and convention is satisfied. That's all there is to it. Laura knows no state secrets, I assure you." She put her arm around Meg's waist. "Thank you for helping to make the evening a success. But do go to bed now—you must be exhausted. I know I am!"

Meg was far from convinced, but she said farewell and retired to her rooms. Delia was kept awake by unsettling thoughts of their proposed income, which, reality told her, would be meager at best. And William was abrupt and impatient; she could not imagine her parents welcoming him as they would Sir Michael McMahon. Finally she knew that she must soon tell Will of her decision to join the Suffragette Movement and become an active member. Delia suspected that he would oppose it violently.

The concert at the Sheldonian was most successful, until the interval. Her conversation with Will started agreeably enough. He asked, almost jokingly, if she found being in love as distracting as he did. For the first time he could hardly keep his mind on his work. Some mischievous devil prompted Delia to reply that in her case it did not matter so much. Even if she achieved the highest marks, and passed the finals with credit, she would receive no degree. Women graduates, even the most brilliant, had to be satisfied with a diploma. The time when they would be accorded the degrees they earned was still far off. Will took umbrage at this criticism of the university's rules. To admit women as students and to allow them every facility to sit the exams was already a significant concession, he felt.

The crowded foyer was hot, and Delia had no fan, other than her program, which she waved to and fro with one hand, while looping up the trailing brocade skirt of her dress with the other as she strolled with Will. The colors in the skirt were faintly iridescent, woven with flashes of peacock green, peach, and gold thread. Many women glanced at it enviously while their escorts admired the lovely wearer.

"I am sure Magdalen will be the last to admit women students to lectures," Delia said provocatively, though her tone was light. "We shall be sitting on camp stools with our ears to the keyhole outside your lecture rooms long after all the more enlightened colleges have invited us to take our rightful place inside. I dare say you even resent the necessity to let us be seated in the examination halls along with the all-powerful male intellectuals."

"That is hardly fair, Delia." Will's voice had an edge. His self-control was not proof against the exciting intimacy of feeling her hand secretly caressing his arm. "Don't ride your hobbyhorse in public, my darling girl. Let me whisper sweet nothings to you instead. Isn't that what all girls particularly enjoy? The sensation of listening to compliments spoken *sotto voce,* so that no one else can hear? As usual, I've left it far too late in the evening to mention how lovely you look in that dress. There is a sort of subdued opaline shimmer in the material that suits you particularly well. Why did you not wear your opal necklace with it?"

"I could not wear it, for I was obliged to sell the necklace only a few days ago." Delia's voice was so airy that for a moment Will did not believe he had heard her correctly.

"Sell it! Why?" He laid a restraining hand on her wrist, gripping it so tightly that she almost dropped her program.

"Let us not discuss it now. I will tell you later!" She had given a totally unsatisfactory answer, as William's frown and compressed lips told her. She did not relish the explanation he would insist on the next day. Poor Delia had just begun to realize that, for two people with strong personalities and beliefs, romantic love might not be enough to ensure a happy marriage. Its fabric must be woven of something stronger: mutual respect and agreement on life's greater issues.

However, William's reaction when he heard the full story, and the extent to which his beloved had become involved, was one of admiration. He began to smother Delia's face in kisses.

"Generous to a fault! But what a sublime fault, my lovely girl. I should direct my anger against that swine Eustace Bradleigh for making you feel such a sacrifice was necessary. We both owe a great deal to his miserable little victim, don't we? It must have taken enormous courage for Elsie to bring you that letter. But since I am fortunately in funds, I shall redeem your necklace immediately, no matter how high a price the jeweler sets on it."

The price was high enough, in spite of that gentleman's protestation that he might not be able to sell such an unusual piece at all. And at the same time Will chose an antique ring of rose-cut diamonds in an ornate setting, which he put away in its crimson velvet box for the day when he could officially ask Lord Grandison for Delia's hand in marriage.

At the first opportunity, William and Delia explored the house Will was so eager to buy. Delia found it enchanting, and she talked all the way back along the riverbank of how they could decorate their new home, until Will covered his ears, saying he was overwhelmed by such precise domestic details.

"You have never mentioned the subject of my paper, which gained the award that will pay for all this furnishing frippery," he observed, half in jest. They had paused at a lock to watch the keeper see a small canal boat through. "Aren't you interested in its contents?"

"I should not understand a word of it, dearest," Delia answered honestly. "My field is the classics, as you know very well. I can translate from the works of any Greek philosopher you care to name, but scientific jargon is beyond me. Don't frown, darling. Please be reasonable . . ." She could see he was hurt, but she could not quite understand why.

"You little philistine." He swung her around to face him. "Don't you know that philosophy means the study and advancement of all human wisdom? Scientists are as much philosophers as any poet or storyteller. I myself am a doctor of philosophy, remember . . ."

Seeing her face cloud, Will dropped her arm. "Why do I harangue you like this?" he reproached himself. "Your lip is trembling, and your eyes are quite moist." He took her hand again and led her a little way along the bank, out of sight of the lockkeeper.

"Forgive me, *cariad*." He drew her close, pressing the length of her soft body to his hard, lean frame, making her tremble, half faint with the communication of his desire.

"I think I must be very tired," he said after a deep sigh. "I've fallen into the damnable habit of going back to the lab after dinner and working there sometimes until dawn dims the electric bulbs."

"I'll try to understand and share your enthusiasms, Will," Delia whispered remorsefully, snuggling her cheek against his muscular chest. "Tell me about your paper while we're having tea. I know Jenkin will have some ready for us. I can't conceive of anything smaller than an atom, but I'll try. The sun's going down already. Oh, dear, it will soon be dark. But won't it be rather nice, sitting by the fire, with the curtains drawn, while you instruct me?"

The prospect was so delicious that William unconsciously drew her more quickly along the towpath, and indeed the sky was purple, fading to lemon and rose behind the farthest spires before they got back to the Carfax.

"Must you work every night?" Delia questioned when they were established in Will's easy chairs, on either side of the fireplace, with a battered but nevertheless elegant Georgian sofa table supporting the tea tray between them.

Will threaded a piece of bread on the toasting fork and held it out to the flames before he answered.

"There never seems to be enough time for my work. Oxford is such a small community. Everyone of consequence knows everyone else, and we are all drawn into the same society, attending endless meetings within our department, and joint dinners with Cambridge men. And now this adorable distraction—yourself."

"Will, the toast is burning!" Delia exclaimed. They both laughed as he flung the charred remnant into the grate and began again. She hardly noticed he had not replied to her timid inquiry.

"I can't rest on my laurels, Delia; no scientist can." He gazed into the fire with a serious expression. "I'm on the track of another discovery, or, rather, a development from my first observation. The Curies have unlocked a vast treasure chest of knowledge, capable of much development, more far-reaching than anyone yet dreams. Perhaps a Pandora's box, from which evil will fly. I sense that there is harm in their radium, as well as good for mankind. Don't laugh at my mysticism; a strange foreknowledge tells me that it is so."

William invited Delia and Laura to tea the next Saturday afternoon, along with a selection of his own most promising students. These tea parties were a regular institution at Magdalen. Most tutors had a favored few protégés, often young men destined for brilliant careers, whom they entertained regularly in this informal manner, and they enjoyed getting to know them better away from the atmosphere of the lecture room. William's guests thought nothing of draping themselves over the settee, or lying full length on the carpet to consume tea made by Jenkin, plus great quantities of buttered pikelets, Cree Cakes, tinker's cake, and other Welsh specialties. Conversation flowed. There was much laughter and discussion of the latest lectures. Finally came a general exodus, with a chorus of offers to see both Laura and Lady Cordelia home safely. Laura accepted an escort as far as the porter's lodge, where Piers would be waiting for her.

The hour that followed was precious to Delia, yet she sensed that Will was becoming gradually more and more abstracted. "What is it, Will?" she asked. "Your thoughts are a thousand miles away."

"No more than a thousand yards!" he admitted ruefully. "Now you will see what a perverse, crusty old bachelor you have taken on. The fact is, I set up an experiment this morning and asked my lab assistant to be sure to come in and take some readings at six o'clock. I can't help wondering whether he remembered . . ."

"Why don't you go and see?" she asked quietly.

His face lit up. "You would truly not mind, my golden girl? It will take just a few minutes, no longer. Bless you." He kissed each fingertip individually and with such enthusiasm that she laughed.

When Will had left her, Delia returned to the sofa and began to look through an old photograph album of his motorcycling club. Rallies, hill climbs, long runs to Devonshire and back. Will mounted and unrecognizable in goggles, bare-headed, triumphantly holding up medals or other trophies, always the tallest of the group. The pictures became blurred before her gaze . . .

The fire sang softly, hissing a little around a log of applewood, and Delia drifted into slumber. When she awoke with a start, the grandfather clock in the corner was striking the hour of eight. Jenkin appeared almost at once when she pulled the bell.

"Beg pardon, milady, but I did knock. I just wanted to take out the tray, but you didn't hear me, I'm sure."

"I was asleep. I had no idea it was so late. Dr. Prynne mentioned that he had to go over to the Daubeny Laboratory, but it was only to have been for a few minutes. That was two hours ago. Do you think he can have had an accident?"

"Not likely, ma'am, but it does seem a long time. Do you wish me to go and find out?" he offered.

Suddenly Delia felt the laboratory was her rival. She hated it, and she wanted to see for herself what temptations it had to offer that would keep her lover from enjoying her company.

"I shall come with you," she said decisively. "I have stayed far too long, and perhaps Dr. Prynne will be good enough to take me home immediately."

The halls of the science building were deserted. A smell of chemicals, like some ghostly emanation, hung about the place. There were many tall and narrow windows, shrouded now with green holland blinds. The gas mantles on the walls burned low, making it a place of shadows in the far corners. Upon entering the laboratory, Delia's first impression was of scrubbed oak workbenches stained with acids, glass-fronted mahogany cupboards filled with delicate instruments, Bunsen burners fixed to open gas jets with worn rubber piping; it was a cheerless, utilitarian place. Even the high wooden stools drawn up to the benches looked hard and uncomfortable. Delia shivered. Her instincts prompted her to turn and run from this cold, impersonal temple of the sciences, but Will had dropped his pencil and looked up, disturbed by their approaching footsteps.

His look of annoyance passed at once when he saw who it was, and he cried, "Impatient girl! Couldn't you wait for me in comfort? Or were you too eager to see what I am about?" His roving glance took in the wall clock, and his expression turned to one of penitence. "Is that really the time? Good heavens, I thought only a few minutes had passed. But now that you are here, let me show you—"

"Will, I think I must go home. As you have so much to occupy you, perhaps Jenkin could walk with me part of the way."

"No, no, my darling. You must come back to my rooms and take something hot to drink. Then I will walk with you myself, and I will not be satisfied until I have delivered you safe to Somerville's gate." Giving a rueful glance toward one piece of apparatus that Delia could not see clearly at that distance, he made a swift pencil note and turned the gas down above the bench where he had been so absorbed in his calculations.

Soon Delia and William were back in his rooms, enjoying a cup of hot China tea. With a practiced hand, he stirred up the fire and added a few pieces of coal. Delia sat silently nearby, her azure gaze hidden by the lowering of her lashes.

"Where would we be without a good coal fire to warm us?" Will spoke, lightly, coaxingly, but she did not respond at once. He flung himself down beside her and possessed himself of both her hands, drawing her with a masterful strength to face him.

"Now you know more of my true character, darling. Time means nothing to me when I am immersed in an experiment. If you had not, quite rightly, come to find me, I would have worked on until midnight and I would not even have noticed whether I had dined. I have asked Jenkin to prepare us a rarebit, by the way. He'll bring it in presently. I hope you like toasted cheese."

Still Delia did not reply. But she raised her eyes to his forgivingly and slowly nodded.

"I might be worse, the prototype of an absentminded professor," he said teasingly. "Like my friend Pierre Curie. When I last visited his home, the cook provided a succulent beefsteak for dinner, which must be a rarity in his poor household. Pierre ate his portion but said nothing. He was too busy thinking of his work. At last the servant could bear it no longer and inquired how the master had enjoyed his meat. He looked at her in astonishment. "'Have I eaten beefsteak? It is quite possible,' he said thoughtfully."

A smile lifted the corners of Delia's mouth, almost in spite of herself. "Now that you have come back to earth, try and explain to me what your new experiments are all about," she suggested. "I understand so little of science."

William leapt up and began to walk about the room, his eyes flashing with excitement. "As you must surely have learned from that governess of yours, all matter consists of atoms, and for a very long time it was taken as absolute truth that they were the smallest parts into which matter can be divided. Your expression shows me that you don't even know what an atom is, my poor darling!"

Delia flushed. "Please explain."

"It is far too small to be seen, even under the strongest microscope, but its nature is very much like that of our solar system." William was being very patient. "It consists of a nucleus surrounded by electrons. Imagine planets, our earth among them, circling endlessly around the sun. That's how electrons circle around the nucleus, eternally and unchanging, or so we thought. But now it looks very much as if the element discovered by the Curies, radium, is different. Occasionally one of its atoms disintegrates spontaneously. In tiny form, it's as though the sun suddenly exploded in our universe! Imagine what an incredible amount of energy such an explosion would release!"

He scanned Delia's face keenly to judge whether she realized the significance of what he was saying.

"We don't know yet how or why it happens," he went on. "But in my experiments using a few grams of radioactive material, I'm trying to find out whether energy is created by this occurrence, and if so, how much."

Will continued striding up and down, warming to his theme. "I'm using a cloud chamber. It's just a glass tank filled with clear water-saturated air. You probably didn't even notice it in the laboratory. But my experiments show that when the nucleus of a radioactive atom splits, the parts fly off at a great speed. You can see it, because the parts of the nucleus, in passing, charge the water droplets in the air of my tank with electricity and leave a trace of fog behind. I've worked many nights on mathematical formulae, which lead me inevitably to conclude that the energy produced by the disintegration of the nucleus is infinitely larger than any energy produced by a chemical reaction, such as burning coal, as we're doing at this moment on our fire, or my burning petrol in the dear old Panther's engine."

He mopped his forehead with a handkerchief, remembering the hours he had spent at his desk over these calculations. "If the Curies had not given me some radioactive material, I could not have made this discovery," he admitted frankly. "If, working with them, I can discover what makes the atom split of its own volition, it might be possible to reproduce the same circumstances and release a vast source of energy, totally undreamed of today."

He dropped down on the sofa beside Delia, his expression clouded by concern. "One thing worries me," he said slowly. "This might be used as a means of destruction more frightful than any we know. Should I pursue my experiments? I hesitate. Meanwhile, I wrote to Pierre and asked him whether we should publish a joint paper. He replied that he shares my interest, but he urges me to publish my findings alone. He is too deeply involved in fitting out his new laboratory, the first he has ever had worthy of his efforts, and in teaching at the Sorbonne. We might have been asked to present our paper on the subject to the Royal Society. I probably will be invited to do so myself." He stroked the girl's white forehead, gazing deep with his strange, brilliant eyes into hers.

"Ah, Delia, to be born in this age! I'm still young, but I have seen already in my brief lifespan an unbelievable expansion of our understanding of nature and its awesome powers. Giants among men like Pasteur, the great conqueror of bacterial diseases; Röntgen, with his astonishing X rays, which penetrate flesh and allow us to photograph the bones and organs of the body; the incomparable Curies, with their new element, radium, unveiling for the first time a substance with apparently magical properties that changes *of its own accord* into others—the power-charged element I am studying. My dearest love, we are at the beginning of a golden age in science; I know it and long to be in the forefront of discovery!"

He kissed her with a passion she found almost frightening.

"Are your experiments dangerous?" Delia inquired.

"No, I can assure you. We are years, maybe centuries, away from learning how to release this new power. First we scientists must persuade the disbelievers that it even exists. Then we must search for a means to reach it, harness it to our needs. My task will be to persuade other physicists that *it is there!*"

At this point Jenkin arrived with their supper, and no more was said of Will's mysterious world, which Delia was only just beginning to glimpse.

Lord and Lady Grandison rarely kept Grayle Abbey open during the winter months, preferring their Park Lane mansion in London until the Christmas festivities began. But the great actor-manager and his bride required a period of relaxation, so Arthur persuaded Louise to desert London entirely for at least the months of November and December and go down to Grayle. A French chef was imported, and a suite of rooms was put in order for the reception of Sir Michael and Lady McMahon.

Before following Natalie's parents to the country, the returned travelers had spent a few days in Park Lane. Michael had inspected his theater, discussed certain pressing business matters with the lessees, and decided to take a short holiday. Only then would he mount a new production at the Clarence with the McMahon Company. This delay was more for Natalie's sake than his own, for he was always eager to be at work, never so happy as when studying and creating yet another role. He wanted Natalie to be well and rested before appearing for the first time on the London stage. As her mentor, he had insisted that she keep up both her singing and piano lessons wherever they might be staying. Under his tuition her stage voice had strengthened and become enriched, so that every word she spoke, even in the lowest register, was clear and musical. Her presence, for so young an actress, was remarkable. He was confident she would take London by storm.

* * *

A carriage was sent from the Abbey to Oxford to collect Delia, most conveniently, on a Saturday morning. She had no lectures until the following Monday. Her translations and essay were all completed and copied neatly in her impeccable handwriting. So it was with a clear conscience that she asked Miss Maitland's leave to spend the weekend at home, promising to attend divine service at Grayle, in the little village church, and to be back for evening dinner. It was required of every female student to go to church regularly on Sundays, and it was one of the few rules very rigorously enforced. But as all the tenants would be eager to see Natalie and her famous husband, the family would be present in full force.

Delia sat, swaying slightly with the motion of the coach, lost in a reverie. Would she find Natalie much changed? The old roles were reversed. Natalie was now the woman of experience, and she herself had everything to learn.

Grayle rose up before her, a bronze crown in a cradle of brown-and-gray velvet, for the sun was not shining, and the verdure of summer was gone. And yet its familiar outline against a sky washed clean of color was noble, as always. Grayle was still home.

Delia ran from the carriage almost before it had stopped in front of the doors, flung wide to receive her, and saw her sister running, too, from the far end of the great entrance hall. They met, crying and laughing, and pressing petal-smooth cheek to cheek. Oddly it was the golden Delia who seemed the younger at that moment, in her simple beige cashmere suit, her soft felt hat of matching beige turned up and away from her pure forehead. Natalie, unbelievably slender, and certainly taller than before, looked as though she had been poured into the figure-fitting coat-dress of purplish-blue, just the color of her eyes. Diamonds winked in the choker clasping her slim throat and in the rings on her slender fingers.

The sisters kissed, then stood apart, hands clasped, considering each other. Their mother came forward.

"Mama, she looks splendid, doesn't she?" Delia cried.

"You, too, darling. Let's join Papa and Michael in the drawing room!"

Chapter 24

The reunion at Grayle began joyfully for them all. Delia observed with wonderment the transformation that had taken place in Natalie during one short year. The artless young girl, ready to fall headlong in love, had become a sophisticated and poised young woman. Where she had once charmed with her innocent freshness, almost unaware of her extraordinary beauty and its stunning impact on men, she was now fully conscious of this power.

Natalie's relationship with her husband, which had begun under such painful circumstances, was obviously now one of perfect accord. To see them happy together, with Michael's fine gray eyes frequently fixed on his wife and often encountering her own loving gaze, was a pleasure so keen that it stirred Delia profoundly.

Louise was in excellent spirits to have both her girls once more at her beck and call, and she was delighted to welcome Michael as a son-in-law. As far as Arthur was concerned, Michael proved to be a man after his own heart—a man who played chess like a master, who could discuss European politics as easily as home affairs, and above all, a man in whose presence his daughter glowed unabashed to display the love she bore him.

Delia was expecting an intimate family party. But her mother had decided at short notice to give a dinner and ball at Grayle Abbey on that Saturday evening. She had hastily invited friends from several large house parties in the neighborhood, and she was putting up others coming down from London for the occasion.

After the first exchange of kisses, congratulations, and compliments in the drawing room, Louise went off to look at Mrs. Ponder's menus for the ball supper. The sisters ran upstairs together to choose their evening gowns, glad of the excuse for an intimate chat. Fortunately, Louise had instructed Flora before leaving London to pack several of Delia's dresses in their luggage.

Complaining in jest that they had been deserted by their womenfolk, Arthur and his son-in-law went up amicably to the library. Michael welcomed such opportunities to cement his growing friendship with the Marquess. The two men seated themselves together at a table where Arthur opened a large atlas and, pointing to the Russian port of Odessa, remarked, "This is where a most significant event recently took place. The Russian ambassador himself informed me that when the battleship *Potemkin* docked, it was in the hands of mutineers. Most of the officers had been shot or tossed overboard at sea." His face darkened. "The few who survived were murdered later."

"While we were in America, I heard little of what was happening in Europe," Michael said ruefully. "It seemed a world away, and the papers hardly thought such events were worth mentioning. Certainly there was nothing about a mutiny aboard one of Russia's warships."

Lord Grandison nodded. "A blanket of silence seems to have fallen over the revolution that failed at Odessa. I do know that one of the murdered naval officers was Count Dmitri Kutschinskiy, brother-in-law to my old friend the Grand Duke Constantine Voroshnikoff." Michael flinched at that name, but Arthur went on. "I have it, in strict confidence, that there had been civil war for two days and nights there before the ship came into port. The Black Hundreds, members of a right-wing secret society, joined forces with the police and military to suppress the disorder and succeeded in preventing the crew of the *Potemkin* from landing and making common cause with the rebel forces. Then some fool shot down the leader of a squadron of Cossacks. Wholesale slaughter followed. Knowing that the rest of the fleet, which had remained loyal to the Czar, must soon arrive, the disappointed mutineers put to sea again and made for the port of Constantia, in Romania." He placed his finger on the open atlas. "There, they scuttled the vessel and sank it with such officers as remained alive still aboard. Dmitri, poor fellow, was drowned." Arthur closed the heavy book with a solemn thud.

"I remember him well," Lord Grandison continued, "from my own visit to Russia with my wife in '86. He was only a youngster, a naval equerry to the Czar, rather a dilettante. He'd probably long since quit the service and never expected to be recalled. But I confess this brings to mind his nephew, young Andrei Voroshnikoff. Has Natalie forgotten him? If harm came to him, would it revive all the old heartaches? My poor nightingale, she pined for that impetuous young devil all last summer . . ."

"Yes," Michael said simply. "She would be hurt. I believe she still cherishes some fondness for him. But why should he be in danger?"

"The Ambassador told me Andrei had completed a token period of service in his regiment. He need not serve—unless he wished it—and cared nothing for putting his life at risk. I can hardly imagine Prince Andrei would be idealistic enough to become involved in such an incident. But he was an impulsive young man, and if Natalie were to hear that he had died for his country, she might be terribly upset."

"I, too, would wish to save her from such a shock," Michael agreed. "Between us, we can make sure she is shielded from it."

He said no more, but the two men understood each other very well. Arthur thereupon suggested that they might ride out together; he spoke in the tones of a man who had confided an anxiety and felt all the better for it.

"A splendid idea, Lord Grandison," Michael agreed. "I like to get a good horse between my knees and your stable has an outstanding reputation."

"A compliment, indeed," the older man replied warmly. "But must we be so formal? In public, if you insist. But when we are alone together, would you call me Arthur?"

"With pleasure." Michael rose and swept the bow that had all London at his feet when he appeared on the stage. He was truly delighted.

* * *

When the girls had closed Delia's bedroom door, they embraced again fondly, ignoring the gowns laid out on the chaise longue.

"Our first real chance for a talk together, darling!" Natalie exclaimed. "Come, let's put your dresses on this chair. We'll decide later which one you should wear. Well, what do you think of him?" She sat down, her face aglow with obvious pride.

Delia laughed. "That is more like my dear Imp! But I needn't ask whether you are happy. It shines from your eyes. To answer your question, my new brother-in-law is a wonderful man, and besides having made Mama his devoted admirer, I believe he is well on the way to winning Papa's approval." Her voice changed. "How did it all happen, Natalie dear? You loved Andrei so much. Did you find one day, quite suddenly, that you were free, able to love Michael as a wife should?"

"Not suddenly. At first Michael was no more than my support and refuge. I didn't love him then as I do now. Over the months my feelings changed. Delia, I believe I already cared for him *in that way,* long before I allowed myself to admit it. . . ."

Natalie let the thick sweep of her dark lashes fall, veiling her eyes, and she bent her pliant body forward over clasped hands. She did not want even Delia to see the great wave of emotion that shook her now, remembering how it had felt that day she had given herself utterly to her husband at last.

It had seemed impossible. Always the imperious, commanding ghost of Andrei had come between them. It had lingered stealthily in the shadows of their bedroom, his voice echoing in her ears like a sigh, imploring her to remain faithful . . . never, never to forget him, reminding her that she was vowed to him for all eternity.

But gradually the knowledge of Michael's affair with the beautiful Maeve O'Malley had eroded her determination to stay true to a mere shadow. She could picture only too clearly her husband's proud masculinity, powerful invasion and royal possession of Maeve's eager body. If only she had not experienced herself all that took place between a man and a woman. Night after night Natalie had lain alone, feeling her own body's heat inflamed by the mock embraces on the stage, but unable to translate her desires into love for Michael.

Then, one night, Natalie had begged Michael not to go. He had been a little surprised by the entreaty so frankly betrayed in the violet splendor of her eyes. For a long time he had known better than to touch her and risk her flinching from him. So, as usual, he had restrained the urge to move closer to his wife. But her voice had come through the open bedroom door, calling him with a longing he had never heard in it before.

"Michael, my darling, please come to me."

He had gone, hesitating before he entered, to behold a vision in black lace, with hair streaming far below her waist and caught behind one ear with a huge full-blown white rose. No longer a virginal bud, but offering its golden heart openly, the petals trembling, almost ready to fall. It was she who had run to close the door behind him and turn the little gilt key in the lock. It was she who had kneeled to draw him down beside her on the bed, slipping the thin blue silk robe from his shoulders and unbuttoning the shirt he wore beneath it. He had not needed to beseech, to entreat and reiterate his right. All her body and soul was in the first kiss she rose to give, her lips opening under his.

Michael did not know, even as he had entered her with luxurious slowness, why the miracle had been wrought. He had accepted it, as regally as she had bestowed it on him. Their lives were changed in that night. The next day, he wrote to accept the offer to appear in San Francisco that had lain on his desk, waiting to be refused.

Maeve had sulked, wept, and wondered why he came no more to her mansion on Fifth Avenue, except to say good-bye. But the two honeymooners, en route for California, had never spoken of her. Absorbed in each other, there was no need.

"You haven't told me anything of your own life, darling," Natalie said. "Do you prefer living in college, and have you found it easier to make friends?"

"In some ways I enjoy it very much," Delia acknowledged. "But I'm disappointed that none of the other girls seems fired as I am by enthusiasm for the cause of women's suffrage."

Natalie looked sympathetic. "I dare not mention it either, in Michael's hearing. In theory, the most intelligent and just of men agree with your ideals; but in practice it's a different matter. I am selfish, I suppose; but just now my career seems more important, to justify Michael's faith in my talent." Color rose in her cheeks. "And to have his child; it's my dearest wish."

"That's perfectly natural, and I'm delighted to hear it," said

Delia. Her thoughts flew to Elsie, and she explained the poor girl's predicament and her own promise to help.

"I won't take a penny from Mama, or Papa either, and the income Aunt Mildred left is only just enough to cover my expenses . . ." She paused, then decided not to speak of her commitment to Miss Bail. "The thing is, I've just enough to pay for Elsie's lodgings and confinement, and for some woman to care for the baby so that she can go out to work afterward. But she ought not to stay in Oxford, where her past is well known. She'll always be pointed at as a fallen woman."

"Quite right." After a moment's thought, Natalie said, "Let me make a suggestion. At the Clarence last week Michael was delighted to see how well our new apprentice, Ted, is doing helping the stage manager. His family lives over a shop in one of those little streets nearby. He and Elsie must be about the same age. Ted's mother would be glad of the money, I dare say, to take the girl in. No one in London knows her. She could make a fresh start there. In fact, she might be needed at the Clarence. We'll find her employment in the theater wardrobe."

Flora disturbed their tête-à-tête to introduce the maid assigned to look after her ladyship for the weekend. Robin was a plump, stolid young girl, Linnet's sister, and next in line of the head gardener's daughters to seek service. Linnet had recently married, as Papa had mentioned to the local carrier.

"Has Linnet a baby of her own, then?" asked Delia.

"Not yet," said Robin, going scarlet, "but soon." Too soon if one counted the months since she married, thought Delia.

But it was not sufficient that Natalie should hear twice that day of young women expecting children. A letter arrived in the second mail from India, twice postmarked, since it had first been directed to New York. It disclosed that her friend, Gwen Halloran, was well into the seventh month of her pregnancy and feeling the hot weather badly. "Liam has engaged an ayah for the baby, which I shall have in the military hospital in Bombay. I'd be grateful for even Aunt Carrie's company just now!" wrote Gwen wistfully.

Natalie folded the letter and put it away. She pitied and yet envied her friend.

At last a decision was made on the subject of gowns. Natalie was to wear silver lace over shot lavender-and-gray taffeta; Delia had chosen gold lace over bronze silk. However, the younger girl was preoccupied. Her happiness was by no means complete.

Michael had teased her, telling her not to be impatient. But it was more than four months since their marriage had been consummated. And his baby in her arms would be worth more than any triumph on the boards, no matter how sublime. An idea was forming in her mind: she was suddenly filled with determination to consult the greatest authority in Harley Street on her apparent failure to conceive. A name rose in her mind: the physician who had attended all the Grandison brood in London since childhood. She went to a writing desk, drew out the thick creamy paper embossed with the family crest, and wrote to him, begging him to arrange an appointment for her the following week.

Louise was at her most agreeable. "It is so pleasant to have my girls under my wing," she said sweetly, turning great dark blue eyes on Delia, whom she had summoned to her bedroom. "I don't believe you have had any new clothes this year. And that gold lace has, to the best of my knowledge, never yet been worn on a dance floor. How do you manage, with so little money to spend on your wardrobe and so few diversions?"

Delia laughed. "Really, Mama! When one has so few diversions, as you put it, one does not need so many clothes. I am quite happy with what I have; indeed, the other girls in college envy me. Most of them are fitted out by village dressmakers, and they have never worn a Paris model in their lives."

Louise pouted. "Well, since it is becoming all the rage for young girls to be bluestockings, more interested in their studies than their suitors, I'm ready to confess I was a little hard on you last year. I was very angry at the time, but it is a changing world, and I suppose I must change with it . . ." Her voice trailed off, and she extended one slender white hand across the quilted rose-satin bedspread, almost apologetically. Delia took the hand and fondled it gently.

"Do look at the list of guests for tonight, darling," Louise went on faintly. "It's on my dressing table. Placing everyone at dinner has quite fatigued me. I've put you next to Uncle Hugo, on one side, and Charlie Haversham on the other, since I dare not put him anywhere near Natalie. Hugo can take Nell Haversham in."

Sheer surprise caused Delia to drop the list she had just taken up. "Surely you haven't invited the entire Haversham family?" she cried. "Isn't that rather tactless?"

"What could I do?" Louise's voice was studied in its pathos.

"Lord Augustus is one of Papa's best friends. Lady Augustus is as dear to me as a sister. They happen to be staying only a few miles away, at the Hamptons' place. How could I fail to invite them? Charlie is on leave, and Miss Eleanor, who is still not settled, to her mother's great distress, is there, too. Oh, yes, and Miss Jarvis, whom you will remember. They are all coming."

"Miss Jarvis—Gwendoline's Aunt Carrie? How did she become attached to the Haversham family?" Delia demanded in injured tones, for she did not like the lady at all.

"Well, she is rich and chaperones Nell for nothing. You know most chaperons are badly off, and they require all their expenses paid, with a discreet gift now and again to sweeten a thankless task," Louise felt obliged to explain further.

"Nell's dowry has been frittered away, I fear, on some unlucky investments. Then that house, the small estate at Banbury, which Charlie bought in expectation of marrying Natalie, has proved an expensive disaster. He cannot either make it habitable or sell it, it seems. Julia has not told me all, but Augustus is in very low water financially. That is the trouble with being only the second son of a Duke; there's no income to go with his title, high sounding though it may be."

"So there will be at least five people both Natalie and I will wish to avoid," Delia could not help saying sarcastically. "Must I go in to dinner with Charlie? Oh, I see you have set your heart on it," she said, seeing Louise's hopeful expression. "Very well, but he must not count on more than one dance with me, and I hope he will have the good sense to avoid Natalie."

As it happened, he did not approach Natalie at all. But Miss Jarvis and Nell hovered reproachfully around her all evening. The elder lady, usually resplendent in crimson or puce, was wearing purple with a somber parure of jet jewelry. At the supper interval she joined the McMahons at their table without being invited and drew out a black-bordered handkerchief to mop her heated brow. "I wonder I have not heard from you with your condolences," Miss Jarvis complained pointedly. "I certainly expected something, even if only a few words. Gwen used to write to me often. I shall miss her letters sadly," she continued in self-pitying tones. "So full of lively descriptions. She made the best of it, but Asmara was a dreadful place to be stationed. Liam should have sent her up to Simla or somewhere else in the hills in her delicate condition. I wrote and told him so, scolded him roundly. He has not yet replied; he's a poor correspondent. But, then, we had nothing in common except Gwen."

Natalie's eyes were enormous pools of anguish in her small face. "For God's sake, what has happened? Tell me!" Delia heard her cry of distress and ran to her side.

Miss Jarvis had risen. "Are you implying that you do not know of my poor niece's death in Bombay? She died in child-birth, and the babe, too. It was more than a month ago. All the proper announcements were in the papers. You must have seen, or heard of it."

"We have been traveling," Michael broke in. "This is a terri-ble shock for my wife. Let me take you upstairs, darling." He led Natalie away from the chattering throng, motioning to Delia to follow them, deeply concerned by the stricken look on the younger girl's white face.

Together they persuaded Natalie to undress and lie down. But she could not seem to stop crying.

She sobbed and murmured incoherently that Gwen had asked her if she knew what marriage really meant, and she hadn't been able to answer. Now it was too late; she would never see her friend again. At last Michael fetched her a sleeping draft and forced her to drink it. Meanwhile, the party continued into the small hours and it was voted a huge success. Nell and Miss Jarvis, although they whispered a good deal together, for once kept silent and said nothing of the pathetic scene that had taken place.

Sunday seemed to stretch out interminably. Delia peeped into her sister's room from time to time, but Natalie still slept heavily. Michael went to her the moment she awoke, then returned with a message that she wanted to speak to Delia, just for a few min-utes.

Natalie was sitting up in bed, her dark gleaming hair loose against a pile of lace-frilled pillows. "I still feel quite light-headed," she admitted, "so don't expect anything I say to make sense. I'm sorry I've wasted so much of our time together, dar-ling. Do you really have to go back to Oxford early tomorrow?"

"I'm afraid I must go, Nattie dear. What a pity that our first meeting after so many months was overshadowed by the terrible shock you had last night. Can't you come over and see me as you used to do when I was staying with the Bradleighs?"

"Of course I will. Is Tuesday too soon? Oh, do let's have lunch together after your morning lecture! I'll call on Olivia Chalfont and then come directly to Somerville College."

Although Delia regretted the delay, at least this would give her a better opportunity to reveal that she had fallen in love with William Prynne.

When Michael entered the room, she sensed, with her newly heightened perceptions, the current of emotion that flowed between these two mortals. Obviously he desired his beautiful wife with a passion of rare intensity, and she responded as ardently. Would it ever be like this between herself and Will? she thought. How wonderful it would be to love like that . . . She stole out, leaving them alone together.

Michael looked at his fragile wife with some apprehension. When he saw her melancholy expression, he spoke with a certain note of censure in his voice.

"You will make yourself ill with grieving, my dearest. Don't give way to it. We'll write together to Gwen's father and Hetty. Then to Liam, poor chap. That's all we can do, except to remember her as she was, on her happiest day. Give me your smile, darling—the smile that would launch more than a thousand ships if there were such a navy!"

She did smile, tremulously, and flung herself into his comforting embrace. Later, when she was alone, Natalie thought again of Gwen's tragic death, and then her own determination to carry Michael's child. If others took the risks of motherhood, she decided, so would she.

Chapter 25

The next morning arrived with soft breezes and puffy white clouds scudding across a sky of aquamarine, making a mockery of autumn's progress toward winter. After Delia had left, Michael suggested to Natalie that a stroll in the park would do her good. By the lakeside they watched the eager approach of a pair of the famous black Grandison swans. Finding the visitors had nothing for them, they set up a strident squawking.

"Swans are extremely vocal, when disappointed," Natalie observed softly. "Perhaps it is a pity that we humans have so many inhibitions about expressing our emotions—especially grief, or anxiety..."

Michael knew she wanted to speak of Gwen and sought an opening. He gave it to her obliquely. "Talking of anxiety, I hardly know Delia, since we have met only once or twice before. But she did not strike me as being entirely at her ease," he observed, stooping to gather up a handful of pebbles, then skipping them one by one across the water. "I caught her frequently looking in your direction, with a quite pathetic intensity, as though you were some Delphic oracle to give advice. Or did I imagine it?"

"No." Natalie tucked her hand under his elbow for warmth as they walked on, for the brightness of the day was deceptive. "I believe Delia had some secret she wanted to tell me, but there was no time." She paused. "I was thinking more rationally this morning about Gwen. You know, judging from the letters she sent me after they reached India, Liam was not such an experienced or appreciative lover as you are, my dearest."

He slid his arm around her slight shoulder. "That is a true compliment. But you are beautiful almost beyond belief, and your own fire kindles mine. Perhaps both qualities were lacking in your friend. I don't mean to speak unkindly of her, or to take Liam's part."

"Darling, I know. But I can't help feeling angry on Gwen's behalf. Married in ignorance, and shocked and disappointed by reality. She was only eighteen—exactly my age! The fate of young wives is often abominable," she went on bitterly. "It is indeed a man's world. So few of them, even doctors, seem to care what we suffer. We have no voice to demand justice. Delia's in favor of women's suffrage. And at this moment, I'm ready to share her views."

"Equal rights for your sex will not remove the curse of Eve," protested Michael. He was only voicing the retort many men were making to the timid complaints of their wives and daughters.

But the tone of resignation in his wonderful voice made Natalie flare out. "What if studies, and research, were directed to lightening that curse, or at least not subjecting poorer women to the endless, inevitable bearing of children their husbands cannot feed, and so many of which die? Possibly it is unladylike to speak so frankly. But, Michael, I want more than anything else to have a baby of our own. Would you object to my consulting a specialist in Harley Street? Our own physician in London will recommend someone."

"Of course I would happily take you to see any medical man you choose, although you are rather impatient. It is only a few months since there was any possibility of our union being so blessed."

They both laughed a little, but Natalie did not swerve from her decision. She then suggested that Michael should enjoy a day's hunting with Papa, while she went off to Oxford alone to indulge in a heart-to-heart talk with her sister.

Louise very much wished to go, too, for she had not seen Delia's new rooms; nor had she spent nearly as much time as she wished with her elder daughter. But her thoughts were uneasily beset by some most disquieting news from Julia Haversham. Augustus was "in deep," Julia wept, and in a fair way to "go under." Friends of the Grandisons simply did not go bankrupt; the old Duke would pay up if he had to, Louise insisted. Julia needed the moral support of her best friend, and Louise could not abandon the poor woman to morbid fears while she herself went gallivanting to Oxford. But she did not confide a word of all this to Arthur. It was strictly between themselves.

At Somerville, Delia had almost given up expecting her sister for luncheon and was about to go in alone to the dining room when she arrived. They ate with healthy appetites, Natalie insisting that it was so long since she had tasted a simple rice pudding with plum jam that she now enjoyed it as much as any French confection. She admired Delia's rooms, and the way her own ornaments had been used to advantage. Miss Margaret Douglas, who hovered purposefully in the corridor until she was introduced, was at her wittiest and most charming. Then, at last, they were alone.

"Come and sit on my window seat!" Delia urged her younger sister to this vantage point, then she began, breathlessly, "Darling, I'm in love. I'm engaged, it's all decided, and it's a secret! He's the most wonderful man," she went on rapidly. "I never thought this would happen to me, but it has. I want you to meet him, now, this very day. I want you to love him, as I do—no, of course not at all in the same way, but it matters to me a great deal that you should like him. Say you will, darling."

For a moment Natalie could say nothing. This was not at all the kind of secret she supposed her sister had been nursing. But she could only be happy at the thought that Delia was on the brink of life's most rewarding experience—the romantic courtship and betrothal every girl dreamed of, followed by a true welding of souls and bodies, such as she had found with Michael. "Could I dislike a man you have chosen to love?" She hugged her sister. "Of course I want to meet him as soon as possible. But why the secrecy? Isn't it a matter for both his family and ours to rejoice over?"

"There are difficulties," Delia admitted reluctantly. "For one thing, he is very forthright in his opinions, and since his own background is humble, though that's a horrid word, he despises people of our class as parasites. He makes no bones about it, and that might easily give offense. He could never dissemble. I'm sure he would not agree to my having a dowry, even if Papa wishes to give it; we shall have to live quite modestly, and Mama will be tiresome about that. Many people in Oxford find him eccentric. But he's a brilliant scientist, a genius, and I absolutely adore him!" Indeed, as she reached this conclusion, Delia's face was alight with an emotion that quite transformed its calm, classic perfection.

"Well, you have never praised a man so highly before," observed Natalie, rather uncertainly. "Why do you find him so attractive?"

"Because he's different from all other men. The first time we danced together he said such wonderful things. Not the usual rubbish about my looks and my deportment. Our steps matched so perfectly, I wished the music would never stop."

Was this the matter-of-fact, cool-headed sister Natalie knew so well, fiercely contemptuous of all attempts to woo her?

"Well, you shall introduce me to this paragon," she said cautiously. "We need not take the maid with us. Remember, I'm a married woman now, and I can chaperon you!"

It was a joke that kept them both laughing all the way in the carriage, and as far as Will's door. To be truthful, both girls were nervous; it mattered so much that Natalie should take a liking to Will, and approve of him, for her opinion would sway Michael's and, indirectly, that of their parents! And Delia was not at all sure that she would like him, if he happened to be preoccupied with his work, or seething with rage against some crass decision by the university authorities, as he sometimes was. But she need not have feared.

William was in his most affable mood and kissed the hand of his future sister-in-law with almost a courtier's grace. But the reason for his high spirits soon became apparent.

"While you were enjoying yourself at Grayle Abbey, I was not idle, my Delia!" he announced. "I actually copied out my paper for the Royal Society on foolscap in a legible hand, and I sent it off. My friend Vernon Harcourt, who is pretty well versed in the society's proceedings, believes I have a fair chance of being invited to go up to London next month and read the paper myself in the lecture hall at Carlton House Terrace. He thinks the committee will be looking for another speaker and will not be hard to convince, provided I have something interesting to say."

He then tried to explain part of his research to Natalie, but she was soon putting her hands over her ears and begging him not to tax her brain so severely. He was remorseful at once. "I must remember that I am not among my students," he reproached himself. "But would you not be impressed if you read paragraphs about my paper in all the scientific journals?"

When Natalie pointed out that she was unlikely to read such stuff, but added generously that she would not insist on his giving a critique of her performance as Ophelia, Delia felt relieved. These two, whom she loved so dearly, were obviously compatible.

When Natalie had returned with her maid to Grayle Abbey, Delia checked the porter's desk for mail. There was a small parcel addressed in a hand she did not recognize that had been posted locally. She took it upstairs and, upon opening it, found a substantial pile of handbills and a brief note asking her to distribute them within the next few days. They were invitations to attend a meeting of the Society for Women's Suffrage.

While Will waited in an increasingly restless mood for an acknowledgment of his paper, Delia distributed her hand bills, twenty or so at a time, without much enthusiasm. She thought it might be heartwarming to address an enthralled audience from the foot of Nelson's Column in Trafalgar Square, flanked by huge bronze lions; but pushing poorly printed sheets stealthily into letter boxes, hoping not to be noticed, was less heroic and, if she were challenged and attacked, perhaps humiliating. But as it happened no one accosted her while she was at her self-imposed task, and William knew nothing about it. Neither did any of the other girls at Somerville, for she decided not to mention it even to Laura.

Michael sat in the doctor's waiting room, suppressing his anxieties; it was already an hour since Natalie had vanished, accompanied by a nurse in rustling, stiffly starched white, into the specialist's inner sanctum. Surely it did not take so long to examine a young woman. He was becoming thoroughly alarmed when the nurse reappeared and invited him to come in and meet the doctor. Michael's first glance was, as always, at Natalie, sitting on the other side of the desk in her customary graceful attitude, with a soft wool skirt swirling around her feet. Her gaze was directed at the window, but as she turned her head back to meet his smile, the look she gave him was so unhappy that his own heart froze.

"Well, Sir Michael, I fear I've had disappointing news for your wife," began the consultant. "Excuse me." He coughed dryly, behind his hand. "I have conducted an examination, and I find . . ."

Michael heard no more. He could see the result in Natalie's eyes. They were pools of emptiness, of quiet despair.

"The unfortunate early miscarriage . . ." That pedantic voice was droning on. It took some time to come to the end of his recital. If her ladyship was so determined to have a child, he counseled them to consider adoption. Better than nothing, wasn't it? And perhaps, sometime, a miracle might occur. Apart from that one problem, a wonderfully healthy young woman. Just a fraction delicate in her nerves, which would bear watching. A tonic, a visit to a spa, a few days in bed occasionally. She should not overtax herself.

Michael cut it short. "Thank you, Doctor. I shall take great care of her."

In the carriage on the way back to Park Lane, he said compassionately, "My dear, does it matter so much?"

"Yes, terribly. By my own selfishness and folly, to deny you an heir? Of course it matters!" The cry came from her soul, where her spirit wept and could not be comforted. He took her hand and they sat together in silence, not seeing the lighted shop windows, the throngs of shoppers, the paper boys, and the flower sellers.

"I need only you, my darling. You have denied me nothing . . . It is your sorrow, your immense sorrow, that hurts me," he said at last. They were already near home. When the horses pulled up, Natalie got out and went up the steps on his arm, as she always did, and into the marble-floored hall with its fine colonnades.

"Her ladyship is receiving in the drawing room," Adams whispered in her ear.

Wearily Natalie unpinned her fur hat, relinquished her muff and gloves, and went in. What point would it serve to go upstairs, to throw herself on her bed in a storm of tears, and make Michael even more unhappy on her behalf?

Louise was pouring tea for her dear friend Julia. Lady Augustus looked depressed, and ill health did not flatter her complexion. Nell, slouched by her side looking glum, greeted Natalie without enthusiasm. There was a desperate glitter in her eyes, as of one who had long glimpsed a certain resigned expression on the faces of her parents and knew herself to be, to put it plainly, on the shelf.

"How have you supported your exile in America?" she asked Michael affably. "It must be dismal to exist so far from . . . well, civilization—unless one is doing one's duty in some part of the Empire, of course." She helped herself to an iced cake. "Even social events pass you by, I dare say. Who dies . . ." She paused significantly. Then she continued: "Who marries and what children are born," she went on brightly. "For instance, Natalie, an acquaintance of ours has recently married. Oh, not in England, to be sure. In Russia."

Natalie had just accepted a cup of tea from her mother's hand. "You are speaking of . . . ?" Her winged eyebrows were raised, her sweetly modeled chin thrust a little forward.

"Why, Prince Andrei Voroshnikoff, of course. There was a long paragraph in *The Tatler,* and pictures of the wedding group, with the bride wearing the Voroshnikoff pearls. It took place in the cathedral at St. Petersburg. After all, the Countess Desirée is niece to the Comte de Paris, and almost a royal Princess herself."

"Natalie is tired. Will you excuse us, Lady Grandison?" Michael inquired formally. "Lady Augustus?" His gaze swept past Nell, as though she did not exist. At the door he turned and said flatly, "And Miss Eleanor. Good day."

It was more than Natalie could bear. She wept then, in the privacy of their bedroom, and begged Michael to leave her on her own. She wept for her lost hopes of a child, and for this final proof that Andrei had deceived her from the very first.

She could not know of the long interviews between the Grand Duchess Natalya and her only surviving son; that, as many times as she appealed to him, he refused her. He would not marry and, above all, he would not marry that prattling little French schoolgirl with the hot, moist, greedy hands.

He had chosen his Princess, and fate had denied her to him. There would be no other. But the order of the Emperor had the force of law. Andrei must marry the bride of his parents' choice, and at once. He must live with her, and speedily get her with child. If the child should be a daughter, he must try again. There must be an heir of the Voroshnikoff blood to carry on their name. But in Andrei's heart he heard the sweet voice of his little nightingale, singing the plaintive old English refrain:

Drink to me only with thine eyes
And I will pledge with mine!

That poignant pledge, never now to be fulfilled between them . . .

Chapter 26

Lord Augustus Haversham squirmed uneasily in the chair that had been placed for him at a discreet distance from Sir James Berryman's desk. The all-powerful chairman of the bank contemplated his guest with the keen interest of an experienced fisherman who had just netted a fat salmon and wondered how long it would continue to gasp and thrash about before going limp.

Berryman's bank had long since become one of the largest in the country. The sign of the white unicorn on a black shield headed its notepaper and it was emblazoned above the solid mahogany door at every branch, of which there were dozens. Though Sir James might prefer to see himself as that most desirable of fabled animals, the magical unicorn, he more resembled a squat black spider sitting at the center of a web in which many a fly was trapped, suffocated, and devoured, all to assuage his enormous appetite. This hunger was firstly for money, followed secondly by a short margin for power, and thirdly for recognition and the perpetuation of his name.

Money was his already, for he was a millionaire many times over. Power he also possessed in no small degree. Financial empires mushroomed at his command, or dwindled and sank from view. Unfortunate investors were mercilessly sucked dry and discarded while his friends prospered. But he had not as yet received the recognition he felt to be his due.

However, Sir James had not given up hope. By obliging his daughter's husband to take the name of Berryman, and withholding the financial reward promised until their son, Clive, was born, he had secured an heir: two grandsons, Clive and Victor, worthy of adoption and well fitted to inherit the peerage that would shortly be announced in the honors list. Steps had been taken to achieve this aim; the title was almost within his grasp, and its bestowal was only a matter of time.

Sir James could now afford to devote his cold and calculating attention to the fourth of his aims in life, and the only other one not yet accomplished. He longed to take revenge upon Lord Grandison, whom he held solely responsible for the suicide of his boy, Francis.

Often, over the years, he had hired investigators to wheedle out some scandal upon which he might base his attack. But there was none; the Grandison family had a spotless reputation. He must strike at them through the plight of a friend. Now the banker had such a friend at his mercy, and the man was in a very sore plight indeed. Typically, Sir James had put young Charlie Haversham under the microscope as soon as it was rumored that the Grandisons intended him for their younger daughter, Natalie. His character was irreproachable, his debts not sizable, and he was no more foolish or easily corruptible than most other young officers in his regiment.

But his father, Lord Augustus, was quite another matter. A personal friend of many years standing to Arthur. So far, so good. Their wives were also friendly. How else had the engagement with Natalie first been mooted, then pushed almost to fruition? That was even better. But, best of all, Lord Augustus was faced with the dilemma of having a great position to keep up without the appropriate income. As the second son of a Duke, he depended entirely on the generosity of his noble father, who disliked him heartily. His Grace had opened his purse strings wider than for many a year, in expectation of a marriage, so eminently creditable to the family, with one of the Grandison girls. When the marriage fell through, the strings were pulled tight, funds were cut off, and the Augustus Havershams entered on a period of lean, all the more painful for following a period of plenty.

The Duke did not particularly like his grandson Charlie, or the young man's mother, whom he had been heard to describe as "that fool Julia." He positively loathed his granddaughter, Nell. So there was no ambassador to plead the cause of poor Augustus. By exerting his influence, which extended far beyond the city, Sir James had made available to Charlie what seemed a nice little country property and saw to it the said property fell into his lap. Once Charlie had bought it, many snags mysteriously appeared, and the place was fit for nothing but to swallow money.

Opportunities for investment were waved temptingly before Lord Augustus. They seemed so golden that his fortunes must rise; then, in the oddest manner, they turned to dross, lost heavily, and left the Havershams poorer than before. Having been accommodated by Sir James, an unusually generous banker whom he looked upon as a decent chap who knew his place, Lord Augustus followed his advice to the letter. At this moment he found himself up to his neck in the mire, and the formerly obsequious Berryman had suddenly become a truculent superior, issuing orders.

Sir James allowed him to wallow most thoroughly, then offered him an olive branch that appeared stout enough to pull him clear of his misery. To his consternation the scheme that had just been outlined sounded overambitious. How was he to persuade dear old Arthur to concern himself with high finance?

"You and Grandison are on intimate terms, I dare say," Sir James remarked thoughtfully.

"Pretty much so." Augustus ran a finger stealthily around his starched collar, which had grown uncomfortably tight during the last few minutes. "But I've a feeling he doesn't like you much. Sorry to say it and all that, but as soon as your name was mentioned, he'd throw in his hand."

Sir James gave a sardonic smile at this card-playing allusion. Augustus obviously knew nothing of the scandal that had been hushed up in '86.

"You will not mention my name. You are to be invited to join the board of a new company. There will be an emolument—say two thousand a year." The desperate eyes of Augustus brightened, then dulled again.

"Wouldn't interest Arthur . . . he's never short of the ready."

"He is not to be approached in that way, Lord Augustus." Sir James could hardly contain his contempt for the oaf before him. "You are to tell him only that the aims of this company are so laudable, he must help to launch it, and that a name of great integrity is required to head the board. Mention the financial consideration for your place on it as being important to yourself, though a fee is of no matter to him. You must enthuse him. There are precedents; peers, even Dukes, who have lent their names to undertakings of the highest endeavor in order to encourage the public to participate."

"What's the undertaking, then?" mumbled Augustus, seeing a way out of his difficulties dangled before his eyes, then snatched away. "Dammit, I still don't get it!"

"The extension of the network of underground railways beneath London, serving two purposes. They keep the roads reasonably free for persons of quality to move about in comfort. They convey workers conveniently to and from their places of employment in all weathers, and at a reasonable cost. What could be more laudable?"

"Ah, yes, very commendable. And am I not to say you invite Lord Grandison to be chairman?" put in Augustus, plainly mystified.

"Do not on any account do so, as I've already told you. It would increase share prices at once if I were known to be involved, and I intend to buy quite a few. The project is put forward by its designer, Mr. Wordsworth Rivers. Here's the prospectus."

Sir James pushed an elegantly printed pamphlet across the desk and watched his visitor flip through it, uncertain whether he was expected to make some comment. "There's a slip of paper inside with Mr. Rivers's address. Kindly contact him and suggest a meeting at your club. He'll enjoy that. Give him a good dinner and listen carefully to what he has to say. Then go to Lord Grandison, tell him Wordy Rivers approached *you* and that he wants Grandison as well. Mention the emolument and that you're in need of it. Play it down a bit; don't admit how badly in need you are, or he might be put off. He must not guess you're up to your ears in debt. Do you understand me?"

"Of course, my dear fellow. Won't let your name pass my lips," Augustus muttered unhappily. Sir James was already using his speaking tube, summoning his secretary. By merely raising an eyebrow, the banker indicated to this pallid individual, who had been his alter ego in business for more than two decades, that he should escort the visitor out and return at once. The mission accomplished, he glided back into the office and stood respectfully by the door, awaiting Sir James's further instructions.

"Think he can carry it off?" Sir James questioned sourly. "Well-bred nincompoop that he is?"

"Oh, I think so, Sir James. Mr. Rivers will see him through. A very persuasive gentleman, Mr. Rivers. Is there something else?"

"Yes. The Havershams have a daughter, haven't they? Bit long in the tooth, been out quite a few years and hasn't landed a catch yet. Rather plain, I believe."

"Miss Eleanor. She would be twenty-one now. No, not pretty, to judge from the picture postcards my wife collects."

"It's time Clive settled down. Young yet to slip his head in the noose, but when I declare him my heir, a bride with a pedigree like hers might help. I want that barony next year. Get Lord Augustus to arrange for them to meet, and make sure the girl knows on which side her bread's buttered. I didn't raise the matter today, for that feeble brain of his can't take in more than one idea at a time. Press him. Remind him about his promissory notes, due next month."

The secretary nodded his head, permitting himself to smile. He understood why, very well indeed. Sir James was a genius, no doubt of it. He knew exactly what he was being ordered to do, and how Lord Augustus would jib at the idea, but he quite relished the task.

Margaret Douglas was delighted to hear that Sir James was coming to Oxford, would be staying at the Clarendon, and had invited Clive to dine with him there. If only the stay were to be prolonged for a day or two, she stood a fair chance of being introduced to the ruler of the banking empire. With her good looks and charm, she was certain she would make a favorable impression; and, with her former devotion to Piers having quite evaporated, the thought of marrying into the Berryman family was positively thrilling.

Clive had explained the quirk of inheritance that made him the heir to Sir James, and the prospective barony. To be the wife of the second Baron Berryman was a dazzling prize for any girl to win, and infinitely more important than being handed a miserable diploma at the end of four years' grinding study. Why had she ever thought the classics Tripos worth striving for? Clive was suave, attractive, and altogether more fun than Piers had ever been.

Her disappointment was all the greater when Clive returned from his dinner with Grandfather James in a most uncommunicative mood. His attentions to her diminished from that day forward, no matter how she flashed her dancing dark eyes or teased and beguiled him. Something had happened to discourage him from declaring his love for her, when he was just on the brink of committing himself. In the course of a few days she knew without doubt that her chance was gone; Clive would not, as she had confidently expected, offer to marry her. Yet she could not begin to guess why.

Pride prevented Meg from admitting to anyone that Sir James Berryman's heir had let her down. But her spite toward him for doing so needed expression. And she had a weapon with which to strike him, for, only the day before that horrid dinner at the Clarendon, he had told her an incredible tale about Sir James, with severe warnings against repeating it, though he fancied there was little chance of that, since Meg's friendship with Delia had considerably cooled. She deliberately approached Delia on the subject.

"I am coming around to your point of view about Clive," she announced with some show of regret. "But, although the fellow adores me, and I can twist him about my little finger, I begin to agree that he's lacking in warmth and sincerity. Besides, his grandfather is little less than a monster. Heaven knows what Lord Grandison did to offend him, but it seems Sir James is still nursing a grudge for some fancied slight dating back to our infancy. He's positively gloating over the shrewd blow he's about to deal your father as revenge. Surely it can be nothing to do with money, for the Grandison family is known to be uncommonly wealthy..."

Delia frowned. Even mentioning her family's vast fortune was in the worst of possible taste. "No doubt it's the sort of thing men think important," she said tersely. "Probably horses. Perhaps he means to outbid Papa for some yearlings he wants to acquire, no matter how high the prices go. That's the kind of petty revenge men take." Her solemn expression relaxed. "Whereas, a woman would be satisfied with spreading the tale that her enemy's fabulous black pearls were not truly black, only dipped to make them appear so!"

"Well, I think you should mention it to your papa," Meg said airily, sure that the arrow had found its mark.

Delia agreed privately, but only nodded, then quickly changed the subject. No matter how hard the other girl probed to learn whether she had managed to extract a declaration from Will, Delia was no longer so naïve as to confide her business to a fellow student, especially the volatile Meg. The exclusion did not apply, of course, to Laura Boscawen, who continued to make possible Delia's almost daily visits to Will's rooms by acting as an extremely youthful chaperon. When she laughingly threw up her hands, protesting that she spent more time sketching views of the Magdalen quad from Dr. Prynne's windows than reading her set books of Ovid and Pliny, Delia began calling alone. Lace curtains were drawn aside. The wives of certain other dons lingered on their way in or out to watch Delia's arrival and prompt admission by Jenkin, but she was too much in love to care.

An answer to Will's submission of his paper to the Royal Society came with flattering speed. Would he present it at the meeting due to take place very shortly? He was more than happy to accept Natalie's invitation to stay overnight in Park Lane rather than at some dreary hotel.

While Arthur and Louise allowed themselves to be fêted at Grayle Abbey by their neighbors, who rarely had such an opportunity, Sir Michael and his wife were pressed to use Grandison House as their own home.

Michael was acutely aware of Natalie's suffering, but he did not know how to assuage it. Often he took her in his arms and stared deep into her desolate eyes. She smiled bravely and said nothing. It was too painful to put her feelings into words. The blow that had been dealt in Harley Street went deep; but that delivered by Nell Haversham struck deeper. Certain that she would never completely exorcise Andrei from her heart until she had Michael's child, that joy was now denied her. Michael made no reference to Andrei, thinking that Natalie preferred him to forget, to write *Finis* at the end of that episode in her life and turn the page.

Besides, he was afire with a new interest, which, for the time, made him less solicitous of his wife. For more than a year he had devoted all his enthusiasm to establishing his darling as an actress of equal rank with the highest, selecting plays that displayed her talent rather than his own. But an actor of such towering ability could not remain in a subservient position forever. The Irish playwright whose first work had failed to establish his reputation had written another play. It was a more polished effort, with witty dialogue and an excellent plot, ending with a surprise twist that would stagger the audience. The part of the hero fitted Michael like a glove. That of the heroine was not quite right for Natalie. But, knowing how much he longed to present the play, she assured him she liked the role, and inferred that perhaps something less demanding was just what she needed. She struggled with the part, reading it again and again, trying to wring some gleam of pure gold from it; but there was no doubt—it was Michael's play, and she could not become as totally immersed in it as he.

So it was an agreeable diversion when she received a letter written in William Prynne's spiky, almost illegible handwriting mentioning the date of his lecture. Had she forgotten her kind invitation? Would it be convenient for him to stay overnight at Park Lane?

Natalie replied at once that she was delighted, that she and Michael would dine at home with him that evening; for both of them were anxious to develop what promised to be a most enjoyable acquaintance.

Natalie had sworn Michael to secrecy when she revealed that Delia was in love with this Oxford don. Therefore it was disquieting news when they learned that Arthur and Louise were returning to Grandison House for a few days, just at the time when William Prynne would be there.

It seemed, wrote Louise, that dear old Augustus Haversham had inveigled Arthur into coming up to town and lending his name to some grandiose scheme for extending the system of underground railways! Arthur approved most highly of the "tuppeny tube," as it was familiarly called, and although he was indifferent to the emolument offered, he quite took the point that his old friend Gus would also benefit and needed the money. He had no idea that Gus was in the grip of his own unscrupulous and implacable enemy, Sir James Berryman. Indeed, Arthur had never realized that Berryman nurtured against him a grudge of quite insane proportions.

There was nothing about the person of Wordsworth Rivers to suggest that he was a monumental swindler. The son of middle-class emigrants to America, and a qualified engineer, he had traveled widely by the time he was forty, including a spell in Australia, where he formed a profitable gold-mining company. He then returned to London, bought a modest home in Ealing, where he established his aging parents, and turned his attention to the building of underground tunnels. He also floated several companies, with such resounding titles as the London Travelers' Transport Corporation and the Metropolitan Colossus Corporation. These companies flourished, borne up by the boom in providing a means for workers who lived ever farther afield from the center of the great city to reach their places of employment. From Clapham, Kingsbury, Campden Town, and Acton they flooded in daily (distances impossible to cover on foot) by omnibus and train, and now by the "tube."

Nearly a decade had passed since the unsuspecting Marquis of Dufferin had been duped by just another such confidence trickster into becoming chairman of the fraudulent London Globe Finance Corporation, which collapsed shortly afterward, bringing down with it a whole group of substantial-sounding concerns whose profits existed solely on bogus balance sheets. The Marquis had been fully exonerated, but he had been liberally spattered first with obloquy by the gutter press. It was a scandal practically forgotten by all, including Lord Grandison.

Wordsworth Rivers was considered almost with awe among financiers. He had the Midas touch. All his schemes succeeded, no matter how ambitious. His charismatic personality did not, however, entirely fool Sir James Berryman. "Pride goeth before a fall," he said sourly to his secretary, pointing to a paragraph in the *Times* that recorded the purchase by Rivers of a palatial property on the river at Kew. "He has expanded his interests in too many directions, spread his capital too thin. Only public confidence keeps his balloon aloft. If that were to come in question, if his empire were seen to be no more substantial than a bag of hot air, he'd crash soon enough."

But events had stolen a march on Berryman's calculations. Already Rivers had amalgamated his two most important companies into one concern, with a capital of more than a million pounds. He now speedily floated a number of smaller companies, all to do with transport, which mushroomed in size because the magic name of Wordsworth Rivers ensured success. But their prosperity was fictitious; like many other entrepreneurs who had known only the smiling face of fortune, he ignored the signs of a recession. The Russian crisis in 1904 and the loss of some lucrative trade with Japan wiped out the early profits. At the same time his pet scheme of enlarging the network of underground railways was becoming an ever-hungry giant, devouring vast sums of money. The rights to build tunnels, viaducts, and stations adjoining peaceful residential properties cost far more than he had anticipated, before ever a spadeful of earth was turned.

Rivers dared not lose public confidence; all had to seem to be well. To avoid discovery, he hit upon a fraud so daring that no one would suspect it. He boosted the assets of one company with funds borrowed from another, then stripped that in turn, entering losses as assets in his balance sheets, and never stayed more than one step ahead of his auditors.

Now, seeking easier concealment by setting up a new holding company amalgamating all his multifarious endeavors, he needed a figurehead. Berryman had suggested Lord Grandison, a capital choice to head the board of the Metropolitan Colossus Corporation. But it was essential that no one, especially his lordship, suspect that this whole edifice was just a house of cards. Rivers was ignorant of the crafty banker's intention to buy shares cheaply in Colossus and sell at a profit on the crest of a wave of public support. Panic would soon ensue when he began to unload. The company would collapse, burying the reputation of Lord Grandison in its ruins.

There was no time to consult Delia on how best to prepare the ground for William's meeting with her parents. Natalie's charm and Michael's easygoing good manners ensured that William took in his stride the first encounter with his beloved's parents. Will bowed over Lady Grandison's hand, murmured a compliment or two, then passed on to meet her husband's critical eye. Michael was unobtrusively at hand to tide over any awkward moment. He had taken a liking to this Welshman with the lilting voice. Whether Will was worthy of his forceful sister-in-law, he had not yet decided; but if a girl who had refused so many men chose to love him, he must be possessed of rare qualities. At the table Will at first appeared preoccupied, but that was natural, for he was still thinking of the unexpectedly favorable reception he had won from his distinguished audience that afternoon. But, realizing how important this occasion was, he rallied to take part in the general conversation. He was soon on the best of terms with Lady Grandison, for he knew very well how to compliment a beautiful woman, and she was one of the loveliest he had ever seen—a cold, glittering beauty whose appearance was quite unlike the warm, ruddy-hued golden looks of his Delia, but still breathtaking in her icy splendor.

But he had less success with her husband. At dinner, Lord Grandison questioned him politely on his paper, but there was no instant rapport between them. Michael, anxious to smooth the way between the two men, introduced the subject of the new company and the financier who had asked his lordship to head the board.

Lord Grandison, rarely loquacious at table, had more than usual to say about his meeting with Wordsworth Rivers and the latter's grandiose schemes. Each time the name of Rivers was mentioned, Michael became more disturbed. He put down his fork, leaving half the smoked trout on his plate untouched. Where the devil had he heard that name? It was unusual and had stuck in his memory. Then it came to him. The New York tycoon, Pierpont Morgan, had spoken of Rivers as an untrustworthy promoter of questionable business ventures.

"There's a fellow who has beaten us at our own game, Michael!" He nodded across the room. "He's a tricky customer. I'll have nothing to do with him. If he offers to sell you the Brooklyn Bridge, ask to see his title deeds first."

"What sort of man is this Wordsworth Rivers, Arthur?" Louise spoke up. "He probably has a commanding presence, but what is his background?"

Arthur replied that he came from humble beginnings, had worked industriously as a mining engineer, and at an early age, without possessing capital, had impressed a banker sufficiently to get backing and sink a mine of his own, despite strikes and walk-outs.

Will was goaded to comment, "I wonder what caused the miners to strike. An increase in wages all around? Shorter hours? Or better working conditions? Perhaps Mr. Rivers was able to pay back that loan with such dazzling speed because he followed the example set by owners in the mining community where I grew up: milking the pay packets to keep the men at starvation level, and their families often below it." His remarks, which had begun jokingly, turned bitter and vitriolic as he spoke. Unconsciously he fingered the scar where the policeman's night-stick had marked him savagely.

Almost at once, seeing Lord Grandison's astonished and displeased expression, Will could have bitten his tongue. It was a tactless, unwarranted attack, made on his host, and at the man's own table. "I beg your lordship's pardon most heartily. Not all mine owners exploit their workers, and I have no reason to charge Mr. Rivers with doing so. Please accept my apology."

"Very handsomely spoken, Dr. Prynne," Louise agreed graciously. But the damage was done. Arthur, seeing the persuasive Rivers through rose-tinted spectacles, felt injured on his behalf. He would not lightly forgive Dr. Prynne, and he hoped this disagreeable fellow was not a particular friend of Delia's.

When dinner came to an end, the host and hostess announced their intention of going out at once to join a party of friends at the theater. Natalie was left behind at her own insistence, to pour coffee for the two other gentlemen and to play the piano for them afterward in the drawing room. While they were sipping their demitasses, Will expressed his apprehension at having offended the man whom he hoped would be his future father-in-law.

"My tongue is sharp when I'm touched on a raw nerve, and I can't control what I say. It has always been my worst fault," he admitted. "What can I do to improve matters between myself and the Marquess?"

"Nothing at the moment, William," Natalie advised. "Let it drop. Papa is too fair-minded not to know that there is a great deal of truth in what you say. He seems to have been quite carried away by Mr. Rivers at their first encounter, but that may not last. Besides, you have Mama on your side. I could tell that she thinks you a most fascinating man, and she can already see herself introducing you to her friends as yet another highly presentable son-in-law."

The atmosphere became less tense. Natalie invited Will to sing with her some of the old ballads they both knew and had loved since childhood. She went to the piano, and her glorious soprano mingled with his fine tenor in melodies that wove golden strands through the silence of the great high-ceilinged rooms of Grandison House. Then she accompanied him while he sang alone, and Michael was quite genuine in his applause.

"You are a man of many parts, William," he said as they shook hands that night. "I confess I am surprised. The cold clarity of a scientist's mind seems almost at odds with your other talents. If the Marquess asks my opinion, I shall tell him that Delia appears to have chosen an unusually gifted man to marry." He spoke lightly, but Will knew him to be sincere and returned the handshake warmly. He was astonished when Michael changed the subject. "I have thoroughly enjoyed this evening, except for one thing," he went on earnestly. "I have heard of this man Rivers before, from no less an expert on company promotion than Pierpont Morgan. And nothing to his credit. I believe his probity would stand investigation, and I am seriously worried that even if I wrote at once to my banking friends in New York, I could not receive a reply before his lordship is irretrievably committed to this enterprise, which will receive enormous publicity in the press. Yet I do not see how I can interfere, unless I have something concrete on which to base my suspicions."

William was quite taken aback. Perhaps his caustic words had been more justified than he knew. "May I do something that might speed up your inquiry?" he asked. "I could approach an old family friend, David Lloyd George, in complete confidence. We practically grew up together, and he was like an elder brother to me. As president of the Board of Trade and a cabinet minister, he may know something about Rivers that we do not. It might be in his power to find out quietly whether your forebodings are justified and, if so, intervene to prevent the formation of the company."

Michael was relieved. "I know Lloyd George myself, but only slightly. If you are friends of long standing and he would be prepared to listen to you, please express my fears, and say that they stem from a recent conversation I had in New York with Mr. Morgan."

Will returned to Oxford and, without delay, made an appointment with Lloyd George for the following week.

Delia's greeting was less rapturous than he would have wished. It was obvious that something was on her mind. He waited for her to unburden herself, but she seemed to hesitate. So he talked on easily, mentioning that he had met her parents at Grandison House.

"I was received very affably by your mama. Her beauty quite swept me off my feet. Of course, it was to my advantage that Natalie and I were already well acquainted, and I had no trouble with Michael. What a handsome pair they make! He's a far more intelligent fellow than I had expected. Somehow I thought he would be rather a dandy, with nothing in his head but poetry."

"And Papa?" Delia prompted anxiously. "How did you get on with Papa?"

"Oh, well enough." Will was not keen to admit that they had crossed verbal swords at the dinner table. "We did not exactly hit it off, but, then, I believe he was a bit wary of Michael at the start."

This slight prevarication satisfied Delia, who now poured forth Meg's story about some plot to injure her father's high reputation.

Promising most convincingly that he and Michael would investigate the matter and see that no harm came to the family name, Will forbade Delia to worry further about such a disturbing piece of gossip. This put her mind at rest for the time being. But she was not entirely deceived by the airy manner in which Will had dismissed his first meeting with Lord Grandison. A few days later when they were inspecting Sundial House together she felt emboldened to return to the subject.

Chapter 27

"My cursed tongue ran away with me as usual!" Will was
striding up and down the empty dining room of his newly bought
property. He rattled the bolt on the French windows with none
too gentle a hand, then thrust his fists deep in his pockets and
stood glaring out despondently at the rain-soaked garden. "I
meant to keep it from you, *cariad*, but I fear I may have fallen
out with your father at the start . . . something admiring he said
about an enterprising mine owner making a fortune out of the
business. I know how these bosses operate—cutting corners on
safety, paying starvation wages, then forcing the men to work
longer hours for the same pittance."

Delia came up behind him and put her arms around his waist,
pressing her cheek to his rigid, angry back.

"Never mind, darling. At least Mama liked you and Papa will
come around, you'll see. Look, doesn't this room appear almost
furnished, even without a table and chairs? It must be the proportions, and the lovely paneling."

They had just come from a sale at Woodstock, where Will had
purchased an entire bedroom suite, a card table and desk, and
some very beautiful Oriental carpets. He had not been as pleased
with these acquisitions as Delia had expected, and seeing him

overcast and moody when they visited the house, she was not surprised by this outburst.

"I'm in a dashed bad mood these days." He swung around remorsefully and, with a masterful gesture, unpinned her soft blue felt hat, and then laid it on the mantelpiece, the better to cup her face in his hands and press butterfly kisses on her creamy forehead and smooth eyelids. "It's the strain of waiting to be officially engaged. If I had my way, we'd just run away and get married without the slightest pomp and ceremony. You're over twenty-one, darling, and God knows I've attained my majority long since. Why don't we?"

"Because the University authorities would have something to say about that, not to speak of my parents." She stood on tiptoes, reaching up to search the corners of his mouth with tender lips and the darting tip of her tongue. He stirred restlessly under that touch, desiring, hardening, barely able to control the need to take her, there and then, pinioned under him on the bare, shining boards. Didn't the girl know how she tempted him? "I'm afraid we cannot avoid having our grand wedding," Delia went on, "whether we wish it or not. Your father, Olwen, and even Anna would want that. As for my parents, they missed the fun of Natalie's wedding; I couldn't deprive them of mine as well."

The time had come for Delia to spirit Elsie away from Stonelea before Eustace could interfere and banish her to the workhouse. Natalie had provided the address of the family in Rupert Street and an assurance that a room was ready and waiting for Elsie, who would be welcome at any time.

While she took tea with Mrs. Bradleigh, Delia explained the arrangement and asked if she might inform Elsie of her good luck there and then. The girl was summoned by an astounded Mrs. Bradleigh, whose natural assumption of her own inferiority where Delia was concerned forbade any protest. If her ladyship had taken over the planning of a fallen girl's future, it must be the right and proper thing to do.

Elsie had been confidently waiting for such a summons. Hadn't Lady Delia said she'd take care of her? But she wept a little, out of sheer gratitude, when Delia informed her of the new home awaiting her where she could have her baby in complete safety, and the post that had been arranged with the wardrobe mistress at the Clarence.

Delia was feeling triumphant as she resisted Elsie's attempts to kiss her, or at least the back of her hand.

"Go along, Elsie, and pack up your things," Mrs. Bradleigh broke in officiously.

When they were alone, the good woman took the opportunity to confide. "Eustace thought he saw you, my dear, putting tracts through a number of letter boxes on the other side of the road. But it could not have been you, dear Lady Delia, of course, who circulated invitations to some horrid women's rights meeting. It is an invasion of the privacy of our homes to deliver such pernicious rubbish as if they were respectable letters, Eustace says. And I quite agree."

Delia soon took her leave, neither denying nor admitting Mrs. Bradleigh's statements. While she struggled to concentrate on her studies, her thoughts kept straying to her unwanted responsibility of delivering those handbills. Could she be criticized, reported to the Chancellor of the university? At last she went to bed apprehensive and heavy-eyed.

Even more disturbing than Mrs. Bradleigh's remarks was a passage in the letter she received the next day from her father. One fateful paragraph leapt to her eyes as she unfolded the notepaper:

> Your friend Dr. Prynne appears to have made a good impression on your mother; but I confess I found the man too much of a radical, with an unruly tongue. To be compelled at my own table to hear all mine owners denigrated, including such a man as Wordsworth Rivers, was most distasteful. Personally, I have no wish to further the acquaintance . . .

Running to Will's side for consolation, Delia was further upset to find him fuming. He, too, had received a letter that seemed to put yet another obstacle in the way of their future together.

"Listen to this rubbish! I've just received a note from a colleague who says he warns me as a friend. I've a good mind to walk around to his rooms at once and give him a piece of my mind."

"Stop, Will. Please don't do anything hasty," Delia implored. "Tell me what it says."

"The whole thing is ludicrous, but the gist is as follows. You have been seen coming and going here, often alone, and late at night. Damnation! I thought we had been so circumspect. I am compromising you, it seems, which would be overlooked—if I approached the right authorities for their sanction to marry you, and we immediately announced our engagement. But there is an impediment. Why can't the fellow write plain prose? Every other word is six syllables long."

"What is the impediment?" Delia hardly dared to ask.

"Why, your suffragist activities!" Will flung the crumpled letter toward the fire, but it fell outside the fender. Delia bent to pick it up, smoothed the paper, and read the words herself. It had come to the attention of the writer, the letter said, that she had joined the Oxford branch of the Society for Women's Suffrage.

"This letter is not official, you understand," he said more gently, seeing Delia's mortified expression. "It is from one of my colleagues, expressing views that are bound to be put forward when I ask for permission to marry you. He advises me seriously to forbid—*forbid,* you note—any further participation by yourself in the activities of the movement."

Delia did not reply. She stood, the letter crushed in a clenched fist at her side, looking into the fire. Why need they be vexed by these sordid considerations, hounded by the hypocritical standards of an outdated society?

"I have to tell you, Will, I've heard from my father that he disapproves of you and would prefer not to meet you again," she said unwillingly.

Will looked taken aback, then keenly disappointed. He folded her in his arms. "Another blow! Come, dear heart, shall we fight them all?"

"No, Will. I don't believe we could win. But I have to think about it very carefully—whether we are wise to go ahead with our plans, I mean. And you should do the same. Maybe . . . maybe we were never meant to marry." Her voice broke, and she could not continue.

Will released her, then moved swiftly toward his desk. He opened a drawer, and came back, proudly holding a little velvet box. "Your engagement ring. Please put it on now, this very moment." He snapped open the catch of the box, and, taking the ruby ring from its satin bed, slipped in onto her finger. "There. 'The Lady Cordelia Grandison is betrothed to Dr. William

Prynne, and the marriage between them will shortly take place.' Is that how the announcement will read in the court circular?"

Delia's face flushed. "Oh, Will, how beautiful it is." But the jewel on her finger was no magic key. They could hardly marry in the face of such universal opposition. Reluctantly Delia drew it off. "I'll put this lovely ring back in its box. It's too soon for me to wear it."

It was hard to persuade Will, but eventually he put the ring away, looking understandably dejected. She kissed him passionately—the only consolation she could offer.

The incident with the engagement ring was followed by a painful interview between Delia and her tutor. For some time her essays had not been as long, as carefully considered and neatly presented, as during her first year. It was obvious that Delia was falling behind the academic achievements of Laura Boscawen and Margaret Douglas. Little wonder, for she found it increasingly difficult to concentrate. Delia wrestled alone with her problem. Will would not ask her to give up her principles and demand that she abandon the suffragist cause.

"If only we were as enlightened here as they are in France," he said. "French women have long had equality with men in almost every field. Marie Curie never received such snubs at the Sorbonne. I hate to admit it, but your so-called sin is to struggle for something we men know in our hearts is unequivocally your right."

The more Will veered toward sharing her point of view, the harder Delia found it to stick by her sincerely-held principles. Why not just give in, resign meekly from the movement? The small devil who sometimes whispered in her ear suggested that after marriage she could once more take up the work. But Delia was too honest to accept this solution. However, the problem had to be set aside.

Will's father and sister Anna proposed visiting Oxford to congratulate him on his academic triumph in winning the Kimberlake Award and presenting his paper to the Royal Society. Rooms were reserved for them in the town, and Jenkin engaged a capable woman to help him with the extra meals at Will's own table. The small establishment was in an uproar.

Delia had certain suspicions about the reason for this visit. Perhaps Laura had let drop a hint about an imminent engagement when corresponding with her mother. A word from Mrs. Boscawen to an interested Olwen and a careless remark passed on to the vigilant Anna were more than enough to bring her straightaway to Oxford to see what was brewing. Anna was just the woman to rush in where angels feared to tread if she thought it her duty to prevent an unsuitable match for William.

Delia's first meeting with the senior Dr. Prynne was, in fact, strained and awkward. She had changed her mind twice about what dress to wear, and then mistrusted her choice of a ruffled blouse and velvet skirt. Laura, who was also bidden to tea, was in despair. They would be late, and Anna hated latecomers! As soon as Jenkin ushered the girls into Will's small drawing room, Delia guessed he had already imparted the momentous news of their engagement. Dr. Prynne, silver haired and looking far older than his years, rose, it seemed reluctantly, to greet her. Anna stood by the fire, clad in unrelieved black, her hands clasped before her. When old Dr. Prynne shook hands, he flashed a sudden glance at Delia from under beetling brows, and the gaze was startling in its intensity.

He is appraising me, she thought, *but clearly not favorably.*

They spoke of William's work, his award, and the honor it had brought him. Presently his father was asking about the series of experiments in Will's cloud chamber, over at the Daubeny, and he seemed eager to see the equipment used and to meet Will's lab assistant. The gentlemen therefore excused themselves. It would take only a few minutes to stroll over the road. . . .

Laura left at the same time, explaining that she had arranged to meet Piers. Promising to be back shortly, the two men left Delia alone with Will's sister, over the empty teacups.

"Will you join me in some more tea, Miss Anna?" Delia invited her. She turned to the bellpull.

"No, I would prefer to talk instead, since we have a little time together," the other girl answered abruptly. Surprised, Delia turned to meet the regard of hazel eyes so like and yet so unlike her fiancé's, ablaze with smoldering dislike.

Anna spoke coldly, almost dispassionately. "Do you really intend to marry my brother? If so, you will certainly ruin his life."

"But, why?" Delia faltered, quite disconcerted by this sudden attack. Then she drew herself up, for she was fully as tall as Anna, and said firmly, "I have already sensed that you do not like me—no, that you positively *hate* me. I want to know why, and what reason you have to make such a wounding assertion."

"Isn't it obvious? Will is a genius, destined to become one of the leading scientists of his age. He should not be held back from fulfilling his destiny by a selfish, pampered wife who will always be clamoring for his attention."

"Ah, now I begin to understand." Delia's own blue eyes flashed cold fire. "You glory in having sacrificed your own youth to the needs of a pair of country doctors, too busy to notice how selfish they are, how unfair toward you. Don't clench your fists and turn away; you know it is true. And you want to see another girl, a victim of your choice, meekly and of her own volition, bound and placed on the same altar."

"Yes, if it is necessary." Anna almost hissed the words. "The wife he needs is one who will put a curb on her tongue, expect nothing of him he is unwilling to give; not a spoiled aristocrat, a seductress who lures him back to her bed with lascivious temptations, when he should keep his mind free of such thoughts."

"I see it quite clearly," Delia retorted. "You are jealous. A self-condemned eternal spinster. That is why you accepted Charmian without resistance. She was too weak in body ever to have been a true wife to William, nor was he in love with her. You hate me because Will desires me—and that you cannot bear!"

"Nonsense," muttered Anna, brushing her hands angrily against her skirts.

"What does Olwen say?" Delia questioned. She knew how much Olwen Griffiths had liked her. "Is she of the same opinion?"

"Oh, I have told Papa, she is a snob, and that husband of hers is a social climber. They applaud the match, sycophants that they are." Cold contempt was apparent in Anna's voice.

"If you dare to set your father against me, be sure I will tell Will of your ugly motives!"

"Too late, dear Lady Cordelia. Besides, he would not believe you. The idea of his son marrying the daughter of an idle aristocrat quite disgusts him."

At this, Delia lost her temper completely. She slapped Anna across the cheek. "How dare you try to come between us, to separate me from Will in this wicked fashion! But you won't succeed!"

Anna fingered the scarlet markings of Delia's fingers. "I shall do so, and you'll regret striking me. Father must take me back to the hotel. Will has achieved nothing by forcing this odious meeting on us." She left the room, slamming the door behind her.

Delia did bitterly regret giving way to her temper, which, though so rarely roused, was on such occasions quite ungovernable. She stretched out on the rug, feeling cold and depressed in spite of the fire's companionable flame. It burned low and still William did not return. At last the door opened softly, and he came in. She turned her head away, afraid to meet his eyes.

He came forward, saying quietly, "Delia, look at me." She did, still rather fearfully, knowing that he was hurt by her gesture of withdrawal. The anger she had expected was there, but she could already sense that it was not against her.

"My darling, when this quarrel between you and Anna has simmered down, it will all come right, I am certain. I have heard her side of it, but know you to be in the right. She has great influence with my father, and I confess she has worked on him against you. They must have known about us for weeks. But he is a kind man, and a just one. When he knows you better, he will love you, too. No, don't speak, *cariad*." He lifted her, carried her to the sofa, and drew her down on his lap, rocking her like a hurt child. "Say that you will come with me to Wales for Christmas," he went on. "We shall stay with Olwen, who is already your friend and champion. We'll only go to Criccieth if I feel convinced you will receive a warm welcome as my bride-to-be, and I have told Anna so. But it is better not to attempt any reconciliation just now. Kiss me, *cariad,* and say yes."

Delia could not refuse, though she hardly believed differences that went so deep would ever be smoothed out.

The next morning, however, Delia awoke with a plan. She must consult Natalie; it would be wonderful to talk over her dilemma in the frankest terms with someone she could trust. Arriving unexpectedly at Grandison House, Delia was directed to the old schoolroom, where Natalie was kneeling on the floor next to her old doll's cradle. She had a baby doll, its wax face much battered, in her arms, and Delia was surprised to see a glint of tears in her eyes.

But in haste to pour out her story, she forgot to ask at once why the loveliest creature in London, with certainly the handsomest and most attentive husband, was crying over her childhood playthings. Natalie assumed her sister's unheralded appearance had to do with Michael's forebodings about Papa's commitment to the new business project.

"Has William spoken yet to his friend at the Board of Trade?" she asked. "Michael is terribly anxious now that the date has been fixed for the issue of new shares, and Papa has promised to read Mr. Rivers's announcement at the shareholders' meeting. It takes place just after Christmas."

"I know nothing of board meetings, share issues, or any other financial maneuvers." Delia sank down beside Natalie. "I've come to see you because everything is going wrong between myself and William. I can't sleep or eat or study, and I need your advice."

"*My* advice! How am I qualified, since I came so close to wrecking my own life?"

"Let me explain. First of all, Papa has written to me an unequivocal refusal to consider Will as my husband. I'm reading between the lines, of course, because we haven't asked for his approval yet. Then, Will's father and his unmarried sister, Anna, are my sworn enemies. Will thinks I can win them around, but I doubt it. They hate all members of our class, especially girls who seek higher education. What would they say if they knew that I campaigned for women's rights?"

"Does the entire Prynne family reject you, then?"

"Only Anna has said so. But William cannot marry and continue his work at Oxford without official assent to his chosen bride, and that will be withheld if I continue to support women's suffrage publicly."

"Poor Delia, I see you are beset on all sides." Natalie put out her hand. "Why must you carry the torch?" she asked at last. "Let others take it up for the time being. Agree with them in your heart, support them behind the scenes. Right every wrong you can, as you did with Elsie. But don't march, carrying a banner, or chain yourself to anyone's railings. Concentrate on just those things men think us best fitted for—being William's wife, having his children. Later, when he's a great man, they won't dare attack him no matter what you do. But, Delia . . . oh, how can I tell you this? Please have a baby soon. Let it be a girl, and make her my goddaughter, for I can never have babies of my own. I'll have to settle for loving yours as if they were mine."

"Who told you this, darling?" The two sisters clung together.

"An eminent doctor in Harley Street," Natalie replied tearfully. "It seems I miscarried and suffered some injury, which can't be repaired. I mustn't even hope. And I wanted it so much, to make up to Michael for . . . everything. For it wasn't his child that I lost. It was Andrei's. There, now I've told you my shameful secret. So Michael is deprived of an heir. He tells me I shouldn't dwell on morbid thoughts, but I can't help it. I only pray Will makes you as good a husband as Michael is to me."

Later, when Natalie was calmer, Delia agreed to withdraw from the movement.

She would renounce her membership for Will's sake. If old Dr. Prynne came to accept her, Anna's strictures did not really count. Her suffragette activities had certainly shocked the dons. Without this black mark against her, the opposition at Oxford would melt away. Only Papa remained to be persuaded, and Natalie believed Michael would do this. "Will wants to elope, or at least marry quietly—and very soon," Delia went on. "He's bought the loveliest little house for us to live in; it's ready now, or will be by Christmas. He seems almost angry with me when I find valid reasons for waiting."

Natalie smiled faintly. "How long has Will been in love with you—since last summer? He's not a boy, Delia. He's a full-blooded man, of experience, I hope. The strain of holding back is unbearable when he wants to make love to you."

"That's what I don't understand. I feel, oh, the strangest urges, wanting to do the most terribly intimate things. What is going to happen? I'm eager, yet afraid of the force that's there between us."

Natalie did tell her, very simply and directly, in terms that Lady Grandison would never have brought herself to use when preparing either of her daughters for their marital duties.

Delia was startled, shocked, but no longer afraid, as one would be of the totally unknown. Natalie then suggested that the wedding should take place at Grayle, perhaps on St. Valentine's Day. If both families could be reconciled to it over Christmas, that would only impose a waiting period of just over six weeks on the impatient bridegroom.

"When your passion rises to meet his, that is the right time to yield. Let it happen naturally, and beautifully, so that it is something you can both always treasure as a golden memory, not one of humiliation and outrage," Natalie concluded.

Delia hurried downstairs, more deeply shocked by Natalie's disclosure of her coupling with Andrei than the nature of the act itself. What was the slumbering beast that lurked in men's bodies, and the awesome power it gave them over the tenderest, purest of women? Had Mama, or worse still, Papa, realized Natalie to have been guilty of the ultimate sin—that she had lain with her lover and already carried his child—on that terrible day when she fled to London in search of him?

As Delia reached the front door she paused to draw on her gloves. Then she heard a soft footfall behind her. Natalie's hand was on her elbow and she just caught the whispered entreaty: "Your first little girl, darling . . . promise me you will call her Gwendoline . . ."

Chapter 28

It was with great difficulty that Delia penned her resignation as soon as she was in the familiar sitting room at Somerville. She could hardly hold back some angry tears, but she knew that Natalie was right—her loyalty to Will must come before the cause. She showed the brief document to him and mentioned Natalie's advice on setting their wedding date. The rest, she felt, was a secret between herself and her sister.

Will was delighted and was at once full of plans for their future. "I'll write to your papa this very day and ask formally for his blessing—not his permission, you note, for we don't need it."

"Please, please be tactful, darling," Delia interposed, fearful that once again he might put himself at odds with her father.

"The epistle I shall write will be masterly, I assure you. I well know what a jewel I shall possess in you, my lovely girl. I need only promise to treasure you with my heart, body, and soul, as you deserve. What more can he want?" With some temerity she allowed Will to put the ruby engagement ring on her finger and let it remain there.

* * *

In spite of all Delia's forebodings, she found the visit to Wales less of a trial than she had expected. But her biggest surprise lay in her conversation with Dr. Prynne as they stood outside the chapel after the meeting on Christmas morning. The weather was turning cold, and powdery flakes of snow were dancing a jig in fitful gusts of wind that blew up the village street.

"You liked the service, I hope?" he asked. "It's plain enough, with none of your high church trimmings, but the singing is good. Welsh voices, you can't beat them." He hesitated, looking away toward his own gate. "I hope you'll enjoy the dinner at home today. Anna's not such a fancy cook as Olwen, but she likes to see us gathered around the family table once a year, as we did at Christmas when her mother was alive. Lovely, she was, a most kind and beautiful lady. And so are you, my dear."

Delia was astounded. "But I thought you didn't approve of me at all . . ."

"Come along, you'll catch cold." He offered her his arm. "It's only a few steps back to the house. The others can catch up with us. I wanted to have this word with you, out of Anna's hearing, Delia *bach*. You mustn't think I forced my youngest girl to lead such a life. Oh, yes, I know what folks say. But it's her choice. There's a perverse pleasure in it for her. A masochistic pleasure, I fear. Do you understand my meaning?" As he tramped along briskly Delia was reminded of Will's determined walk. "It was best to let her have her own way," he went on. "She spoiled Charmian, you know; she almost snatched every task away from her, rather than sit idle for a moment herself. Made the girl feel more useless than she was. Ah, here's the gate. *Croesl!* Be welcome to our house, Delia. I know you'll make my son happy." The light kiss on her cheek assured her that his words were sincere; a wealth of happiness filled her, and she felt nothing but optimism for her future with Will.

On the way back to Oxford, Delia was struck with a sudden desire to see her future home at once. "If the train isn't late, could we drive to Folly Bridge straight from the station and see the house again?" she asked Will shyly. From the moment they entered, Delia was enchanted. Mrs. Ford, the local woman engaged to look after it, had everything in perfect order. Even a fire had been lit in their bedroom upstairs. The feather pillows and eiderdown she had purchased were laid around it to fluff up be-

fore being put away in the linen cupboard. Will drew her closer
to the warmth, his eyes telling her without words that he found
her wondrously beautiful. His hand fondled her breast, at first
timidly, then insistently. At once she drew back.

Then she was conscious of the most extraordinary sensations,
a shocking desire to press herself close to him, to let her own
hands wander from their half-defensive position against his
chest. To let them slide around the back of his neck, draw him
toward her while she molded the length of her body against his.
Would she feel the hardness, the threat of a weapon Natalie
had described, and which she feared? But did she fear it? A
wild curiosity invaded her, sent tremors between her thighs,
made her almost writhe, first gripping her own limbs convulsively together, then parting them, instinctively moving closer to
the unknown source of his manhood. She gulped, her throat con-
stricted, her mouth dry. "I love you," she faltered. "Love you,
love you . . ."

She dropped her hot face on his shoulder, knowing that she
was shamelessly offering herself to him; then she tried to strain
away.

But he wound his fingers in the golden tresses, keeping her
breathlessly close, body to wildly throbbing body. "Only a few
weeks," he murmured. "Our wedding night. But, God in heaven,
Delia, how I want you now." He was pressing brief, burning
kisses on her temple, moving down her cheek to her bosom,
encountering the lace frill that edged her dress; her own hands
were fumbling with the row of buttons that fastened it, opening
the tiny hooks and eyes, rending the delicate lace. His hands
followed hers blindly, while she sought his mouth, both of them
with eyes now closed, feeling the butterfly caress of lashes, and
then his lips were there, on hers. She was seeking to part his
clenched teeth, for he was almost groaning, so fierce was the
battle within him not to take her at once, in the firelight and the
intimacy of their future home.

She felt him go very still for an instant. Then his mouth
clamped down on hers, sweeping her into a whirlpool of surrender to his passion. Her clothes were ripped away. His mouth was
cruel on her breasts, his hands bruisingly strong, forcing her
thighs apart.

But it was exultation she felt, not pain, and the wonder of
submission, even while she whimpered a little under his attack.

He pinned her down. The first thrust was agony, but then it was perfect, all undreamed-of pleasure. There was no shame, only amazement that men and women were so fashioned, and that it seemed exquisitely right. Delia felt the hot surge of Will's fulfillment, experienced with wonder the sensuous questing touch of his fingers that brought her own. He sighed and slowly drew away. She drifted on a delicious sea of fatigue, the aftermath of their union, in his arms.

It seemed ages later that they returned to Oxford. They were silent during the drive back into town. Once Will murmured in Delia's ear, "Forgive me for my impatience, my selfishness. Say that I did not hurt you too much—at least that I did not disgust you, my golden girl!"

And she replied, seizing the hand that fondled her and kissing it fervently, "No, no, my dearest one. I wanted it, too. You were wonderful."

A pile of letters and several parcels were waiting for Delia at Somerville: delayed Christmas greetings and presents from her family, including a Japanese ivory fan of exquisite delicacy from Natalie, and a letter from her father. It read:

My dear Delia,

 Your company was missed over Christmas by the boys as much as by Mama and myself. We were all disappointed that you chose to spend the festive season with Dr. Prynne's family instead of with us. The holidays were not cheered for me by receiving the news of your impending marriage. I cannot bring myself to refuse, but I would really prefer that you should not be married from Grayle and oblige me to give you away in such haste. The truth is, though I dare say you will find it unpalatable, that I cannot immediately approve of the match. Must you rush into it? Perhaps I might come to like William better, in spite of his radical views, in the course of time. Both Natalie and Michael think well of Dr. Prynne, and your mother remains, to my surprise, open to persuasion in his favor. If you are prepared to wait six months, I will reconsider my attitude then, and it is my sincere hope that in time I shall be convinced, my darling child, that you have chosen a man who will make you happy. Perhaps you will convey my feelings to him in the meantime.

Delia put her hand unconsciously to her breast, where the lace was torn and a small button was pulled away from the fabric of her dress. The supreme experience, which had crowned her love for Will, now seemed far away. The censorious opinion of her elders, the world at large, towered over her threateningly.

When Delia was summoned the next day to Miss Maitland's sitting room, she was astonished to find William seated there with a glass of Madeira in his hand, and to receive congratulations on her engagement from the principal. Saying that Dr. Prynne had some further joyful news to impart, Miss Maitland tactfully left them alone together.

William had noticed Delia's subdued demeanor, but he had attributed it to a certain shyness, now that their future plans were to be generally known. Or, perhaps she was remembering their lovemaking of the previous evening. He could not wait to produce a folded sheet from his pocket, saying triumphantly, "Delia, I still can hardly credit it. The president of the Royal Society has written to say that the members have unanimously decided to elect me a fellow. What an honor. I believe I shall be the youngest of that august assembly by a good few years! It is an accolade I never hoped for at such an early stage in my career. Miss Maitland was sure I would be offered another lectureship at once."

For a moment Delia was speechless with delight. Then she flung her arms around him, murmuring, "My clever, brilliant sweetheart, I'm so proud of you!"

"This news certainly ought to impress your father," continued Will, much gratified. "I know you haven't heard from him yet, and neither have I. But could you write and let him know?"

"I don't think it would help," she admitted dejectedly. "He has already replied to me, making it clear he does not approve entirely, and he insists on a long engagement, so that we may be quite certain we are suited." She turned away, flushing painfully. It was like a blow in the face that Papa had chosen to ignore Will's own letter.

"It makes no difference to my intention," he said steadily. "Provided he gives me permission, I intend to consult Lloyd George, on your father's behalf, about the company Rivers intends to float. The connection between his name and that of Berryman may be tenuous, but it's highly suspicious."

He took up a folded newspaper, which lay on Miss Maitland's

table next to the decanter of wine. Quickly scanning the financial pages, he gave an exclamation of dismay. "Good God, Delia! Details of the shareholders' meeting are advertised here, and your father's name is mentioned, too! It's only a week away! If there is anything unsavory about the venture, there is no time to lose. We have to find out and warn Lord Grandison if necessary. I'll call on David at once without an appointment; even if he's busy, he won't refuse me."

"Let me come with you, Will," Delia pleaded. "If I don't, Papa may not even see you. Or you might lose your temper and say something to him you would regret afterward. Oh, anything might happen!"

Will was not anxious to involve Delia; but at least her presence would ensure him a hearing. He agreed, hoping devoutly that Michael had already paved the way by convincing the Marquess that serious doubts existed about the honesty of Wordsworth Rivers.

Will had anticipated not being invited to stay in Park Lane by booking a room for himself at the Great Western Hotel. At Grandison House, Lord Augustus Haversham was standing with his back to the fire in the library, solemnly observing the progress of a game of backgammon between Michael and his father-in-law. When Delia and Will were respectfully ushered in by Adams, Arthur rose.

"Delia, I am amazed to see you. And to what do I owe this honor, Dr. Prynne?" he inquired stiffly.

Michael had no intention of letting tempers flare up, so he broke in, saying, "No doubt William has some interesting news for us, Arthur." He, too, had risen and, with frank deliberation, took Will's hand and shook it. "Have you seen Lloyd George, then? I myself have sent two telegraphic messages to Morgan in New York, but I have had no reply."

Michael hesitated, on the verge of saying more, but he glanced at Lord Augustus, who muttered uncomfortably, "Family matters to discuss, eh? I'll be off, then, Arthur."

"Wait, Gus, don't leave us." Each of Lord Grandison's words was chosen with icy calm. "Delia, go upstairs to your mother. I insist. Matters of business do not concern young ladies."

"Mama will be happy to see me, I know, Papa—even if you are not," she said rebelliously, than marched out of the room and headed up the stairs.

Louise was more than happy to see Delia, and she embraced her elder daughter tenderly. "What an opportune moment for you to arrive, my darling. Do join me in a cup of chocolate! Have you brought your fiancé with you?" she inquired with a teasing glance.

"At least you acknowledge our engagement, Mama," said Delia despondently, unpinning her hat. "Do you really like William?"

"Extremely, and I have told your father so time and again. I shall wear Papa down, you'll see. If you two are prepared to wait . . ."

"But we are not. Our house is furnished, our servants engaged. Why should we wait?" Delia's voice rose plaintively above her mother's. "We have set our hearts on an early wedding. Papa should be grateful to Will for making sure that he's not becoming innocently involved in some wretched scandal."

Then, knowing how much her mama would be pleased, Delia went on, "Will is a great admirer of yours. There is nothing cold or didactic about my scientist; he appreciates beauty keenly, and he thinks you one of the loveliest women he has ever seen."

Louise bent her head, graceful as ever on that long, swanlike neck. The clean lines of her throat and exquisite profile were outlined against the sapphire velvet of the quilted headboard behind her. "Rubbish, Delia—or, at best, arrant flattery. I am approaching my fiftieth year, darling."

"Age has not dimmed your beauty, and I don't believe it ever will, Mama." The girl spoke sincerely, for, indeed, Lady Grandison's looks were as breathtaking now as ever. Pausing at the door, Delia's attention was caught by a silver-framed photograph; it portrayed the Marchioness in the splendor of her youth, clad in rose-colored satin. She was holding the little Natalie on her lap, an adorable three-year-old in starched muslin with lavender ribbons, though the sepia print did no justice to the painstaking hand-coloring that had been added later. Delia, a grave ringleted child in a dress that matched her sister's, leaned over her mother's shoulder, caressing the younger child's arm with a protective air.

She spoke impulsively. "May I take this? Will would love to see how Natalie and I looked as children."

After Delia had carried off the photograph, Louise suddenly started up in bed, a hand flying to her cheek. "I had quite forgotten," Louise murmured fretfully to herself, for there was no one to hear. "How foolish of me to let that photograph out of my sight. Well, perhaps no harm will come of it. After all, the past is over and done with."

Downstairs in the library, Michael was inwardly expressing the same hope.

"Sure you don't wish me to leave?" Lord Augustus spoke after a full minute of weighty silence. "We could lunch together tomorrow."

"You're also involved in this matter, as it happens," his host replied sarcastically, resigned unwillingly to the inevitable discussion. "Perhaps you should hear what accusations have been leveled against Wordsworth Rivers—without any proof, I may say—"

"By your leave, Lord Grandison," interrupted William, sketching a jerky bow, his face taut with annoyance. "If Michael's friend Morgan, who must be one of the most knowledge-able bankers alive, says Rivers is a rogue, it should be given serious consideration. But what worries me far more is a piece of gossip repeated to Delia by one of her friends about Sir James Berryman. It came from a girl who's hoping to marry his grand-son Clive. It sounded as though he has borne a grudge against you for many years, and now he thinks he has found a way to ruin you. Could this be because you are about to enter his special domain—the arena of the Stock Exchange? The coincidence does give some cause for alarm."

At the mention of Berryman's name, Lord Augustus started, and his florid complexion turned to a mauvish shade of gray. He began to speak, then checked himself.

But Arthur was determined to hear him. "You are to be on the board of the Colossus yourself, Augustus. I met Rivers at your behest. Do you think there can be a word of truth in these allega-tions? Could there be anything amiss with the new company? And how could Berryman possibly be involved?"

Lord Augustus gulped and made feeble waving gestures, as though submerged by a sudden wave and seeking to find the surface of the water. His instinct was to flee, but the blood of heroic ancestors who had fought on the same battlefields as those of Lord Grandison flowed, even if turgidly, in his veins.

"Arthur," he panted, clapping a hand to his bulging waistcoat in the vicinity of his heart. "I'd better make a clean breast of it. I never meant to involve you in anything to your detriment, old chap. I don't know what the connection is, or if Rivers is a wrong'un, but the fact is, I'm in Berryman's hands. Nasty fellow . . . bought up some rather pressing promissory notes of mine. Due any day now. It was he who put me on to Rivers, and made it an absolute condition of calling off his bloodhounds that I should talk you into heading the board of Colossus." Augustus drew out a handkerchief and began to wipe his forehead and balding pate. "Rivers had never thought of asking you, he said, but he wanted to oblige Berryman," he went on miserably. Then he brightened. "I expect the crafty old blighter is buying a lot of shares in the new enterprise. Wants a well-known name like yours to launch it, eh? There can't be anything sinister in that!"

There was no answer to be found to his plea in Lord Grandison's frozen expression. Michael looked, frowning, from one man to the other before he glanced, seeking an opinion, at William Prynne. Could there be some unholy alliance between the banker and Rivers of which Augustus had been the unwitting tool? Almost imperceptibly William nodded.

"This is the first I've heard of Sir James Berryman as your enemy, though he does have the reputation of being something of a shark. But the matter definitely needs sifting, Arthur." Michael addressed his father-in law in that rich, persuasive voice of his. "There might be nothing in it, just that Sir James knows you're the ideal man for his purpose and doesn't care to make a direct approach. Some clash between the two of you years ago, perhaps. However, that remark of his about ruining you—I don't like it at all."

"Please allow me to go to the president of the Board of Trade on your behalf," Will said earnestly. "David Lloyd George is an old and dear friend; otherwise, I'd not suggest it. But he's the one man who might know if there's anything shaky about the company's backing. I'll lay the facts before him and ask whether he advises you to withdraw your support from the flotation while there's still time."

Lord Grandison could not bring himself to look at Will. "Such a worthy scheme," he said wistfully. "The extension of the underground railway. It would be a boon to Londoners. Surely there's nothing that old curmudgeon Berryman can do to hurt me through it." He was not yet ready to admit that the silver-tongued Rivers might be a trickster, the company worthless, or that his support was being used by Sir James to blacken the name of Grandison.

But he felt the first deep pang of doubt. Whether he disliked William Prynne's politics or not, and resented the way Michael had sided with him, it was just possible the fellow had the right of it, as far as both the banker and Rivers were concerned.

"Investigate, damn you!" he cried with supreme lack of logic. He strode out, forgetting Augustus, ignoring Michael, and a moment later they heard his study door slam behind him. He flung himself down into a chair behind his desk to ask himself whether he had been duped by a rogue, and whether he would be lucky enough to emerge unscathed. Also, he had to consider the unpalatable possibility of accepting a scientist and a radical into the family.

William found David Lloyd George in his bedroom, sitting in an armchair by the fire, wearing an old smoking jacket, a voluminous scarf around his throat. The operation he had undergone to remove his tonsils should have prevented further infection, he growled hoarsely to William, but there he was, laid up for weeks, nursing a damned quinsy again.

William wasted little time on expressing his sympathy. He plunged into the story of his engagement to Delia, her father's opposition, and the present quandary.

Lloyd George looked thoughtful. "I can't interfere directly. But I get information on the state of the Stock Exchange from all kinds of sources. Most of these bankers have some trusted secretary or assistant whom they send out to sniff the wind for information. These lackeys meet for a chat after office hours, and a great deal of business is done as the result of their gossip. This Berryman has some such assistant, you may be sure. As it happens, I'm in touch with a man who probably knows him well." He took his card from a desk drawer and scribbled a few words on the back. "That's to introduce you. Get in touch with him directly, and ask him to sound out Berryman's chap to see what's going on. Promise him a pony, at least, if he ferrets out anything interesting."

"Twenty pounds?" expostulated William. But it might be worth it. He left immediately and threaded his way toward the city and Queen Street, where the man he was searching for might be found.

Lloyd George returned to his chair by the fire. He made a mental note to invite Berryman to come to his office. A hint would be sufficient that when the banker's name came to be considered for a peerage, his character must be unblemished. Any scheme to manipulate the flotation of a company for the wrong motives would be a serious bar to granting it. It wouldn't even be necessary to mention Lord Grandison's name. Berryman would have to forgo his revenge, or his peerage—one or the other. . . .

The Manchester Arms, a gloomy public house in Lombard Street, did a great deal of trade after six o'clock in the evening. The tables in its private bar were well spaced out, enclosed in booths that had long been proved completely soundproof; it was the perfect place to converse without being overheard. The customers, almost exclusively clerks to wealthy stockbrokers, bookkeepers in the employ of merchant bankers and the like, enjoyed meeting there to relax and brag a little after a harassing day of bowing, scraping, and leaping to the orders of their irascible employers.

Sir James Berryman's creature sat over his pewter pot of brown ale, in conversation with a particular friend of his. To enhance his reputation he was enlarging on his employer's despotic personality, hinting that many a business magnate shook in his shoes when Sir James requested him to call—a command that no one dared disobey. Behind the doors of that office in Threadneedle Street, under the sign of the unicorn, fortunes were made and lost; men of affairs became wealthy or were ruined, as Sir James saw fit.

"Going well, is it, Colossus?" inquired his friend. "My gentleman, now, doesn't fancy Rivers at all. Won't let him get his foot over our doormat. Sir James must fancy him a great deal, if what I hear is true." He paused significantly.

The creature shook with silent laughter. "Not involved at all, my old cockelorum. If he is, it's done through nominees, that's all I can say. He doesn't like Rivers either. Thinks he's a man of straw, as they say. But he's ready to buy, when the shares come on the market. I can always tell when Berryman's in the mood to buy. The question is: Will he hold? There's more money made by selling at the right time than by buying."

"Ah, so that's the way of it," observed his companion, emptying his beer mug. "Will you have another? No? Well, then, neither will I. The wife likes me to get home early these dark nights."

Nothing more was said, for it would have been indiscreet. But later, at the Red Mill, a more salubrious pub in Shepherd's Market, a pony changed hands. "He'll buy, and send the shares sky high. Then, when they've jumped to twice the issue value, he'll sell and throw them all on the market at once. The market will take fright, every investor from bishop to bank clerk will want to get out, and the shares will plummet. The company will go bust, mark my words. A sly bastard, Sir James. He might even buy again at rock bottom, then nurse the company around. But it's not likely. More of a funeral undertaker than a nurse is Berryman."

"I see. So the public who invested and lost their money would be inclined to blame the chairman for painting too rosy a picture of the company's prospects?" William asked.

"Dare say. I'm off now, guv'nor." The informant slid away, grasping four crisp, crackling five-pound notes in his avaricious hand.

Michael decided to postpone his departure from Grandison House. He knocked at the study door, and after a moment he heard a gruff indication to enter. When he saw that his visitor was Michael, Lord Grandison gestured toward a chair on the other side of the room.

"Come to tell me I'm an ungrateful, bad-tempered old stick-in-the-mud?" he growled defensively.

Michael sat down. "I don't think you appreciate what a remarkable fellow this lover of Delia's is," he began mildly. "What do you really have against him? Of course, he's unduly sensitive about the wrongs of the miners, having seen firsthand how the poor devils are ground down by the owners. He got that scar over his eye in a baton charge, when the police were hitting out indiscriminately at a few miserable demonstrators. He almost lost his sight. But that didn't stop him from going on with his studies and eventually winning the highest academic honors. The work he's doing now is the stuff pioneers dream of; I'm certain he's at least a decade ahead of our time in his discoveries . . ."

Lord Grandison gave a grunt that might be taken for agreement.

"And only today I've learned that he's received national recognition. He's been made a fellow of the Royal Society."

Arthur could not help being affected. And he began to feel a little guilty that he had taken such an instant dislike to William

Prynne. He knew he owed a great deal to William for the energy he expended in tracking down the sinister power behind the scandal that was in the wind. He already knew in his heart that their suspicions would be proved right.

"I will agree to meet the man again and get to know him. If Delia loves him, I'm prepared to revise my decision about attending the wedding. I may give her away after all!"

"Don't you think you should see her and tell her so?" Michael could speak with the voice of an angel when he chose, and perhaps he was the only man alive who could have wrung compliance to this course from the reluctant Marquess.

When Delia came to her father, he was standing, his hand resting on the oak mantelpiece carved with the Grandison coat of arms, staring into the fire.

"You wrote me a very cruel letter, Papa," she said in a low voice.

"I felt you were making a mistake. I only asked you to wait, just a little while, to make sure that you would be well-matched with your William. He's not an easy chap to get on with. Wait a few months, my dear . . ."

Delia faced him defiantly. "No, Papa, I can't agree to postpone the wedding. Will and I feel so certain, and we're so much in love. We're not children." She came closer, and in spite of her declaration, she nestled against him, as she had when she was quite a little girl. "Do him justice, Papa. He'll be a great man one day. You'll be proud of him."

Her father looked down at her. He had never seen this daughter of his so lovely, so radiant, her eyes of that deep azure blue aglow with confidence and happy anticipation.

He gathered her to him. "Let it be as you wish, my darling." He laid the benison of his kiss on her fair head.

William came back to Park Lane very late and very tired. He had returned to the home of David Lloyd George for a further conference. And it was no coincidence that the new company was never launched and that the enterprises of Wordsworth Rivers came under careful scrutiny by the Board of Trade. As a result, some of them failed. A few prospered in a modest way; but the new meteor in the financial sky was seen to fizzle out like a spent firework after a bonfire-night party. The name of Wordsworth Rivers was no longer held in awe.

However, the disgruntled and grasping Sir James did eventually receive his barony, and the highborn wife he desired for his grandson. Eleanor fell head over heels in love with Clive Berryman. She did not dislike his coldness; it acted as a spur to her own passion. And he came unwillingly to enjoy her crass demands for the good things of life, including her insatiable sexual appetite. It was said of them that they deserved each other, though not always in flattering tones.

As for the straits in which Lord Augustus found himself, Arthur discovered that these were more severe than he had imagined from occasional hints that were dropped to Louise. It was the Duke's duty to do something for his second son, and Arthur accosted that tight-fisted autocrat in the robing room at the House of Lords to tell him so. It was a short but white-hot exchange, with a great clashing of verbal swords, from which both emerged sufficiently shaken to require a strong whiskey-and-soda to recover.

But Arthur devoted the proceeds of selling the yearlings from his stable that season to the benefit of Gus and Julia, a fact quite unknown to Louise or any other living soul, except his legal adviser. And, having been extricated from the mire, Lord Augustus was the delighted recipient of a much improved allowance from his noble father.

Chapter 29

Having returned to Oxford with Will in triumph, Delia was unpacking her valise. Her mind was so preoccupied with the strange turn of events that had taken place in their lives during the last twenty-four hours that she did not even hear a light knock, until Meg had slipped into the room.

"Your fire is smoking, and it's wretchedly cold in here," she began in a critical tone. Then, with a quick change of mood: "But you are above worrying about creature comforts, I know, and how I envy you for it."

The truth was that Meg found herself rather lonely since her own affair with Clive Berryman had ended abruptly. Since relinquishing Piers, although not without some tears and tantrums, to Laura, she really had no reason to be jealous of Delia.

"What a charming portrait," she went on in her most winning tones, taking the frame that had just been unpacked from Delia's hands. "Your mother, the famous Snow Queen, I suppose. One can see, even in tinted sepia, that her hair is more silver than gold; at least it has caught a certain icy glitter from the photographer's lights. What pretty little creatures you and Natalie were. Those dark curls of hers clustered around that sweet oval face, and the enormous eyes peeping out rather shyly under such a

329

fringe of lashes. Was she about three then? You must have been no more than seven years old yourself at the time."

Meg turned the frame to catch the gas lamp's glow. "Oh, the glass is cracked. You must have packed it carelessly, my dear girl."

In fact, Delia now realized with some annoyance that her steel-pointed buttonhook, quite indispensable for the speedy fastening of high-barred shoes and boots, had pressed too hard against the fragile glass.

"Be careful, Meg. You might cut yourself," she said swiftly, vexed that Meg had caught her in even this trifling kind of inefficiency. It was not yet so long since a maid had always packed for Delia, with many careful folds of tissue paper between each item and the next.

"I believe I have a spare frame of the same size." Meg was, in her turn, annoyed with her own swift tendency to criticize. What a pity, just when she most wished to conciliate Delia. "Let me lend it to you," she went on in a gently persuasive manner. "I have banished the picture, which once had pride of place on my mantelpiece, of myself with Clive and Piers on the river, since both my swains have transferred their allegiance to others." She laughed to show that this comment was made in jest, but it sounded rueful, and Delia felt a surge of pity. It was a loan Delia felt obliged to accept, for she knew Meg was more hurt than she cared to admit.

Together, the girls unscrewed the back of the damaged frame, removed the thick white card behind the photograph itself, then the shards of broken glass. Another picture, which had been hidden behind the first, slid out onto the desktop. A strikingly handsome woman as dark as Louise was fair, and wearing magnificent black pearls, stared haughtily up at them. She was holding by the hand a boy of some four years, still in skirts, as was the custom of the day, who bore a startling resemblance to little Natalie.

Delia turned the picture over and read the inscription, written in a nervous hand, with many flourishes: "To my dearest friend Louise, from Natalya—myself with my darling Andrushka on his fourth birthday." Below was the date, May 10, 1887. There were a few more words: "Constantine joins me in hoping that we may meet again soon with you and Arthur."

Meg was already reaching out to take it, as Delia, suspicious at once of the truth, yet disbelieving the evidence of her own eyes, laid the two photographs side by side. "What an extraordinary likeness there is between that child and Natalie!" cried Meg. *"They might be brother and sister."*

"No, no—merely distant relatives." Delia spoke mechanically, but the strength seemed to be draining out of her. Her hands were icy, the fingers too numb to intervene when Meg possessed herself of the long-concealed photograph and calmly studied the inscription. The resemblance between the two children did not immediately mean anything to her, but Meg's quick perception sensed some scandal, which she determined at once to uncover.

"Well, you are obviously not in a mood to talk," she said kindly. "My poor Delia. Some world-shaking events must have taken place in London. Did your parents finally give their consent to your marrying Dr. Prynne? And, by the way, did you find out why your father quarreled with the odious Sir James? Oh, I see I am tormenting you when you are tired and perhaps not quite yourself."

Delia clenched her fists agianst her skirt until the nails dug unmercifully into her soft palms. "I am tired," she acknowledged in a colorless voice. "But the visit was most successful. My parents are quite reconciled to the engagement, and they even approve of our plan to marry on Saint Valentine's Day. As to the other matter, it turned out to have been quite trivial, and my father has nothing to fear from Sir James. I won't come down for dinner tonight, Meg. I'd rather go to bed early if . . . if you will excuse me now."

When Meg had left her, with a calculating glance and tightly pursed lips, Delia sank down on the desk chair. Again, she compared the two children's faces, remembering how she had missed Mama and cried for her that summer her parents had spent in Russia. How thrilled she had been afterward, when the baby sister arrived to share her nursery. The hair, so unlike her own, fine as black silk, that curled around the infant's forehead. Feelings of outrage stirred in her breast.

Gradually the enormity of it all dawned on her consciousness. She knew the true reason why her mother had been adamant that Natalie could not marry Andrei and had influenced Papa with all her might to refuse also. The word *incest* was too ugly to be spoken out loud. But Delia was no longer entirely innocent and naïve. If she had hesitated to believe it possible, the proof lay in

Lady Grandison's own conduct—namely, her implacable refusal
to let her younger daughter marry the Grand Duke Constantine's
son. They must be half brother and half sister, as Meg had suggested. "Papa could have been won around, I know it," she whispered to herself. "His convictions were not so deep-seated. If
Mama had pleaded Andrei's cause, Papa would have given in.
He, who could deny nothing that my poor Imp truly desired! It
was Mama's decree that the marriage should not take place."

Had her mother suffered, she wondered, to see her guilt ex-
piated by the heartbreak that had nearly driven the inexperienced,
defenseless young girl out of her mind? Delia crouched by the
smoldering fire, shivering in spite of the paisley shawl she had
dragged from the sofa to wrap around her shoulders.

Eventually the sense of shock and revulsion abated. She could
even find it in her heart to pity Mama. For, if Lady Grandison, a
woman of such stern principles, had sinned, she must have suffered a private hell of shame.

Papa must never uncover this secret. Delia decided that she
would not seek to know more, would never challenge Mama, nor
breathe a word to Natalie that might hint at the scandalous nature
of her love for Andrei. An incestuous love—Delia shrank from
the word, from the very thought. She rose, the cold making her
fingers clumsy as she swung the kettle on its trivet over the sulky
coals. She made herself hot tea and drank it, her teeth chattering
a little against the cup.

It was not until she lay huddled in bed that another anxiety
rose, specterlike to haunt her. Had Meg grasped the significance
of the two photographs? Surely not, for Delia had never spoken
to her of Natalie's blighted love affair, which had ended so dra-
matically in an elopement with another man. She concluded that
Meg's comment had been an idle one, and she fell asleep at last,
exhausted.

Delia's conviction that Meg had thought no more of the matter
was rudely shattered at luncheon the next day. She took the chair
beside Delia's and began a lively discussion. Somerville students
were expected to converse on academic subjects at mealtimes,
rather than those of personal interest. Delia was unusually silent,
keeping her eyes on her plate, and would not be drawn into the
conversation.

When the other girls had departed, Meg risked a rebuke by

whispering, "I believe I know the identity of that fascinating woman in the photograph we found yesterday. She had such high Slavic cheekbones and such a haughty air. I saw a picture of her in *The Tatler* last year at her son's wedding. Much older, of course, but one could not mistake the Voroshnikoff pearls. It was quite a grand occasion, graced by the Czar and Czarina. No doubt there is a connection with your own family. The aristocracy of Europe are all first or second cousins. I am intrigued; do ask your mother which member of the Grandison clan married one of the Voroshnikoffs."

"I'm not really interested. Our family tree has so many branches, I cannot remember which twig became entwined with another of that particular name. I must hurry, Meg. Laura will be waiting for me at the lodge."

Meg scented an intriguing mystery. She went off to write to an elderly aunt in Edinburgh whose one delight was gossip concerning high society and its titled members.

The answer came within a few days. By looking up ancient and now yellowed editions of various magazines, Aunt Clara had assembled an interesting collection of facts. The Grandisons had paid some kind of unofficial state visit to Russia in 1886, and photographs had appeared of Arthur in British naval dress uniform standing next to the imposing figure of a high-ranking Russian naval officer, the Grand Duke Constantine Voroshnikoff, on the quarterdeck of the *Potemkin*, pride of Russia's fleet. The Marquess and his wife had returned to England in the late summer of that year, and Natalie was born some seven months afterward.

There was no proof, of course, Meg told herself. But even a breath of scandal was bound to circulate like wildfire. Nothing would please Sir James Berryman better than to be in possession of this juicy piece of gossip, which, if it were common knowledge, would undoubtedly come to Lord Grandison's ears. What a triumph for the banker to place an indelible stain on the reputation of that family without fault or reproach, whose name never appeared in the gutter press. Some impudent journalist would be eager to state that he had it on the best authority that the actress of worldwide renown, Lady N. McM. was not, in fact, the daughter of straightlaced Lord G., but some mad Russian aristocrat who had seduced her mother eighteen years earlier. No names mentioned in full, of course, only initials. Sir James had many connections with the press, and he could ensure that such a scurrilous rumor was widely printed and read. An action for libel was unthinkable. The last thing a noble lord would wish was to draw even more attention to it by dragging his name through the law courts. To know that she had unwittingly brought this about would punish Delia for diverting the attention of Piers first to herself and then to Laura.

Clive Berryman was still in the running. The Scottish girl nurtured a fading hope that she might revive the interest of Sir James Berryman's heir. She had never known why he had cooled off so suddenly. At any rate, she longed to see him again. After rejecting various wild plans, she penned a short note inviting Clive to go riding with her. The country was so pretty in this frosty weather! Would he hire a couple of hacks for Saturday morning?

Meg knew that Clive rode well and enjoyed showing off his prowess. It was a harmless suggestion, and he saw no reason to refuse, although it was hardly Meg's place to issue the invitation, which should have come from him. But he was not insensible to the charms of the delightful Meg, very slender in her black habit, with beckoning eyes and cheeks rosy from the cold. He had not meant to turn her thoughts to the time of their courtship, but carelessly suggested a ride they had often taken together when he was toying with the idea of asking her to marry him. They were quite alone after a gallop across a deserted meadow with hoarfrost asparkle on the grass. On the fringe of a small wood, both riders dismounted, and Meg perched on a stile, bewitching as ever. Clive leaned against the fence, idly swiping at his riding jacket with a stylish little whip.

Meg savored the moment, imagining her companion's reaction to the tidbit she intended to let slip—oh, so cleverly—without hinting that Sir James would be eager to hear of it. She wanted to win the old man's approbation. And how could he fail to approve of the girl, who in all innocence had stumbled on a misdemeanor that would shame the Grandisons and confided it to Clive as something to be shared among friends, rather than be published abroad. That it would be published, she had no doubt; nor did she feel the slightest compunction where Delia was concerned, for the disclosure could never be traced back to herself.

She was silent, wondering how to introduce the subject of the telltale photograph. Clive moved nearer and casually laid his hand on the slim ankle so enticingly close to his shoulder. God, but he wanted her. He was within an ace of making a complete fool of himself, he thought. This must stop, once and for all.

"I'm glad you suggested riding today, Meg. Such spiffing weather," he drawled, unobtrusively removing his hand. "Besides, there's something I want to tell you . . . been wanting to tell you since Christmas, seeing that we are rather close friends." He cleared his throat, his usual polished calm deserting him. "Fact is," he went on jerkily, "I am getting engaged. A bit young, I suppose, to contemplate double harness. But the granddad is keen, and that's pretty important, as you know. Name's Eleanor Haversham, daughter of Lord Augustus Haversham. The old Duke, her grandfather, has a fine place at Tring. They've invited me down during the next vacation for port and inspection. But I expect he'll give us the go-ahead. What do you think, dear girl?" He couldn't stop talking, knowing that he sounded idiotic and almost hating Meg because he knew that every word of this revelation must pierce her to the heart.

Meg did not at once reply. She seethed inwardly, longing to strike his smooth cheek with her own whip, to punish him for the humiliation he had inflicted. Her mind raced. But there was a way to punish him! To say nothing, to hug the knowledge to herself that his miserable granddad would have paid dearly to possess, then always she'd be able to remember that she had had it in her power to give Sir James his revenge and had deliberately withheld it.

"If the poor girl can put up with you, I suppose everyone else will be delighted," she said curtly. "It's cold here. Do help me down. Let's get back to town and get rid of these animals."

He obeyed, then helped her to remount, and she stepped into his cupped palms and went up like a bird into the saddle. He thought of Eleanor's podgy limbs and awkward gait and sighed. But a fortune was hanging in the balance, and Clive Berryman could not turn his back upon it.

When she entered the college, some instinct prompted Meg to go straight to Delia's room. The fire still burned smokily, and her sharp eyes discerned shreds of cardboard, not quite consumed at the edges, through the bars of the grate. Did she only imagine that Delia's sapphire gaze had the moisture of recent tears? Well, she need cry no more.

"I've been riding with Clive Berryman." Meg tossed her veil

and hat on the sofa. "What a bore he's becoming. Getting engaged to some dull girl his grandfather has picked out for him. By the way, remember that old photograph we came across? I think you ought to get rid of it, if you haven't already. A bit startling, when you put the two pictures together. I shan't mention it to a soul, of course."

She saw Delia's face, which had been so strained, change and brighten. No matter, she thought cynically, it was true enough. But it had been a close thing. She went out in a whirl of black serge skirts.

Delia was never to know how close to exposure and retribution Lady Grandison had been. She knew only that as one grew older, idols began to fall. Natalie, so pure, a songbird with dazzling spotless plumage, the very image of innocence. Mama, the cold and icy goddess, whose subjects dared lay no finger on the edge of her glittering gown, much less on the satiny white flesh of her body. Both made reckless sinners by desire, as she was now herself. And Papa, the all-wise and heroic family head, who had been duped and made a cuckold without realizing it. Only stalwart Will remained, in her eyes, worthy to be worshipped. And he must not know the truth. At that moment Delia took on herself the heavy burden of a secret that she would never share all her life long, except with Michael, who perhaps knew it already. Nor would she speak of it to him; never acknowledge that they were both aware of a bar sinister across the Grandison escutcheon.

For the first two weeks of February rain swept the country. Then, on St. Valentine's Day, a watery sun emerged in a tremulous, pearly sky. Meanwhile, the Grandison family's private railway carriage had made the long journey to Cornwall and, under the supervision of John, the head groom, had returned loaded with early spring flowers from the Scilly Isles.

Grayle Abbey and the village church were decked with snowdrops, narcissus, and tiny daffodils of the same variety that would bloom a month later in Wales. Evergreen garlands woven with creamy flower heads and pale yellow ribbons festooned the lych gate and the ancient Norman arch at the church door. More fragrant blossoms looped with ribbons adorned each pew, so that their fresh scent was everywhere.

Delia's dress of snowy white lace was perhaps not her right to wear, for the union that had made her William's bride already brought them together again twice on a wave of ecstasy before the great day. Each time his passion was more confidently expressed, and Delia's response more schooled in its ardor.

Silently she thanked her younger sister for the advice that had helped to make the beginning of her married life so joyful. She thought of Gwendoline Jarvis as she slipped into her satin-lined bodice, then waited for Flora to fasten myriads of small buttons. Gwen's letters to Natalie from India were pathetic evidence that her initiation into marriage had been a loathsome ordeal, and thereafter a constant disappointment that had settled into a distasteful routine. Then had come pregnancy, a welcome relief from hateful marital duties, and its tragic conclusion. Gwen had not ceased to love Liam, but love had brought her no happiness. Natalie had spoken of this sad conviction with much bitterness.

Marriage was to be a paragon of joy and equality for Delia and William; they shared an understanding of each other's views and needs, and the glory of expressing their physical adoration of each other's bodies would not lessen with the years. Even now, their passion was too demanding to be concealed.

After the wedding breakfast, flattering toasts, and eloquent speeches, the great hall at Grayle had been cleared for dancing. As they slowly revolved around the floor in a formal embrace, the bride and groom had eyes for no one else.

"My Delia, what have I done to deserve you?" whispered Will, his lips tantalizingly close to his wife's radiant face. The heavy fringe of golden lashes dropped, veiling the blissful expression in those sparkling eyes.

"Everything!" she murmured. She raised her firm little chin, yearning to join her mouth to his. He could not resist the invitation, and he dropped the lightest of kisses on her soft, sweetly curving lips. A ripple of indulgent laughter and clapping followed them around the room, but in their world of private delight the happy couple hardly noticed.

When the celebrations were at their height, Delia and William intended to slip away. They were to spend a few days at Natalie's house in Sackville Street, in the midst of theater land, to see the latest shows and be cosseted by her excellent domestic staff. While the world imagined them on honeymoon in Paris, they would quietly return to their own Sundial House and begin life there together.

From her vantage point in the minstrel's gallery, Louise looked down upon the colorful throng of guests dancing below. Most were tenants of the estate, with a sprinkling of local gentry, friends from London, and the visitors from Criccieth. Delia's fair hair was still crowned with a bridal wreath of narcissus and snowdrops. The flutter of her gauzy white train billowed out over her arm; Will's smooth brown head was bent toward the bride's as they whispered endearments. She gave a tremulous sigh of relief. No one had suffered, after all, because of her past indiscretion. Arthur and all her children were happy. Still surveying the crowd from above, Louise caught sight of Natalie, in primrose tulle, lights glancing from the diamond combs she wore under a circlet of fresh flowers. She was surrounded by the best-looking men in the room, all anxious for one glance, one smile, one flash of those drowned-violet eyes. . . .

Michael came up behind her and offered his arm. "Shall we join the dancers, Louise?"

She nodded, laying her slender fingers on his sleeve, and they descended to the dance floor. As they made their way through the crowd Louise noticed the group clustered almost too closely around Natalie, and that one young man had possessed himself of both her hands and was kissing them in turn. She spoke with a touch of asperity as they began a slow waltz.

"My little nightingale has become such a bright theatrical star that I hardly recognize her. I must compliment you on the success of your new production, Michael. It does you both credit. And, fortunately, Natalie is unlikely to have her head turned by so much adulation." She swept up her own skirt by its loop, ready to float into the dance with her handsome son-in-law. They turned several times before she said in her most queenly manner, "Have you not thought of furnishing a nursery in that charming new house of yours? Natalie needs a babe or two to keep her safe at home for the next few years. To anchor her, so to speak, my dear boy." She was speaking half in jest. "Why don't you see to it?"

But Michael swung around, so that she was forced to drop his arm. He looked startled and hurt. "Has Natalie not told you of our disappointment? I believe it almost broke her heart," he went on bitterly. "She miscarried, you know, soon after we reached New York. An eminent specialist in Harley Street told her only recently that she can never have a child."

Louise paused in horror. How tactless, how wounding a remark she had made. But Natalie had not chosen to share this sad secret with her.

"I truly did not know; I'm sorry." Her lips trembled. So there was retribution after all. But it had fallen, not on her own guilty head, but on that of her innocent daughter.

Michael was profoundly aware of her distress. "Don't reproach yourself too much, Louise. We've come to terms with it." He was alarmed by her sudden pallor, her remorseful haunted look. However, with a tremendous effort, she rallied. Convention and a lifetime of training in correct behavior came to her aid. She danced on, but she was in torment. How had she dared to imagine that her sin would never find her out? Why was Natalie, the child of Constantine's illicit love, condemned to endure this punishment for her mother's wrongdoing? Louise felt the first throbbing pain of a violent headache stab her temples.

Soon she was compelled to withdraw, bowing her elegant head to left and right, acknowledging the congratulations of their guests. It had been a beautiful wedding, everyone was saying.

But in the privacy of her bedroom she sought oblivion in the stream of drops that she poured with a shaking hand from the laudanum bottle.

Natalie and Michael slept, too, in the tower room. They lay entwined, her head on his broad shoulder and the ebony masses of her hair loose about them both. Suddenly she started up, crying out that someone had called her, that she must go at once on a journey, and she was not ready. Nothing was packed!

He soothed her, saying that it was only a nightmare. He lit the wax candles in the branched candlestick by their bed to chase away the shadows. Natalie shuddered, looking about her fearfully. Presently she was reassured that no one lurked even in the farthest recess, and she consented to lie down again in the shelter of his arms.

Sleepily she whispered into the warm curve of his neck, "It was Andrei, Michael. Shall I ever escape from him?" His hand tightened on hers.

"Don't think of it anymore. Rest, my beloved," he whispered.

When morning came, he woke to find that she had left him and was kneeling on the window seat, the curtain drawn back, staring toward the east. Outside all was still gray and misty. She turned to him a face in which sorrow and immense relief were blended.

"I think it's over, Michael. He'll never call me again."

Three thousand miles away Prince Andrei Voroshnikoff had gone riding across the *taiga*, the prairie that stretched for hundreds of versts on every side of the remote estate where he had chosen to live. His wife Desirée never ceased to complain that Simbirsk, the nearest town, was nothing but a provincial hole. A dreary little town on the Volga, and a world away from St. Petersburg!

Sparks flew from his horse's hooves when they struck an occasional stone, and its breath froze on the air, for winter still held Russia in an iron grip.

It had become Andrei's habit to ride until he was exhausted, and then to call at some peasant's hut, swallow a fiery draft of vodka, and chew on some black bread.

He never returned until dark; what was there to draw him back? Although he visited his sulky wife's bed each week, as the Czar had bidden him, there was no sign of a child to bless their union. Today he was particularly restless. He turned his horse's head toward Simbirsk. There was a tavern where the tziganes danced their wild gypsy dances to the music of the violin and balalaika. For a few roubles he could drink himself into forgetfulness.

He struck his horse's rump, urging it to a headlong gallop. A long ride lay before them and already dusk had fallen. They reached the town gate just as it was closing. A cart, laden with oak logs, that had been delayed by a broken axle was rumbling through. But he rode straight at it. Who would dare bar the way of Prince Andrei Voroshnikoff? The wagoner did not see him in the gloom or hear his thunderous approach.

Andrei hurled his mount at the narrowing space. The horse took fright and reared up, afraid of being crushed against the iron-studded gatepost. His rider was thrown to the cobbled paving stones, the wagon lurched crazily, and part of its load fell across his chest. A flash of agony, and then all pain dissolved. Andrei felt nothing, did not even know that blood was welling up in his throat.

Terrified, the townspeople dragged him into the hallway of the nearest house, sent messengers to summon the doctor, to fetch Desirée. The doctor was still kneeling by Prince Andrei when his wife arrived in an anxious flurry of sleigh bells. She flung herself down beside her husband, seizing his limp hand, brocaded skirts stained at once with his lifeblood, fast ebbing away.

"He does not suffer, Highness, for I think his back is broken," whispered the doctor to comfort her.

Andrei still could turn his head. He looked toward the kneeling girl and his face was lit with wonder. "The troika bells! I knew you would come, my princess. We'll ride away together in the snow and the silence . . . and . . . never be parted again."

Desirée understood only one word for she had never troubled to learn English. "What do you mean, Andrushka? There is no troika!"

But she waited for a reply in vain. A trickle of blood flowed from that proud mouth, and the handsome features were set forever in an expression of ineffable joy.

When Arthur came wearily to bed, he found Louise sunk deep in slumber, with tears half-dried on her cheeks. He bent to kiss her, hardly surprised that she did not stir.

It had been an exhausting but triumphant day. Louise remained in his eyes the most beautiful of women and the best of wives. He owed her so much. She had given him four children of whom he was truly proud. His splendid sons, and the daughters so dear to his heart. He had to acknowledge, Arthur thought hazily through mists of fatigue and champagne, that guided by her, the girls had chosen excellent husbands, fine fellows.

He was too tired to undress. Sitting comfortably in the chair by Louise, holding her hand, he drifted into slumber.

Epilogue
1910

Lord Grandison's girls were taking tea with their father on the terrace of the Ritz Hotel. There was a fine view from their table across the Queen's Walk to Green Park, where the trees were now in full leaf.

Arthur sat between his beautiful daughters, still youthful himself in figure but gray-haired now and with an air of melancholy distinction. The group, which drew many curious glances, was completed by a pretty child seated on the knee of a slender, charming young girl.

All were in mourning for the passing of King Edward VII and for the golden Edwardian era coming to a close. A couple seated nearby whispered together, aware that the dark beauty must be the famous stage star Lady Natalie McMahon, now praised on both sides of the Atlantic.

Four-year-old Gwendoline was restless and, climbing down, ran around the table to Natalie, who lifted her tenderly, saying in mild reproof, "Gwennie, poor Hetty will think you are tired of her company. And she is so patient with you. Say you are sorry."

"Yes, I am. But I love you best of all," piped up the little girl

343

bravely. "That is, after Mama." Her small face, framed by golden curls under a big straw hat lined with white lace ruffles, was flushed with embarrassment. Natalie hugged the child, smiling at this frank avowal. Hetty blushed in her turn and shook her head, saying that she needed no apology.

She was a shy creature, who owed much to the kindness of the Grandison family. Miss Jarvis now spent most of her time with the Clive Berrymans at their estate in Berkshire. Lady Grandison had presented the girl at court and found that she pleased Justin even more than Natalie; for he had come to care deeply for Gwendoline's younger sister. She now lived with Delia and Will at Sundial House, and was much concerned in the upbringing of Gwennie and her two little brothers, who were left at home on this mournful day.

Lord Grandison sat silent, his head bowed, and took no part in the conversation, though his eyes were kind when he turned his head toward his little granddaughter, or glanced at either of his own lovely girls. His gaze lingered particularly on Natalie. He saw Delia often, but his nightingale had been absent for more than a year in America, since Michael's purchase of the Brady Theater.

Each member of the group felt it keenly that they were meeting to mourn the passing of a loved one. To lighten their mood, Delia inquired how her protegée from the Woodstock Road in Oxford was faring.

Natalie looked rueful. "Oh, Elsie has left the Clarence, and is very much missed by our wardrobe mistress, for she'd become a wonderful seamstress. But she received an offer of marriage from a young widower. He observed that Elsie was an honest, hard-working girl and an excellent mother. I hear that she rules her husband with an iron hand."

Remembering the scrawny waif at Stonelea, Delia could hardly credit it. But Natalie was now asking what had become of her own college friends, Margaret and Laura.

"Meg did not marry after all. We have lost touch. But Laura made a match of it with Piers Douglas and they have started a preparatory school for boys at Woodstock, which is very successful. Laura has become quite pretty and plump and intends to publish a volume of her poems, or so Piers tells me."

"And the Bradleighs?"

"You would never believe it. Eustace took to walking along

the river after dark and peering into our windows. Will scared him off on several occasions. Then he must have tumbled into the water, for the lockkeeper fished him out one night half drowned. It seems he had suffered a stroke, for he practically lost his power of speech and the use of his right hand. Mr. Archibald had to pension him off. But almost directly afterward, Bessie's aunt Bella died. It turned out that she had only spoken of leaving her fortune to a nephew, to ensure that Eustace had no reason to wish her dead; Bessie got everything. So she invited Martha Bail to live with them, and now the two ladies order the household between them. Eustace is confined to an invalid chair. Stonelea is the center of suffragist activities in Oxford. Martha soon made a convert of her sister; and, of course, the erstwhile master of the house is powerless to prevent it."

There was a pause while tea was poured and handed around. Thinking of the unhappy Bradleighs, Delia could not help contrasting their situation with that of Will and herself; and Natalie's with Michael. But then neither she nor her sister led lives entirely untouched by sorrow. Natalie still longed in vain for a child of her own, and Delia herself was precluded from taking any active part in the fight for women's rights. Will's position in the public eye made it impossible.

But it was her father they must think of now, his future plans.

"The memorial service for Mama was most touching," said Delia wistfully. "Do you feel it is wrong, Papa, to take tea in such a public place? Perhaps we should have reopened the house in Park Lane."

Lord Grandison shook his head. "Natalie and Michael are staying here, at the Ritz, and I have no wish to reenter that house where your mother and I lived so much of our lives together. Let it remain closed. I am happier with my dear old friend Hugo just now at his place in Acacia Grove. Besides, we leave together next week for a tour of Italy. We've rented a villa on Lake Como for the summer. Louise always loved it there."

"We have wondered so much," Delia began, anxious to change the painful subject yet unable to leave it, "if you could bring yourself now to tell us a little more about Mama's death." Her voice faltered. "Your letters were so brief, and the newspapers were frightful . . ."

Lord Grandison reached and touched her hand. "You have a right to know all I can tell you," he brought himself to acknowledge. "Because of the new links between Britain and Russia, it was wise to show that visits might be freely exchanged between the two countries. At the personal request of His Majesty and the Prime Minister, we accepted an invitation from our old friends the Voroshnikoffs, whom we had not seen for many years. In fact, your mother did not really want to go. By pure chance she went driving one morning alone with the Grand Duke in his carriage. But I was told by a bystander, who saw it all, how a young student stepped forward to throw a bomb, believing Louise to be the Grand Duchess Natalya. Constantine flung himself in front of her and was fatally wounded. My poor darling began to scream. Another man, on the other side of the street, leveled a pistol and shot her through the heart."

His voice broke and he covered his eyes with his hand, unable to continue.

"It was a mistake, Papa," Delia apologized. "I shouldn't have asked you to speak of it."

"I have made many mistakes myself," he said, looking from one to the other of his daughters. "But I shall never cease to reproach myself that I allowed her to drive with Constantine that day. No one knows better than I how dangerous these mad fanatics are. They care nothing for their own lives. But I thought, as English visitors, Louise and I would be safe." He rose abruptly. "Here's William, and Michael with him." He was patently relieved by the interruption.

Gwennie had already seen her father and ran to clasp his knees, for he had to bend to take her in his arms and to drop a kiss on Delia's cheek. Then he was bowing over Natalie's hand. Both men greeted Lord Grandison in subdued tones.

"We've seen Julian and Justin off on their train to Dartmouth," Michael told the Marquess before seating himself next to his wife. "They're both very anxious that you should be present at Julian's passing-out parade. He has high hopes of winning the sword of honor."

His Lordship showed a passing spark of interest. "I shall certainly come back from Italy for that occasion if he does!" He was very proud that his sons had chosen to enter the Royal Navy.

He was proud of his girls, too, though they had not followed the paths he and Louise had at first planned for them. There was no denying that they each had chosen a perfect partner in life, and they were happy.

Had he made Louise, his lovely Snow Queen, as happy? he wondered. Perhaps she had never fully returned the physical expression of his passion, but he was certain she had loved him and him alone. He would willingly have faced the assassin's bullet in her stead.

Mercifully he was always to remember her like this. The secret love, with its trail of tragic events, died with her, united at last in the arms of the Grand Duke Constantine.

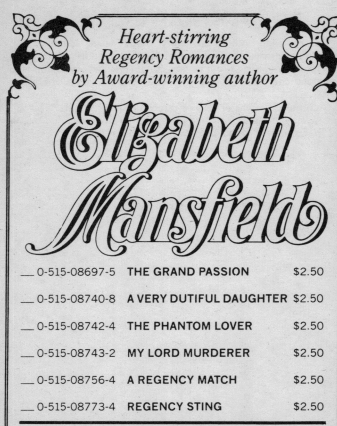